Mary D. Brooks

In The Blood
Of The Greeks

Intertwined Souls SERIES

BOOK 1

Sydney, Australia 2015

ISBN-10: 0994294506
ISBN-13: 978-0-9942945-0-0

Edited by:
Rosa Alonso

Cover by:
Jazzy "Aiglon" Trafficano

Illustrations by:
Lucia Nobrega

Photography by:
KT Jorgensen

Models:
Kat Cavanaugh (Eva Muller)
Penny Cavanaugh (Zoe Lambros)

AUSXIP Publishing

Sydney, Australia
www.ausxippublishing.com

Intertwined Souls SERIES

To my dear friend Evelyn Elephan –
your courage and strength was
an inspiration to me. Peace and Respect

ACKNOWLEDGMENTS

Rosa Alonso – *I've always said that an author needs a Rosa in their corner. Thank you for being a superb human being and above all, a fantastic editor and dear mate.*

Jazzy Trafficano – *Your talent is extraordinary, your generosity is amazing and above else, your friendship means the world to me. Thank you.*

Joy Scavo – *Funny as hell, a joy to be around and an incredible human being. Thank you my friend.*

Penny Cavanaugh – *the maker of dreams coming true. Muchas gracias senora!*

Kat Cavanaugh – *Thank you for indulging my reality! You are a kind and gentle soul.*

Invictus

Out of the night that covers me,
Black as the pit from pole to pole,
I thank whatever gods may be
For my unconquerable soul.

In the fell clutch of circumstance
I have not winced nor cried aloud.
Under the bludgeonings of chance
My head is bloody, but unbowed.

Beyond this place of wrath and tears
Looms but the Horror of the shade,
And yet the menace of the years
Finds and shall find me unafraid.

It matters not how strait the gate,
How charged with punishments the scroll,
I am the master of my fate,
I am the captain of my soul.

William Ernest Henley

PROLOGUE

 pril 16, 1941

Thunder boomed overhead and across the valley as the night sky was lit up with exploding artillery shells in the hills surrounding the small farming town of Larissa, Greece. This once sleepy town was the scarred battlefield between the Allies who were defending the town and the oncoming juggernaut that was the German army.

When the Italians tried to invade Greece, the invaders had been defeated. Great jubilation had resulted in a joyous celebration that stretched for days. In the town, the pride over the news that the Italians had been beaten back flourished amidst the sorrow for the fallen.

But after the euphoria of the victory against the Italian invaders had faded, the Greek government realized that the Axis powers had not been defeated, only stalled. The government stumbled from one crisis to another, trying to starve off the inevitable. What they feared the most happened in the spring of 1941, a day that many Greeks had been anxiously anticipating for months.

The Germans had arrived at the outskirts of Larissa and were raging through the hills and valleys like hungry locusts. The British, Australian, and New Zealand soldiers kept the Germans at bay until they could hold them no longer, and now a retreat was in progress.

Burning cars, trucks, and bodies of soldiers and Greeks littered the roadways as the battles continued.

A young girl stood outside on a clear night, gazing at Mount Ossa in the distance. The sound of falling shells and the rumble of tanks thundered in the background.

Zoe Lambros looked up into the heavens for a long moment, closed her eyes, and prayed to God for victory. She crossed herself on finishing a prayer she was certain God would listen to. He had to. He was on their side.

Zoe was a carbon copy of her mother, Helena, with long red-colored hair that reached her waist and green eyes her father had said reminded him of emeralds in the sunlight. She was barely five feet-four inches, with a slight frame.

Zoe noticed their plough horse, Zeus, was standing next to the wagon. She wasn't sure why the horse was out so late and she walked the few yards to the tall animal. "Loud night for you, Zeus," she said and patted the horse.

The horse shoved his head towards Zoe and she giggled at the animal's playful nature. "I'm absolutely certain that the Germans will be defeated. We defeated the Turks in 1821, then the Italians. Now it is the Germans who will feel the full force of our brothers... God is on our side, and as Father Haralambos often says in church, 'If you have God on your side, you don't need anyone else.'"

A thunderous explosion made Zoe jump a little as the noise reverberated through the night. "Oh, that must have destroyed several of those Germans tanks."

"Zoe, come inside, child." Helena Lambros, a slim redheaded woman with sparkling emerald colored eyes came out of the farmhouse and put her arm around her daughter's shoulders.

"I was talking to Zeus, Mama. I think we are winning. Listen to those rockets. That's the Allies—they are winning and we are beating those horrible Germans like we beat the Italians!"

Helena's gaze turned to the mountains and sighed. "God willing, we will all come out of this alive."

"We will. Father H said we have God on our side and that means we will win."

"Don't call the reverend 'Father H.'"

"Why?"

"It's not respectful. He is a man of God and we should show him respect."

Zoe gazed up at her mother with a dubious look on her face. "I don't think God minds."

Helena grinned and shook her head. She kissed the top of Zoe's head. "You are going to give me a lot of grief as you grow older but I love you."

"I love you too," Zoe replied as she put both arms around her mother's waist and hugged her. "Why is Zeus outside?"

"Papa is going to hitch the wagon to Zeus and we are going to Thieri's cabin."

"Now?"

"Yes. I want you to come inside and help pack."

"Why are we going to Thieri's cabin?"

"Zoe, we don't have a lot of time," Helena replied and kissed Zoe on the top of her red-gold head before going back inside.

Zoe scowled. She looked back at the horse and gave him a final pat. "I don't know why we are going to Thieri's cabin but we will be seeing the Germans being routed. I love Athena's Bluff, Zeus. We will have a really good view of the Germans from up there."

Zoe patted the horse one more time and walked back to the farmhouse. She found the living area piled high with blankets in several bundles and two suitcases sitting near the kitchen.

Zoe navigated around the suitcases and entered the kitchen. The smell of homemade bread permeated the room. Five loaves were cooling on the table and another two were in the oven. Her mother had taken out pickled vegetables that were stored in jars from their pantry.

Helena gave Zoe a white bed sheet which had been ripped into long strips. "Take these to Papa and tell him I'll be ready in about thirty minutes."

Zoe collected the makeshift bandages and quickly walked the short distance to her room. She knocked and entered when she heard a faint 'come in.' Lying on her bed was Jimmy Peterson, a young Australian soldier, a few years older than her. His right trouser leg had been torn from the knee down, and a large bandage was wrapped around his lower leg. Zoe grimaced when she saw the blood that had seeped through the bandages.

Three men were sitting near the bed. Zoe's father, Nicholas Lambros, was a tall, broad shouldered man with thick curly black hair sprinkled with white at the temples. His golden brown eyes crinkled in delight on seeing his youngest walk in.

Sitting next to Nicholas was Apostolos Kiriakou, her brother Theodore's best friend and the town only surviving medic, although Zoe didn't think he was a real doctor. Next to Apostolos was another Australian soldier. They had been at the farm for the last three days trying to get Peterson well enough to travel. Sergeant Clarence Timmins spoke Greek but with a very strange accent, much to Zoe's amusement.

Nicholas stood and took the bandages from Zoe. He gazed lovingly at his daughter and smiled down at the upturned face. "I'm so proud of you. You have been a big help to our guests and God will reward you for your loving spirit. Don't be afraid."

"I'm not afraid, Papa. Our friends and our brothers will beat them back to where they came from, won't you, Sergeant Timmins?"

Clarence turned towards Zoe and smiled. "We will win, little sister."

Nicholas bent down and kissed the top of Zoe's red hair. "God willing, we will be victorious."

"Mama said she will be ready in thirty minutes."

"Good. Now I'm going to change the bandages. Why don't you take Sergeant Timmins and help him load the wagon?"

"Alright." Zoe nodded and waited for the soldier to join her before they left the room. He greeted Helena before he picked up the blankets and headed outside. In no time and without Zoe's help, the wagon was ready.

"So how is the picture coming along?" Clarence asked as he sat down on an upturned bucket near the barn.

"Drawing!" Zoe corrected him and chuckled. "How did you learn Greek?"

"My grandmother is Greek."

"Where is she from?"

"She was from Constantinople and then they threw them out and she went to Egypt."

"Is that why you have a funny accent?"

Clarence rocked back and laughed at Zoe's question. He shook his head. "No. That's my Australian accent. My grandmother met my grandfather, who is an Australian, and they went to live there."

"Say something in Australian?"

Clarence gazed down at the inquisitive young girl and smiled. "Bonzer sheila," he replied in English. He smiled at the total confusion on Zoe's face. "You are an excellent young woman," he translated.

"Bonzer sheila," Zoe mouthed and giggled at the unfamiliar

sounds.

"You should come to Australia, ZoZo."

Zoe laughed at the affectionate nickname Clarence had overheard from her father. "I want to see what's out there beyond Mount Ossa."

"At the moment, a lot of bad men."

"After you defeat the bad men, I want to come to Australia and see that bridge...oh." Zoe stopped and fished around in her pocket and brought out the photograph that Clarence had given her. She then raced into the barn and came back with her sketchbook. Flipping through the pages she found the artwork for the Sydney Harbour Bridge. "This is for you."

Clarence took it and smiled. "Wow, this is beautiful. Can I keep it?"

"You like it? Yes, you can keep it."

"One day you are going to be a great artist. I will take you to this bridge."

Their conversation was interrupted when they were joined by Nicholas and Apostolos. Zoe watched the men as they loaded a truck and put a blanket and hay to cushion the ride for the wounded soldier. The time had come for them to leave.

"Papa, are you going with them?"

Nicholas took Zoe's hand and walked her to a nearby chair. He sat down and took his daughter in his lap.

"I have to go with Apostolos and the boys around the gorge to evade the Germans."

"Why can't Apostolos do it? I thought you were coming with us to the cabin."

"I want you and Mama to go to the cabin. Don't come down until I come to get you. Alright?"

"Alright, but why do you have to go?"

Nicholas hugged Zoe tightly. "I know a secret way around the gorge. Do you remember the summer we went hunting and Theo caught that wild pig? That's where we are going."

They sat in silence for a moment, gunfire and exploding artillery sounding louder and closer. Zoe sniffed and grimaced at the smell of gunpowder in the air.

"You will be back, right?"

"I will be back."

"You promise?" Zoe asked as she looked up at Nicholas. "A promise is a promise, Papa."

"No, I can't promise, little one. No one can promise—"

"But Papa—"

"Zoe, we are going to try and stop the Germans but you have to do your part. You have to be strong and be like Persephone Andrakakis."

"She was ferocious and a hero in the war of Liberation!"

"That's right. You have to be like her. Whatever happens, my little girl, you have to be strong. You have to be courageous and never let anything stop you. If I don't make it back, your mama is going to need you."

Zoe stared at the ground for a long moment. "I don't want you to go."

"If I don't go, my baby, how are we going to win this war? Remember the brave men and women during the Liberation? They had to go and fight for our motherland." Nicholas turned Zoe's face towards him. "Have I told you how much I love you?"

"Yes, this much." Zoe threw back her arms. "I love you even bigger. Bigger than Mount Ossa!"

"Only that much?" Nicholas teased, making Zoe laugh. He tenderly kissed her on the cheek. "Be brave, be strong, and listen to Mama while I'm gone. Can you do that for me?"

"Yes, Papa but—"

"Shh." Nicholas wrapped his strong arms around Zoe and kissed her on top of her head. "Be brave."

"Yes, Papa." Zoe used the back of her sleeve to wipe her eyes.

"I will be brave."

"I love you and never forget how much. I will always love you. You are my favorite daughter."

Zoe looked up at Nicholas, her emerald eyes glistening with unshed tears. "I'm your only daughter."

"That's why you're my favorite," Nicholas replied as he gently tapped Zoe's nose. "Now I have to get up and say goodbye to your mama. It may be a few days before I come to the cabin."

Zoe stood and watched Nicholas walk towards Helena, who was anxiously standing by the wagon. He put his arm around her waist and even in the darkness Zoe could see how much they loved each other. She had never seen anyone look at another person the way her parents looked at each other.

They quickly boarded the wagon and after saying another round of goodbyes, Nicholas led Zeus towards the road leading to Athena's Bluff and relative safety.

CHAPTER 1

May 1942

Helena strode purposefully up the slight incline. She glanced at the fields, fields that had once been sown with wheat or cotton but were now sadly neglected. Not that she wanted it that way, but the war had made life in Larissa overwhelmingly oppressive. She was not a farmer and she struggled without her beloved Nicholas to tend to the fields. She was an artist and sold her art in town to buy the meager food rations. She sold her work to the Germans or to the Italians who had been stationed in the town. Reluctantly, she had sold her favorite painting, one she had painted for her Nicholas as a present. It was now enjoyed not by her husband, as she had intended, but by the German commandant.

Helena stopped, lifted her head up to the heavens, and surveyed the coming storm. She shook her head and trudged up the hill to the small farmhouse she shared with her daughter Zoe. As she walked, waves of memories swept over her, as they had every day of her life since the beginnings of this hated war.

Helena was a widow, just another casualty of the war. Though only in her mid-thirties, she looked far older, a legacy of the long war against first the Italians and then the Germans. Both enemies had exacted their price from her family and her community. Her red-colored hair had started to gray prematurely.

She was a strong woman with firm beliefs and a faith in God that gave her the strength to continue after the death of her beloved husband Nicholas, and sons Michael, Thieri, and Theodore. Her three beautiful sons, strapping young men, had died on the front lines defending Greece against the invading Italian army in Albania, a sacrifice that no mother should ever endure.

Her concern for the welfare of her surviving child prevented her from joining her departed husband and sons.

The men of the community who survived went underground to fight the Germans the way their forefathers had fought against the might of the Ottoman Empire. The subversive opposition in the countryside grew and, although the Germans scoffed at the news of the Greek Resistance, their numbers were bolstered with each passing day. For many Greeks, the notion of being an enslaved people was an abomination. The oppressive yoke of the Ottoman Empire had been overthrown in 1828, and many of the older men told tales of the heroic deeds of an earlier generation of Greeks that became part of the Modern Greek psyche.

Helena hoped Zoe would get married and then she might be able to have a man around the farm, although that prospect was severely limited. Zoe was thirteen, nearly fourteen years old, and very capable of setting up a home of her own. Helena had seen to that. The girl knew how to sew and cook, to clean and take care of a household. Helena was very proud of her daughter and was sure that she would make a very capable wife. Standing in the way of that dream was Zoe's reluctance to accept any of the men who were suggested by the town's matchmaker.

Earlier in the day, the scenario had been repeated with Zoe, who once again dashed the hopes of her mother. Kiria Despina, the town's matchmaker, had made the trek to the Lambros farm to inquire about Zoe's availability. Once again she went away shaking her head and without a firm commitment. Helena was certain Kiria Despina would tire of trying to find someone who Zoe would accept.

Helena smiled when she saw her daughter waiting for her at the gate. "Have you finished your chores?" She asked, knowing full well Zoe hadn't. Zoe was perfectly capable of spending the whole day reading or sketching.

Zoe nodded. "Some," she replied, although not very convincingly, since she got a stern look from Helena. "Did the pigs buy it?"

Helena sighed. "Yes," she said sadly. "Kiria Despina said they wanted it."

"How much?"

"Enough so we won't starve." Helena ruffled Zoe's hair. "Kiria Despina is worried about you."

Zoe leaned against the fence and looked up into the dark heavens. "I don't care."

"Zoe, she is going to get tired of coming here and asking. She's running out of boys! What was wrong with Dimitri?"

Zoe sighed. "He's too tall and he's old enough to be my grandfather."

Helena stared open mouthed at Zoe. "He's too tall?"

"Yes." Zoe smiled. "I don't like tall boys."

"You don't like tall boys," Helena repeated. "You don't like short boys, or boys with brown hair, or boys with black hair." Helena counted on her fingers the many variations of boys Zoe had rejected. "Child, are there any boys you do like?"

Zoe shrugged.

"One day you will have to settle on a boy because you're going to be left alone and nothing is worse than being left on a shelf, especially for a young woman," Helena once again reminded Zoe, although she knew there were worse things. But she needed her daughter to get married, for both their sakes.

"One day I'm going to meet someone who will be just right." Zoe smiled. "You'll see, Mama. Kiria Despina won't have to ask twice."

"I hope so, I certainly hope so." Helena shook her head and walked inside to start on dinner. "Go and feed the animals."

Several hours later Zoe heard Helena's exasperated voice. "Zoe Lambros, where are you, child?"

Zoe was fed up with feeding the animals and cleaning the house. There were much more interesting things to do. All she wanted to do was go down to the river, take a book, and read. Theodore, the youngest of her older brothers, had given her a copy of Oliver Twist that he'd found in Athens. It was one of her most prized possessions, a well-read book with dog-eared pages. Zoe had gone behind the chicken shed for some quiet time; it had a tiny overhanging shingle that protected her from the rain. She groaned when she heard her mother's voice.

"Yes, Mama," Zoe muttered and got up from the ground, leaving the book behind in a small, safe cache so that her mother would not see it and yell even more. She rounded the corner to find Helena glaring at her.

"You know you have to help me get these chores done! Were you reading again?"

"I'm going to see the world one day," Zoe mumbled, repeating what she had told Helena many times before, much to her mother's annoyance.

"The only place I want you to see right now is your room. Clean it up."

"But, Mama—"

"Zoe, please, don't argue with me." Helena let out a frustrated sigh.

"I'm going to leave here one day. You'll see."

Helena decided to humor Zoe. "Where would you go?"

"Away, far away from Larissa and Greece. I'm going to travel and see the world. I want to paint, learn, and become somebody."

"You are somebody." Helena put her arm around Zoe. "You are Zoe Lambros, a little too rebellious at the moment, but generally a good girl."

"I want to leave."

"And leave me alone?"

Zoe looked up into her mother's eyes. "You'll come with me." She smiled. "I want to see what's over there." She pointed to the mountains. "I want to know what's out there beyond Mount Ossa."

"What's out there, little one, are the Germans."

"I want us to leave," Zoe mumbled as she picked up a stone. She looked at it and threw it against the barn.

"We can't leave, my love. We can't go anywhere."

"Why can't we go to live with Aunty Stella?"

Helena sighed deeply. "You know travel is dangerous, especially for a woman and a child on their own."

"I'm not a child. I'm nearly fourteen. I'm old enough to get married."

"Yes, you are old enough but it's not safe. I hear stories of what happens when women are caught by the Germans, and it's not something I would like to experience."

"Why can't Aunty Stella come here?" Zoe persisted.

"What did I just say about single travelers?"

"Aunty Stella is fearless. She travelled to Athens and she's a doctor."

Helena put her arms around Zoe and laughed. "You are precious. Just because someone is a doctor doesn't make them invincible."

"No, but Aunty Stella is."

"Oh, my precious child, I wish we could join Aunty Stella in Thessaloniki but that won't happen," Helena said as she hugged her daughter. "Have you seen your cousin Stavros?"

"Not today. I'm going into town tomorrow. You haven't changed your mind, have you?" Zoe looked at Helena, who had an anxious look on her face. Zoe turned to where her mother was looking and saw the reason.

A column of vehicles was passing through on the dirt road throwing up a cloud of dust in their wake. The distinctive and despised swastika of the Third Reich emblazoned on the doors heralded the arrival of more Germans.

"Who is that?"

"The new commander," Helena replied. "I heard he was coming in today."

Zoe grinned as she watched the procession pass through. "Helgberg got a very nice send-off by our boys."

"Zoe, you shouldn't be happy about someone's death."

"Yes, I can. If they are German pigs, I will dance on their graves with tambourines." Zoe started to dance a jig as she swirled around the courtyard amongst the chickens.

Helena shook her head and laughed. "My little one, war is not a dance."

"No, but this is our country. This is my country and they are invaders. We will beat them like we beat the Turks." Zoe looked at Helena and held her hand. "Don't worry, Mama, once this war is over, I'll get married to a nice boy and everything will be just fine."

CHAPTER 2

*E*va Muller gazed out of the window at the woman washing her clothes out in their front yard. The woman was dressed in black from head to toe. The new commander's house was situated slightly on a hill overlooking several houses. Most of them were commandeered by the Germans as Officers' quarters but a few were left to the villagers to remain.

Eva was Major Han Muller's daughter, a tall, dark haired, blue-eyed young woman of twenty-two. She glanced at her cane, which was leaning against the wall, and shook her head slightly at her predicament. She watched the woman freely moving about and envied the villager's freedom.

Eva turned at the sound of her bedroom door opening expecting her nurse to walk through. A smile spread across her face when she saw a friendly face instead. Nurse Frieda Ackman, a middle-aged tall woman with blond hair and twinkling green eyes, walked in a crisp white uniform.

"Frieda!" Eva exclaimed as she grabbed her cane and walked the short distance to her former nurse.

"Well, there you are!" Frieda replied and opened her arms to

Eva. "They told me you were up here. My goodness, why did they put you up the stairs?"

"My father's idea to strengthen my back. What are you doing here?"

"Sit and I'll tell you." Frieda put her arm around Eva as they walked over to the bed. "Now, how are you?" She asked and took Eva's hand.

"I'm alright."

"You don't look alright to me," Frieda replied and gently tipped Eva's face towards the light. "You haven't been sleeping."

"That hasn't changed since you last saw me. I can't sleep."

"You're not taking your medications; that's why you can't sleep. You look very tired."

"It must be the Greek air," Eva replied with a slight shrug.

"Yes, people wanting to kill you wouldn't be all that healthy."

Eva shrugged a little at the true nature of the statement. "What are you doing in this backwater?"

"I'm on the way back to Athens and decided to stop to see you."

"Are you staying long?"

"No, I'm leaving tonight because General Rhimes wants to be in Athens tomorrow," Frieda replied. "Did you get my letter?"

"I did." Eva nodded. "It was such a blessing to get it."

"I'm glad. I missed you so much." Frieda tenderly patted Eva on the cheek. "I have brought some presents for you."

"You have?"

"I went home with General Rhimes and whilst there, I dropped in to see your aunty Marlene."

Eva's smile widened at the mention of her adopted aunt. "How is she?"

"Oh, she's well. She's missing you so much and wants to give you this." Frieda leaned over and tenderly kissed Eva on the cheek. "She also sent me some letters for you and a special letter from Willie."

"Is he well? Is he home? Where is he stationed?"

"Slow down." The nurse held up her hand and laughed lightly at Eva's questioning. "He is well, he's not home, and he was stationed in Italy but has moved out. I'm going to see if General Rhimes can find out and I'll let you know."

Eva's face creased into a smile on hearing her friend's name. "I miss him so much."

"Marlene gave me some photographs and..." Frieda stopped and took a handkerchief out of her pocket. She laid the handkerchief in her lap and opened it up to reveal a silver ring and a gold cross. She looked up to see Eva's eyes glisten, a smile creasing her face.

Eva took the ring in the palm of her hand and gazed at it for a long moment. "My mother's ring," she said in wonder and looked up at Frieda in amazement. "You brought it to me."

"I did. Marlene wanted you to have it as well as your gold cross. You left that behind after your accident."

Eva felt her stomach clench at the memory of how that gold cross had been ripped from her neck. The ornate silver ring in her hand was far more important to her than the memories. "Aunt Marlene had the ring?"

"Yes, and she knew you would want it. Marlene wants you home to care for you but she knows your father wants you here."

"I want to go home. Why can't I go home, away from this war?"

"I know you do, sweetheart. Your father's wish is for you to be with him, and being on your own in Berlin in your condition is just not the sensible thing."

"I wouldn't in this condition if my father didn't take me to Paris with him. I wouldn't be in this condition if the French Resistance hadn't bombed the house. I wouldn't be on my own. There's Aunty Marlene, my grandmother and Uncle Wilbur."

"Your grandmother has gone to Bonn and Uncle Wilbur is trying to keep AEMullerStahl in business--"

"But--"

"We've had this discussion before, Eva. Your father wants you near him."

"In this god forsaken little hellhole," Eva muttered.

"Yes, in this godforsaken hellhole because he loves you and doesn't want you to be alone."

Eva shook her head. "I'm sure he does."

"I know you think they don't care, but they do. Let's not go into this again."

"No." Eva shook her head. "Are you sure you have to leave?"

"Yes, I'm sure. Before I forget, I left instructions with your nurse--"

"Nurse Gestapo," Eva said with a little more venom that she intended.

"Nurse Gestapo?" Frieda laughed. "Your uncle has reviewed her recent notes about your progress. He wants you to walk--"

"Does he know where I am?"

"He does."

"He knows that I'm in the middle of a war zone? In the middle of a shitty little town that just needs the opportunity to kill me?"

"No one is going to kill you."

"I'm in a war zone!"

"I know you are, but you are a civilian."

"Right." Eva nodded. "So all those people we saw lying dead in the fields as we were coming in were soldiers?"

Frieda sighed heavily. "Darling, you must stop talking like this. It is talk that will get you killed, but not by the Greeks."

"I know," Eva mumbled. "I'm more than likely to get shot by my own father."

"Eva!"

Eva merely stared at Frieda. "I can't run anymore. You know

how much I loved to run. I can't even walk properly without looking like a demented cripple."

"I know, but that's in the past now. You have made a remarkable recovery from your injuries and you have to focus on the now. You can walk."

"With the help of my cane."

"You are not confined to a wheelchair like we thought you were going to be. Remember that? You can walk, and the more you walk, the faster your recovery will be. You were very lucky that bomb didn't kill you."

"Yes, very lucky," Eva muttered under her breath. "Will I run again?" She asked hopefully.

"No, you won't run again."

"So what's the point?"

Frieda got up off the bed and took a couple of paces. "Why did you fight to live?"

"I don't think I had a choice."

"Yes, you did. You chose to live rather than die. There is a reason you are still alive. One day you will find that reason."

"I'm a cripple in a war zone."

Frieda shook her head. "No, you are a young woman who has been recovering from your injuries after a bomb blast that almost killed you. Give yourself time to heal."

"I have a lot of time to heal here."

"Yes, you do, and you need to get out of this house. Your uncle wants you walking."

"Great, let Uncle Dieter come over here and walk through this village," Eva replied sarcastically. "What does Uncle Dieter want me to do?"

"He wants you to walk every day beyond this house."

"Where to?"

"I don't know, Evy. I saw a church on the way here. Why don't you make it a goal to walk a bit further from the house and eventually get to the church and back?"

"Where is this church?"

"There're two," Frieda said with a slight smile. "There's one near the center of the village and another just out of the town."

"So I walk to the church."

"Yes, and you go in, have a bit of rest, speak to God, speak to the priest or the nuns and then you come home."

"Hm."

"It will help."

"Hm."

"I'll have a talk to your father about that when I go downstairs and also about hiring a maid to help you."

"Good luck in finding one of those in this village. I think they would rather kill me than help me."

"There you go again with the talk about killing you."

Eva stared up at the ceiling in exasperation. "I know they want to. It's not in my head. I can feel it."

"You are far too pessimistic. It's not that bad and you will have your guards with you."

Eva shook her head. "To the church and back?"

"Yes," Frieda replied with a triumphant smile. "It will help your back. If you can find a swimming pool--"

"Frieda, this place is lucky to have running water."

"Is there a river?"

"There is, but I'm not swimming in it."

"Alright, no swimming. You stick to the walking for now."

"Can I have my letters?" Eva asked with a slight smile.

"I have something else for you as well."

"What's that?"

Frieda took out a small package from her pocket. "Uncle Wilbur said that--"

"Chocolate!" Eva exclaimed as she ripped open the wrapped box.

"Chocolate." Frieda laughed as she watched Eva's face beam with delight. "I know your addiction."

"Uncle Wilbur loves it too." Eva stuffed two squares of chocolate into her mouth and munched happily.

"Amazing what a little drug can do," Frieda said and then laughed as Eva hugged the bar to her chest.

CHAPTER 3

Zoe sat outside the house on an upturned wooden crate and watched the soldiers coming and going from the house across the street. She had a white fabric in her hand, and as she embroidered a pattern, she would occasionally glance up at the soldiers and then back down to her handiwork. She had a great memory—she wasn't sure how it worked, but she could recall everything she saw. She casually glanced down at the watch Stavros had given her.

Zoe's attention was drawn to several soldiers nearly falling over themselves at the entrance to the house. Moments later a tall figure emerged dressed in a black cloak with a hood to cover their head. Zoe scowled and looked up into the heavens. It was a warm, sunny day and there were no clouds in the sky to forecast a weather change, and it wasn't cold either.

"What an idiot," Zoe muttered. The tall figure talked with the guards for a few moments. It was when the cane was produced that Zoe stood up straighter. She had seen that cane before. Very slowly as to not arouse suspicions, she tapped the door behind her, where her cousin was sitting.

"Stav, come out here."

"Now?"

"Now. I want you to see something."

The door to the house opened and Stavros came out feeling his way with a cane. Zoe stood up and offered him her seat while she leaned against the wall. Stavros' "war injury" provided cover for his activities in the Resistance.

"Who is that?" Zoe asked. She decided to sit down on the wooden floor and watch the hooded person.

"Muller's daughter."

"Who?"

"Clean your ears out. I said Muller's daughter," Stavros replied. "Her name is Eva Muller; she's 22 and a cripple."

"What's her dress size?" Zoe teased Stavros.

"I'm not partial to German whores so I don't know," Stavros joked under his breath, making Zoe giggle. "Kiria Despina told me."

"Despina's nice although she is always trying to marry me off. Too bad she is forced to work there for those pigs. Why would you bring a woman into a war zone?"

"You're a woman," Stavros reminded Zoe as he glanced down and smiled at her.

"I live here."

"I don't know why the Nazi brought her here. Maybe Despina is wrong and she's his wife."

"She doesn't look like a cripple," Zoe muttered, but moments later rethought her assessment. One of the soldiers held out a cane which Eva took. "Well, look at that, she is a cripple," Zoe said a little louder than normal. She was more than a little surprised when her comment caused Eva to momentarily stop at the top step. The guards didn't pay any attention to Zoe but Muller's daughter did react. Zoe saw it and smiled.

"Zoe! Lower your voice."

"They're Germans, Stav, they can't speak Greek," she whispered.

"If they can't speak Greek, why are you whispering?"

Zoe grinned and watched Eva laboriously coming down the four steps. "Her shadows can't, but the cripple can speak Greek," she said quietly.

Stavros glanced at Eva in confusion and then back at Zoe. "Zo, the sun's getting to you."

"No. My head is fine." Zoe absentmindedly tapped her head with her hand. "She understood what I said."

"Are you sure?"

"Oh, yes, I'm sure." Zoe nodded and watched as Eva finally got down the steps. She spoke to the guards for a moment before they backed away from her and stood behind her. Zoe was intrigued by this new arrival. The new commander had only been in the village for a few days and Zoe had not seen his daughter at all in that time.

"Come inside."

"No, I want to watch the show," Zoe mumbled as she helped Stavros get up and go inside. She resumed her seat on the overturned crate and saw that Eva had only taken a few steps. She sat up straighter when she saw a gust of wind rip the hood off Eva's head.

"So now you have a face," Zoe muttered.

Eva's long hair disappeared into her cloak. Zoe was mesmerized by the color. She was expecting Eva to be blonde, but she wasn't. Her hair was midnight black with the barest hint of blue as the sun hit it. The artist in Zoe was amazed; the Resistance fighter was intrigued. Eva stopped as the guard put her hood back on and they resumed their slow journey.

Zoe followed Eva's tortuous slow walk to where the house ended and the intersection began. "I wonder what color your eyes are," Zoe mused. "Not bad for a cripple."

Eva stopped and took a breath. She said something to her guard and for a moment Zoe thought it was about her. It wasn't. A few minutes later they resumed their journey. Just as Zoe got up to go into Stavros' house, Major Hans Muller appeared at the entrance. Zoe stopped and sat back down.

Muller was a tall, stocky man in his late forties. Zoe looked into his face as he stood on the landing, waiting for his daughter to come to him. *She sure doesn't look like her papa*, Zoe mused. There was a coldness to him, even for a Nazi. He didn't try to help Eva up the stairs but stood there watching her.

"What an ass," Zoe muttered.

Eva stopped and looked up at Muller. They exchanged a few words which Zoe couldn't quite decipher. Muller did an about face and went back inside the house leaving Eva to walk up the stairs and follow him.

Zoe sneered as Eva's journey up the stairs was taking an extraordinary amount of time. "I'm going to turn fourteen by the time that woman reaches the top step," she muttered and got up and went inside the house.

"So did you enjoy the show?" Stavros said from the window while he continued to watch.

"I thought you said you weren't interested in German whores?"

"I'm not."

"Why are you watching her? Has she reached the top step yet?"

"Yes."

"We should go outside and give her a gold medal. That's an Olympic event."

"What is?" Stavros turned away from the window.

"Slow walking." Zoe giggled. "My god, that took forever."

"Do you care?"

"Nope."

"What did Muller say to her?"

"I don't know." Zoe shrugged and sat down at the table.

"I couldn't hear."

"Why don't you go home and pretty yourself up a little bit?"

"Huh?" Zoe stared at Stavros. "What did you just say?"

"I said go and wear a nice dress and do that thing you do with your hair. Apostolos is coming tonight."

Zoe continued to stare. "What do I do with my hair?"

"You know, that girl thing you do and it looks all nice and pretty."

Zoe smiled. "You are such a boy. Now why do I have to pretty myself up and do that thing I do with my hair?"

Stavros sat down heavily on the chair and rested his head on the table. "Zoe, can we not play this game all the time?"

"You're the one who wants me to pretty myself up."

"Can you please go home and get ready?"

Zoe chuckled. "Mama's going to find this funny."

"Your mama has the patience of a saint."

"I'll let her know you said that." Zoe came round to where Stavros was seated and ruffled his curly black hair. She smiled at her cousin, who looked up at her. "You have to stop trying to match make."

"Apostolos is sweet on you."

"I'm not sweet on him. He's too old."

Stavros let his head drop to the table. "Yes, yes, yes, I know. You don't like how old he is, nor his height, you don't like his dark hair, and you don't like his blue eyes."

"He's not right."

"He can't help being eight years older than you."

"Not that, silly."

"If it's not his age, nor his height, his hair color or his eyes, what is it this time?"

"He has an accent."

"What?" Stavros asked incredulously and started to laugh. He slapped his thigh as the giggles overtook him. "He doesn't have an accent!"

"He's from Athens."

"So?"

"They have a different accent."

Stavros shook his head slowly, causing his curly hair to swing. "How do you know Athenians have a different accent? You've only met one."

"That's enough."

"Zoe, go home and wear that beautiful dress your mama made for you. We have business to discuss tonight."

"Are we going out?"

"Not tonight, but maybe tomorrow night. There's a new batch arriving tomorrow. That's why Apostolos is coming over."

"Can't he send a messenger with the information?"

Stavros smiled. "He is the messenger. He's making a special effort to come and see you."

"Oh, joy," Zoe muttered as she raised herself up and kissed Stavros on the cheek before picking up her bag and leaving the house.

CHAPTER 4

*T*wo weeks later

A low rumble thundered across the valley, threatening rain, and dark clouds hovered menacingly over the mountains. The sound of raucous laughing and curse-filled humor hung in the night air as Stavros and Zoe lay hidden in the brush. In front of them was the barracks that housed the officers of the occupying forces, the pride of the Third Reich. A car was parked outside the house, and a lone soldier leaned against the hood of the car, oblivious to any danger, his rifle slung over his shoulder. The smoke from his cigarette drifted a little as a light breeze rustled the trees nearby.

"What the hell, man, just take a piss and go inside," Stavros muttered quietly as he gazed at the German. His hair was hidden underneath a black beanie. He glanced to his left and winced. "Sorry, Zo," he said. His dark eyes turned back to stare at the soldier as he stretched out his body flat against the ground.

Zoe lifted her head just a little to take a look at the soldier. She had just barely got her eyes above the brushes when Stavros' hand reached out and pushed her head back down.

"What the hell are you doing?"

"Having a look," Zoe whispered as she swatted away Stavros' hand.

"If he had been looking this way… Your red hair could be seen from across the valley!"

Zoe stuck out her tongue at the impertinent way she was being treated. She also wore a black beanie, but it was insufficient to hide the unruly curly hair that peaked out.

"I'm going to shoot the bastard if he doesn't move."

"Can I?"

Stavros glared at Zoe and shook his head. He parted some brush so they could have a look at the soldier. They watched the soldier stub out his cigarette into the ground and for a moment he stood there looking out into the valley. Zoe resisted the urge to groan in frustration as the soldier hefted his rifle across his back and went back inside the house.

Stavros dragged his rucksack through the dirt and sat up, being extremely careful not to be seen from the windows of the officer's quarters. He glanced at the house before turning his attention to the reason they were there. He took out four dynamite sticks with a timer attached. He shook his head and Zoe looked at him with concern.

"What's the matter?"

"The car is too low; I can't get under," Stavros whispered and pointed to the car, which would not be able to hide his almost six-foot frame.

Zoe lifted her head and focused on the car. "I bet I can go under that."

"This is dynamite—you could blow yourself up."

"Now why would I do a stupid thing like that?" Zoe hissed. "I can be very useful, Stav."

"I know you can but this--"

"Well, I don't see you getting any shorter or leaner." Zoe glared at Stavros. "We want this to happen, right?"

"Yes."

"Right, tell me what I have to do."

Stavros sighed and glanced down at the time bomb. "Go under the car and position it, and make sure it won't fall off."

"How will it fall off if I make sure it won't?"

Stavros shook his head slowly as he set the timer. "I promised Theo I was going to keep you safe."

"Well, that's a silly thing to promise," Zoe replied. She gave Stavros a kiss on the cheek. "I promise not to blow us up so you won't have to break a promise to my brother."

"That would be good."

Zoe took the bomb and started to crawl out of the brushes. She was hidden from view of the window for a good portion of the way under the car, except in one area where there was an unobstructed view. She watched the window and waited until the soldier that had his back towards her moved. She quickly crawled under the car, which indeed was just right for her slender frame.

Zoe took the bomb and began to fasten it to the undercarriage. She stopped moving when she saw a flash of light spread across the ground. She froze and tried not to move as several men left the house and congregated just meters from where she was hiding. She closed her eyes and tried to calm her galloping heart from escaping out of her chest.

Zoe felt the long excruciating wait drag on as the men lingered. At one point someone dropped a lighter which landed just near the rear tire, making Zoe's eyes widen in fear. She tracked the man's hand that felt along the tire and captured the lighter. His hand was a short span away from her head. She held her breath when the man dropped the lighter again, but this time he didn't pick it up and kicked it under the car instead. The lighter hit the tire, ricocheted, and came to rest against Zoe's arm.

Zoe watched the booted feet of the soldiers move off and she exhaled. Her head was pounding from the anxiety. Without wasting any more time, she finished affixing the dynamite and began to crawl out. She flattened herself against the ground and looked up into the window from under the car. Seeing no one at the window, she crawled out and scampered back into the brushes where Stavros was waiting.

"Oh, god, Zo," Stavros whispered and smothered her in an embrace. "Are you alright?"

"I nearly wet my pants." Zoe giggled and glanced up at Stavros with a triumphant grin. "Fumble fingers nearly made my heart stop."

Stavros leaned in and kissed her on the cheek. Before he could say anything else, the door to the house opened and five officers spilled out into the night. The two Resistance operatives watched as the men went into the car.

"Good night, boys," Stavros whispered and tried to glance at his watch in the darkness. He could barely make out the time. He had set the timer for five minutes past midnight. It was now midnight and the officers were on schedule. "One good thing about the Germans—they are punctual."

The car spluttered to life and stayed motionless for a few minutes. Stavros motioned for Zoe to start crawling backwards as the time was counting down and the car was still there. Just as they had gone several meters away, the car began to move.

Zoe grinned and began to count down. A minute later the car exploded, sending a fireball into the air. "Hope Hell is welcoming," she muttered.

"Amen," Stavros replied and crossed himself. "Come on, Zo, I promised your mama you would be back before midnight."

"You and your promises," Zoe said with a smile as Stavros ruffled her hair. He took her by the hand and they fled away from the explosion.

CHAPTER 5

*S*ix months later.

Captain Jurgen Reinhardt winced at the expletives that reverberated around the room. It wasn't the first time he had heard his commander scream, but not at quite that volume. The ambush of the new squad had caught them by surprise, even though they were anticipating trouble from the Resistance. They were always anticipating trouble.

Reinhardt flinched when Major Muller came within inches and screamed. "What happened?" He yelled, waving a flyer in front of the captain's face. Reinhardt watched as the veins stood out starkly against the redness that enveloped Muller's face and neck. "Well, are you going to answer me or are you going to stand there mute?"

Muller had already read the flyer that the Greek Partisans had produced. It was indeed the same as the one he had flung through the window moments before in rage. It proudly accepted responsibility for the bombing of the train tracks. The major made a snorting noise and crumpled the flyer in his hand.

"We lost the train tracks again and the train fell down the gorge," Reinhardt stammered.

"How many did we lose?" Muller yelled.

"Fifty men and four officers."

Muller closed his eyes and continued to yell his abuse at the Resistance. He threw the door open, startling the two guards standing outside the office.

"Where do these men think they are? A resort? Why wasn't there anyone on guard?"

"I don't think--"

"Make sure that never happens again!"

"Yes, sir."

"Actions speak louder than words, Reinhardt."

"Yes, sir," Reinhardt stammered, and then glanced towards the open door.

"Round them up and I will give the Resistance my answer."

"Round up the men?"

Muller glared at his second in command. "Round up the villagers."

"Where do I take them, sir?"

"The field near the town square. That's a good place for it."

"Yes, sir. How many?"

"Everyone," Muller said and then left the office and headed to the next room down the small corridor. He knocked on the door and entered.

Nurse Edith Ratsger was seated at her desk in the small room that doubled as a bedroom and her office. She was a petite middle-aged woman with deep-set blue eyes behind wire-framed spectacles. Her long blond hair was up in a tight bun under her white nurse's hat. She and Muller were dear friends, and when Eva needed a nurse Muller thought of his friend Edith, who he knew was a very good nurse and was able to travel with them to France and then Greece.

"Edith, you wanted to see me?"

"Was that you bellowing a moment ago?" Edith asked with a slight smile.

"Yes, that was me." Muller sat down on Edith's bed opposite her chair. "Did you hear about our men?"

"I did. Those poor boys. I heard that the Resistance has blown up that line a few times. It has to stop, Hans."

"I know. I'll make them stop. Can you write to their parents and I will sign the letters?"

"I could but I think you should give that job to Eva; it will help with her recovery."

"How will it help?"

"It will give her something to do other than brooding in her room. Now, how are you going to stop the Resistance?"

"I'm going to send a message to the Greeks. They will be made to listen."

"Hm." Edith took off her glasses. "Would you like me to come with you?"

"Yes, if you want to. It would be good for Eva to see a strong woman standing up to these animals." Muller shook his head. "Now your note said you wanted to see me?"

Edith put her glasses back on and nodded. "It's about Eva."

"What has my daughter done now?"

"I have been thinking about Eva's care--"

"What about her care?"

"I think you should hire a maid."

"What's wrong with Despina?"

"She's the housekeeper and has enough to do around here without being Eva's maid as well."

"Hm. She had one in Aiden and in Paris before the bombing. Unfortunately, she died in the blast. Does she really need one?"

"Eva won't allow me to help bathe her," Edith replied. "She is quite adamant about it but I know she finds it difficult with her condition."

"Yes." Muller nodded. "I don't know—that is something for you and her to discuss. I won't force her to have a maid, especially here. You will need to convince her of that."

"There is my problem."

"Eva is a stubborn woman, but for this matter let her make the choice."

Edith nodded. "There is one more thing."

"Yes?"

"I found quite a few pills thrown away in the garbage and I know they belong to Eva."

Muller leaned forward on the edge of the bed. "Are you sure they're hers?"

"Yes, quite sure."

Muller sighed. "What was I saying about my daughter being stubborn? What medication is it?"

"Pain medication."

Muller shook his head. "She would rather be in pain than take the drugs?"

"She tried this in Paris and I let her get away with it."

"What happened then? You didn't tell me about this."

"Hans, you don't need to know everything. If it's important I will tell you. It lasted a few days until she couldn't hold out anymore and she started to take them on her own," Edith said with a smile.

"That won't always work."

"I know, but eventually she does buckle."

"Alright, I will have a word with her. Other than her being stubborn, how is she?"

"It's a difficult place for someone like Eva."

Muller nodded. "She will just have to adjust."

"She is trying and she has been exercising more with going out of the house. This is a good thing." Edith reached out and touched Muller's hand. "Dieter wants her to move around, and walking will ease the pain in her back."

"It will?"

"Yes. She needs the exercise."

"General Rhimes' nurse Frieda said she saw a church not far from here. She thinks it would be a good landmark for her to reach."

"I agree with Frieda. By the way there's a nice lookout not far from here…"

Muller grinned as he held Edith's hand. "You found a lookout after being here for a few days?"

"I didn't find it on my own." Edith smiled at the look she was getting from Muller. "Despina told me about it. It's called Athena's Bluff—beautiful location overlooking the valley."

"Hm, maybe when the mayhem dies down a little, we could go up there and have a look?"

"Oh? When do you anticipate the mayhem dying down a little? You don't even sit down to eat properly and you're going on a picnic with me?" Edith teasingly asked.

Muller chuckled. "Yes, that's true. That will have to wait. So you want to send Eva to this church and then to Athena's Bluff?"

"Yes, it would be good for her to get out and it will strengthen her legs and back."

"Alright. I'll have two guards escort her when she's out." Muller got up to leave and started to walk away when he stopped. "Edith, have you noticed anything I should be worried about?"

"I would tell you if I did. There is nothing to worry about." Edith nodded. "Dieter's therapy has worked, so *that* won't happen again. Didn't he tell you?"

"Dieter told me that the therapy worked and that Eva was cured. I don't know though...."

Edith took off her glasses and regarded Muller for a moment. "Dieter has been experimenting with his method of eradicating unwanted personality traits for a long time. He has worked with some of the best. Now, many of us as little children stuck our hand in a fire, didn't we?"

"Of course."

"Once we got burnt, we realized that sticking our hand in the fire wasn't a good idea because it would hurt," Edith patiently explained. She held up her hand to forestall Muller's question. "We know that if we continued to put our hand in the fire, we would cause ourselves pain."

"Unless you were a 'useless eater.'"

"Hans! I really hate that phrase."

"It's true," Muller responded with a shrug.

"Need I remind you that my brother was wounded during the Great War and was crippled? I dislike that phrase."

Muller sighed. "I'm sorry Edith, I wasn't referring to Konrad. He is a war hero."

Edith dabbed her eyes with her handkerchief. "I love our Führer, but I dislike that phrase."

"I know." Hans moved to sit next to Edith and put his arm around her shoulders to comfort her. "I'm sorry."

"Where was I? Oh, yes, we don't go around putting our hand in a fire. We learn by experience, and Dieter has perfected his conversion therapy so that Eva is physically very ill when..." Edith stopped when she saw Muller's furrowed brow deepen. "Do you want me stop?"

"No." Muller shook his head. "Explain it to me."

"When someone like Eva is physically attracted to a woman it would be the equivalent of her sticking her hand on an open flame—it would hurt her. Eva's interactions with women are fine as long as she doesn't have any physical feelings for them."

"She can interact with you or any other woman without the hand in the fire reaction?"

"Yes. If Eva has any feeling of a sexual nature, then Dieter's therapy will trigger the pain response."

Muller looked down at his hands for a long moment and nodded, feeling uncomfortable about discussing Eva's mental lapse. After a long moment he looked up at Edith. "How do we know if this has worked?"

"Dieter tested Eva back in Aiden. She was married to Erik for two years and he believes she's cured. It's worked, Hans. I've treated a few patients that had similar mental problems such as Eva and they have been cured. It's a mental problem that is easily fixed."

"What about here?"

Edith smiled at Muller's reluctance to believe the conversion therapy had worked. "I will be keeping an eye on her and she will be tested. I saw Eva and Captain Reinhardt kissing yesterday. They have been flirting since he joined you after the bombing."

Muller smiled broadly at such good news. "Really?"

Edith chuckled. "The normal response to that revelation would be one of shock and dismay that your little girl is kissing a boy."

"Yes, it would be, but I don't have a normal little girl."

"She is normal. She lost her way but she's back now."

"Good, maybe I should--"

"No, you should not meddle. Let the young man court her without having her father looking over his shoulder," Edith gently reprimanded her friend. "Eva is finally jumping back into the pond."

"She can jump in the pond if she wants as long as she doesn't jump in the other pond."

"That won't happen."

"I hope you are right."

"Don't worry, Hans."

"Good," Muller replied as he rose to leave.

"Are you taking Eva with you?"

"Yes."

"It is raining; maybe you should leave her here."

"No. I want her there. Having you there will show her what strength and courage is all about," Muller said as he opened the door and left to go find Eva.

The windows rattled as the wind got stronger outside. The unseasonably warm May weather of yesterday had deteriorated overnight. Eva sat in her desk beside the window and watched the rain splatter against it. She hated Larissa. She hated the backward villagers who didn't bother to hide their hatred. She knew she would; that wasn't the surprise. She wasn't sure if the villagers pitied her or out rightly despised her on her sojourns outside.

Eva's attention was drawn away from her thoughts of the humiliating 'walk' when she heard Muller talking to one of the soldiers outside. Moments later, he entered the room she had been given as a small office. She wasn't sure why she needed an office when she had a bedroom, but she wasn't about to question her father on that or why she was placed upstairs and not downstairs.

"Get ready. We are going out."

Eva mentally sighed as she got up from her seat. "Father, it's raining--"

"I'm well aware that it's raining. I can see it," Muller tersely replied.

"I don't want to go outside," Eva mumbled as she looked down at her hands.

"That is not your decision to make."

Eva looked up at Muller. "Father--"

"Did you not hear what I just said to you?"

"Yes, sir."

"Think of it as an extension of what you have been doing."

"It was dif—"

"Don't show weakness." Muller grabbed hold of Eva's cheeks and held her face in a vice-like grip. "You are a Muller, god dammit! Behave like one. We do not show weakness," he growled as he came inches from her face. "Do you understand me?"

Eva swallowed her fear and blinked back the tears that threatened to spill. "Yes."

"Yes, what?"

"Yes, Father," Eva said as Muller released his grip. She dropped her eyes and stood with her hands clasped together in front of her.

"Your uncle wants me to give him reports on your progress. You will continue this regime, as I said, but you won't do it piecemeal. You will walk to the church every day. If it takes you an hour or four hours, you will do that. If you have to stop every five steps, do it, but you will walk to that church and beyond. Edith tells me there is a nice lookout just out of town. I want you to aim to get to the church and to that lookout."

"Yes, sir."

"Sergeant Franz will continue as your guard. You are not to leave the house without him. Do you understand?"

"Yes, sir."

"You will not pull the same stunt by leaving on your own like you did in France. We have discussed this more than a few times but you seem to want to disobey me."

"I won't disobey you."

"Good, because the next time you do it, I will have both guards shot. Their deaths will be on your head and you will have to write to their mothers to tell them why. Do you understand me?"

"Yes, Father."

"Good. Now as for your walks, you can take as long as you like to get there and come back. Your uncle wants you to get stronger. You've spent a lot of time healing in Aiden and then France. It's been a difficult time and you have resisted your uncle's advice." Muller sighed and sat down on the sofa. He took off his hat and ran his hands through his short blond hair. "You are too stubborn, Eva. Erik was too much in love with you to follow Dieter's instructions and you spent years doing nothing in getting stronger."

"I don't see--"

"I don't care what you see or don't see. You will listen to your uncle's advice. He is your physician and he knows what you can and can't do. Had you listened to what he was asking you to do, you would be able to walk more easily."

"It's a bit hard to do when I can't move properly," Eva muttered.

"Whose fault is that?" Muller asked as he leaned back on the sofa and regarded Eva. "I know I said I wasn't going to mention this again because you have been cured of this sickness, but you shamed me and your mother by being with that woman. Did you not consider that this would come to the light?"

"Father--"

Muller rose from the sofa and stood in front of Eva. He stared into her sky-blue eyes. "Your uncle tells me this deviant behavior has been cured and I want to believe him. If you give me a reason to doubt it, I will not be as merciful as I have been in letting you live."

Eva swallowed audibly and nodded. "I am cured, Father."

"I hope so. Now Edith has told me you are refusing to take all your medication."

"They make me sick; I feel funny when I take them."

"Are we going to have this discussion again? You will take your medication or I will be forced to have the medics give it to you with you strapped down to a bed. What do you prefer?"

"I will take it."

"Good. Now what is this about you not wanting a maid?"

"We are in the middle of a war zone--"

"I'm well aware of that. I just lost good men to the Resistance when they blew up the train line. What does that have to do with your reluctance for a maid? You had one back home. Never mind, I don't have time for this. If you want a maid, tell me when you are ready."

"I will."

Muller gazed at Eva for a moment. "A little bird has told me that a certain young captain is courting you."

"Yes." Eva nodded bashfully.

Muller nodded. "Good. I will tell him to behave himself."

"Father! Please don't make him nervous; he's already scared of you."

"Good, a young man should be scared of the father of the young lady he is courting. Now get dressed and wear something warmer."

"Where are we going?"

Muller stopped at the door and turned back. "To teach the Greeks a lesson."

"It's raining."

"Yes, I know, I can see."

"But--"

"Eva." Muller stopped at the door and sighed. "Get ready," he said and closed the door behind him.

Eva leaned against the desk and dropped her chin down to her chest as the pain from her back injury overwhelmed her. Standing up to Muller took a lot of effort. His threats were real. She was living proof that he could inflict the pain he threatened her with. He would kill her if he wanted to without any remorse.

Eva glanced back at the window when it rattled as thunder boomed overhead. Someone was going to die today and there was nothing anyone could do about that.

CHAPTER 6

*E*va looked up at the dark sky and waited for her guards to get themselves organized. She stood outside the house just under a tree which afforded her some shelter from the rain. A car was standing by to take them the short distance to the town square. They didn't need a car, since the field where the villagers were being assembled was a few minutes' walk. Eva didn't think this was for her benefit. She smiled when she saw Reinhardt exit the house and put on his hat.

"You're going to need a hot drink after this," Eva whispered when Reinhardt joined her at the bottom of the steps.

Jurgen Reinhardt was what Hitler envisioned the Aryan race to be—a tall, muscular young man of twenty five, blond-haired, with blue eyes and a devotion to the army; a career soldier. He had been Major Muller's right hand man since joining him in France and now in Greece. He smiled when he saw Eva and put his arm around her. "Your father just had a chat with me."

"Oh, dear."

"Hm. I think I need something stronger than a hot drink," Reinhardt said with a slight smile. "He's given us his blessing."

Eva mentally sighed. "Remind him next time he yells at you."

"I don't think I'm going to remind him of that," Reinhardt replied as he tenderly brushed a leaf that had fallen on Eva's hair. "Why are you out here in the rain? You should go back inside. There's no need for you to be here."

"Papa wants me to be there."

"Ah, well, that explains it." Reinhardt looked around at the assembled men. "I won't be able to be at your side but I'm sure Franz will protect you," he said as he watched Eva's guard heading their way. Sergeant Henry Franz was a giant of a man who towered over Eva's six foot two frame. His helmet covered a bald head. He had thick blond eyebrows over deep-set green eyes.

"You are to escort Fraulein Muller when we get to the field. Do not let her slip, do not let her fall, do not let her get wet. You are to protect her."

"Yes, sir," Henry replied, causing Eva to smile. Henry's quiet voice was in stark contrast to his size. Eva turned to Reinhardt, who had put on his hat and adjusted his uniform. "Go and organize your troops."

Reinhardt smiled, hesitated for a moment before he kissed her gently on the lips and walked away to assemble the men.

"It's going to a very wet day, Henry."

Eva looked around at the soldiers and also at the villagers who were heading in the direction of the field. She wondered if they knew what awaited them. Would it make any difference if she told them to run, to escape? More than likely she would get them killed and herself. She turned to Henry, who was standing very close to her holding an umbrella. The umbrella looked ridiculously small compared to his size.

"You're getting wet."

Henry smiled. "I'll live."

"We're going to be sloshing through the mud."

"I know, but if need be, I will carry you."

Eva nodded, well aware that Henry was capable of carrying her if there was any trouble at the execution of innocent lives. The thought made her sick to her stomach—innocent lives would be snuffed out on the say so of one man. She involuntarily shuddered at the impending deaths. Orders were being barked out and Muller had descended down the stairs wearing his gun holster. Henry held out his arm for Eva to hold as she slowly made her way to the car.

Riding with them was Major Bonhoffen, who had arrived in the afternoon. Eva felt nothing but a dread come over her whenever Bonhoffen was in her vicinity. He was brandishing his pistol and smiled menacingly at the villagers who passed him. He was a much-despised man, a violent and irrational German. Eva had witnessed his brutality first hand in France. She had seen people shot dead in retaliation for Resistance activities without remorse. It was Bonhoffen who insisted that the soldiers' deaths in Larissa needed to be avenged, and Muller agreed.

Zoe and her mother Helena walked slowly towards the field. As she looked around the small farming community, Zoe carefully watched her fellow countrymen walking quietly to the town center. They were subdued. Memories arose of balmy summer nights walking along with her friends, memories of carefree days when the worst that happened was a boy yanking her hair and being generally a nuisance.

Those boys were no longer there, no longer part of her life. Zoe felt her throat constrict and tried to swallow the lump in her throat but couldn't. Tears threatened to spill but were kept back by sheer will. She didn't want those German bastards to see her cry. She didn't want to show any weakness. It was also the last thing she wanted for her mama to see. Too many nights were spent crying over the deaths of her brothers and her father. Zoe mentally shook herself and glanced at Helena, who was talking animatedly with her cousin.

Zoe's attention shifted as a group of soldiers passed by. She wondered when the nightmare would end. To the Germans, the Greeks were a stubborn people who refused to surrender when all was lost. To the Greeks, the Germans were going to know that the country was not going to be subjugated without a struggle, without exacting a heavy price from the occupying force.

The town gathering had become a regular occurrence with the German commander. Major Helgberg was a sadistic man who took delight in torturing the populace. News of his death was met with muted delight—they knew another monster would take his place soon enough. They were right and a demon had taken up Helgberg's mantle for brutality, if the stories everyone had been hearing were true.

They arrived at Maragos' Field, which was now an execution field—it was where many innocent villagers had been murdered and the soil was drenched in the blood of the Greeks. Zoe sighed and looked down at the brown sludgy mud under her feet.

The Κομμουνιστικο Κομμα Ελλαδας, the Communist Party of Greece or KKE, had established a formidable Resistance group and was active in the countryside surrounding Larissa. The Communists had years of experience in working underground and thus formed the best Resistance to the German occupation. The extensive cave system in the hills was used by the KKE to escape and hide from the Germans. Once organized, they hit back at the invaders by blowing up train tracks and disrupting the German supply lines from Athens to Thessaloniki. Other attacks were made by small groups of men descending from the mountains and raiding German troops when they least expected it. The KKE was soon joined by other Greek Resistance groups such Ethnikos Dimokratikos Ellinikos Stratos– National Republican Greek League or EDES — and Ethniki kaí Koinoniki Apelefthérosis — the National and Social Liberation or EKKA.

These attacks brought the wrath of the Germans on the civilians. The German policy of retaliation was to kill civilians and destroy their villages. Helgberg had directed these retaliatory actions in Larissa and the surrounding areas until the Resistance killed him.

Zoe glanced around her at familiar faces, faces that betrayed their fear. She saw old men and women barely being able to stand, huddled in the rain. The young children clasped their mothers' hands. Some were too young to know what was to come. She felt sick as she glanced at her own mother, who had her eyes closed and was silently praying.

"I love you, Mama," Zoe whispered. She took hold of Helena's hand.

Helena opened her eyes and smiled. "I love you so much, my child. Have faith in God; we will be all right. Saint Achillius will protect us," she said and leaned down and kissed the top of Zoe's red-gold hair.

Eva's shoes made that awful sloshing noise as she traipsed through the mud to get to the field. Henry held her arm and he was true to his word. Eva felt at times as if he was holding her up instead of her walking on her own. Assembled was a large group of women and children, their eyes darting back and forth, uncertainty and fear written on their faces. She could not look at them; she felt their fear and wanted to call out for them to run but there was nowhere to run. She kept her eyes down, not daring to look up and meet any of the villagers in the eye.

Eva was wet and cold. The cold wind penetrated deep into her bones and she shivered uncontrollably. Henry held the umbrella and shielded her from the drizzly misty rain that had now turned into a downpour. The wind had picked up and occasionally would turn the umbrella inside out. Muller and Bonhoffen were standing near the car and looked happy. Bonhoffen laughed as an old woman slipped in the mud, which only sickened Eva even more. She could barely breathe as she slowly made her way to where Muller told her to stand.

Eva swallowed and closed her eyes while Muller's voice screamed orders as he came closer. He was enjoying the terror he was inflicting; she could hear it in his voice.

Eva opened her eyes and focused on the first villager that stared back at her—the girl that had called her a cripple. Fiery green eyes met her sky-blue ones. Defiance stared back at her, daring her to do something, but Eva was just as helpless as the girl. The young girl's hatred was palpable—it almost reached out towards her and defied her to act. Eva looked away, unable to watch the heart-rending scene that was to unfold before her. She gazed out into the horizon and watched the rain come pelting down—anything but the ugliness she was going to witness.

Zoe's gaze fell on their much despised commander when he emerged through the crowds, his pristine gray and black uniform neatly creased. Zoe looked at the mud, then back at Muller, and sneered. She was about to go down and collect some mud to welcome him properly when Helena's hand held her.

"Don't," Helena whispered. "You're going to get us killed."

Zoe rolled her eyes and clasped her hands together instead. A wry grin formed on her lips as she envisioned applying the mud herself. She was abruptly brought out of her daydream when the sound of a gunshot pierced the air making her jump.

"As you have all heard by now, we don't have a train line. The reason you are all here, is because I want you to send a message to the Resistance."

Zoe's attention shifted from the murderous, ranting Nazi to the woman standing a few feet away from him. Zoe turned to Stavros. "That's the cripple," she whispered as she gazed at the woman.

Eva's long black cloak covered most of her body, and luckily for her, a soldier stood with an umbrella over her, shielding her from the rain that once again fell. Zoe shivered as the rain pelted her in the face. Her coat had long since been soaked. She kept staring at Eva, whose angular face was barely visible in the gloom and shadow of the cloak and umbrella, and she was surprised when Eva turned her gaze towards her.

Their eyes met and Zoe glared back in defiance. She was almost tempted to reach down and pick up the rock that she could feel under her foot. The woman just stared. Didn't move, didn't blink. She just stared at Zoe.

Zoe jumped at the sound of the gun going off. To her utter horror, this time the German's aim was not in the air but directed at a feeble old man. In the blink of an eye, the old man crumpled to the ground, the blood streaming down his face. His eyes gazed up into the sky, unseeing.

Zoe turned to see that it wasn't Bonhoffen who had fired but Muller. He was brandishing his pistol and stamping his barbarous authority. There was no rhyme or reason to the execution and Zoe wanted to disappear, to hide from the utter senselessness.

The villagers panicked, but couldn't escape, as the field was surrounded by German troops. Those that tried to flee faced either Muller's gun or the guns of his troops. Zoe watched in horror as the young and the elderly fell.

Then the unthinkable happened. Muller stepped in front of Zoe and her mother and looked at them. Blue eyes met green for a very long moment. Helena put her arms around Zoe and held on tight. All Zoe could hear was the sound of the beating of her heart. All she could see was the look of utter hatred in Muller's eyes.

"So you see, Greeks will die for the soul of every Aryan hero who is killed," Muller was saying, but Zoe could barely discern what he was talking about, the sound of her heart was thundering so loudly in her ears.

Zoe's gaze shifted to Eva, who had once again turned and was watching her. Zoe could almost hear a voice in her head telling her to keep watching—*keep looking; don't look away*. She swallowed her fear as Muller came within inches of her head. The gun was so close to her face that she could smell the gun smoke, but she didn't move. She didn't look away from Eva, who was staring back at her. Zoe didn't look at the monster that was a hair's breadth away from her.

Zoe wanted to hide her face from this madness. She held tight to Helena and prayed to Saint Achillius, hoping against hope. But she could not stifle the sound of the gun popping so close that she felt the bullet rush past her when it exploded in its next victim.

Mama.

Zoe felt Helena's arms release their grasp, and to her horror, she saw her beloved mother slump to the ground. A dark crimson stain spread across Helena's chest. The madness continued around her as she held her dying mother to her chest, the blood mixing with the mud, caking her legs. *Oh dear God, Mama!*

Zoe's soul was shattered that very moment. Everything that was, everything that she was going to be, perished as her mother's life ebbed away. She held Helena, who was talking to her, trying to tell her everything in those few seconds that they had left.

"Be brave," Helena whispered, unable to breathe as the pain in her chest was overwhelming.

"I will take care of her," Stavros vowed as he knelt beside Helena.

Zoe was oblivious to everyone except Helena, but then a sound, something incongruous to the pain and death surrounding them, made her look up. To her utter horror Eva was chuckling as she walked away from the carnage along with the German butcher.

In that instant between life and death, Zoe's purpose in life crystallized. She looked down at Helena's face and rocked her back and forth. "I promise I will kill them. I will," she repeated, over and over. Nothing else had meaning any more. She was going to exact her revenge for Helena's death and kill the woman that laughed as her mother lay dying. "I promise you, Mama, I will kill them. I promise," Zoe kept repeating as Helena passed away.

"Zoe."

Zoe opened her eyes to find the village priest, Father Panayiotis Haralambos, his black robes covered in crimson stains, looking at her. "You can let go now," he said gently as he tried to pry the dead woman from Zoe's arms.

"No." Zoe shook her head. "No," she murmured while Father Haralambos gently separated her from Helena's body. He picked

Zoe up, cradling her in his arms, and Zoe curled up against his chest. She buried her head against his neck and sobbed. Father Haralambos looked back at Stavros, who was kneeling next to Helena, and nodded before walking away from the carnage.

CHAPTER 7

*S*ix months later.

The sound of crunching leaves was the only distraction for Zoe as she walked purposefully away from the cemetery. She had dodged a few patrols—the last thing she wanted was to tangle with yet another group of soldiers. She was sick of them, sick of their superior attitude and even sicker of their machismo. She used to take delight in setting small booby traps for the soldiers and would often hide and watch her handiwork. Since her mother's death, Zoe had a new purpose and it wasn't to annoy the Germans but to inflict as much damage as she could.

Zoe pulled the coat collar tighter around her neck as the wind picked up and she hurried along. Her frequent visits to the cemetery had started soon after Helena had been killed. Someone had told Zoe that the dead could hear the thoughts of the living, mostly to console her, but she had latched onto the idea for dear life. She was a common sight in the cemetery, cleaning the graves of her parents and brothers, talking to herself and drawing as she sat for hours. Many thought she had lost her sanity and pitied her.

Zoe was lost in thought until a hand touched her on the shoulder and she jumped in surprise. "Whoa!"

"Zoe, where were you?"

"What?" Zoe turned to find Father Haralambos standing beside her, his long black robes reaching to the ground and his large gold cross glistening in the sunlight. His normal headdress was replaced with a beret, which looked a little out of place. "Nice hat," Zoe muttered.

"You were daydreaming again," Father Haralambos teased. He had become a surrogate parent to Zoe after Helena's death. He had given her a place to stay, and he had cared for her during those long months when she just wanted to lie in bed and refused to move at all.

"Father," Zoe said as she bowed and kissed Father Haralambos' hand in reverence. She may have lost her faith in God on that godforsaken day when Helena was killed, but she still loved and respected the priest.

"I want to speak to you."

"Why?"

"It's an important matter and we need to speak inside." Father Haralambos indicated the church, which made Zoe scowl. She had not entered Saint Spiridon Church, the only church in the village, since Helena's death. "Please?"

Zoe didn't reply but walked up the stairs reluctantly. She stood still for a moment and, without thinking, crossed herself before entering. Father Haralambos smiled.

"Alright, I'm here." Zoe folded her arms and waited impatiently.

"We don't see you at church these days. Is something wrong, my child?" Father Haralambos' blue eyes bore into Zoe. He knew the answer to his question but wanted to reach her, to try to get her faith restored. He knew he had a difficult task ahead of him. He didn't believe Zoe's faith had entirely died—it was just buried in a very deep hole.

Zoe stared up at the icon of Jesus and then back at Father Haralambos. "I have no use for it."

"You have no use for your faith?"

"There is no God."

Father Haralambos nodded. "So sayeth the fool."

"What?" Zoe asked sharply.

"My dear child, the Bible says that those who don't believe in God are fools."

"Well." Zoe sighed. "I'm a fool then. I have to get going, Father."

"I need to speak to you." Father Haralambos smiled and polished his cross against his black robes.

"What about?"

"Please, don't go out tonight."

"Stavros has a big mouth. It's a miracle he hasn't killed himself," Zoe muttered.

"He confided in me and he was worried. He was a little--"

"Let me guess, he was scared?"

"No, he was concerned."

"It's not the first time I've gone out with the Resistance."

"No, it's not but--"

"Stavros doesn't want me to go because he thinks I'm still a young child. That child died when my mama was murdered." Zoe's brow furrowed as she glared at Father Haralambos. "What have you been doing, Father?"

Father Haralambos stroked his long beard and smiled. "I can honestly say I have never killed a man so I don't know that is like, but you are losing your soul."

"I can't lose what I don't have. They took it from me."

"I love you and I don't want to see you get hurt, or worse—get killed."

Zoe sat down heavily on a chair and gazed down at the floor. "What would it matter if I got killed? There's no one left to mourn me if I do."

"Now that's a silly thing to say. Stavros, myself, the village, your aunty Stella. So many people would miss you."

Zoe looked up and blinked in the glow of the candlelight. "I want to be with Mama and Papa. I don't want to be alive anymore. I want to join them."

"Is that why you're going out tonight? You want to get killed?" Father Haralambos gently asked as he pulled a chair and sat down opposite Zoe. "That's suicide, Zoe. God hasn't given you the right to take your life."

"It's alright, I'll let the Germans do it," Zoe flippantly replied.

"You will not go to heaven to be with your mama and papa if you do that. Suicide is a severe sin and one that should not be flippantly entertained."

Zoe looked up at the crucified Christ and sighed. "So no killing myself with the help of the Germans?"

"No. If you choose that path, God will know."

"So, Jesus didn't kill himself with the help of the Jews?"

"Zoe!"

"What?" Zoe held up her hand and pointed to the icon of Jesus. "He let them kill him. He could have escaped but he let them. That's the same thing."

Father Haralambos shook his head slowly. "Are you making out that you and Jesus are the same?"

"Well, he let the Jews kill him with the help of the Romans.

Those…" Zoe stopped and looked sheepishly at the priest. "Those bad Italians, they are a terrible lot."

Father Haralambos laughed; he just couldn't help it. His laugh echoed in the chamber. "You always make me laugh."

"You mean when I'm not exasperating you." Zoe grinned. She took a deep breath before she asked her next question. "Is it a sin to kill people, Father? Is it alright if I go out tonight and shoot these bastards—"

"Zoe! You're in church! Please, don't swear."

"Sorry," Zoe mumbled. "Isn't it a sin if I kill these nasty men?"

"Those who kill by the sword, die by the sword."

"What does that mean?"

"It means that if you kill, you may get killed yourself and I don't want that to happen to you," Father Haralambos explained. "Yes, it is a sin to take another human's life, but we are at war. I believe God is on our side. We fight not for riches or glory but we fight for the greater good. We fight to save our enslaved brothers and sisters. This is a just fight."

"Even those without a sword die by the sword. My mama didn't have a sword and she's dead."

"Yes. Not everyone who passes away wields a sword, but this is war."

"Why don't you join in the fight, Father?"

"Remember the scripture about not letting your right hand know what your left hand is doing?"

Zoe nodded.

"You do not know what I'm doing. That's how it should be. The less you know, the better it is; for your safety and mine."

"Are you saying you're in the Resistance?"

"I'm saying you shouldn't ask too many questions," Father Haralambos replied with a tiny smile. "Now I want you to promise me that tonight you won't try to sin."

"Um—Father, I'm trying to kill Germans. That's a sin."

"I'm talking about a far greater sin. Your eternal soul depends on you not committing that sin."

Zoe melodramatically sighed. "Yes. I promise I won't."

"Good. I know you have been taught that your 'yes' means 'yes,' and your 'no' means 'no,' so I will take you on your word."

"Not that I will be around for you to tell me off." Zoe giggled and almost immediately stifled that giggle on seeing Father Haralambos' stern look directed at her. "Alright, I won't do it."

"Thank you. I also want you to take care of Stavros. He worries about you so much and you give him much to worry about."

"Stavros is a good man. I'll try not to worry him too much."

Father Haralambos put his arm around Zoe and kissed the top of her head. "I love you very much, Zoe. God loves you as well. Now go home or else Stavros will worry where you are."

Zoe left the church and, walking quickly, rounded the corner toward home. She stopped and looked up into the heavens. "Why is it that my plans just don't work out? A sin this and a sin that." Zoe was a little annoyed but also somewhat pleased Father Haralambos had taken an interest in her, and she walked cheerily back home.

The wind was blowing her long red hair into her eyes. She absentmindedly brushed back the strands as she turned toward the sound of a black car coming to a stop across the road from where she stood. A young soldier held the door open and Major Muller got out with a scowl on his face. He always wore the same expression.

Zoe was about to enter her small house when she caught sight of a familiar figure coming up the cobblestone street. A sneer curled her lips. The distinctive, tall figure of Eva Muller made its way slowly up the street, her head bowed. She wore a cloak; Zoe had never seen her without the garment on. Eva wore it even on hot summer days. On a few occasions she had seen Eva without the hood up but never without the cloak on. Now the hood covered her head, but it was unmistakably her.

Zoe's hatred for Muller's daughter was well known in the village and she had already been prevented twice from killing her, much to her disgust. The entire village was very much aware of what had transpired at the massacre six months before, even though no one could recall Eva except Zoe. Zoe tried to tell them that Eva had laughed while their families were dying. Many thought Zoe was still in shock and in grief over the loss of her mother.

Eva reminded Zoe of her brother Thieri—tall and slender with raven-black hair that surrounded an angular face and a dimpled chin. Eva's blue eyes were mostly cast downward as she went about her business, not eager to make eye contact with anyone. Wherever she went, she had two soldiers shadowing her, ready to protect her in case anyone tried to harm her. Not that they could have protected her if the Resistance really wanted her dead.

Zoe continued to watch as Eva passed and, without thinking, knelt and picked up a small rock. She fingered the stone in her hand for a moment, and saw an opening in between the two soldiers. It was perfect—Eva's head was in the middle and in a perfect location. Zoe drew her arm back and threw the rock, hitting Eva square in the back of her head. A thud echoed back to Zoe, who grinned and jumped in triumph as Eva stopped and slowly turned. Eva lowered her hood and stared at Zoe in surprise. Zoe continued to grin, oblivious to the very real danger that she could be shot where she stood. One of Eva's guards, the one Zoe had nicknamed Goliath, advanced towards her, his rifle in his hand, and the other aimed his gun at her, waiting for their mistress' signal.

Outraged blue eyes met stormy green and held for a few moments. Eva lowered her gaze but not before Zoe noticed, much to her surprise, that her eyes glistened with unshed tears. Eva turned back without a word, mumbled something in German to her guards, and walked away. Her guards quickly followed her down the street. Goliath looked back at Zoe and glared before he turned his attention back to his charge.

Zoe stood transfixed at the doorway, watching the retreating figure. She was mesmerized by Eva's demure behavior. Not quite the image Zoe had envisioned. "The cripple is really a mouse. Fancy that." Zoe chuckled and shook her head in amazement. She had barely opened the door to her house when she was pulled inside and the panel was forcibly shut behind her.

"What in the name of God are you trying to do?"

The door shook as Zoe was held against it by Stavros. His black hair and dark eyes made him appear malevolent but Zoe knew he had the kindest of hearts. At that very moment he was snarling at her, and despite the situation, Zoe couldn't help but giggle.

"Stop laughing, woman!" Stavros implored. "I saw you hit Muller's daughter. Are you mad?"

Zoe looked up at the ceiling with a grin on her face, savoring the memory of the incident. "Did you see me bop her on the head, Stav? Now that was such a great throw!" She said excitedly. "Whap!"

Stavros sighed. "Zoe..."

"I didn't think I would hit her. It's not my fault the rock hit the cripple on her thick head." Zoe chuckled.

"You could have been shot--"

"Ah." Zoe held up a finger to stop Stavros from continuing.

"But I wasn't."

"Keep that up, and one day you will be on the other end of the bullet."

"Well, it's not going to be today." Zoe chuckled. "Whap!" She slapped her hand gently over Stavros' head. "I wish Theo was still here so I could show him how my aim has improved." Zoe laughed.

Stavros shook his head. "Killing Muller's daughter isn't going to help."

"Are you going soft on the Germans?" Zoe teased only to get a scowl from Stavros.

"I'm not one to go soft on the Germans, but all your attacking his daughter will do is get us all killed. That demon is already demented. Do you want him to kill us all?"

Zoe looked down at her scuffed shoe. "It would be easier than living like animals."

Stavros hugged Zoe. "I'm sorry I got rough with you. I was terrified of what they might have done to you."

"Don't worry about me, Stav," Zoe mumbled.

Stavros grinned. "Who else do I have to worry about?"

Zoe shrugged. "Find yourself a girl, and then you can worry about her."

"I'll always worry about you, ZoZo." Stavros laughed as Zoe slapped him on the head for the use of a nickname she loathed. Her brothers had affectionately given their little sister the name and, to her utter dismay, Stavros continued to use it when he wanted to tease her.

Zoe tried to change the subject away from her and her stone throwing. "Major Kookhead didn't look too happy."

"The new officers have arrived." Stavros made the sound effects of bombs going off, which had Zoe grinning.

"Big kaboom?"

"Very big kaboom." Stavros grinned.

"Does she go anywhere without Goliath?"

"Zoe, please, drop the idea. It's only going to get you killed."

"I can't," Zoe mumbled and picked at the cracked wood on the tabletop.

"Why can't you? She's nobody."

"I promised Mama that I would," Zoe replied solemnly. "If she's nobody, why can't I kill her?"

"Because if you do, Muller will kill a hundred of us, that's why. Is she worth one hundred of your countrymen?"

Zoe shrugged. "No," she said reluctantly.

"Good, I'm glad we finally got that sorted out." Stavros sighed with relief. The relief was short-lived when he saw a mischievous look on Zoe's face. "What?"

"What?"

"Spill it. I know you want to," Stavros said as he was gently pushed away by Zoe.

"I had a chat with Kiria Despina and they are looking for a maid."

"Who is?"

"Major Kookhead."

"You want to work for that animal? I thought you said--"

Zoe grinned, the edges of her green eyes crinkling in delight. "Once I get close to her, then I can kill her when the time is right," Zoe said and rubbed her hands together.

"Did you hear anything I just said to you?"

"Yep, I heard you. If the need arises, I'll be in the right place at the right time," Zoe reasoned. "Kiria Despina thinks that they will be hiring someone soon. I knew that it was perfect. It's a message from God."

Stavros groaned. "You don't believe in God anymore."

"I'm beginning to see the light," Zoe said with a grin. "Stav, don't worry. You already worry too much," she admonished him and walked away chuckling.

CHAPTER 8

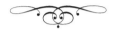

The room was in semi-darkness and a light breeze ruffled the threadbare curtains. A golden glow illuminated the area from a candle as Zoe sat hunched over at the table and stared down at the paper. The pencil in her hand flicked across the page, seemingly of its own accord, and the shape of a woman's face appeared moments later. There was something about the eyes that she found mesmerizing.

Zoe stopped and looked down at the drawing. The eyes looked lost and alone in contrast to the image of the woman; her presence. Zoe took a deep breath and let it out slowly. She looked into the eyes of a demon but saw no hatred. She wanted to see the hatred, wanted to see into the soul of the devil himself. She was certain that she was going to find Satan. But that evil was not there. She had wanted to draw the beast but instead she was staring down at the face of a lost soul. Her mama used to tell her that an artist could see a person's soul through the eyes—you just needed to look and see the invisible become visible. She wasn't prepared for the look of complete innocence that stared back at her. Eva's eyes did not reveal a demon possessed soul. They didn't reveal anything other than her feelings at being struck by the rock.

"What are you hiding?" Zoe asked the drawing. "Pah!" She hit herself on the head. "Stupid." She pushed the drawing aside, pushed back her chair and went to the window.

Zoe pulled back the curtain as she looked past her reflection in the window. Her attention was drawn to the soldiers who were changing guard across the street, and then to the top floor. She knew the layout of the house since she used to play in it before the war. The light was still on, which was unusual. The occupant went to bed early according to Zoe's surveillance. The room next to the bedroom was dark. That was the study. Zoe had seen Eva reading by the window a few times. Her attention went from the still lit bedroom to the unmistakable figure of Major Hans Muller leaving the house and walking briskly towards the next house, where Zoe had figured out he slept. Eva, Despina and the a few select guards slept in the main house. Moments after Muller had left, a woman stepped out of the shadows and just as quickly walked to the same house as him. Zoe shook her head in disgust. Her attention was once again drawn to the upstairs room where the light went out.

"I'm going to kill you. I swear it on my mama's grave. I'm going to kill you," Zoe muttered, and watched the swastika flag flutter in the wind.

Zoe glanced at the clock behind her and frowned. She could barely read the numbers on the clock face but she knew it was very late. Stavros had not returned from his meeting with Apostolos and the local KKE Resistance group. She turned back to the window and scanned the street anxiously, hoping that Stavros had not been stopped by the hated patrols. The Germans were enforcing the curfew, but Stavros found that if he acted dumb, sometimes the soldiers wouldn't pick on him.

The unmistakable figure of Father Haralambos hurriedly

walking down the street caught Zoe's attention. His black robes billowed around his legs as he quickly made his way towards the church. Zoe wondered why the priest would be going to the church at such a late hour unless he was there to alert the village of more deaths. Zoe was sure she would be hearing those bells in her sleep for years to come.

Zoe hated that sound, for it meant that another mother had lost her son in the war. It was the practice of the church to ring the bells whenever a mother found out that her son had died fighting for the motherland. Larissa had lost too many of her sons and daughters.

Zoe stared down at the retreating figure of Father Haralambos. How those words were burned into her memory: God and country. She remembered the day so clearly. It was in May 1941. She saw her first German soldier and realized that God hadn't listened to their prayers, nor would He. She had stopped believing. Whenever Father Haralambos asked her, she echoed the words of Metaxas and said, "No!" She found that rather fitting. That had been two years ago and many things had changed in those years.

"What are you doing?" Stavros asked as he came up beside Zoe and put his hand on her shoulder.

Zoe was startled and jumped. "Stav!" She slapped Stavros' hand.

"Hey, I didn't creep up on you," Stavros protested. "I made a point of being noisy coming up the stairs, since I knew you wouldn't be asleep and I didn't want to scare you."

"You're lucky I didn't have my gun in my hand."

Stavros smiled and kissed Zoe on the cheek. "Just what I need, a hole in the head."

"I didn't see you coming down the street." Zoe pointed to the window.

"I didn't." Stavros smiled. "I took the back way."

"The back way?"

"The less you know about it, the better." Stavros chuckled and ruffled Zoe's hair. He set down the supplies he had brought before crossing over to the table and sitting down in the chair. He picked up the drawing and whistled in approval. "Pretty."

Zoe looked down at the drawing. "She's the devil."

"Looks awfully cute for a devil. You are obsessed with Muller's daughter. I like the dimpled chin."

"I'm not obsessed and I hate dimpled chins—they look silly," Zoe replied and turned back to the window. "I just want her dead."

"Please, can you stop thinking about how to kill this woman?" Stavros took the artwork and looked at it again. "Wow, nice eyes."

Zoe scowled. "Is that all you can see?"

"What do you want me to see?"

"Evil."

"No horns or tail." Stavros chortled, got up from his seat, and went to the supplies.

Zoe pursed her lips and went back to her drawing. Taking her pencil, she drew in the horns. "They don't suit her," she muttered.

"Draw something nice," Stavros said as he cut the bread. Food was getting scarce for everyone but the occupation forces. As the war dragged on, the Germans were left well fed and the Greeks starving.

"Maybe," Zoe mumbled and put away the drawing. "Did you see Apostolos?"

"Yes. Apostolos met me and gave me a bottle of his new brew." Stavros uncapped the bottle and had a sniff before filling two cups with the liquid. Olives and feta cheese were the two items they could get their hands on easily. Zoe looked down at her meal and sighed. When the war ended, she was going to keep away from olives and feta cheese for the rest of her life.

"What is this supposed to be?"

"Well, according to Apostolos, it's the next best thing to ouzo. He said it was his best brew yet."

They ate in silence until the church bells startled them. Zoe looked over at Stavros and they both crossed themselves. Stavros poured some of the alcohol into a cup and took a sip, making a face as he swallowed.

"Those bells, Stav. I'm going to be hearing those damn bells for the rest of my life. We didn't know the horror that would come to us. Metaxas may have been right not to let the English land. Koryzis made a very big mistake," Zoe said quietly. Arxigos Ioannis Metaxas was the leader of the National Socialist Regime and the man who stood against Mussolini's ultimatum to invade Greece and ensure Italy's safety against an English invasion. It had been Metaxas' refusal to bow to the Italian dictator and his fervent "NO!" that created a Greek hero in 1940. The Greeks stopped the Italians from invading and after that victory, Metaxas suddenly died. Zoe had seen him briefly while he was in Larissa for a visit, and she liked him on sight. Her brothers didn't like his politics, but Zoe couldn't be bothered with that.

"No. Metaxas was wrong, not Koryzis. We should have let the English come. We might as well have told Hitler to invade us."

"He was going to invade anyway." Zoe shrugged. "I never liked Koryzis. He killed himself. What kind of Greek kills himself?"

"I don't know. We relied on God to save us as well," Stavros whispered.

"You know something?"

"What?"

"There is no God."

"So says the fool."

"So I've been told. I'm a fool then and so are many others," Zoe replied. They sat in silence for a long time with the candle flickering.

"We are so bright and cheerful." Zoe smiled at Stavros and gently hit him on the arm. They laughed. "You know, Stav, we are way too depressed to be Greeks. I think we are Russians in disguise."

"Ah, but we are Greek and we do depression well. We've had a lot of practice. Joy is for another time and another place."

Zoe stopped smiling and looked at Stavros. "And you are too young to be without joy. It makes your black eyes even blacker."

"I don't think that's possible. As for the joy...we will find our joy after the war," Stavros mumbled. "Until then, we try and rid our country of the krauts." He picked up the glass and took a swallow. "I swear Apostolos wants to kill us with this brew."

"Maybe we can give it to the Germans and the war will end," Zoe said as she took a sip herself and didn't know whether to swallow or spit it out. She winced as the burning liquid went down her throat. "This tastes worse than his other brew." She wiped her mouth with the back of her hand. "Did Apostolos have any news?"

Stavros looked down at the liquid and swirled his cup. "The Germans killed twenty men and women from Nea Smirnea in revenge for the truck bombing. We lost Andreas. He was..." Stavros threw the cup against the fireplace, where it shattered. "Apostolos thinks we have a collaborator in our midst-- maybe from the KKE." He ran his fingers through his hair in frustration.

"I don't believe the stupidity of the KKE and, of course, all the other Resistance groups, such as EDES and EKKA. They were fighting amongst themselves, each trying to outdo the other. All the while, the Germans were killing our people and raping ourcountry."

Zoe went over and collected the broken pieces of the cup and put them in the paper bag. She looked back at Stavros, who had his head down. "When is this madness going to end?"

"He also told me that they are rounding up Greek Jews. He

said they are being shipped somewhere."

"Why?" Zoe asked, drying her hands with a towel and then sitting down opposite Stavros.

"I don't know. Apostolos told me that the three British and New Zealanders they helped escape last week told him some stories when they were in Trikala."

"What stories?"

"They say that the Germans are shipping Jews like cattle, that they have seen men, women and children in boxcars, heading I-don't-know-where."

"Do you believe it?"

"There's no reason for the Allies to lie about this. The Germans are capable of horrendous crimes; we just have to see what they do to our people."

"Are you going ahead with the bombing?"

"Yes, of course. We have to. If we can get the supplies in, we can go and play blowups," Stavros said and banged on the table, startling Zoe.

"If we have a collaborator in our midst as Apostolos thinks, won't they know what you are going to do?"

"I don't know, Zo. I know I can trust you and that's the extent to which I trust anyone." Stavros looked at Zoe and smiled. "I know you're not with the KKE."

Zoe gave Stavros a mock glare. "That's not funny, Stavros Kalanaris! Those communists! Come on, do I look like a Stalinist?"

"No, you're too cute to be a Stalinist," Stavros teased Zoe and tugged strands of her long hair. "Apostolos asked about you."

Zoe rolled her eyes. "Again? All that shooting must really affect his ears. I told you, he's far too old for me."

Stavros chuckled. "He's only eight years older than you."

"That's old," Zoe replied and took a sip of the drink only to find she did indeed still hate the taste, but swallowed anyway.

"He really is a nice boy."

"I don't want to get married. We have a job to do, and the last thing I want to do is get married!"

"I want you to get married and stop being involved in the Resistance. I don't want you to get killed," Stav replied solemnly. "Apostolos has a huge farm near Trikala."

"Is that supposed to impress me?" Zoe asked.

"He really is sweet on you. It's not the farm--"

"If someone wants to marry me for the farm, well, they are going to be disappointed," Zoe replied. A large dowry was a status symbol in the village and many girls tried to accumulate their "treasures" to impress their prospective husbands. Zoe inherited (by virtue of being the only remaining family member alive) the Lambros farm, her brother Theodore's house, where she lived with Stavros, and a small cabin which belonged to her younger brother, Thieri. It was a large dowry and one that was quite impressive. Zoe was never fond of the idea that a woman should have a large dowry; it made her feel as though she was property herself.

"Apostolos is already impressed." Stavros grinned and winked at Zoe. "He knows you have a farm and well--"

"Mary, mother of Jesus!" Zoe exclaimed and shook her head. "I'm not interested in him. How many times are we going to have this marriage talk? I'm sick of it."

"I promised your mama that I would look after you. Anyway I told your mama that you would get married before I did," Stavros said quietly. "How about Yiannis?" He asked.

Zoe rolled her eyes. "He's shorter than me!"

"You are a difficult woman to please."

Zoe smiled. "Thank you."

"That wasn't a compliment."

Zoe continued to smile. "When I'm ready to get married, I'll know."

"Will I be an old man by then?" Stavros teased.

"Probably." Zoe chuckled. The two cousins looked at each other and started to laugh. Stavros finally went to his satchel and pulled out some plans as Zoe watched him in the dim light.

"It's too bad you have to bomb Kiria Vasos' house."

"Well, she will forgive us. It's not her house anymore. It's a barracks. We will get to do some cockroach exterminating."

"I want to come with you."

"No."

"Why not? I came with you on the last one."

"You came with me because you are too stubborn for your own good and you hounded me." Stavros took the sting out of his words by ruffling Zoe's hair and giving her a kiss on the cheek. "I don't want to lose you, Zo."

"Didn't I do a good job?"

"You did an exceptional job but I need to keep a promise. I made a promise to keep you safe and I can't do that if you go on bombing runs with me."

"Everyone must pitch in."

"Yes, everyone must, but we all have our roles. Your job is to keep an eye on Muller and your meticulous recording of the guard changes will come in handy."

Zoe sighed deeply. "That's a useless exercise."

"You really think so?" Stavros asked and brought his chair closer. "When the time is right, that house is going to get blown up and when it does, everyone inside goes up with it. Your spying will be one of the reasons it will be the end of Muller. Like we did with the other pig, his turn will come."

"And the demon's spawn?"

Stavros looked up at the ceiling, brought his hands together, and entreated the higher being. "Oh God, please, do something about my cousin!"

Zoe grinned and gently slapped Stavros across the back of his head. "Stop that, you silly boy. He's not going to listen to you."

Stavros brought Zoe in for a hug and kissed the top of her head. "I want to keep you safe. Let me do that. What's going to happen tonight will more than likely mean we fight these bastards close up. This is a man's job. It's no place for a woman."

"I can do that."

Stavros stopped what he was doing and looked at Zoe. "Zoe, sometimes just listen to me. I'm older than you and I'm a man."

"Well, of course, you're a man so I must listen to you," Zoe responded sarcastically. "I never heard my papa talk to my mother that way."

"Your mama, bless her soul, didn't want to go out and shoot German soldiers."

"You are not my head."

Stavros smiled and lowered his head to study the plans before him. "I pity the poor man who will have to control you when you finally decide on the poor fellow," he said teasingly.

"I pity the poor girl who has to put up with you," Zoe responded lightly, knowing the conversation had become too serious. "I still want to come with you."

"Clean your ears out. I think we have some olive oil in the cupboard. I said no."

"What are you not telling me?"

Stavros took out his home made rolled cigarettes and lit one. He offered one to Zoe, who shook her head. He took a drag of the cigarette before he replied. "I think I may know who the collaborator is."

"Who is it?"

"I can't tell you right now, but I will know more tomorrow. Apostolos is meeting with Manolas and Vangellis."

"Someone from Larissa?"

"Yes."

"What happens to them?"

"They are tried, and if they are found guilty, they are executed." Stavros watched Zoe's face carefully. "I don't want you in the middle of anything. I want you to stay here. Can you do that for me?"

"Yes." Zoe sat down heavily in the chair and folded her arms across her chest.

"And I don't want you to kill Muller's daughter--"

"Are we back to that again?" Zoe scowled. "It's not the same thing."

"Yes, we are back to that. This is different, these are soldiers."

"So is she. She was there when the lunatic Muller was killing us. She laughed when my mama was dying."

"I didn't see that. No one remembers seeing that." Stavros took Zoe's hands and held them. "You were distraught."

"I know what I saw. I know what I heard and that bitch was laughing."

"This is eating you up. You're going to get killed." Stavros tried once again to convince Zoe to alter her plans.

"What's eating me up is that she's living the high life while my mama is dead, while my brothers are dead, while my papa is dead and while Greece is dying. That's what is eating me up." Zoe clenched her fist and banged it on the table. "I'm going to kill that bitch. I know she reports what everyone does to the butcher."

Stavros put down the plans and looked incredulously at Zoe. "She reports back to her father?"

"Yes," Zoe replied and shrugged. "You never know," she said at the look Stavros was giving her.

"What does she tell him? How many candles were lit for the fallen?"

"I don't know but she goes there so much, I bet she counts," Zoe replied.

Stavros shook his head and went back to the plans.

"I'm worried about you."

"I don't care if I die. I just want her dead." Zoe pushed back her chair. "I don't care what happens to me."

"Do you care what will happen to those left behind?"

"We all have to go sometime," Zoe muttered and turned her back on Stavros to stare outside. He joined her at the window. He put his arms around her and held her close.

"I don't want to go any time soon and I don't want you to go," Stavros said quietly. "She's not worth your life."

"I made a promise," Zoe whispered.

"I made a promise as well," Stavros replied. "I promised your mama that I would keep you safe."

"Why did you do that?"

"Because I love you and you're my cousin. You are all the family I have left." Stavros kissed Zoe on the cheek. "Please, promise me that you won't do anything."

Zoe sighed and shook her head. "You made a promise?"

"Absolutely." Stavros crossed himself and kissed the cross that hung around his neck.

"I'll think about it," Zoe muttered.

"Why don't you go to bed? I've got some work to do."

"You don't want company?" Zoe asked and looked up into Stavros' dark brooding eyes.

"No, that's alright. Go to sleep."

"Be careful, Stav." Zoe went up on her toes and kissed him tenderly on the cheek. "I'll see you in the morning," she said and walked out of the small kitchen.

Eva sat with her back to the window as a slight breeze blew in ruffling the white lace curtains. The smell of rain hung in the air as she stared at the open book in front of her. She had been "reading" the same page over and over but her mind was elsewhere. The lump on the back of her head made sure she wouldn't forget the green-eyed girl in a hurry.

"EVA!"

Eva looked up quickly at her father, who sat meters away from her. The last thing she wanted to do was aggravate Muller. He wore a scowl on his face, one she was very familiar with. "I called you twice! Are you going deaf?"

"No, Father," Eva replied quietly. "I was just thinking."

Muller grunted and went back to signing some papers. "Did you hire a maid, as I told you to?" He asked, not looking up from his work.

"No, Father."

Muller stopped what he was doing and looked up at Eva. He took off his glasses and held them in his hand whilst not breaking eye contact. "Why don't you ever listen when I tell you to do something?"

"I don't want a maid."

"You need one."

"Despina helps me and she's--"

"Hire a maid," Muller repeated before returning to study the report in front of him. After a moment, he stopped and looked up again at Eva. "Why didn't you tell me about the rock being thrown at you?"

"I didn't think it was important," Eva replied quietly. "You had your hands full."

"It could have easily been a bullet," Muller chastised Eva. "You are far too casual with the villagers."

"I don't--"

"Next time something like that happens, your guards have

orders to kill," Muller said and went back to his notes. Had he looked up he would have seen a very dark look being directed at him by Eva.

"Father, it was a simple case of a girl throwing a rock."

"Go to bed, Eva," Muller muttered.

"Yes, Father." Eva picked up her book and got up rather stiffly. Her back was aching and she gingerly began to cross the room.

Muller watched her over the top of his glasses. He pursed his lips. "What's the matter?"

"Nothing, Father, it's just a little stiffness," Eva replied as the ache in her back sent dagger-like pain shooting down her spine and down her legs. It made her sick to her stomach. But she wasn't going to admit any weakness in front of Muller.

"Should I call Nurse Edith?"

Eva shook her head. "No, I'll be fine. I'll be going to bed."

Muller watched Eva leave the room and for a long moment he stared at the door. He decided it was time to contact his brother, Dr. Dieter Muller, to discuss his daughter with him. It had been a long time since he had talked to Dieter about Eva. He scribbled a note to himself and absently tapped the pen against the papers he held in his hand. His musing was cut short when Captain Reinhardt entered, saluted, and waited for his commanding officer.

"Did you read these reports?" Muller asked, indicating the pile of papers on his lap.

"Yes, sir."

"How reliable are they?" Muller looked at Reinhardt over

the top of his glasses.

"Well, as reliable as the KKE can be, sir."

"That doesn't tell me anything, Captain."

"I think they are reliable."

Muller looked down at the papers in front of him. "Let them."

"Sir?"

"Are you deaf, man?"

"No, sir."

"I said, let them. Get the troops out first, of course. Then have a reception awaiting the Greek dogs."

"Yes, sir."

"You can go." Reinhardt turned to leave. "Reinhardt, don't kill them. I have other plans."

"Yes, sir." Reinhardt saluted and left.

Muller sighed. He was tired of the war, tired of the Resistance movements. He picked up his wine and sipped it, contemplating life after the war.

CHAPTER 9

*S*chnell! Schnell!"

"Anschlag oder ich schieße!"

The command was followed by gunfire and the sound of screams and abuse emanating from the street below. The commotion woke Zoe from her sleep. She was disoriented at first, as she struggled out of bed and pulled back the curtains. The tableau she saw before her made her blood run cold. A man lay on the road, his blood already staining the dirt, his life ebbing away. A German soldier stood above him. Zoe jumped when the soldier fired into the prone man.

Zoe was shocked and craned her neck to see further into the street. To her horror, she saw three men nearby with their hands above their heads, surrounded by soldiers. "Oh no," Zoe whispered in shock. "Oh, dear God, no," she uttered as she met Stavros' eyes. They looked at each other and he nodded before being led roughly away.

Stavros was in the hands of the Germans and there was nothing Zoe could do about it. She could scream and holler until she was hoarse, but the image of the dead partisan, his blood staining the ground, was too much for her to bear.

"You don't exist! It's all lies!" Zoe cried out against the god who didn't exist for her. "I'll get you out, Stav." She had no idea what she was going to do but she was determined to try something. Even as she was getting dressed, she was forming a plan to break them out. She stopped and sat down heavily on the floor. "Who am I kidding?" She asked as she began to cry. She was helpless to do anything.

"Damn you, God!" Zoe yelled and thumped the floor with her fist. "I hate you!"

The light streamed though the open window and woke Zoe, who had succumbed to her tears and fallen asleep on the wooden floor. She felt a little dazed and then the previous evening's horror came flooding back.

Zoe got up and began to cry again. She dressed mechanically and walked out to the kitchen. There was a note on the table. Her hands trembled as she picked it up.

"You know what I want for breakfast? Fresh eggs, lots of honey, good Greek coffee, and to sleep as long as I want — but not in that order. Don't worry about me, little one. Everything will be alright. Kiriakos came tonight. Apostolos couldn't come—his younger brother Notarios was killed and he took him home. Kiriakos, Antonios, myself and Giorgos will be going earlier than planned. We should be back after things have calmed down in a day or so. While you are waiting, do something about my breakfast order."

Zoe stared at the note for a long time. She didn't want to believe what she had seen during the night. She wanted to believe it was one huge nightmare, a nightmare within a nightmare. She went over to the small weapons cache they had and picked up a small handgun. She was going to kill that demon spawn and she didn't care if she died trying.

Zoe closed the door behind her and listened to her own footsteps echoing in the quiet of the early morning as a light drizzle began to fall. She slowed when she approached the prone figure on the ground. The Germans had not picked up the body, leaving it out in the rain as an example of what happened to anyone who resisted them.

Zoe crossed herself despite her thundered admonitions to a god she claimed she no longer believed in. She pulled the shawl around her, put her head down, and walked swiftly to her destination. She rounded the corner and slammed into Father Haralambos' ample figure, which caused her to drop her bag.

The gun fell at Father Haralambos' feet.

"I'm so sorry," Zoe said as she knelt to collect her bag and the gun.

Father Haralambos looked around and then helped Zoe up. "Where are you going, my child?"

"An eye for an eye--isn't that what your precious Bible says?" Zoe spat, trying desperately not to scream.

"No, it doesn't say that, little one," Father Haralambos replied. "Well, not exactly."

"Don't. Call. Me. That." Zoe looked into Father Haralambos' eyes and ground out the words, regretting losing her temper with him.

"Alright, I won't call you that. You're a woman now," Father Haralambos said with a twinkle in his eye. "Come with me."

"No."

"You want to stay out in the rain? You can if you wish, but

I'm old and I don't think I'm going to get any younger or drier staying out here."

The drizzle had turned into a light rain and Zoe mutely followed Father Haralambos into the church. She halted for a moment and then crossed herself, more out of habit than belief, before going by the altar.

Father Haralambos watched her in silence for a few moments. "You still believe."

Zoe looked at the priest and shook her head. "No, I don't. It's a bad habit."

"Are you trying to convince yourself that you hate our Lord and to deny Him in your heart?" Father Haralambos asked quietly, watching the young woman as he lit a candle.

"What do you care, Father? You are wasting your time. There are Greeks dying out there. Don't you hear them? You sit here and you preach about love and forgiveness. Who do I forgive?"

"We all do our part. We all sin, and we all need forgiveness."

"Do you know about loss? You're not married." Zoe flailed her arms in rage. "You can't know the loss of your wife or children. You don't know what it's like to wake up and find out your loved one has been captured by the enemy. You don't know, do you?" She stared at Father Haralambos and then looked up at the statue of Christ on the cross, shaking her head in disgust. "Will you be there for Samia tonight when Giorgos is six feet under? His blood has stained the ground. Will you forgive the animal that killed him?"

"Sometimes it is best if our left hand does not know what our right hand is doing."

"Are you going to join us to free Greece?" Zoe offered Father Haralambos the gun. "You can use both hands."

"I am doing my part. Now you have to do yours."

"I already am. You say that those who don't believe there is a God are fools. You know, Father, I'm a fool. But I'm a fool who is going to do her part to save our country."

"Is that why you crossed yourself when you came in?"

Zoe didn't answer for a moment. She fingered the gun in her hand. "I told you that's a bad habit I picked up."

"Killing is not the answer," Father Haralambos said quietly as he watched Zoe.

"Yes, it is. Killing is the only answer."

"There must be an end to violence, and you shooting people won't put an end to this war; it will prolong it."

"My only reason for living is to kill that damned bitch."

"Don't swear in church," Father Haralambos gently admonished. "You can't kill innocents."

"Innocent!" Zoe yelled. "That damned bitch isn't innocent!"

"Zoe! Don't swear in church."

"I can't sit and watch. Someone has to pay. An eye for an eye, and I want to be the one to pay them back," Zoe said bitterly.

"It's not for you to judge and not for you to be the executioner."

"Why not? Because you say so?"

"Don't start killing." Father Haralambos took the gun from Zoe and pocketed it in his robes, much to Zoe's disgust.

"You're wrong, Father. I have killed and I'll kill again. I'm following in the footsteps of Kolokotronis—he knew how to stand up to tyranny and he won. I'm going to stand up to tyranny."

"By killing an innocent woman? Is that how you are going to win this war?"

"That's how I win my war. I'm fighting my own war and I'm going to win it," Zoe replied as she sat down on the floor and crossed her legs. "This is my war and there will only be one winner here."

"It won't be you."

"What would you have me do? Lie down and let them do what

they want?"

The church doors opened and a young man raced in. He knelt and crossed himself and then went hurriedly to the priest. "Father, Father!" The young man was breathless. He bent forward trying to catch his breath.

"Take it slowly, Phrixus."

"They are rounding up everyone and sending them to the town square! They posted an announcement that our brothers who were caught last night will be hanged! I was told to come here and tell you. Hurry, Father!"

"No! Do something!" Zoe got up from the floor and yelled at Father Haralambos.

"I can't do anything, my child."

"Hurry up, Father, please! They want everyone to be there or else they will start shooting people."

The three of them hurried out into the busy street as the residents were herded towards the main town square. The German soldiers ringed the plaza and a scaffold stood in the center. The scaffold had become a permanent fixture in the plaza and was in constant use after every Resistance attack. The sounds of grieving and of babies crying could be heard over the murmur of the townspeople. Zoe looked around and froze when four soldiers passed by, flanking three shuffling men. She hardly recognized the prisoners—their faces were badly disfigured by bruises. Father Haralambos held Zoe in his arms as Stavros shuffled away from her. Stavros looked back and tried to smile at Zoe, but the attempt turned into a grimace.

The soldier coming up from the rear pushed Stavros along with the barrel of his weapon and he nearly fell into the mud. They slowly climbed onto the platform of the scaffold. The crowd fell silent; only the sounds of a dog barking and a child crying could be heard.

Major Muller walked through the crowd, his guards

pushing people aside, and stood next to the scaffold. A guard held a black umbrella over him to keep him dry. Muller tapped his black boots in a small puddle, clasped his hands behind his back, and looked out into the crowd. "I see Father Haralambos is here. Father, would you give these men the last rites? I am a God fearing man and I think that would be fair," he said as he gazed at the falling rain.

His arm still around Zoe, Father Haralambos whispered in her ear. He looked around and spotted Despina and beckoned her to be with Zoe. Despina came up behind Zoe and embraced her as Father Haralambos went up the steps to the scaffold. He began to administer the last rites. All three men bowed their heads. The youngest began to cry as the priest made the sign of the cross on their foreheads.

"Be brave, my boys, and know we will continue the fight for you," Father Haralambos whispered to each man as he placed a kiss on his forehead.

"Hurry up, Father, I don't have all day," Muller commanded. Father Haralambos shuffled and deliberately slowed as he descended the stairs and went and stood by Zoe and Despina. He held Zoe's hand.

"This is a warning to any who wish to defy me." Muller raised his voice and lifted his arm, then dropped it. The executioner saw the hand signal and pulled the lever. The scaffold ropes creaked as the three men hung lifelessly in the plaza.

Zoe closed her eyes and began to cry, Father Haralambos holding her. A tiny voice was heard singing. It was soon joined by all those assembled in defiance of the Germans.

We knew thee of old,
Oh, divinely restored,
By the lights of thine eyes
And the light of thy Sword

Zoe looked up, her face tear-stained, and realized the villagers were singing the Ymnos eis tin Eleftherian, The Hymn to Freedom, the soul-inspiring national anthem of the Greeks, their only way to be defiant as the rain continued to pour. She looked up at her dead friends and began to sing.

From the graves of our slain
Shall thy valor prevail
As we greet thee again—
Hail, Liberty! Hail!
Long time didst thou dwell
Mid the peoples that mourn,
Awaiting some voice
That should bid thee return.
Ah, slow broke that day
And no man dared call,
For the shadow of tyranny
Lay over all.

The voices swelled as one while Muller looked on, his face set in a scowl. He turned to walk off, then stopped and faced Captain Reinhardt. "Leave them up there."

"Yes, sir!" Reinhardt saluted as the villagers continued to sing in open defiance.

And we saw thee sad-eyed,
The tears on thy cheeks
While thy raiment was dyed
In the blood of the Greeks.
Yet, behold now thy sons
With impetuous breath
Go forth to the fight

Seeking Freedom or Death.

From the graves of our slain
Shall thy valor prevail
As we greet thee again—
Hail, Liberty! Hail!

The breeze coming through the window caused the curtain to brush against Eva. The strains of the song washed over her as she leaned against the windowsill. She closed her eyes and prayed for the souls of the men who had been killed. Yet, even more bloodshed. Her tears ran down her cheeks for the men she never knew but whose pain she felt. She listened to the anthem being passionately sung by the defiant Greeks. *While thy raiment was dyed in the blood of the Greeks.*

Eva stared out into the rain. Seeking Freedom or Death... *There is no other option, is there?* Eva thought. Her musings were cut short by the noises downstairs of Muller returning from the plaza and yelling orders.

CHAPTER 10

*S*ix months later.

A rooster crowed as the sun made its slow progress to start the morning. Eva walked down the cobblestone streets, her cane echoing as it hit the ground. She was aware of the furtive glances and some openly hostile glares she was getting from the villagers. Most of them were used to seeing Eva, clad in her dark cloak and hood, her two very large shadows behind her. Henry was the taller of the two and he slowed his cadence to match Eva's slow walk. Next to him was Barkow, who stood at just over six feet but was dwarfed by his fellow soldier. With those two behind her, Eva felt somewhat protected. No one greeted her as she passed, not that she was expecting them to, and some spat on the ground before she passed making sure she noticed. Nevertheless she was a common sight for those who woke up early to tend to their chores.

Eva stopped for a moment to catch her breath and smiled when she saw their housekeeper, Despina, walking towards her.

"Good morning, Kiria Despina," Eva greeted her in Greek,

aware that the villagers closest to her could hear her. She used the respectful Greek phrase to denote the housekeeper was married. She made sure she was using the phrase correctly.

"Ah, Miss Eva. You know the church is just a few meters down there." Despina greeted Eva with a smile. She pulled her cardigan across her body as the wind picked up a little, bringing with it a blast of cool air. Despina was a plumb older woman in her mid-fifties, with salt and pepper hair worn up in a tight bun. Her brown eyes crinkled when she smiled at Eva.

"Today is the day," Eva replied happily.

"It is, it is. You should be very proud of yourself."

Eva nodded her appreciation at Despina's words. She lowered her voice. "Is it difficult for you to be seen speaking to me?"

Despina shook her head. "No, sweetheart, it's not. You are not the enemy."

"Your fellow villagers don't seem to agree with you."

"Don't you have enough to deal with at home without worrying about me?" Despina asked as she touched Eva's hand. "Don't worry about me. Now, you have just a few meters down that way to get to the church."

"Thank you, you're very kind to me."

"You're a very kind and gentle young woman. It's not hard to be kind to you. Now once you have mastered the church, you can go all the way to Athena's Bluff."

"How far would it take me to get there?"

"It takes me half an hour at a slow pace."

"That's my next goal once I reach the church," Eva said and smiled when Despina took her hand.

"I'm quite sure you will be doing that soon. Now I have to get going to get these eggs back to the house and get breakfast ready."

Eva watched Despina walk away and sighed. "Sergeant Franz."

"Yes, Fraulein?"

"The church is just up the road there."

"Yes."

"I'm going inside once I get there."

"Alright. I haven't seen inside a Greek church—"

"No." Eva looked at Henry. "A German soldier inside a Greek church would anger many of the villagers; we don't need that happening. You and Barkow stay outside."

"Fraulein Muller, I must object—"

"Don't worry. Even the Communists, who don't believe in God, would never enter a church to kill."

"There's always a first time," Henry muttered under his breath, causing Eva to smile.

"You worry too much. If the Resistance wanted to kill me, they can easily do it here on the street," Eva replied and turned. She mentally sighed when she heard Henry's aggrieved growl. "Your mere presence behind me is enough to scare Ares Velouchiotis," Eva added, regarding the Greek Resistance leader she had heard so much about.

"Velouchiotis is a coward."

"Let's hope you are right because I do not want to meet this fellow—a passionate Greek is always trouble," Eva said as Henry came up and walked next to her. "What are you doing?"

"We are coming up to where there are children playing. I do not want them to throw any stones at you," Henry replied. Barkow also took up his position on Eva's other side.

"I don't think the children will do anything."

"Other than call you names?" Henry muttered.

"Names can't hurt you."

Henry glanced down at his charge and shook his head. "Maybe I should put my helmet on your head?"

Eva lowered her head and concentrated on walking without falling over. "Yes, that would be a good look."

Henry glanced around and sighed as they walked past the children, who did indeed call out but they didn't throw anything.

Eva stopped when she turned the corner and the church stood before her. Its white facade was marred by bullet holes. The sky blue dome stood in contrast to the white with the white cross above it. Six stone steps led up to the ornate doors. Eva looked around but the street was empty.

"I'm going in."

"Fraulein—"

"Please, stay out here. I told you I don't want the Greeks to feel more aggrieved than they are. I doubt the priest is going to kill me either."

"Alright, but I will have to tell Captain Reinhardt."

"I already told him I was going to visit the church," Eva said before she turned and slowly walked up the steps. The two guards quickly walked up the steps behind her and took their place on either side of the door. Eva shook her head a little, and lowered the hood of her cloak as she entered the church.

The light from the lit candles cast off a warm glow to the outer sanctuary of the church. Eva was surprised to see the seating wasn't regular pews as she was used to, but chairs. The floor was a polished marble all the way to the altar. The walls featured prominently the saints and Mary, Mother of God. Above the stone altar was the Crucified Christ. Eva bowed her head and crossed herself as she approached the altar.

Eva sat down at the closest chair to the front. She rested her hand over the cane's handle and looked up at Christ's icon. A door opened next to the altar and she saw a man come out. Clad in a black cassock with a gold crucifix around his neck, his long beard and pillbox hat made it quite obvious who he was.

"Good morning, Father." Eva stood up and approached the priest.

"Good morning, my child," Father Haralambos replied without any noticeable surprise on his face that Eva was speaking to him in Greek. Eva bowed slightly and took his hand.

She kissed it as was customary for the villagers on greeting their priest.

"Ach, you shouldn't bend down like that with your bad back," Father Haralambos gently said. He led Eva back to the chairs.

"What do you know about my back?"

Father Haralambos' blue eyes gentled as he gazed at Eva. "A priest hears stories."

"Ah, yes, I almost forgot—'the German cripple.'"

"I have heard that, and I have watched you take your early morning walk. It's not an easy walk for you but you have managed quite well. Are you happy with your progress?"

"I'm a little proud of myself this morning," Eva admitted. "I think most of the village knows about me at this point," she said to Father Haralambos, who had taken off his hat. His black hair had slivers of white throughout and he had tied it back in a ponytail. "You're not surprised I can speak Greek."

"Not really. Kiria Despina has told me you speak Greek. She has very nice things to say about you." Father Haralambos smiled. "Would you feel more comfortable if I spoke German?" He added in German, which made Eva's eyes widen in surprise.

"You speak German?"

"I do. I can also speak Italian and French. I love languages."

"That is so surprising."

Father Haralambos chuckled as he clasped his hands. "Yes, you don't expect that from a village priest."

"No, I didn't expect it."

"Most people don't, so that's alright."

"Father, what's your name?"

"Father Panayiotis Haralambos. I have the right first name for a priest, no?" He smiled at Eva, who gazed at him quizzically. "Panayios means Holy. I know your name and what it means. It's Hebrew for life and the first woman Almighty God created."

"I saw you when we first arrived."

"Hm, as did I. It was a horrible way to arrive into a town, especially for you."

"Father, do you listen to confessions?" Eva asked quietly, ignoring Father Haralambos' recollections of the blood bath that followed her arrival. She looked around at the icons on the wall. "You must have seen a lot of death since the war started," she said, and turned to Father Haralambos to see his eyes glisten in the candlelight.

"I have seen a lot of death, yes. I listen to anyone who wishes to confess, Fraulein Muller."

"Please, call me Eva. I feel like I can talk to you almost like I've known you my whole life."

"Why do you say that? We've just met."

"I just feel it. I trust you."

Father Haralambos smiled. "Trust is earned, Eva, but I'm happy that you can confide in me."

"Can we talk here?"

Father Haralambos looked around the empty room. "You can. Sister Maria is not due to start her scripture class for another hour or so."

Eva stared up at the crucifix for a long moment before she turned her attention to Father Haralambos. Their blue eyes met and Eva looked down at her hands. After a few minutes she looked up again. "Father, are you in the Resistance?"

Father Haralambos gazed at Eva for a long moment. His face revealed nothing and Eva was worried she had just made a terrible mistake.

"Are you confessing to me or am I confessing to you?"

"A little of both."

"Ah. Why don't you tell me your confession?"

Eva nodded. "When I was in France, I had the opportunity to help Father François in Paris," she whispered and looked around the church hoping her guards had listened to her and stayed outside.

"Where are the two young men who shadow you?"

"Outside. I hope."

"Hm. You helped Father François, and what did you do to help him?"

"I forged my father's signature on identity papers," Eva replied softly. "I'm a very good forger."

"I see. How did it come about that you were helping Father François?"

Eva gazed at Father Haralambos, the edges of her mouth slightly curled before she looked away. "He was helping Jews escape."

"That is a very noble effort; the work of angels. Is there a need to confess such a good deed to me? I would think that it was a good thing what you did to help others."

Eva looked back at Father Haralambos, who was looking at her with a noncommittal gaze. "You do know what I just confessed to you, right?"

"Yes, I am aware that you just told me that you collaborated with the French Resistance. I'm not going to tell you that you are wrong, because it's not wrong what you did."

"No, I don't feel bad about that."

"You do know what the confessional is used for?" Father Haralambos sincerely asked and smiled when Eva sighed and looked up at the ornate ceiling.

"Father, I think you are not making this easy."

"What am I not making easy? So what are you expecting me to say? Do you want to confess because you have sinned against God? Hardly. Do you want to confess because you feel bad about saving someone's life? Do you want me to be shocked that a German woman just told me she did the work of angels?"

"No," Eva said resolutely. "I want you to tell me how I can help you here."

"You want to help me in my church? I don't think the villagers would be all that happy to see you helping out."

"Father!" Eva threw up her hands in frustration. "You are being—"

"Cautious?" Father Haralambos suggested. "How do I know you are not a spy? How do I know that your father didn't send you to me?"

Eva frowned before a smiled creased her face. "You already know or else you wouldn't have asked me those questions."

Father Haralambos gazed at Eva for a long moment. "Eva, you do not know me and yet you come to me and confess that you betrayed your country by collaborating with the French—"

"I didn't betray my country."

"You betrayed someone."

"I don't see it that way."

Father Haralambos nodded. "You collaborated with the French, and that is punishable by death. You are aware of that?"

Eva nodded. "I am aware of the penalty. My life is not worth more than a Jew nor is it worth more than a Greek. I did it because it was right."

"And you hate your father," Father Haralambos quietly added. Eva turned away from him but he gently turned her face towards him. "You are doing the work of angels no matter the reason."

"It is not because of my father. It is because of my guilt."

"Your guilt? What have you done to feel guilty for?"

"You have heard of Kristallnacht?"

"Yes. Even in a Greek village I heard about the dreadful night; unfortunately one of many such nights and days."

"I was part of it. I was there and did nothing. I didn't try to save an old Rabbi's life and stood by and watched. I can't stand by and watch people be killed and not do anything again," Eva quietly explained as her voice broke with emotion. "There is too much death. Standing by and not doing anything is the same as pulling the trigger."

"It is, but what if someone betrays you?"

"My life is meaningless. There is no happy future for me. I'm like a bird in a cage—no escape. I envy the villagers. They will escape once this war is over. I'm just stuck in a cage." Eva swallowed audibly and closed her eyes. "What's left is resistance. If I can help someone escape, then this gilded cage I am in has meaning."

"Oh, my precious child." Father Haralambos put his arms around Eva as she broke down and wept in his arms. His soothing words were totally lost on her while the emotional walls she had built around herself came crumbling down and lay at the priest's feet. Eva felt safe in his arms and was slightly embarrassed by the rush of emotions that overwhelmed her.

"I'm sorry, Father." Eva wiped her eyes with the back of her hand.

Father Haralambos caressed Eva's dark head and then kissed it. "You are a brave young woman. It takes a special person to put themselves in harm's way."

"I have to do something."

"I understand your reasoning."

"Can you help me?"

Father Haralambos nodded. "I can help you and we can help those who you want to help. There are many Jews in Larissa and the surrounding hills. They need fake papers. I have been trying but it's very difficult."

"I can help you. Let me help."

"Yes. We will work together."

Eva smiled. "Thank you, Father."

"What happened to Father François?"

"He's no longer alive. He was killed before we left for Greece."

CHAPTER 11

The wind rushed through the open window in the cabin while outside it caused the trees to sway, and one in particular was making Zoe quite annoyed. It was hitting the side of the wooden cabin making a scraping noise.

Zoe lay near the window on a bed that felt more like a cement block when compared to her more comfortable bed back at the house. A woolen blanket covered her, and although she was cold, it didn't matter to her.

The cabin was a large L shaped cabin built in the woods. It was her brother Thieri's cabin. He had cut down the trees and painstakingly built it as a present to his soon-to-be fiancée, but he never got the chance to present the house. The war with the Italians saw him volunteer along with his brothers Michael and Theodore. All three brothers died in that battle with the Italians.

The main room was the dining room and entrance, and off to the side was a bedroom, although there was a skeleton frame in place and no wall. Thieri didn't have time to build the wall, but the small section was the bedroom. Another smaller room was going to be the kitchen; that too was not finished.

Zoe put her hands behind her head and looked up at the ceiling. The only family she had left was Aunt Stella in Thessaloniki and her cowardly uncle Dion, who had shipped himself off to America as soon as a hint of war was talked about. Zoe stared at the spider which had taken up residence on the corner, where it had spun an intricate web. The spider had become a silent companion while Zoe had raged against God, the Nazis and cowards in general.

Zoe chose the cabin to let out her anger because of its seclusion. She didn't want to see anyone, didn't want to speak to anyone, and definitely did not want anyone's pity. She screamed out her anger and pain alone in the woods and took an axe to a tree, and when she wasn't yelling at God, she sat for hours on Athena's Bluff watching the majestic scene before her, its beauty totally lost on her.

"Damn you to hell!" Zoe screamed. "I hope you all burn for eternity!"

There was silence except for the wind rustling the fallen leaves outside. Just silence.

"Are you tired of my yelling, Calliope?" Zoe asked the spider, her voice a little husky.

The spider ignored the human down below and just sat in the corner minding her own business.

"You have a great life, Calliope." Zoe continued her one sided conversation. "You sit there, not caring about the Germans, the Greeks, the flies." Zoe sat up and swung her legs to the edge of the bed. Her feet touched the dark red flokati rug, her favorite rug, which had been brought up from the farm after her mother died.

Zoe got up and stretched. She closed her eyes as the breeze from the open window brushed against her face. She could smell the hint of rain in the air. She went to the window and looked out. The "bedroom" overlooked Athena's Bluff, and on any other day Zoe would have admired the view, but she didn't care for it at that very moment.

Zoe turned away from the window and grabbed her skirt. Sitting underneath the skirt was her gun. She gazed at it for a long moment before she turned and got dressed.

"I suppose I'll have to catch something if I don't want to starve." Zoe glanced up at the spider. "If I catch a rabbit, do you want the leg or the breast?" She shook her head at her own silliness and picked up the gun.

"Come on, Athena, we have work to do," Zoe said to the gun. She stuck the gun in a rucksack and slung it over her shoulder. She opened the door and blinked as the sun hit her eyes.

Zoe ventured outside towards the large fallen tree, which was located away from the walking track that led up the hill. It was obscured by the thick trees and perfect for Zoe's makeshift lavatory. She went about her business and covered up the hole in the ground with dirt and leaves in time to hear footsteps.

Zoe quickly hid behind the large tree trunk and grabbed her bag, which had been sitting on top of the fallen tree. She could not see who was coming up the track but she could hear them. One set of footsteps and then a scraping noise.

Zoe lowered herself onto her belly and waited.

Eva stopped and sighed. This trek up the hill was tougher than she had thought. The incline had tested her legs and her back but she was determined to get to the top. From what Despina had told her, it was one of the most beautiful parts in Larissa. Larissa's beauty was totally lost on Eva and she doubted anything could be beautiful there.

Eva had told no one of her little trek, and she had left the house before the town had a chance to rise. She did get a few raised eyebrows from the guards but no one stopped her. No one wanted to be the one to stop Eva Muller, daughter of Major Muller, and question where she was going. She was hoping this would be the case and was very relieved when she didn't see her regular shadow, Sergeant Henry Franz.

The walk from the village to Athena's Bluff was long and tiring, but Eva was determined. Halfway there she thought she had lost her mind, but she continued forward. She felt compelled to go up that mountain.

Eva stopped just before the clearing and leaned on her cane. Her back and legs were screaming at her to stop. She took a deep breath and walked into the clearing.

What she saw took her breath away. The clearing was a short distance to what had to be Athena's Bluff. The lookout was surrounded by trees but at the base it was flat with several boulders on either side. An overhanging tree cast its shadow over the outcrop.

"This is beautiful," Eva muttered as she took several steps forward. She stood gazing out at the valley below. A train weaved its way through Tempe Gorge and through the trees. The Pinios River ran through it. She took a step forward and looked down at the rocks below. She stood there mesmerized. Could she? It would end it all for her and that is what she wanted. She was alone and there was no one to stop her.

Zoe smiled for the first time in days. She glanced up into the heavens with a gleeful look on her face. She mouthed 'thank you' to whoever was answering her prayers. This one place, at this time. Just her and Eva Muller. Alone. No bodyguards, no means of escape except down the gorge.

Zoe pulled her bag closer and took out her gun. She kissed the barrel and smiled. She lowered herself behind the tree and very quietly made sure the gun was loaded. Having checked that it was, she lifted her head above the fallen tree. Eva was still on the ledge, almost transfixed by the view.

Just stay put, Fraulein, just stay put. Zoe aimed her pistol, and having Eva in her sights, she fired. The gun clicked and nothing happened.

Zoe suppressed the urge to scream as she lowered herself behind the fallen tree again. She checked the gun. Not finding anything wrong with it, she shook it before she half rose to take aim. Eva had moved. She was now standing near the boulder, which made the shot a little harder since the tree branches were in the way, but Eva was still visible.

Alright, let's try this again. Zoe took aim and fired. Nothing. The gun jammed once again Zoe was about to stand and rush Eva. They were both going to fall down the gorge but Zoe stopped. She looked around the spot where she was and for some unknown reason she hesitated. Someone else was in the brush behind her. She sat back down and turned hoping to see a friendly face, but she was alone.

Alright, Zo, you have lost your mind. Without a word, Zoe was about to stand when she heard someone running up the hill. A man's tread and one in a very big hurry. She quickly hid behind the fallen tree.

Sergeant Henry Franz woke at 4 am. Unable to sleep due to someone yelling in the distance, he tossed and turned until he decided to get up. Being quiet so as not to wake his roommate, he dressed and grabbed his boots from outside.

Henry sat on the front step of the main residence as silence descended on the village. "Ah, so now everyone shuts up, when I'm awake," he muttered as he put on his boots.

Henry stood up and for a moment wasn't sure what to do. Taking a cigarette from his pocket, he lit it and set up walking towards the sentry at the gate. The guards nodded to him as he walked out and down the street. Since he had some time before Eva woke, he would check with his friend Anton, who was on duty, and see if he had had any luck in the poker game the previous evening.

Henry noted the villagers were starting to wake but it was still generally very quiet. To his surprise, an old woman was walking towards him with a smile on her face. That had never happened to him. Usually it was a scowl, or they just turned their backs on him. Henry stopped and looked behind him to see if there was someone else who the old woman had seen. Seeing no one behind him, he turned back to the old woman, who had stopped in front of him.

"Good morning, Sergeant."

"Good morning, *yiayia*." Henry used the affectionate and respectful Greek term for grandmother.

"You're up early."

"I am. So are you."

"I'm always up, never sleep anymore," the old woman said and touched Henry's hand. "Are you trying to catch up with that young Fraulein you guard all the time?"

Henry blinked. "Fraulein Muller?"

"Yes. How many young women do you guard?" The old woman gazed up at Henry.

"You saw her this morning?" Henry asked, ignoring the old woman's cheeky question.

"Yes."

"Are you sure it wasn't yesterday? We did take an early morning walk—"

"She was walking alone, and unless you were invisible, it was this morning."

Henry groaned internally. *Oh, Eva, don't do this to me again!* "Do you happen to remember which way she went?"

"Athena's Bluff."

"Where? How do you know that?"

"Where does this road lead?" The old woman indicated with her hand.

"To the church."

"The church is not open. It's too early even for Father Haralambos."

"What's beyond that?"

The old woman sighed and shook her head. "Athena's Bluff."

"What's that?"

"Follow the road, young man, and you will see," the old woman replied with a smile and patted him on the arm before she walked away.

Henry looked back for a moment before he turned and took off running down the street, his footfalls echoing down the cobblestone street. He did indeed follow the road and then the road stopped. He wasn't sure where to go until a farmer showed up in his cart and gave him directions to Athena's Bluff.

"Eva!"

Eva turned at the sound of her name and shook her head.

"What in God's name are you doing?" Henry asked as he leaned against the tree to catch his breath. "I should get more fit."

"Early morning walk."

"Early morning run to an early grave." Henry wiped the sweat from his brow and sat down on the boulder. "Your father is going to kill me when he finds out."

"My father has other concerns."

"I thought we agreed you wouldn't do this again."

"In France," Eva replied with a slight smile as she sat down next to Henry.

"What are you doing here?"

"Admiring the view," Eva replied as she gazed at the vista before her."

"Can we go back to the house before your father unleashes the demons from hell and then we can talk about it?"

"I like the view."

"I would like to stay alive for my next birthday. Come along." Henry took Eva's hand.

"Alright. Let's go." Eva smiled at Henry as she took his arm and they trekked back the mountain, oblivious to the hidden Zoe.

Zoe couldn't quite believe the scene before her. The useless gun lay at her feet and any chance of her killing Eva was as dead as her gun.

In absolute frustration, Zoe kicked the log at her feet. "God damn it!" She muttered as a rabbit hopped into the open. She gazed at it for a moment before she picked up her gun.

"Aren't you lucky this gun is useless," Zoe addressed the rabbit and pointed the gun. She pulled the trigger.

It fired.

To Zoe's amazement, the bullet struck the rabbit and it fell where it stood. She shook her head, looked at the gun, and with a heavy sigh went to pick up her breakfast.

CHAPTER 12

*T*he saint's eyes moved. Eva was sure of it as she stepped forward and looked into Saint Peter's eyes. The artist had created an illusion that made her smile. She was alone in Father Haralambos' office, so she took some time to admire the art in the form of various icons that were displayed around the room. She loved art and the room was decorated with several pieces. Daniel and the Lions were displayed prominently and she noticed the same style in both artworks.

"His eyes move."

Eva turned to find Father Haralambos leaning against the doorjamb with his arms folded. "I thought they did but I wasn't sure. That is really beautiful work."

"It is. It was created by one of our own here in Larissa."

"I would love to meet him. I love art and artists always fascinate me," Eva said as she turned back to the artwork.

"Unfortunately she is no longer with us," Father Haralambos replied as he shut the door and placed a ribbon to indicate the room was being used as a confessional. He walked forward to come and stand next to Eva. "She passed away a year ago."

Eva stood still for a moment. "She died at my father's hand."

"She did. Helena Lambros. She was a very talented artist—"

"There's a painting in my room of the valley with Lambros on the corner."

"How do you remember that?" Father Haralambos sat down at the nearby chair.

"It's in the same style. It's a beautiful painting and it's the last thing I see before I go to sleep. It's very peaceful and she evokes a time when this place was just a sleepy village," Eva quietly explained. "It talks to me."

"Yes, I remember that painting."

The two remained quiet for a moment before Eva pulled out a folded piece of paper out of her cloak and handed it to Father Haralambos. "That makes four, right? That means the whole family can travel?"

Father Haralambos nodded and smiled at Eva. "That does make four. They will escape."

"How much love that father has for his daughters that he didn't want to leave them behind until everyone's papers were in order," Eva said with a touch of amazement in her voice. "To have a father like that..." Eva took a breath. "I'm really glad."

"You have made a difference to these people. The last six months have been heaven-sent for them."

"We may have a problem."

"How so?"

"Nurse Gestapo—"

"Eva, your nurse has a name," Father Haralambos gently scolded. "She does a lot of good in looking after you."

Eva looked up at the ornate ceiling and sighed. "Nurse Edith," she amended and gazed back at Father Haralambos with a smile. They shared a quiet laugh. The last six months had been both a comforting and an increased joyous time for Eva. She had found a friend in a hostile village. Her well-guarded friendship with

Father Haralambos had given her some respite from the hate.

"What is the matter with Nurse Edith?"

Eva giggled. "Other than her unrequited love for my father?"

"I don't think it's unrequited."

"Father!"

"Ah, didn't you know the village priest knows everything that happens in a village? The confessional gives me more than enough gossip." Father Haralambos smiled. "Now what is the matter with Nurse Edith?"

"She was asking Sergeant Franz about my visits here and how long I'm staying."

Father Haralambos nodded as he stroked his beard, lost in thought. "It's interesting that she asked the young man who has a crush on you."

"Pardon?"

Father Haralambos chuckled. "My dear, have you not seen how that young boy's face lights up when you are around?"

"Um—no."

Father Haralambos nodded. "Take it from me—the boy has a crush on you."

"Just what I need."

"It's not a bad thing. You are only a few years older than him. Now how do you know that Nurse Edith asked him?"

"He told me. He said she was asking how long I'm in the church and why he didn't come in with me. She also wanted him to tell her if I was speaking to anyone outside."

"Do you think she suspects?"

Eva looked up at the crucified Christ for a moment. "I don't know. I think she will continue to snoop around. I didn't call her Nurse Gestapo to be mean. She is like the Gestapo."

"This is going into a dangerous phase."

"I can handle it."

"No, Eva, you cannot handle this on your own. I know you are very brave and you have given quite a number of people a chance at escaping. We have to be even more careful now."

"Are you saying I should stop?"

"No, of course not, but you can't be seen coming to the church as frequently as you have been. Even the villagers have noticed."

Eva gave Father Haralambos a wry smile. "The villagers notice if I sneeze and then they know that I've caught a cold long before I do."

A quiet chuckle echoed in the room as Father Haralambos nodded. "You have made an impression on the village." He looked at Eva with a worried expression on his face. "My job is to protect you."

"No. Your job is to protect those poor souls."

"I'm sorry," Father Haralambos said and looked down at his black robes before he turned his attention back to Eva. "Since when did you become the village priest?"

"Father!"

"Eva Muller, my job is to protect you and to protect them." My job is to know when you are in danger."

"I'm not in danger. Nurse Edith is just being a little gossipy."

"No, your dear nurse has your father's ear and that means he will hear her suspicions and act upon them," Father Haralambos said. He took Eva's hand and held it.

"So what do we do?"

Father Haralambos sat motionless for a long moment as he stared at the painting of Daniel. "You haven't hired a maid, have you?"

"No. I don't want any of the villagers to get anywhere near me."

Father Haralambos looked at Eva with a knowing smile. "Someone from the village already has."

Eva frowned for a moment trying to discern what Father Haralambos was talking about when it finally dawned on her.

Her face creased into a smile. "I don't count you as part of the village."

"No? Do I live somewhere else?"

"You know what I mean." Eva gently tapped Father Haralambos' arm. "A maid will see all of me."

"Unless she was blind in one eye, yes, she would."

Eva couldn't help but shake her head. "You don't understand."

"I understand. I do. We all have scars, little one. Some of our scars are visible and some are invisible. The invisible ones are the worst," Father Haralambos gently said as he put his arm around Eva. "What those demonic people did to you is horrible but you can't let them win."

"The visible ones are just as bad."

"I'm sure they are, but we have a problem here that will become extremely dangerous. You have to get a maid."

"What good will a maid be to me?"

"A maid can go to church without rousing suspicion."

"You want me to hire someone in the Resistance?" Eva asked incredulously. "Do you realize that those people want to kill me?"

"No, they don't. The Resistance doesn't want to kill you. If that was the case, they would have killed you twelve months ago."

"Wonderful," Eva replied as she let her head fall back against the back of the chair. "Do you have someone in mind?"

"I may have. The less you have to do with me and the church, the less suspicious Nurse Edith will be. You need to start on your journey to Athena's Bluff."

"I've been there already."

"You have?"

Eva nodded. "Yes, I went last week."

"That was not nice, Evy, to do that."

"I know but I had this idea in my head…" Eva stopped when she realized she had said too much. One look at Father Haralambos told her he understood the reason she had gone to the outlook just out of town. "You don't have to say it."

"But I will."

"I know. God knows."

"God knows," Father Haralambos agreed as he gently tipped Eva's face toward him. "He knows, but taking your own life is a sin."

"I didn't."

"I know. You're still here to talk to me!" Father Haralambos replied, making Eva smile. "You are making a difference and saving lives. One day, you will see, your goodness and loving kindness will be rewarded."

"I'm not after a reward. I just want my life to end."

"For someone who wants to end their life, you are reaching out and helping others. That's a little different to someone who just doesn't care. No." Father Haralambos shook his head. "Your life has value and meaning. You are loved—"

"By one person, you." Eva gently poked Father Haralambos in the chest.

Father Haralambos took Eva's hand from in front of his chest and kissed it. "No, dear child, there is one far more important than me that loves you. God loves you. There is no one more important than that. No matter what the world does, God loves you."

"It always feels I'm alone."

"But you're not. He always sends someone to help you, to guide you. He sent me and I know He will send others. You are never alone when you have God's love."

Eva bowed her head. "A nun befriended me in Aiden and she said the same thing."

"Oh?"

"Sister Abigail. She was this tiny thing and old. She was feisty too, and told the lamest jokes I've ever heard." Eva laughed at the memory of the old woman who had comforted her so much when she needed it the most. "She told me that when I needed God, He was always there."

"He is there. He sent Sister Abigail and now He sent me. God knows what you require."

"Hm, if you say so."

"Indeed. Now you must go back to Athena's Bluff and make that a priority."

"The maid will bring the identity papers to you?"

"That is what I had in mind," Father Haralambos replied as he put the forged identity papers Eva had given him in the drawer of his desk. "I will arrange for you to meet your new maid and then she will come to you at the house."

"If I must have a maid, then alright."

"Good. Now when you were here the other day, you said you wanted to ask me something?"

Eva ran her hand through her dark hair and wondered if it was the right time to ask; there was no harm in asking. "I don't know if you can help me with this."

"Why don't you ask me and then will both know."

"You're the village priest and like you said, you know what happens in the village."

"I do. Sometimes I wish I were deaf," Father Haralambos joked, making Eva feel a little less uncomfortable. "We are friends. You can ask me."

"Major Hans Muller is not my father."

"He's not?"

"No, he's my stepfather."

"I see."

"I don't know who my real father is. My mother and this man were courting and they were intimate."

"Yes, you are the living proof of it."

Eva's eyebrows rose. "You are not a typical priest."

"I'll take that as a compliment, thank you. So your mother

and this mysterious man courted, were intimate and then what?"

"Then I don't know. I don't know what happened to him. Mama was from this village. I think my stepfather chose to be stationed in Larissa in a sick, twisted way of proving something. Or maybe he just thought he would hurt me or maybe it was just luck."

"He is a very strange fellow."

"Sadistic bastard--" Eva put her hand over her mouth when she realized she had sworn in front of the priest and in a church. "I'm sorry, Father."

"It's perfectly alright on this occasion, since he is a sadistic bastard."

"You know everyone in the village. You would have been here when my mother was here."

"What's your mother's name?" Father Haralambos got up from his seat and stood in front of a bookcase.

"Her name was Daphne. Her parents were Eva Theresa and Petros Mitsos."

Father Haralambos stared at the ground. Eva watched him as he twisted the gold cross that hung down his chest. After a long moment, he looked up and smiled.

"Let me tell you a story." Father Haralambos smiled when Eva groaned in frustration.

"Do you have to tell me one of your stories now? Can we talk about this question?"

"Yes. Have patience little one." Father Haralambos sat back down. "A very long time ago, a sheepherder fell in love with a young woman, much younger than himself. As is customary, the woman's family had already picked out a husband for her. The young woman, as things go, didn't want to listen to tradition. Her heart fell in love with the sheepherder, even though he was older and a very poor sheepherder at that. Her father was against this union, so they called a halt to it, much to the deep and aching sadness of this sheepherder and the young woman. There was a slight problem. She was pregnant with his child."

"You are talking about my mother, aren't you?"

"Indeed." Father Haralambos hesitated. "Daphne was sent away before anyone learned she was with child. It was a miracle of sorts, because it's hard to keep a secret in such a small village as this. Her father wasn't going to allow them to marry, so he sent his daughter away from the village and away from the sheepherder. I don't know where he sent her, and I don't know what happened to her."

"That doesn't tell me who my father is."

"Ah, but I haven't finished the story yet." Father Haralambos looked into Eva's eager blue eyes and softly said, "The sheepherder lost his one true love, or so he thought, and decided that no other would, or could, replace her in his heart. A little melodramatic perhaps, but he loved her so." He cleared his throat and said, "So the sheepherder decided to enter the priesthood..."

Father Haralambos watched as the realization surfaced on Eva's face. "You! You're my father?" The shock was evident in her voice, although her eyes were bright with excitement at the news.

"I am your father," Father Haralambos answered and smiled. "And you are my daughter. You are more beautiful than I had imagined."

"You are my father?" Eva repeated as she put her hand over her mouth and stared at Father Haralambos. "Why didn't you run off with my mother?"

"I was a poor sheepherder. Where would I go? Petros Mitsos was a war hero, a revered man in the village."

"Do you think my father knows about you?"

"I doubt it," Father Haralambos replied with surety. "I almost blurted out your mother's name when I first saw you."

"You knew I was your daughter?"

Father Haralambos closed his eyes and took a deep breath before he opened them again to see Eva's eyes gaze back at him. "You are the spitting image of your mother. There is no denying who you are, Evy. When I saw you for the first time, I knew who you were."

"You didn't say anything."

"What was I supposed to say? 'Hello, I'm your real father and not that fool that is standing next to you.' Is that what I was supposed to say?"

Eva shook her head. "You have known who I am for the last twelve months."

"Yes, but I didn't know if you knew that Hans Muller was not your father," Father Haralambos reasoned. "There were times when I wanted to say something but I held back. The time was not right."

"I wasted so much time."

"No, you didn't waste them. You and I became friends and God has answered my many prayers. He does give you what you desire at the appropriate time." Father Haralambos crossed himself and then brought the cross up to his lips and kissed it.

They looked at each other for a moment before Father Haralambos took Eva into his arms and held her against him as he kissed her tenderly on the top of her head.

CHAPTER 13

"Zoe! Zoe! Zoe!"

"I'm here, Klim," Zoe called out from the other side of the cabin, where she was skinning the rabbit she had caught. She heard running footsteps and a dark haired boy hurtled around the side of the cabin and came to a screeching halt, his shoes skidding on the rocks.

"Zoe!" Klim bellowed as he tried to catch his breath.

"I can hear you. Don't yell."

"Apostolos wants to see you."

"That man won't take no for an answer," Zoe muttered under her breath as she placed the skinned rabbit aside. "What does Apostolos want?"

"It's important."

"How important is it?"

Klim sighed deeply and pulled Zoe's shirtsleeve. "Zoe," he whispered and was cut short by Zoe's raised eyebrow.

"Why are you whispering? We are alone up here unless you think the trees are collaborators."

Klim scanned the trees and turned back to Zoe. "It's about the collaborator."

"Are you absolutely sure Apostolos said collaborator?"

"Yes."

Without a word, Zoe went back into the cabin. She picked up the sack she used as a makeshift bag and also her gun. She closed the door to the cabin and hurriedly walked down the track. Klim quickly followed.

They did not speak as Klim led Zoe to the designated location just a little way out of town to the north. Leaving Larissa and following the road, Zoe's mind turned to Stavros, who had promised he would take care of her, a promise he would now never be able to keep owing to the traitor amongst the Resistance. Zoe wanted to know who it was that had betrayed them. Now she was going to find out and demand justice—justice for her cousin and the others that he had betrayed.

Klim walked hurriedly along the path and through dense bush land until they came to a cave, one of the many caves that littered Larissa's hills and were last used during the war of Liberation from the Turks.

"Zoe, you're here. I wasn't sure if you were going to be at the farm or at Athena's Bluff," Apostolos said. "Come with me."

Zoe didn't have a chance to ask questions. She just followed Apostolos through the cave and onto the other side, to an area dense with bush land. In the middle of a cluster of trees was a clearing.

"Let's sit for a minute."

Zoe wasn't in the mood to talk but she reluctantly sat down on a fallen log. Apostolos sat beside her.

"I want you to know that I feel your pain. Stavros was like a brother to me and his betrayal cuts me to the bone." Apostolos reached out and took Zoe's hand. "What I am about to tell you will not be easy."

"What is it?"

"We know who the traitor is."

"Klim told me that you did. Who is it?"

Apostolos remained quiet for a moment and glanced to the two men who had walked out of the cave. He shook his head and they went back inside.

"Vassili Petrakis," Apostolos quietly said as he cast a worried look at Zoe. She stared at the ground for a long moment. "Zo—"

"I want justice."

"I know you do and we will mete out justice but—"

Zoe shook her head. "I want justice by my hand."

"No. No, Zoe. No, never."

"You are not listening to me. I'm not asking you. I'm telling you."

"It's too much of a burden to bear. I cannot allow you to do this."

"I'm not new to the Resistance. My father told me to be brave and to do what is right. I know what he meant; I didn't at the time but I do now."

"I know." Apostolos covered Zoe's much smaller hand with his own. "I was with your father and he was courageous and strong but he would never want me to give you this heavy burden to bear."

"My father isn't here," Zoe quietly responded. "I am here. Blood for blood, an eye for an eye."

Zoe and Apostolos looked at each other before a noise made them look up. Father Haralambos came out of the cave and slowly made his way towards them. With a slight nod, Apostolos got up and walked away, leaving the priest and Zoe alone.

"Does Apostolos think you will change my mind?"

"I don't know what you have decided. I came to give the last rites."

"You are going to give the last rites to a collaborator?"

"We are all God's children. Vassili made a mistake. He will pay for that mistake but it's not my job to be his judge."

"Pah!" Zoe picked up a stone and threw it against the cave wall, where it bounced.

"What have you decided?"

Zoe took Father Haralambos' bible. "The Bible says, an eye for an eye, a life for a life."

"An eye for an eye? Is that what you want to do? You want to exact vengeance?"

"Blood for blood," Zoe replied. "Vassili was Stavros' cousin. He betrayed his own cousin. He is my family. It is my job."

"You have been through enough—"

"Who do I give this job to, Father? Apostolos? He has been through a lot as well. We all have. None of us knew that we were going to be in a war but here we are. Who do you want me to give it to if not me?"

"You are far too young to make such a decision."

Zoe gazed sadly at Father Haralambos. "I was young and naive once. I'm not anymore."

"You are determined to do this?"

"Yes. I know am I am right." Zoe sat down and took a deep breath. For a long moment she didn't say anything. "Are you with us or against us?"

"I'm doing God's work. God is on our side, so yes, I am on your side."

"Good. Go and give that bastard the last rites so I can send him on his way to hell."

Father Haralambos pulled Zoe into his embrace and held her. Zoe shook her head trying not to let the tears overwhelm her but she lost the battle. She sobbed against his black covered shoulder.

Zoe sat alone in the cave, her eyes fixed on the ground. She could hear Father Haralambos' voice from outside the cave talking to Vassili. Her heart beat loudly in her ears and the enormity of what she was about to do made her hands shake. She closed her eyes and tried to steady her nerves. She opened them again to see Apostolos had sat beside her.

"It's time."

"Did you learn anything?"

"Nothing we didn't already know."

"Has Father H finished?"

"He has."

"Right." Zoe stood. Her knees trembled under her pants but she stood still waiting for the fear to subside. "I'm ready."

"You don't have to do this. Let me do this for you? Please." Apostolos put his arm around Zoe's shoulders. "Allow me to take this burden from you."

"No. I know you care about me, but—"

"I don't just care about you, Zo. I love you," Apostolos replied quietly. "I asked your father for your hand in marriage."

"I know." The corners of Zoe's lips curled but she refrained from smiling. She had suspected Apostolos had asked her father. Nicholas Lambros was a very happy man after he came out of his barn with Apostolos a few days before their world exploded. Now she knew why—her father had given his blessing.

"You do?"

"Yes. Stav told me how sweet you were on me."

"Your father gave me his blessing. I know Theo would have

given me his blessing as well. Is that a yes, you will?"

Zoe shook her head as she gazed up at Apostolos. "Tolis," she addressed him using a nickname she had for him when she was younger. "You are my friend and have been for a long time. I love you."

"But?"

"I love you as my brother." Zoe smiled sweetly and cupped his bearded cheek. "You and Theo were like brothers and that's how I see you. I love you because you want to take this burden off me. It's what a brother would do, but you can't."

"I understand," Apostolos replied. He leaned down and kissed Zoe tenderly on the cheek. "I am going to be jealous of the man that wins your heart."

"Pity the poor man," Zoe replied with a quiet chuckle. She picked up her gun and held it in her hand. "Let's do this." She took Apostolos' hand and they walked through the cave and into brilliant sunshine.

The clearing was now surrounded by members of the Resistance. Father Haralambos stood to the right, his Bible clutched firmly to his chest. In the center of the clearing was Vassili, tied to a chair and with a black hood placed over his head.

Zoe took a deep breath and slowly exhaled. Her legs felt like lead with each step she took. She was meters from Vassili. "Take the hood off."

"Zoe--" Apostolos stopped when Zoe glanced at him. He removed the hood.

Vassili Petrakis was a black haired man who resembled her cousin Stavros so much it made Zoe's heart ache. His dark brown eyes met hers and he blinked.

Zoe gazed at Vassili for a long time before she took a step forward. "Why?"

Vassili turned his tear stained face away from Zoe, who wondered if he was ashamed or remorseful for what he had done.

"I did it to save my family."

"You did it to save your family," Zoe repeated. She knelt beside his chair and gazed into his eyes. "You did it to save your family?"

"Yes."

"We were your only family. Stavros was your first cousin. That was your family. I don't believe you. How much money did they give you?"

"I'm sorry, Zoe." Vassili pleaded with Zoe. "Please, don't do this."

"Why don't you want me to do this?"

"You are my family."

"You are not my family. Do you see everyone here?" Zoe pointed to those gathered around. "Every one of them is my family. They were your family and you betrayed them. You are our Judas. You betrayed Stavros and you betrayed all us of us for thirty pieces of silver."

"I'm so sorry."

"I know you are." Zoe cupped Vassili's cheek. "I know you are, because you were found out."

Zoe stood for a long moment. "Look at me." Vassili turned his head and gazed at her, tears running down his face. "An eye for an eye, a life for a life."

Zoe raised her gun, she blinked back the tears that threatened to become a river, and then she fired.

CHAPTER 14

$\mathcal{E}$va entered the church. As usual at this time of the morning it was very quiet. She saw Sister Maria lighting a candle off to the far right of the room. Eva made her way across to the altar. She stopped for a moment, bowed her head, and then crossed herself before moving away and heading to Father Haralambos' office. He looked up from his studies and smiled when he saw Eva through the open door.

"I have some news." Eva reached into her cloak and brought out two identity papers and handed them to Father Haralambos, who came around his desk.

"Ah, this is good. I'm glad you're here. I want to introduce you to your new maid."

"I'm afraid my church visits are going to be very limited."

"Ah, did Nurse Edith convince your father—"

"Stepfather."

Father Haralambos smiled. "He is still your father. Now did Edith convince him?"

"Yes, as we feared."

Father Haralambos put his arm around Eva and led her away

from the office towards the back. He opened a door which led into pitch darkness.

"You have a cellar?"

"Yes, Father Alamanios used to store his collection of wine down there before the war and now we just use it for storage."

"Where are we going?"

"To meet your maid," Father Haralambos replied as he lit the oil lamp. "Now do you want to stay up here? There are a lot of steps."

"How far down is it?"

"About twenty steps."

"I'll come down with you," Eva replied taking Father Haralambos' offered arm.

"Zoe, it's just me," Father Haralambos called out as they descended.

"I'm in the wine room," Zoe's muffled voice filtered back up.

"She sounds very young," Eva whispered.

"She's fourteen but works hard and has a good heart. I'm quite sure she will like you and you will think she's a little too chatty."

"I'm not chatty, Fath—" Zoe came out of the wine room holding an old bottle and stopped dead when she saw Eva's tall form behind Father Haralambos. "What in God's name is the cripple doing here?" She spat out, and then she turned and went back inside the wine room. Moments later she came back out with a gun and aimed it at Eva's head.

She fired.

The gun jammed.

Zoe swore and glared at the gun and fired again at Eva. "For the love of Christ! This is the second time this stupid gun hasn't worked on this bitch. She-demon," she muttered as she checked the barrel of the gun.

"Put the gun down, Zoe, and what have I told you about swearing in the house of God?" Father Haralambos shielded Eva from the enraged young woman.

"No! Get away from her, Father, or else."

Father Haralambos stood his ground. "Or else what? You will shoot me? Here? In the house of God?"

"The gun is cursed, so you're safe."

"Zoe Lambros!" Father Haralambos exclaimed in outrage. "That is not what I expect from you!"

"Sorry, but the sight of this bitch makes my blood boil!"

"The sound of your swearing is going to send me to an early grave! Haven't there been too many deaths already today?"

"This will be a justified death. Now step away from her."

"Do you think I can't call on my guards at this very moment?" Eva asked in Greek as she peered over Father Haralambos. She wasn't sure why she wanted to goad Zoe but she couldn't help herself.

Zoe shook with rage and leveled the gun at her.

"Your gun doesn't work, little girl."

"I am cursed with a stupid f--," Zoe stopped herself from swearing and then glared at Eva. "What is the cripple doing here in the holy of holys!"

"Since when has the wine cellar been the holy of holys?" Father Haralambos asked shaking his head in astonishment.

"It's in a church."

"My god, you are insufferable!" Eva exclaimed. "Father, I can't work with this child!"

"I'm not a child, you Nazi cripple!" Zoe spat out, and before she could react Father Haralambos reached out and grabbed the gun from her hand. "Father!" Zoe protested.

"I told you, no swearing in church. Now sit down and listen." Father Haralambos pushed Zoe onto a crate. Eva chose to stand as far away from her as possible.

"You can't expect me to be in the same room with this..." She was about to swear again but stopped herself. "With this...

whore!" Zoe gave up and threw her hands up.

"Why not?"

Zoe looked at Father Haralambos as if he had grown another head. "Were you not at the hanging? Or did you forget giving the last rites to them?"

"I haven't forgotten. It's not what you think. You remember when I said it is best if our left hand does not know what our right hand is doing?"

"Yessss." Zoe let out a frustrated breath. "What does that have to do with...her?"

"Zoe, Zoe, Zoe. You need to cultivate patience."

"Father, Father, Father," Zoe mimicked Father Haralambos sarcastically. "I need to get out of here before I kill someone in this church." She tried to get up, but Eva had moved and was standing before her. She was pushed back down by the tall woman.

Zoe pushed her hands away in disgust. "Don't touch me!" She yelled. "I don't want your bloody hands on me."

"Stop behaving like a two year old and listen to Father Haralambos before you give yourself heart failure. At this point I vote for you to continue but I don't think Father Haralambos would like it," Eva told her in Greek, but Zoe's response was to bolt to her feet and spit at her. The spittle landed on Eva's cheek and dribbled down her neck. She wiped it from her face with her hand.

"So you can speak Greek. I knew she was a spy! I knew it!"

"My god, you are an imbecile!" Eva retorted and wiped her hand against her cloak.

"Zoe!" Father Haralambos exclaimed and took out a handkerchief from his robe and handed it to Eva. "Need I remind you that you are in the house of God!"

"It's okay, Father." Eva wiped the spittle from her face. "We are dealing with a child having a temper tantrum. I understand her hatred even though she can't articulate it without sounding like a drunken whore."

"What would you know about hatred other than being the one doing the hating?" Zoe snarled and crossed her arms over her chest. "You're a Nazi whore and a spy. You can fool the priest but you don't fool me."

"Oh, no! You brilliant child, you have found me out. What am I going to do now! Oh, no, the game is up." Eva mocked Zoe and shook her head.

"Ladies!" Father Haralambos got in between Eva and Zoe and glared at both of them in turn. "Will you please treat the church as Switzerland and call a truce? Zoe, I think you owe Eva an apology."

"Like hell I do!"

"Zoe." Father Haralambos shook his head. "You need to calm down."

Zoe paced around in a circle trying to calm herself. "Father, if I didn't know better, I would say you were a collaborator."

"We now go from imbecile to moron," Eva muttered.

"Eva! I want the both of you to stop talking," Father Haralambos pleaded and pointed to the upturned crates. "Both of you sit down."

Eva sighed deeply and took the largest upturned crate and sat on it. Zoe took a crate on the opposite site and continued to glare at Eva.

"Zoe, this is Eva Muller."

"I know who she is," Zoe spat out bitterly. "Fraulein Muller is the devil's spawn."

"No, you don't know who she is. And stop interrupting me!"

"Zoe, what Father Haralambos is trying to say is that I'm not the person you think I am."

"Oh, that's even better. I don't know who Father Haralambos is, you're not who I think you are, and you expect me to sit here and believe it? By the way, I'm not who you think I am either. In fact I'm a German spy sent here to live a miserable life as—"

"Do you remember when Lucas had to warn the British airmen that the Germans were trying to find them?" Father Haralambos sat down and pulled Zoe down with him, clasping his hands over hers.

"Yes. We got them out in time but what—"

Father Haralambos pressed his fingers to Zoe's mouth to quiet her. "How do you think we got that information?"

Zoe shrugged, pulling Father Haralambos' fingers away from her mouth. "I don't know. Maybe Fraulein Muller gave you the news," she said sarcastically. "This is worse than that drama Petrakis put on last summer. That stank too."

Father Haralambos looked at Eva, who nodded at him. Zoe looked between the two of them and sighed. "A few months ago I approached Father Haralambos and gave him the news about the airmen whose whereabouts were being sought by the Germans."

"Oh, how noble of you, Fraulein," Zoe mockingly responded. "Is that your good deed for the week?"

"Zoe!"

"What? Father, are you telling me that she gave you the information? Do you really want me to believe that?"

"Yes," Eva said simply.

"Oh, right, and I believe it because Fraulein Bitch tells me."

"Why is it so hard for you to believe?" Eva asked.

Zoe's eyebrows hiked in surprise. "Oh, I don't know, could it be that you're the enemy!" She yelled at Eva.

Despite the seriousness of the situation, Eva laughed, knowing it would probably make Zoe even more enraged. She didn't know why she laughed, but she did. The sight of this fiery and fearless petite young girl made her want to applaud, which was a very odd reaction. She continued to smile when Zoe stood up and stepped over to her.

"I'm going to kill you," Zoe said very slowly. "It's not a threat. I swear on my mama's grave, I am going to shoot you."

"Not with that gun, you won't," Eva responded with a sneer.

"You have a smart mouth for a cripple."

"You're a feisty little thing, aren't you?" Eva asked, which only earned her a growl. "Feisty and stupid. Almost as entertaining as a two year old."

"Someone should shut that smart mouth of yours," Zoe spat back.

"It won't be you. You can't reach it," Eva responded and then chuckled.

"Eva is my daughter," Father Haralambos announced. Zoe turned to him with a look of disbelief on her face.

Zoe blinked. "Your what? You have a daughter and it's her?"

"See, I'm not Satan's spawn, I'm his spawn," Eva said on seeing Zoe's green eyes darken in anger. The vein in her neck pulsed to such a degree, she was certain Zoe was going to indeed have heart failure.

"Eva! You're not helping." Father Haralambos admonished, and turned to Zoe, who was now completely outraged.

"You are a priest!"

"Yes, I know I am."

"Priests don't have sex."

Father Haralambos smiled. "There are more things in heaven and earth."

"Huh?"

"That was William Shakespeare."

"Who?"

"An English poet..." Eva began to explain, but was silenced by the hate-filled look she was getting from Zoe.

Zoe let out a frustrated growl. Shaking her head, she bolted up the stairs and out of the church into a downpour.

"Oh, great!" Zoe looked up into the heavens, now soaked.

The rain fell steadily as Zoe thumped the ground in frustration. She was cold and angry. Angry with Father Haralambos for taking Eva's side and angry with herself for not killing her when she had a chance. She splashed through the mud and sat on an old motorcycle that lacked a wheel. Muddy water had pooled in the sidecar and she watched the rain fall. The old motorcycle was a project she was helping Father Haralambos with.

Father Haralambos stood under the overhanging shingle and sighed. "Zoe, come back inside. Eva has left and we really need to talk." Please."

"No," Zoe mumbled and straddled the bike.

"Getting wet won't help. You're going to catch a cold."

"So what?" Zoe replied. "If I die from a cold or if I die from a German bullet, what would it matter?"

"It would matter to me." Father Haralambos held out his hand. "Come back inside. We have to talk."

"What's left to be said?"

"You would be surprised." Father Haralambos smiled as Zoe got off the bike and made her way towards him.

Zoe accepted the towel from Father Haralambos and dried her hair. She followed him inside the small office. With the towel around her wet hair, she stood by the window, her head resting on the glass as she watched the rain falling lightly against the pane, making a kaleidoscope trail down the window. She sighed as she traced a droplet with her finger, disappointment weighing heavily on her shoulders. "You've complicated matters."

"Oh, how so?"

"I was going to kill her," Zoe said quietly. "I had it all planned out. I was going to avenge my mama's murder. Now you tell me she's your daughter. How can she be your daughter? You have never married. Priests don't marry and they don't commit fornication. That isn't right."

"I have never lied to you about anything. Why am I going to start now?"

Zoe shook her head. "I don't know. How can she be your daughter?"

"That answer is not for today. I want to talk to you about how you are a useful member of the Resistance."

"Yeah, right." Zoe continued to watch the rainfall. "Very useful, and I have the most useless gun ever made."

Father Haralambos got up and walked over to Zoe, gently placing his hands over hers. "You can be very useful."

"If I was useful, why didn't I help Stavros or Kiriakos or Antonios? How useful was I to Giorgos or to the others who have died?" Zoe turned and looked at Father Haralambos, her green eyes glistening with unshed tears.

"You can't stop the war by yourself, my child. It's going to take the might of the Allied powers to deliver the deathblow to the Nazis. Just as a hand needs the rest of the body to accomplish its desired action, so do we. We need the Allies to help us to defeat them. You are useful."

"How? I haven't done anything, apart from a lot of crying and watching my friends die."

"You were very brave. Brave enough to have witnessed the death of your friends so they left this earth knowing their lives were not in vain. And you are here for moral support to your friends who still live. It takes a lot of courage to continue when death is all around you. Don't cry for the dead, for they are with our Lord in Heaven. Cry for the living who need your help. Remember the job I recommended you for?"

"Yes, how can I forget that?" retorted Zoe sarcastically.

"Why do you think I recommended you to Eva?"

"Because I can clean and cook?" Zoe replied bitterly.

"Indeed you can, but Eva is going to need someone to help her to get us any information she comes across that would be useful in our struggle. She has noticed that her nurse and her father have been watching her closely, so she might want you to deliver the information. So, what do you say?"

"I won't kowtow to the Germans. I don't care if one of them is your daughter!"

"It doesn't matter that she's my daughter. What matters is that we need you. You need to put aside your anger and understand that you will be doing your comrades a service and possibly saving lives as well. Can you see how you are needed here?"

"Yes."

"Killing Eva would only have caused more deaths to our brothers."

Zoe shivered as the darkest memory of her life once again made its way to the surface to torment her, a torment so painful that she was not even aware of the tears silently rolling down her cheeks. Nor did she feel the embrace of Father Haralambos as he tried to comfort her. Zoe was completely absorbed in her torment and in her memories.

"It's going to be alright, Zoe. We have lost too many loved ones, I know, my child. We can grieve for them, but they are in a better place."

Zoe wiped away the tears and accepted the handkerchief Father Haralambos had handed to her. She nodded her thanks and sighed. "Remember that day my mama died?"

Father Haralambos nodded.

"My belief in God died with her," Zoe whispered.

"I know, my child, I know."

Zoe sighed again loudly. "What do I need to do?"

"Eva is expecting you, so I suggest you go and get cleaned up and report to Kiria Despina." Father Haralambos stood up and wiped a tear from Zoe's cheek. With a twinkle in his eye he chuckled. "And try to be meek and humble when you are talking to Major Muller."

Zoe glanced up at a drawing on the wall. It had a shaft of light descending from above, illuminating the figure of Daniel in the cave with lions around him. "Well, I think I'm about to learn what Daniel felt like. Although those animals were tame compared to Major Muller."

"You have a guardian angel like Daniel did."

"Well, if I do, then I need to report him for not being on the job," Zoe replied as she continued to look at the painting.

"Would you like to pray with me? I know you don't believe in our Lord, but I do, and I would want you near me as I ask for His help," Father Haralambos said, taking her hand.

Zoe nodded. "All right, Father, but I have to warn you, once our job is done, I'm going to kill the b—erm—I'm going to kill your daughter."

"I know you will."

"Right. You do know that when I say I'm going to do something, I do it."

"I know that."

"Good. Now let's get on with the prayer so I can go over to Satan's lair."

As they knelt, Father Haralambos put his arm around Zoe. They bowed their heads and he offered a prayer.

CHAPTER 15

*Z*oe straightened her shirt one more time and then rounded the corner. As she spotted the major's residence, she wiped her sweaty palms along her skirt. The house was hard to miss; it was the largest estate in Larissa. It used to belong to the Faksomoulos family, who had owned property from Athens to Thessaloniki before the war with the Italians. Danalos Faksomoulos saw the coming troubles and packed up his family and fled. Zoe had thought him a coward and it was fitting his estate would be occupied by similar cowards and murderers. There were two properties—the larger house where Major Muller made his base, and the small house, once used as a guest house, where Zoe knew that Eva Muller was located. For as long as Zoe could remember, the guest house was always called 'the small house' but it was a misnomer. The 'small house' was larger than two normal village properties.

A small stone fence separated the property from the street. Standing on guard next to the front gate were two soldiers. Zoe scowled as she approached the gate, and to her surprise, the guard nearest the gate latch opened it and let her in.

Zoe walked through and proceeded to walk up the driveway. She stopped momentarily and looked back at the guards. With a slight shake of her head, she resumed her journey.

Slowly, Zoe made her way up the stone steps where two other soldiers stood guard before the entrance. Above them the Nazi flag hung limply in the drizzling rain. One of the soldiers brandished his gun and pointed it at her. She stopped when she was about to take the final step to the landing. She looked up at the sky. *Now would be a good time to show up, guardian angel.*

Zoe was prepared for a long drawn out argument but instead the door opened and the soldier she recognized as being one of Eva's bodyguards stepped out. She inwardly groaned on seeing Henry. The extremely tall, bald man with piercing green eyes crooked his finger at her to follow him.

"I listen and obey," Zoe muttered in Greek as she stepped through the threshold. The house didn't look any different, other than the swastika which adorned the main entrance, from what it had been when she had visited the house as a young child. She was expecting more guards than the two outside and the two inside, but was very surprised not to see any others.

Henry stopped suddenly, causing Zoe to nearly crash into his broad back. He turned around and faced Zoe.

"If you throw as much as a rumpled piece of paper at Fraulein Muller, I will kill you."

Zoe looked at Henry's face. "How long did you practice that, Goliath?"

"I mean it."

"Yes, I know," Zoe patted henry on the hand, surprising both herself and him. "I've watched you walk next to her for months."

"That was a lucky throw."

"You should have given her a helmet."

"I should have shot you," Henry growled back. He opened the door to an office downstairs and indicated for Zoe to walk through.

Zoe entered the room, which looked quite sparse—a desk sat in the middle with a solitary lamp on the left hand side. That was it. There was nothing personal about it to indicate its owner and the room was devoid of anything to suggest someone actually occupied it.

"What's this?"

"This is Captain Reinhardt's office."

Zoe studied the room again and slowly shook her head. "It's cold. There's nothing to say who it belongs to. He doesn't even have a piece of paper on his desk." She bent her knees slightly and tilted her head to the side to inspect the desk surface. "It's also dusty."

Henry sighed as he looked at the ceiling. "Do you always talk so much?"

"No, not always. When I'm throwing rocks, I am very quiet." Zoe smiled when Henry gave her a disgusted look.

"I don't know why they are hiring you. You are a menace."

"You're worried I'll want to kill her."

"No, I'm not worried."

"Really?"

Henry stared at Zoe. "You won't get another chance. I will kill you first."

"How old are you?" Zoe asked expectantly.

"Why?"

"I want to know."

"You're very strange."

"No, I'm just bored," Zoe replied and inspected the room to find a spot to sit down. There weren't any chairs other than the one behind the desk. "Where is your master?"

"He is busy--"

"Killing people."

"Stop that," Henry admonished and lowered his voice.

He glanced behind him at the open door before he turned to a very bemused looking Zoe. "You want to help Fraulein Muller, don't you?"

Zoe gazed up at Henry and looked behind her for a moment before she turned her attention to him. "I am Frau Muller's maid."

"Fraulein Muller," Henry corrected.

"Evil bitch from Berlin, yes, that one."

"Stop that!"

Zoe grinned. "You like her."

"Stop talking."

Zoe observed Henry. His green eyes narrowed as she gazed at his face. He avoided her for a few moments but then lost that war with himself.

"What?" Henry asked finally.

Zoe's response was cut short when Captain Reinhardt entered the room and took a seat behind the desk.

"I'm Captain Reinhardt," Reinhardt introduced himself in German and glanced briefly at the piece of paper in front of him. "You are Zoe Lambris?" He asked in Greek, taking Zoe by surprise.

"Lambros." Zoe scowled at the very obvious mistake in her name.

"Zoe Lambros," Reinhardt repeated and sat back in his chair. "Are you a good maid?"

"No. I've never been a maid before."

Reinhardt looked up with a slight smile. "I'm quite sure you will learn very quickly. Where are your belongings?"

"My what?"

"Your suitcase."

"Why?"

"You are moving in. Didn't Kiria Despina tell you?"

Zoe glanced at Reinhardt with a very confused look on her

face. "I live right across the street."

"Yes, I know you do, but you will move into this house."

"Like hell I will," Zoe muttered and glared at Reinhardt. "I'm a maid, not a servant."

"That's the same thing," Henry muttered under his breath just barely audible for Zoe to hear. He tried to hide a smirk when Zoe glared at him.

"Fraulein Lambros," Reinhardt said reverting to German. "You are moving into the top floor of this house to be with Fraulein Muller. Do you understand?"

"Yes."

"Good. How old are you?"

"Fourteen."

"Can you read and write?"

Zoe glanced at Henry, who was standing to attention and deliberately not looking in her direction. She turned back to Reinhardt. "Yes, can you?"

Reinhardt burst out laughing. "You are very funny. I like you. Sergeant Franz, take Fraulein Lambros to Fraulein Muller."

Zoe glanced back at Reinhardt, who was still chuckling as she left the room. They turned the corner and found the stairs.

Eva sat at her desk, her long, raven hair falling across her face as she looked at the photo she held in her hands. The smiling face of a young girl, her arms around an older woman, looked back at her. Eva remembered, so vividly, the day that photo was taken. She had been excited to join the Bund Deutscher Madel, the League of German Girls from fourteen to eighteen years of age. She raced home to tell her beloved mother how she and her friend Greta had signed up.

They found out they were going to parade in front of their leader and the following months saw them practicing how to march in formation. The night before the big day, Greta had stayed over and neither of them had slept. The following morning, thousands of Hitler Youth paraded before the Führer.

Eva closed her eyes and could still see the stands at Nuremberg, the banners flying in the breeze. Adolf Hitler stood at the podium, waved at them and said, "You, my youth, are our nation's most precious guarantee of a great future and you are destined to be the leaders of a glorious new order under the supremacy of National Socialism. Never forget that one day you will rule the world!"

The cheers had reverberated from the stands as thousands of young voices were raised in enthusiastic response. And then Kristallnacht happened.

Eva shook her head at the memory and sighed. "Oh, Mutti, you would have been so ashamed of me," she whispered to the woman in the picture as she brushed away tears. She put the photo aside and went back to the letter in front of her. A photograph of a young soldier lay on the side. She picked it up and gazed into the young man's earnest face.

She looked up at the sound of knocking, and quickly composed herself. "Enter."

The door opened and Henry entered. Behind him came Zoe, clutching her bag. "Fraulein Muller--"

"Just a moment," Eva said not bothering to spare more than a glance at Zoe. She finished writing the letter and put her pen aside. She stood and walked around the desk and sat on the edge of it while she watched Zoe look around the room.

"You can go, Franz."

"Fraulein--"

"Franz, you can go. She won't attack me."

Henry scowled and held his ground for a moment before he turned and walked out. He closed the door behind him.

"So, this is how our slave masters live," Zoe stated flatly as she looked around the well-furnished room. She smiled grimly when she caught sight of a painting she recognized well.

"My mother painted that," Zoe said proudly. It had been the last painting Helena had sold before her death.

"She was very talented," Eva replied and glanced at the painting of the countryside.

"She was," Zoe whispered, cleared her throat, and then continued to look around the room. A desk was positioned near the window and a light breeze blew the curtain over the chair.

Zoe looked up at a photograph on the nearby wall and peered at it. She recognized Eva quickly as the gangly teenager with her dark hair in a ponytail who was taller than the man and woman standing on either side of her. The man wore a black hat which contrasted with his silver hair. A salt and pepper moustache gave him a comical look. He wore a dark suit and had his overcoat folded across one arm while the other was wrapped around Eva. The older woman wasn't looking at the camera but smiling proudly at Eva, who had a medal hanging around her neck.

Still looking at the woman, Zoe realized she had never seen anyone wear so much jewelry in her life. She leaned in and scrutinized the pearls that were around the woman's neck. A peacock pendant also caught Zoe's eye.

"Find anything interesting?"

Zoe jumped a little at the nearness of Eva's voice and she glanced back at Eva, who hovered nearby.

"That's you?"

"Yes."

"What's the medal for?"

Eva let a crooked smile grace her features for a moment. "Running."

Zoe glanced back. "Hmm," was all she said, and turned back to the photograph. She stared at it for a long time. There was something about the man that reminded her of someone, but she wasn't sure who or why. "Who are these people?"

"You ask a lot of questions."

"Are you going to tell me?"

"Do I have to?" Eva responded, her tone a little irritated by Zoe's inquisitive nature. "They are my grandparents."

"Your grandfather has gentle eyes," Zoe said, still gazing at the photograph. "Is he a Nazi?" She smiled when she heard Eva's sigh behind her. She had to work with her, but Father Haralambos didn't say she had to "behave" the entire time. Annoying Eva Muller was going to be fun, making her time more enjoyable.

"No, he was not a Nazi."

"He looks like one except for his eyes." Zoe cocked her head to the right and continued to gaze at the photograph.

"Can you stop looking at the photograph like you're going to find the meaning of life behind it?"

"Is it bothering you?"

"No, it's not, but I find it strange that you would look at it for so long."

"What are their names?"

"None of your business."

"Does he answer to Herr None of Your Business?" Zoe quipped, getting a very irate look in return.

"No, his name was Alexander Muller, and before you ask,

he passed away when I was fifteen years old."

"I'm sorry for your loss." Zoe abruptly ceased her teasing and noticed a flicker of uncertainty cross Eva's face. "Is your grandmother still alive?"

"She is, I think?"

"You think?"

"Can you stop interrogating me?"

"How else will I get to know you while I'm working with you?"

"You're working for me."

"No." Zoe shook her head. "You are deluded. I'm working with you. Remember, this maid business is all pretense."

"No, it's not. I do really need a maid."

"Oh, wonderful!" Zoe rolled her eyes. "Why do you need a real maid for?"

"To be a maid, silly," Eva replied. "You do know what a maid does, don't you?"

"Do I look like I'm the village idiot?" Zoe scowled.

"No, you don't."

"I know how to sew, how to clean, how to cook. My mama taught me how to be a good wife some day. Do you know how to do all those things?"

Eva shook her head. "No, none of those."

"Thought so." Zoe made a snorting noise and turned back to the photograph. "Your mama had a maid to do all those things for you?" She asked sarcastically.

"Actually, yes, she did." Eva was smiling when Zoe turned in surprise. "I'm not going to apologize for that."

"You better marry someone rich or else you will be doing the cleaning, the washing, and the cooking."

"If I need marriage advice, I'll call you."

"You could always hire me as your maid," Zoe quipped, then chuckled at her own joke. She turned away and finally stopped staring at the photograph and focused her attention on the artwork nearby. It was one of her favorites, Bartolomé Esteban Murillo's The Beggar Boy. She studied it for a long moment.

"You like that?" Eva asked. "Bart--"

"Bartolomé Esteban Murillo." Zoe finished the artist's name and looked back. She gave Eva a knowing smile. "My mother was an artist, remember?" Her eyes went to her mother's artwork before returning to the piece in front of her. "This was one of her favorite pieces."

"You are full of surprises."

Zoe watched Eva for a moment. "You speak fluent Greek. Where did you learn how to speak Greek?"

"My mother taught me." Eva sat down on the couch and motioned for Zoe to join her.

"Oh, yes, I forgot, you're the bastard child," Zoe retorted, ignoring Eva's request.

Eva took a deep breath and flexed her fingers. "How did the meeting with Captain Reinhardt go?" She asked, ignoring Zoe's last comment.

"Other than him not getting my name right, he asked how old I was and if I could read and write."

"You can read and write?"

"Of course! We're not all illiterate here, you know," Zoe said defensively. "I also know how to speak German," she muttered.

"I'm sorry; I didn't mean it that way."

After a beat, Zoe looked at Eva. She reluctantly took a seat, but at the far end of the couch. "You never know when speaking German could be useful for a Greek. Do you know how to read and write?"

Eva smiled. "Yes, I know how to read and write."

"Well, you can't cook and sew, but at least you can read and write. Your husband will be proud."

Another long sigh made Zoe smile inwardly. *This is going to be so easy.* After a few minutes of uneasy silence, she asked, "What were you doing before I came in?"

"You ask too many questions."

"Yes, it's how I find out things."

Eva glanced at Zoe and shook her head. "I was writing a letter to a mother back home."

"Why?"

"He was killed last night," Eva responded tersely. "I write to all the parents after their sons have been killed or injured."

"Ah!" Zoe nodded. "That's how you know how to copy your father's signature."

"I don't sign those letters—my father does."

Both women lapsed into silence for a few moments until Zoe couldn't stand the silence. "So why are you betraying your Fatherland?"

Eva looked down at her hands, twisting the ring on her finger. "I have my reasons."

"What? Did Daddy not give you what you wanted?"

"Zoe, we are on the same side. I don't want to fight with you."

Zoe shook her head. "You don't get it. I'm not on your side. Your side killed my mother and I hate you."

"Why do you hate me?"

"Because you are a callous bitch."

"You don't know me," Eva replied, sounding hurt by the bluntness of Zoe's answer.

"You were there when my mother was killed. I saw you." Zoe looked up to find a very confused Eva looking back at her. "I heard you."

"You heard me? I don't understand."

Zoe was not fooled by the innocent look. She was expecting it. Here was the demon she hated with all her soul, the woman she wanted to kill to avenge her mother's death, and she was staring back at her with the most puzzled expression on her face, as if she truly didn't know what Zoe was talking about. Zoe nodded. "I have to hand it to you—you're good."

"I really don't know what you're talking about."

Zoe was angry. Angry with the woman sitting opposite her calmly denying what she had done. "When my mother lay dying, I heard you laughing. I saw you," Zoe said and waited to see if Eva reacted.

Eva sat back and shook her head. "I have never laughed when anyone was dying. I most certainly did not laugh," she said vehemently. "I wouldn't do that."

"I wasn't expecting you to admit it." Zoe shrugged. "You're a Nazi and Nazis have no heart."

"You have me all worked out, don't you? You think you know me," Eva replied angrily. She stood up and walked over to her desk, turning her back on Zoe. "You don't know anything," she said quietly.

"I know what I saw and what I heard," Zoe continued, unfazed by Eva's emotional outburst. "I can't deny that."

Eva took a deep breath, exhaled slowly, and regained her composure. She turned around to find Zoe was staring at her. "You are wrong. I wasn't laughing."

"Someone was laughing," Zoe replied.

"I'm sorry about your mother's death but I didn't laugh."

"You didn't even know her. How can you be sorry?" Zoe stared at Eva. "I know what I heard." She stood and walked over to Eva and looked up defiantly.

"You are a Nazi and yet you want to help the Resistance. It doesn't add up. I don't buy 'Father H is my father and that's why I'm doing it.'"

"Why is it difficult to believe?"

"You are the enemy."

"You're right in that I'm not helping because of Father Haralambos," Eva replied. "I'm helping the Resistance for my own reasons. My reasons that are none of your business."

"Very noble," Zoe replied. "I couldn't care less about your reasons."

"Have you ever changed your mind?"

Zoe stared at Eva for a long moment. "Yes, I've changed my mind many times. I've changed my mind about killing you although that could change again."

Eva shook her head slightly before continuing. "I changed my mind about Hitler and about the Nazis."

"So you're telling me that when you found out who your real daddy was, you jumped ship?" Zoe asked sarcastically.

"You're not going to be easy to get along with, are you?" Eva blurted.

"No," Zoe replied. "Get used to it."

Eva sighed. She was getting tired of Zoe's antagonism. She had enough hate to deal with in her life, and adding one more person who hated her was just overwhelming. Father Haralambos had told her that Zoe was going to be doggedly determined to hate her no matter what. She thought the priest was stretching the truth a little, but she could see that winning Zoe's trust was going to be difficult, if not impossible.

"Do you know about the 'Night of Broken Glass'?" Eva asked, motioning for Zoe to resume her seat on the couch.

"No." Zoe shook her head. For a moment, she ignored the Eva's request, but then she sat down again.

"Kristallnacht," Eva said in German. "It was a night of shame. Our group had assembled and a few of the older girls and boys heard about a plan to scare the Jews. Greta, she was my best friend, wanted to go." Eva went to the window and stared out. "Greta wanted to go and she wanted me along, so I went. Mutti thought I was at Greta's house." Eva tried to collect her thoughts. "I remember standing in the courtyard of a synagogue which had been set on fire. My friends were laughing and joking. For the first time I was ashamed to be in the Bund Deutscher Madel."

"You killed Jews?"

Eva didn't turn around but continued to stare outside. "No. I helped to burn a few houses and a synagogue... I watched as a rabbi was beaten. I watched and did nothing. I might as well have been the one who dealt the blows." Eva was lost in her memories and she mentally shook herself as she continued. "I helped my friends destroy people's lives and I didn't stop them."

There was complete silence in the room except for the noise of the soldiers outside though the open window.

"I stood by and did nothing. I ran all the way home and that's when I found out my mother had been killed."

"How?" Zoe asked, her voice no longer sounding angry.

"Someone thought she was a Jewess and shot her," Eva said, trying to regain her composure before turning around to face Zoe.

"Oh," Zoe whispered.

"So we both know how it feels to lose our beloved mother," Eva said. "You're not the first to lose their parent." Eva slowly lowered herself onto the couch again.

"Is that when you decided to work against the Nazis?"

"No. It was after I went to join my father in France," Eva replied. She wasn't about to reveal everything about herself to Zoe.

"Remember what I said about killing you?" Zoe quietly asked.

"Yes." Eva nodded. "I remember. It's not something I can forget."

"I meant it. You are everything I hate."

"You don't know me. How can you hate me?" Eva reasoned.

"I don't need to know the devil to want," Zoe stopped for a moment, "her dead."

"Hitting me with a stone in the head won't do it," Eva remarked wryly. "That just gave me a lump."

Zoe smiled.

"Why didn't you? Why did you choose a rock and not a bullet?"

Zoe took a deep breath and exhaled slowly. "I didn't have my gun when I saw you," she replied honestly.

"Lucky for me."

"I also don't think your life is worth a hundred souls."

"Oh."

"You represent everything I hate," Zoe said again. "How did you find out your real father was Father H? Did you roam the Greek countryside asking every priest you met if he was your real father?"

Despite the sarcasm, Eva found the question funny and chuckled, which only caused Zoe to scowl. Eva composed herself but couldn't help the smile that creased her face. "You have a unique way of expressing yourself."

"It's a gift." Zoe shrugged and folded her arms across her chest. "So, what's the story?"

Eva paused and got up from her seat, went to her desk and took a photo. "This is my mother," she said and gave the photo to Zoe.

Zoe looked at the black and white photograph of a striking woman and a younger version of Eva. Without a word, Zoe handed the picture back. "So that's how Father H knew who you were."

"My mother was from this village." Eva looked down at the photo and sighed.

"What's her name?"

"Daphne Mitsos."

Zoe scratched her head in thought for a long moment. "I don't know her."

"I didn't think you would. She left Larissa in 1919."

"So your mother was from this village and you instantly thought your father was the local priest?" Zoe asked with a puzzled expression.

"No, the local priest knows everything about a village so I asked him if he knew who my father was," Eva replied. She could tell Zoe would need a lot of convincing to believe her good fortune.

"You just happened to find the local priest, who was your real father?" Zoe asked incredulously.

"Yes."

"A priest doesn't marry, you know that, right?"

"I don't think it's my place to tell you the story. It's none of your business. The truth is that Father Haralambos is my father. If you don't want to believe it, that's up to you, but it's the truth."

"So out of all the folks in Greece, or even in this village, you found him." Zoe shook her head. "This is really worse than that Petrakis drama."

When it was put that way even Eva found it difficult to believe. "Yes. I would like to think of it as divine intervention, but I suspect Major Muller chose to come to Larissa."

"Why?"

"I don't know."

Eva remained quiet; there wasn't anything she could say to the young woman. They sat in silence for a while, each in their own world of pain, trying to come to grips with their own demons. For Eva, the gentle chimes of the antique clock were a decided relief, for they had broken what had been a puzzling train of thought. It was strange. Here she was, raised in a life of privilege as the child of a Nazi officer, educated in the best schools and yet in some strange way, she was overwhelmed by the feeling that she somehow did not quite measure up to this intense peasant girl with the soft green eyes, whose face was as beautiful as her name.

But there was more to it than that and Eva knew it. Already she sensed that there was something about Zoe. Something that was sparking emotions in her that she had not felt in a long time. Yes, it was indeed strange. In fact, as she sat there in the thick silence, it finally occurred to her that she admired Zoe's courage and passion. The fire in her eyes when she spoke about the things she loved and her commitment to her homeland. How she spoke about the love for her family and her friends.

Cupping her hand, Eva stared down at her perfectly manicured nails as if they encompassed in this moment all that made up the universe. For what seemed like an eternity after the clock's chime, she continued to sit there silently alongside the equally mute Zoe.

Eva found Zoe captivating, and had they been in another time and place, she wondered if they could or would have been friends. She wondered if the only thing in Zoe's heart was a burning desire for revenge, for swift and terrible retribution for what had been done to her homeland and to her mother. And who in God's name could blame her?

Finally, in a voice so low Zoe had to strain to hear, Eva said, "You realize, of course, the risk you are taking."

"Life is full of risks, both great and small." Zoe stared deeply into Eva's eyes and slowly added, "For all of us."

"Yes," said Eva, returning Zoe's mesmerizing gaze. "I suppose that is true. Well, I think Father Haralambos was right. You are perfect for the job."

"Aren't you scared that I may turn around and kill you anyway?"

"You may, but that's another risk I'm prepared to take."

From down the hall the heavy tread of Despina reverberated as she labored up the stairs. Eva stood up and in a clear voice asked, "You understand, then, what is expected of you?"

"Yes, Fraulein Muller," Zoe meekly replied, standing up as well. "I assure you, I am a quick learner."

As they heard the hesitant knock on the door, Eva said, "Good. You will begin your duties immediately."

"Yes, Fraulein Muller."

"Come in, Despina."

In a voice that seemed perpetually out of breath, Despina said, "Your lunch is ready, Fraulein Eva."

"Very well," pronounced Eva. She turned to Zoe and said, "At the moment I'm going to finish writing those letters. Will you please bring it up to me?"

"As you wish." The tone of Zoe's voice was properly respectful, but as their eyes met, Eva thought she detected just a hint of grim amusement in Zoe's expression.

"This way," Despina panted.

Without looking back, Zoe followed her out the door and down the hall. Eva stood at the door and watched Zoe as she patiently followed Despina as she waddled down the hall, and then as they disappeared down the steps. When they were gone, Eva's gaze lingered for a moment or two before she quietly closed the door.

CHAPTER 16

Zoe sat at the kitchen table and looked down at the dark wooden top, deep in thought. She was sitting in the house of her mama's murderer. God was mocking her—He had to be for her to end up here. Being a servant to the murderer's daughter, or was that his stepdaughter? Zoe didn't know what to believe or who to believe. Father Haralambos was not going to lie to her; there was no reason for it and he was a man of God. Despite losing her faith in God, Zoe still respected the priest. She couldn't fault him for believing in a cruel God who had robbed her of everything. No. Father Haralambos had been like a father to her, and for that she wasn't going to thank God. God had nothing to do with it. Nor did He have anything to do with the kindness and love that was shown to her by Kiria Despina—the older woman had looked out for her and became her adopted aunt. Zoe seldom bestowed the honorific 'aunty' to anyone she didn't feel was deserving of that honor, but she felt Despina had earned that title. Greeks were very quick to bestow the term 'aunt' or 'grandma' but Zoe didn't think it was right to honor someone because they had lived longer than she had. Respect was earned as far as she was concerned.

"What are you muttering to yourself about, child?" Despina came round the table and sat down. She set down the tray table that had some toast and two eggs on a plate.

"I wasn't thanking God for Father Haralambos and you," Zoe explained with a slight smile when she saw Despina's exasperated look.

"You must not mock God."

"Really? Why not?"

"He is the Almighty--"

"Almighty who sits on his hands, you mean? He is responsible for all of this." Zoe flayed her hands up in the air. "He is responsible for not listening to our prayers. Remember those?"

"Zoe--"

"We prayed this day would not come. We did. We prayed, we lit candles, we prostrated ourselves on the ground, and we begged. What did that get us? It got us war, it got us death."

Despina put her arm around Zoe's shoulders and leaned in for a kiss. "You have not lost everything. You have me and Father Haralambos, and we both love you a great deal."

"Hm." Zoe nodded and then gazed at Despina with a smile. "I love you too and I'm sorry you have to work for these demons."

"Not all of them are demons. Especially young Eva."

"Demon's spawn."

"Zoe!"

"What? It's the truth."

"We need to have a talk about that later. Take the tray up to Eva. She should be up now even though they had a late night."

"Why?"

"Why, what? Why should you take up the tray? You are taking the tray up because you're her maid now."

Zoe sighed. "I know that, but why did they have a late night?"

Despina smiled at Zoe. "Sometimes, even in a war zone, there is some happiness. She got engaged to Captain Reinhardt last night."

"Oh." Zoe nodded as she got up from her seat. She placed a towel over the tray and looked back at Despina. "Reinhardt must not mind that she's a cripple."

"Zoe!" Despina exclaimed as Zoe chuckled and left the kitchen with the tray.

Zoe was still chuckling when she approached the steps. Two soldiers were standing at the bottom of the stairs; both were smoking and were standing around casually. She passed them without a word and was a little curious as to why they were not at the top of the steps as they had been the previous day.

Zoe cast a backward glance at the soldiers, who were oblivious to her curiosity. *Hm, that is odd, but maybe it's not normal they were up there yesterday. Wonder if they thought I would kill the cripple.* She adjusted her hold on the tray. Taking a sniff of the flower in the mini vase, she approached Eva's room, which was the furthest away from the stairs. *What an odd place to put a cripple.* The door to Eva's room was slightly ajar.

Zoe was about to tap and enter when she stopped cold. She could hear the bed creaking but there was something else— a low moan, almost the sound of a wounded animal, but she wasn't sure. It sounded like someone was in pain. She glanced behind her wondering if she should call the guards from downstairs. She put the tray on a nearby chair and was about to enter when she stopped just as her hand touched the door.

She heard a man's low and deep voice speaking in German. She frowned and leaned towards the door, placing both hands very lightly against it. The creaking, the low moans, and a man's voice made Zoe's eyes widen. The noises inside became a little louder and she finally understood what was going on.

Zoe let go of the wooden door and took a step back as if the wood had exploded into flames. She glanced around her to see why the guards were not coming up, since they obviously knew what was going on. She took another step back and the floorboard creaked, making her shut her eyes tightly and grimace. Fortunately for her, the sound was not going to be heard by the two people inside the room. She took the tray from the chair and hurried down the corridor and down the steps to get as far away from the room as possible.

The two guards heard her coming down the stairs and looked up with matching smirks. As Zoe passed them, she could hear one of the soldiers laugh and make grunting noises. She looked back and stuck out her tongue at them, which only made them laugh harder.

Zoe entered the kitchen and put the tray on the table with a loud bang, causing the vase with the flower to come crashing to the stone floor.

"Argh! I'm going to go deaf or blind or something!" Zoe yelled and shook herself all over. She put her hand over her eyes. "This is going to be the death of me!"

"Zoe! My dear, what is going on in here?" Despina asked as she hurriedly entered the kitchen.

Zoe had now found where Despina kept the vinegar and brought up the bottle to her lips and took a large swallow. The liquid burned her mouth and she grimaced.

"Yuck!"

Despina looked at the tray minus the vase and then back at Zoe, who was shaking her head. "What are you doing?"

"I'm trying to get the mental image of the cripple and her fiancé out of my head, that's what."

"How are you going to do that? By drinking my vinegar?"

"Yes, but it's not working. Argh." Zoe sat down heavily in the chair and put her head down on the table. "Yuck."

Despina sat down next to Zoe and put her hand on her shoulder. "What did you see? Did you walk in on them while they were kissing? I have interrupted them a few times like that."

Zoe lifted her head and gazed at Despina. "Don't they believe in locking the door?"

"That door doesn't lock."

"Why not?"

"I don't know, but it doesn't lock. That's why there are two security guards at the top of the stairs. They are there to protect Eva."

"Well, those two idiots were at the bottom of the stairs today."

"So, did you find them kissing?"

"No." Zoe shook her head. "I thought she was in pain and I was about to enter to find out and then I stopped. They were having sex."

"Oh," Despina replied, a tiny trace of a smile was trying not to develop into a full-blown laugh at Zoe's expense.

Zoe looked up with a scowl. "Don't laugh at me. Just because I'm a virgin doesn't mean I don't know what sex is."

"I'm not saying you don't know but it's not something that is wrong. They are engaged and I don't know how Germans go about their business but it may be customary for them to engage in sexual intercourse before they get married."

Zoe shuddered and put her head back down on the table, letting her forehead touch the wooden surface. "If sex sounds like that, I don't want anything to do with it."

Despina burst out laughing and put her arm around Zoe's shoulders. "Oh, my dear girl, you make me laugh!"

"It's true, Aunty. She sounded like she was in pain. Never mind him—I think he was having a great time."

"Most men have a great time."

Zoe clapped her hands over her ears and shook her head to rid herself of the mental image. "That's just going to make me sick."

"When two people love each other, they make love after they are married, but we are in a war, so you never know."

"She didn't sound like she was enjoying it."

Despina smiled. "What did she sound like?"

"She sounded like she was in pain; that doesn't sound good to me. She sounded like my dog Athena just before I put her down. Do you remember my dog Athena? She was in constant pain."

"I don't think it's the same sound." Despina cupped Zoe's cheek and smiled. "You will understand once you find the right boy."

"I have far more important things to worry about than falling in love in the middle of a war."

"Yes, you do, and you can't kill her."

"I don't know what you mean," Zoe replied keeping her head down and worrying a sliver of wood from the table with her fingernail.

"Everyone has heard about your hatred for this woman. Even Grandma Alamnos knows and she's been deaf for years."

"I don't think I've made that a secret, Aunty."

"No, you haven't. I'm quite sure several villages further south know of your hatred for her as well. You are mistaken to think that Eva laughed when your mama was dying."

"I know what I heard."

"You think you do but when we are grieving, we tend to hear a lot of things. I remember when my Pericles died—I thought I heard angels calling his name."

"They were calling his name; he was a great man," Zoe said and took Despina's hand. "He and my papa were the finest men

God ever created."

Despina nodded and crossed herself. "Thank you, sweetheart. I still miss my darling Pericles. Zoe, you can't continue to hate. Yes, we must cleanse our soil of these Germans but the hatred will eat you up."

"It won't eat me up," Zoe replied quietly. "I am on a mission of vengeance and that is what keeps me going. I wake up in the morning and all I think about is killing her. It's better than waking up and wanting to be dead."

"You can't kill Father Haralambos' daughter."

Zoe lifted her head and gazed at Despina. "You know about that?"

Despina smiled affectionately at Zoe. "Sweetheart, the gray-haired ones in the village remember Eva's mother, Daphne. Eva is the spitting image of her mother."

"She is?"

"Oh, yes. Daphne was a very beautiful girl and all the boys wanted to marry her. Daphne was a really gentle girl with a good heart. My oldest daughter, Kaliope, and Daphne, along with Alexandra, were best friends."

"So the cri—" Zoe stopped when she saw the disapproving look she was getting from Despina. "So Eva is Greek?"

"No. Not fully. Daphne's mother was German, and her father was Greek. You have heard of Petros Mitsos?"

"Of course, who hasn't? He fought during the Liberation and was a hero."

"Petros Mitsos is Eva's grandfather. Unfortunately for Daphne she fell in love with Father Haralambos, before he was a priest, and they committed fornication. Daphne's mother Eva Theresa was distraught, as was her father. It brought great shame to the family."

"Poor Father Haralambos."

"Yes. He asked for Daphne's hand in marriage but Petros was

adamant that he would never marry his daughter."

"So she married the German instead? That's a great choice."

"Well, a father never knows what will happen to his daughter once he gives her away. The poor family is cursed."

Zoe's scowled at Despina's words. "Cursed? What do you mean? Are they all crippled?"

"No, they are fine. Eva is not a cripple. She had an accident and her back has been severely damaged."

"If that's the case, why does her father have her upstairs! I get tired walking up those steps so I don't think she's going to find them easy to navigate."

"I don't know, I didn't ask him. When you help her bathe you are not to say anything about her scars. She feels very self-conscious about them. You would feel the same way if they were your scars."

"Alright, I won't mention them." Zoe nodded. "Why do I have to help her bathe? I don't feel like seeing her naked."

"That's your job. You are her maid."

"Oh." Zoe sighed. "Why is the family cursed?"

"Oh, that." Despina crossed herself and kissed the crucifix that hung around her neck. "It's a very long story but Eva Theresa's aunty Erika was in an asylum; she was totally mad. She could speak to the dead and see the future."

"Isn't that what Kiria Danallis does?"

Despina smiled. "Kiria Danallis makes all that up—she's just a gypsy with nothing better to do. No one can foresee the future. Father Haralambos says that God doesn't give this gift of prophecy anymore to His chosen. That ability now comes to humans via Satan and the demons. These people are possessed."

"So did this Aunt Erika really speak to the dead?"

"I don't know, but she was locked up for a long time. Daphne had a younger sister called Theresa. She was a quiet and kind young girl but she was demon possessed, the poor child."

"Wow."

"Eva Theresa didn't know what to do and in the end they had to send her to Athens because the priests couldn't cure her. It was the turn of the doctors and they tried everything."

"Did they make her better?"

"Unfortunately young Theresa died in a tragic fire at the asylum so we will never know. Then Daphne fell pregnant and well, their troubles continued."

"That is a very cursed family."

"They are. Now we have young Eva. Her mother was murdered, and then Eva suffered a very bad accident. She was married to a young doctor for two years and he died when he was sent to war. Now she has found happiness with Captain Reinhardt. She deserves some happiness."

"So is that why I shouldn't kill her, because she found happiness with a German?" Zoe asked incredulously.

"No, you shouldn't kill her because she hasn't done anything to deserve your wrath."

"She laughed when my mama was dying."

"Sweetheart, you can't kill Eva. If you do, all the work she is doing with Father Haralambos will be in vain."

Zoe stared at Despina for a long moment. "How do you know about that?"

"Father Haralambos told me. He needed someone to look out for Eva but I couldn't do it on my own. I need your help. We all need your help."

"I'm thwarted at every turn," Zoe muttered. "I'm not going to like her. Just because I'm helping her doesn't mean I'm going to stop hating her."

"No one is asking you to like her. You just have to help her and the rest of us to help those poor people escape."

"Alright."

"Good. Why don't I make you something to eat and also get

Eva something else since those eggs are cold by now?"

"She's going to need her strength," Zoe muttered under her breath.

Despina chuckled as she got up from the table to make breakfast for Zoe and another for Eva. Zoe watched her and then left the kitchen and shook her head at how she was once again thwarted in her attempts to kill Eva.

CHAPTER 17

Zoe covered the breakfast tray once again with a towel and lifted it off the table. She glanced at Despina, who smiled at her while she was cleaning potatoes in the sink. She left the kitchen and slowly made her way back up the steps. This time the soldiers were standing to attention, one at the foot of the staircase. The guard gave her a cursory glance. Zoe was quite certain he had winked at her, but she made sure to keep her eyes forward and not look back.

At the top of the steps Henry, the guard Zoe had nicknamed Goliath, was standing to attention. He had been missing from this morning's antics but he was back in his usual post. He nodded briefly as Zoe passed him.

Zoe stopped midway down the corridor and leaned to the right. The door was open. *Well, they must have finished.* She looked back at Henry, who was staring at her. He was smiling, which surprised Zoe. His features changed and he looked so young that she almost forgot he was the enemy.

Zoe turned her attention back to her task at hand. Her job for the morning was bringing breakfast for Eva, cleaning Eva's room, and then helping her bathe. She took a moment to will herself to be civil, although she wasn't sure how she was going to do that.

"I have--" Zoe entered the room and stopped dead.

Captain Reinhardt was fully dressed in his uniform and the two lovers were kissing, but Eva's robe was open. Reinhardt had a possessive hold of the back of Eva's head, his fingers entangled in her black hair. His other hand was obstructed from view by Eva's robe but there was no denying what he was doing to his fiancée. In the seconds Zoe went from entering the room to shutting her eyes and turning around, she saw Eva's breasts, bare stomach, and one very long leg. Zoe was embarrassed she had caught the two lovers.

The two lovers stopped immediately as soon as they saw Zoe, who had turned her back on them and was staring at the floor and wondering how easy it would be to kill both of them if she had a gun.

"Ah, this is my cue to leave," Reinhardt said with a slight laugh. Zoe heard him kiss his fiancée. To her utter amazement, Reinhardt ruffled her hair in passing her out the door. For a long moment Zoe didn't move, unsure what to do.

Zoe turned around and scowled. "Ever thought of using a lock on the door?"

"Ever thought of waiting to enter before you enter?" Eva replied and tightened the sash around her robe. "I have my breakfast in the next room, never in my bedroom," she said and walked out, leaving Zoe to stare at her retreating form.

Zoe did a mock Hitler salute at Eva's retreating back and shook her head. "Stupid bitch," she muttered as she followed her into the drawing room, where she had initially met Eva as her new maid.

The room had more light than the bedroom. Zoe spotted the table nearby and put Eva's tray on it. Eva paid no attention to her at all. She stood by the window looking out while Zoe arranged the tray. Zoe looked up to see Eva's reflection in the windowpane. The mid-morning sunshine caressed her black hair, which cascaded down her back. Zoe was transfixed by the colors of dark blue and black.

"Do you have to stare at me?" Eva asked, not bothering to turn around.

Zoe was not embarrassed at being caught. She merely shrugged off Eva's terse question and was about to answer when Nurse Edith walked in. She glanced at Zoe for a moment.

"Do I know you?" Edith asked.

"No," Zoe replied in German.

"This is my new maid. Her name is Zoe Lambros," Eva said as she came away from the window and took a seat on the sofa.

"Ah, yes, Major Muller did mention you. I'm Nurse Ratsger. I am Fraulein Eva's nurse. Do you understand what I am saying?"

Zoe gazed at Edith's severe face and then looked at Eva, who had slightly turned away, but Zoe could see her grim look. She turned back to Edith and nodded.

"Good." Edith turned away from Zoe and took Eva's arm. "I leave for one day and I come back to some happy news!"

Eva nodded and brought up her hand to reveal the ring Reinhardt had given her. "He proposed last night."

"He is a wonderful man," Edith said as she gazed at the ring.

"He is," Eva replied as another nurse entered the room. She was in her early twenties and appeared to be friendly. She was a tall woman with blond hair that was tucked under her nurse's hat. She stood respectfully next to Edith, who was removing some items from her bag. Eva looked briefly at the nurse without acknowledging her presence.

"Eva, this is Nurse Alana Langstein," Edith said without being asked. She glanced up at Eva, who was staring at Alana. "Nurse Langstein, excuse Fraulein Muller's rudeness. She dislikes all nurses."

Alana's dark blue eyes crinkled and she smiled at Eva. "Well, I hope we can change that." Zoe watched the interaction completely fascinated by Edith's behavior and her lack of respect for her employer.

"I have seen you around," Eva said as she looked up at Alana. *Who is she? I've never seen you around.* Zoe was eager to find out. She had sat down at a nearby chair and watched. She was mesmerized by the tone in Eva's voice and her eyes. Her mama used to say that an artist can see into a person's soul by looking into their eyes. Eva's eyes betrayed her true feelings, and Zoe wasn't sure why Edith couldn't see Eva's contempt for her. Zoe could clearly see it. *You are in a lot of pain and you definitely don't like this new nurse.* She was intrigued by the way Eva was standing. It was obvious to her untrained eye that Eva's back was giving her a great deal of problems.

"Did you forget to take your pain medication?"

Eva sighed and shook her head. "No, I didn't forget."

Edith turned to Alana. "Eva is not an easy patient to treat. She will, at times, not take her medication."

The two nurses exchanged glances, which made Zoe lean forward in her chair, eager to decipher the latest mystery.

"Did you run out of your medication?" Alana asked Eva as if she was talking to a child.

"No."

"You just didn't want to take it?" Alana took Eva's hand and held it.

Zoe's eyebrows lifted at Alana's actions. Edith was either oblivious to Alana's behavior or it was premeditated. There was something very wrong in the whole interaction but Zoe wasn't sure what it was.

"I don't like how they make me feel."

"We've had this conversation before. Her injuries won't get better if she doesn't follow medical advice. She's been a rather stubborn patient even in Aiden, although now that I think about it." Edith stopped for a moment before she turned to Eva and smiled. "You were never a good patient—you couldn't stand to stay in bed."

Alana made a clucking noise and Zoe immediately hated the way it sounded. "Medications always made me feel ill as well, but I think we can fix that little problem."

What happened in Aiden? Where is Aiden? Zoe kept a running commentary on the conversation going on around her. She wasn't even sure why she was in the room. Curiosity won over the need to stay silent.

"What happened to you?" Zoe asked, which got all three women to turn to her.

"Eva suffered a severe injury to her back several years ago in Berlin which took her a great deal of time to recover from. She was treated by her uncle, Dr. Muller. Whilst we were in France with her father, the house they were living in was bombed by the French Resistance. Major Muller suffered some minor bruises but Fraulein Muller's room was destroyed and she was caught up in the blast."

Wow. You really are cursed. Zoe momentarily felt sorry for Eva.

"It was a blessing that Dr. Muller was in France at the time. I heard from Dr. Baer that he is a true healer," Alana exclaimed and took Eva's hand. "Nurse Edith will update me on everything I need to do to make you feel better. It's remarkable how far you have come, especially after the bombing. Dr. Muller is so proud of you."

Why are you going to be kept updated about her, Nurse Blondie? You are just strange. All you Nazis are just strange. Zoe mentally sighed.

"Yes, it's been a difficult recovery," Eva replied tersely.

"She also happens to be the most stubborn patient I've ever had to treat, but I do remember Dr. Muller telling me about a nurse that seemed to get Eva to listen, which was quite a feat."

Eva turned her gaze at Edith and stared at her for the longest time. "His name was Karl."

"Yes, that's his name. Karl. Good looking young man, wasn't he, Eva?"

Eva turned away and nodded. "Yes."

"He was rather sweet, if I remember correctly, but Erik won your hand, right from under the young man's nose, no less!" Edith continued her story to Alana, oblivious to Eva's very obvious discomfort in talking about Aiden.

"I was wondering what had happened to you." Zoe couldn't help herself and spoke to Eva in Greek.

"I wasn't born a cripple," Eva replied, causing Zoe to merely gaze at her.

Edith watched Eva and Zoe for a moment before she focused her attention on Eva. "Are we going to have another round of this?" She asked and glanced at Alana. "I can hide it from your father for a short time but he is not going to be happy."

Eva let her head drop and slowly shook her head. "What does it matter to my father if I don't take my medication?"

"He loves you. You know that and it hurts him if you don't look after yourself."

"Well, we can't have him feeling hurt," Eva replied sarcastically. The comment earned her a raised eyebrow.

It's a brief act of defiance. You are staging your own mini resistance war. Zoe watched Alana get handed the syringe. *That didn't last very long but it was worth a try.* Her thoughts were interrupted when Eva looked up as if she had sensed Zoe's thoughts. She gazed into Eva's eyes for a long moment, and for a brief second she saw a flash of anger and then it was gone.

"An old friend of yours will be dropping in this week," Edith said as she set out a syringe on a towel on the sofa. She looked up to find Eva staring at her. "Dr. Uta Baer will be stopping in on her way to France."

Eva blinked rapidly and her eyes completely betrayed her rising panic. Zoe noticed her shoulders slump and that all too brief defiant act was gone. *This Dr. Baer terrifies her.*

Eva took several gulps of air, her distress clearly evident to everyone in the room, although the two nurses were not reacting to it.

"Eva, darling, she is just coming to see how you are. That's all. It won't involve any treatments. I promise you that. Dr. Muller can't make it, which is most unfortunate as he would love to see you," Edith said as she let go of the syringe and reached out for Eva's hand.

Zoe's gaze never left Eva's face, which was quite ashen. *Who are Dr. Muller and Dr. Baer? They are not people she wants to see, but the nurses are not noticing this?*

"I have been sending him such glowing reports about your health that he wanted to come and see for himself but he's been unable to get away. Dr. Baer was in Thessaloniki and then she's going to Athens, so this would be a perfect time to come visit us."

"Who are Dr. Muller and Dr. Baer?" Zoe decided to ask. Her curiosity had won out and she wanted to know who these people were more than she wanted to observe.

"Dr. Dieter Muller. He is Major Muller's brother and a world-renowned physician. He treated Eva in 1938. Dr. Baer treated Eva in France after the bombing."

"Who?" Zoe asked, not understanding the more difficult German words.

"Satan and his little helper," Eva muttered in Greek. Zoe's eyebrows rose at Eva's words and she glanced at the nurses, who were oblivious to the statement.

"Where is Dr. Muller?" Zoe said in German. She didn't want to give away Eva's honest answer. One look at Eva's anxious demeanor was enough to tell her Satan and his little helper terrified her.

"He's stationed in France," Eva replied and looked down at her hands. She twisted the ring on her finger, completely lost in thought.

"Dr. Baer is looking forward to seeing you," Edith said before she took hold of the syringe and gave it to Alana. The needle caused Zoe's eyes to widen.

Without a word, Alana pushed up Eva's sleeve from her robe and gently wiped a patch on her upper arm with white gauze. Eva pulled her arm away from Alana's grasp momentarily. Alana's response was to take Eva's arm without a word.

Ah, Blondie, you're not so nice, are you? Zoe watched the interaction.

"I know you hate injections and would do anything to get out of them. I could get your father to give them to you if you want. Is that what you want?"

Eva shook her head at Edith's very real threat. "No."

"No, I didn't think you would." Edith watched Alana bring the injection to Eva's arm and slowly push it in, causing Eva and Zoe to wince in unison.

While Alana tidied up after herself, Zoe's gaze remained with Eva, who had closed her eyes. Zoe noticed the Eva's hands shake, as whatever she had been given was causing her distress. Zoe was about to say something when Eva's hands clenched. Edith looked down and didn't say a word. She merely prepared some pills from her bag. She stood up and walked to where the breakfast tray lay and poured Eva a glass of water. She came back and helped Eva sit up to take the pills.

There was no defiance, no act of resistance. Whatever resistance Zoe had seen, it had disappeared.

For a brief moment their eyes met and all Zoe could see was surrender in Eva's eyes.

What really happened to you? Eva closed her eyes; her hands were clenched.

"What did you give her?'

Edith gazed down at her charge and brushed Eva's dark hair from her eyes. "Nothing you should concern yourself with."

Zoe wasn't sure if Edith cared for her patient or not, but whatever was going on, it wasn't what she was expecting.

Just what I need; more complications. Zoe watched Edith get up from the bed and repack her bag.

CHAPTER 18

"W asn't there anywhere smaller they can put me?" Zoe asked as she stood in the doorway of the room that was assigned to her. The room was located next to Eva's bedroom, which didn't please Zoe, or Eva for that matter, but that's where Major Muller wanted her. It wasn't exactly a room. It was the tiniest room she had ever seen.

"Zoe--" Despina put her arm around Zoe's shoulders.

"My chicken coup at the farm is bigger than this," Zoe muttered as she stepped into the room. A bed and a single wooden chair, acting as a bedside table, took up half the space of the room. "Why can't I live across the street?"

"Major Muller wants his daughter's maid to be close by."

"I live across the street. That's close." Zoe was undeterred by Despina's reasoning. She went to bounce on the bed and was surprised to find that it was rock hard. "Ouch, my butt did not like that."

Despina leaned against the doorjamb and shook her head. "This is not a holiday at the seaside."

"They could at least give me a soft bed," Zoe muttered. She

noticed her legs dangling off the side of the tall bed. "These people are giants. Look at the height of this bed!"

"I don't think the Germans brought their beds halfway across Europe," Despina entered the room and hurried Zoe off the bare mattress.

Zoe made a face as she got off the bed and watched as Despina put a clean white sheet, a pillow, and a blanket. "I don't like this place; it's very cold."

"It gets that way in the evening."

"No, I don't mean the house is cold, but there isn't any warmth to the people. I know the Nazis are cold but this is like the Pinios in winter. Almost frozen." Zoe sat back down on the bed, mindful this time of the hardboard beneath the mattress.

Despina gazed at Zoe for a moment. "Your job is not to try and understand these Germans. Just get some rest tonight."

"Doesn't her majesty need anything tonight?"

"Zoe! You need to show some respect."

"Respect is earned, Aunty. I'm not going to respect that Nazi bitch or anyone else in this house."

"I live here too." Despina raised an eyebrow at Zoe's comment.

"Except for you."

Despina sighed and crossed herself. "Goodness, child, you are going to get yourself killed talking like that."

"Nah." Zoe waved away the suggestion. "They need a maid and no one else is stupid enough to do the job."

Despina smiled, stepped forward, and kissed Zoe on the top of her head. "You are a brave young lady, little one. I know what it means for you to be in the same house as that evil creature. You are doing God's work."

Zoe raised her eyes and met Despina's gaze. "I'm not doing God's work—I'm doing the work of the Resistance. God has nothing to do with it."

Despina put her arms around Zoe and hugged her.

"I remember when you were born. Your mama held you in her arms and you were screeching so loudly, I think the next village could hear you. She named you Zoe because that's what you were—a new life. You were so full of life. For me and the rest of the Resistance, you are doing the work of God."

Zoe didn't say a word; she couldn't. The mere mention of her mother and the reality that she would never again see her again made her physically ill. She tried to swallow the lump in her throat and sighed deeply as she lifted her gaze towards the ceiling.

Despina tenderly kissed Zoe's cheek. "My darling Zoe, your mama would be so proud of you. Now get some rest. It's going to be a busy day tomorrow."

"Why?" Zoe asked hoarsely.

"We have visitors staying with us. Now get some rest," Despina urged Zoe and gave her a parting kiss on the head and walked out of the room.

Zoe watched Despina leave and the door close. Her meager possessions were lying at the foot of the bed. There was no wardrobe to hang her clothes, but a clothesline attached to two hooks on other side of the room. With a shake of her head she began to unpack the small suitcase she had packed after going back to the house across the street.

Zoe worked purposely to hang up the clothes and arrange her two pairs of shoes neatly in the corner. It didn't take her long to arrange things the way she wanted them. Her sketchbook and pencils were neatly laid out on the chair. She sat down on the bed and watched the afternoon shadows creep along the floorboards. She brought the chair towards her and flipped over the book to the nearest blank page.

Zoe smiled as she picked up her pencil. The Resistance had another tool at their disposal that most of the Germans were unaware of—Zoe's photographic memory. Relying on that gift and her ability to draw, she started to draw the house plans that she would complete as she was taken to various areas that she would be going. The Resistance could use those plans for a later bombing the same way they had used her skills with the first German commander. She stopped drawing when the sound of a soldier's voice reached her from outside. The evening curfew had begun. Several minutes later gunshots were heard in the still night air, making her shake her head at the apparent loss of yet another life.

Zoe put down her pencil and went to the window. She pulled back the curtain and looked outside. She didn't see anything out of the ordinary. She could see the guards stationed at the gate and beyond that her own house. She smiled on seeing young Dimitri standing at the window.

Marika and her son Dimitri were homeless. The Germans had taken over their modest home for their use, not caring what happened to the widow and her son. They were looked after by the Church but that was not a home. Zoe quickly thought of them and the now vacant house. She had spoken to Father Haralambos and arranged for them to move in.

Marika was Zoe's link to the Resistance and could send for her, if needed, to get the message out. Zoe's movements were going to be watched even more carefully now that she was working at the house.

Zoe's attention was drawn to the line of cars that had stopped in the courtyard. "I bet that's not King George who is visiting," Zoe said aloud as she watched a soldier rush to the passenger side and open the door. A tall woman exited the car and was greeted by Major Muller with a kiss on the cheek.

Zoe let go of the curtain and hurriedly ripped the page from the sketchbook. She folded the page and stuck it under her thin mattress for another time. She crossed the short distance to the door, opened it, and stuck her head out. Henry talked quietly with another soldier for a moment before the soldier went back down the steps. Henry turned and caught Zoe's attention.

"Do we have royalty visiting?" Zoe asked as she opened the door fully and stepped out.

"Royalty?"

"Long line of cars outside."

"Oh, that. No, not royalty."

"Who?"

Henry stared at Zoe for a long moment. "Why do you need to know?"

"Why are you going to keep asking me why I'm asking?"

"Because I need to know."

Zoe smiled knowingly. "That's my answer."

"I should have shot you," Henry replied as he ran his hand over his bald head in frustration.

"Who is here?"

"Go back inside and mind your own business." Henry put his hands on Zoe's shoulders and gently pushed her back inside the room. "You ask too many questions."

"Because I need to know," Zoe quipped giving him a sly smile.

"You're going to get yourself shot."

"Would you miss me?"

"I would miss my bed bugs more," Henry muttered and closed the door, leaving a grinning Zoe in his wake. Moments later Zoe crouched against the door and put her ear against the wood.

The sound of footsteps and muffled chatter filled the corridor. Zoe cracked open the door and found herself staring at the back of Henry's leg. He had positioned himself outside her door and she was unable to discern who was on the landing.

Zoe backed away from the door with a puzzled expression on her face. Whoever it was, they were important enough for Major Muller to greet them. She went back to the drawings she had hidden under the mattress, and on the opposite side of the house layout, she started to write what she had just seen.

CHAPTER 19

Zoe strode towards the cemetery with her head down as the wind whipped around her red hair. Zoe pulled the warm coat tighter as slowed her pace when she saw an old woman cleaning weeds from her mother's grave. She watched the woman, her face obscured by a black headscarf—a common sight among the old women out of respect for their dead loved ones. Zoe hated the color. She preferred bright colors like yellow, light blue or orange, but her favorite was fire engine red. At her mother's funeral Zoe refused to wear black. She wore a bright orange skirt and a dark blue shirt. Naturally the old women of the town were scandalized but many thought the child had lost her mind and made allowances.

On getting closer to her parent's grave Zoe noticed the old woman's white hair peeking out from the scarf.

"Hello?"

"Oh, good morning, my little Zoe!" The old woman turned. Her smile creased an already lined face and her big brown eyes crinkled. She was short and rail thin. Zoe never forgot a face but she was having a problem in remembering who the woman was and where she lived.

"Do I know you?"

"My name is Aretha Palakalios," the old woman introduced herself and chuckled at the confused look on Zoe's face. "Your aunty Stella sent me."

"Oh!" Zoe's scowl turned to a happy smile when she heard her aunt's name. "You're from Thessaloniki?"

"I am, I am. Come, let's sit down." Aretha looked around and spotted a crate near a tree. "Ah, a crate, how convenient."

"I use it to sit and talk to my parents," Zoe responded as she took off her coat and placed it on the damp grass before she sat cross-legged on the ground. Aretha sat down on the crate. "So, my aunt Stella sent you, *yiayia*?"

Aretha smiled. "She did."

"Why couldn't she come herself?"

Aretha crossed herself and kissed the silver cross that hung around her neck. "Ah, my dear child, Stella has been caught up in some troubles of her own."

"Oh? Does she know about Mama?"

"No, we didn't get the news in Thessaloniki, I'm sorry to say."

"So Aunty Stella doesn't know about me being alone?"

"No, my darling, she doesn't. Stella is up to her neck in trouble with the Germans. She's the personal physician to the commander in Thessaloniki."

"Well." Zoe shook her head, a slight smile appearing on her lips. "I think this is the first time I feel sorry for a German since this war started."

Aretha chuckled in response to Zoe's comment. "She is a little on the exuberant side."

"So does that mean she won't be coming down here?"

"No, my darling Zoe, she can't."

"So, I'm on my own," Zoe muttered as she picked up the blades of grass that peaked out from the edges of her coat. "I was wondering what had happened to her."

"You're not alone. You have Father Haralambos looking after you--"

Zoe continued to stare at the grass she had clipped and played with it in her hand. "How do you know about Father Haralambos?" She tilted her head a little and regarded Aretha. "Did you come into town very early? Father H is in church every morning at five."

"No, it was very late. Two boys from the Resistance brought me into town because it was after curfew and they found me on the road. They told me about you."

"You walked from Thessaloniki?"

"I tried to run but I ran out of puff." Aretha grinned at Zoe's exaggerated eye roll.

"You've been spending far too much time with my aunty Stella."

"She's a good girl and hopefully, if she doesn't kill the commander out of sheer lunacy, she may live to the end of the war."

"So, how is she?"

Aretha nodded slowly. "She was bereft after Timmy died."

"Did you know my uncle?"

"No, but Stella told me so much about him. She still mourns for him. The two boys wanted to know why I was walking into town and I told them I was looking for the Lambros farm."

"You were walking in the wrong direction."

"Apostolos, handsome young man, told me, but he said it was alright, since you were not there."

"Did Apostolos tell you about Mama?" Zoe asked as her gaze turned to the makeshift headstone bearing her mother's name.

"He did. These Germans are savages. He also told me what a brave young woman you are. I think he's very fond of you." Aretha patted Zoe's cheek. "He seems like a sweet boy."

Zoe shook her head and sighed. "Oh please, don't start. He is far too old, he's too tall and those light blue eyes of his just look unnatural."

"The boy has blue eyes. Is that terrible? How old is he? He can't be more than five years older than you."

"He's eight years older. That's old."

"Ah well, yes, that's old," Aretha said with a slight smile. "Now let's forget about Apostolos, since you think he is too old, too tall and his eyes are too blue. Tell me how you are faring so I can tell your aunty Stella."

"Are you going back?"

"I am. I came to see how you and your mother were faring. The news I take home with me is not good but Stella will want to know how you are."

Zoe sighed and looked around the cemetery as the early morning sun started its climb casting the cemetery is a golden hue. Her attention was on the distant figure of the undertaker going about his early morning chores. After a long moment she turned to Aretha. "I am alive."

"Apostolos tells me you are working for the Germans."

"Apostolos also has a big mouth. For a Resistance leader, he needs to learn to shut up," Zoe muttered as she picked up a twig and rolled it between her fingers.

"So it's true?"

"Yes. Our local priest--"

"Father Haralambos?"

"I think if the Germans ever capture Apostolos, he is going to start telling them everything they want to know before they even ask," Zoe said with a shake of her head.

"Now, now, Zoe, he was just trying to be helpful."

"Father Haralambos talked me into working for the Major's daughter. I suppose you know about Major Muller?" Aretha nodded and Zoe continued. "Well, I'm working for his daughter, the lunatic Eva Muller."

"Oh dear, the poor woman."

"She's not really a lunatic, although judging from what Kiria Despina told me about her family--"

"The Germans?"

"No, seems her mother was from Larissa. Lunacy runs in the family."

"Oh, that's terrible."

"I'm surprised Apostolos didn't tell you that," Zoe said, giving Aretha a cheeky grin. "I'm working for the lunatic. That's alright; the whole place is like one huge lunatic asylum."

"No, darling, a lunatic asylum is not like Larissa. I've seen lunatic asylums and they are not the same."

"You have?"

"I have visited many a poor soul in those horrible places. Trust me, little one, you don't want to see the inside of one."

"Well, *yiayia*, this place is lunacy. The Major's daughter is crazy. One minute she talks to me calmly and the next she gets angry for no apparent reason."

"It's a little strange to be in a war zone."

"As I said, the family is crazy."

"Why are you working for them?"

Zoe looked at Aretha with a slight smile. "So Apostolos left something else out?"

"It was late at night and the poor boy can't remember everything." Aretha chuckled.

"It has something to do with the Resistance."

"Ah, say no more. The less said, the better. You never know who might be listening."

"Well," Zoe looked around at the quiet cemetery, "my job is to be Fraulein Muller's maid. I haven't been her maid yet and it's been four days since I started. I've been helping Despina and not being a maid."

"Why is that?"

"Seems a friend of the family came to visit and this woman has been helping the cripple--"

"Zoe!"

"What? She is a cripple. The doctor friend is helping her, although it hasn't helped her disposition. Eva Muller is a rather disagreeable woman."

"Oh, dear."

"Hm, I don't care, really. This doctor has been really nice to me and gave me some sweets yesterday. I was in the kitchen cleaning potatoes for Kiria Despina and she comes in, sees I'm alone and then leaves. She comes back in with a small package in her hand."

"Just like that?"

"Yeah, just like that. She sat down and started to talk to me. I almost forgot she was German; she was very funny. She then gave me the sweets."

"Hm, interesting."

"One of the very few Germans I like."

"Why was she nice to you?"

"I don't know. Maybe she was bored or she got tired of Eva's temperamental ways."

"Are there other Germans you like?"

"Goliath," Zoe replied and laughed at the confused look on Aretha's face. "His name isn't Goliath, but that's what I call him. He's very tall--"

"We know you don't like tall men," Aretha quipped making Zoe laugh. "You have a very beautiful laugh."

"Thank you. You make me laugh."

"We need that occasionally or else life becomes too dark. Tell me about Goliath?"

"He is the crazy one's bodyguard. He is really a nice boy although he keeps threatening to shoot me."

"That doesn't seem nice."

"I think it's become a joke between us. I don't know why it became that way but every time I annoy him, and I annoy him a lot, he threatens to shoot me. I think he's smitten with Eva."

"Do you?"

"Hm. Every time she's near him, he gets this funny look on his face. I want to slap him but he's too tall so I can't." Zoe shook her head slowly. "My brother Michael used to say that there were three stages of love."

"Only three?"

"That's what he used to say. He said the three stages are," Zoe held up three fingers, "Like, Heavy Like and Deep Love. Michael said when you get to stage three, everything is lost and they could shoot him, because he would be useless. I think Goliath is at number three."

Aretha smiled as she reached out and held Zoe's hand. "My darling, that boy is probably at stage one. Deep Love is never that quick and it takes a lifetime to get there."

"I don't know anything about that since I've never been in Like, Heavy Like or Love. I don't know how that feels like and right now I don't want to know."

"You will, one day. When that lucky boy comes along, you will know it. It will come into your life like a train and run you over when you least expect it."

"Great, I'll get run over by a train. Something to look forward to. Is that what happened to you?" Zoe asked and indicated the dark clothes Aretha was wearing.

"It is and it was extraordinary. Your day will come."

"Pah." Zoe dismissed that notion. "I have to get back to the house to help Despina, can you come back with me--"

"No, my darling, I have a long journey ahead of me. The blue eyed boy you don't like is going to take me home," Aretha replied as she got up from the crate. "I have quite a few stories to tell Stella when I get back."

"Safe journey, *yiayia*, and tell Aunty Stella I love her."

"I will, my darling, I will. Be safe." Aretha tenderly cupped Zoe's cheek. "Keep your eyes on the road ahead and never waiver. You will find happiness one day where you least expect it."

"Hm, please don't tell me it's with a blue eyed boy."

"No, I won't tell you it will be with that blue eyed boy but you will find that special someone," Aretha said with a knowing smile. "Be well, be safe, and laugh when you can," she added before she took hold of Zoe's shirt and tugged for the youngster to bend for a kiss on the cheek.

Without another word, Aretha took her cane, which had been leaning against the tree, and slowly made her way out of the cemetery. Zoe stood at the graveside, smiling as she watched her leave.

CHAPTER 20

"Of course this has to be on the top shelf," Zoe muttered as she stood in the walk-in pantry and looked up at the high shelf. In her hands she held the flour that Despina had given her to go and store.

Zoe put the flour on the nearest shelf she could reach and stuck her head out the pantry. Henry was about to walk past when she pulled his jacket.

"Stop doing that!"

"How else am I going to get your attention?"

Henry glared at Zoe. "How about using my name?"

"Goliath, can--"

"My real name. My name is not Goliath."

"It should be," Zoe replied and looked up at the scowling soldier. "Oh, come on, you like it."

"I do not," Henry responded and followed Zoe into the pantry. "This was not built for midgets," he said as he gazed up at the high shelving. Zoe gave him the flour, which he effortlessly placed on the top shelf. "My name is Henry."

"No, it's not."

"I know what my name is."

"It's Heinrich."

"It is not."

"What kind of name is Henry? That doesn't even sound German."

"Why do you always have to be so disagreeable?"

Zoe grinned. "It's fun and I like you."

Henry looked down at Zoe and smiled. Just as he was about to respond, they heard Nurse Edith's voice. Henry sighed heavily and put his finger to his lips to indicate to Zoe not to speak. Ever so quietly as to not betray their location, Henry turned off the light. The door was slightly ajar and he didn't attempt to close it.

"Wh—" Zoe's question was cut short by Henry's large hand, which he placed gently over her mouth.

"Don't talk," Henry mouthed as Edith and someone else stopped just barely feet away from the pantry.

"Do you have to leave, Uta?"

"I must, unfortunately. Dieter wants me to come back and I can assuage his concerns about Eva."

"I didn't have any doubts."

"You are such a gentle soul, Edith. Sometimes those treatments don't always work and further work needs to be done, but you are a soft heart."

Edith laughed, and Uta joined her. Inside the pantry, Zoe froze. That laugh. The same laugh she had heard the day her mama was killed. The laugh she thought belonged to Eva. Zoe scowled.

"So you have no doubts?"

"None."

"Have you told Hans?"

"I did. I'm satisfied she is cured."

"Are you worried about that maid?"

Zoe's eyebrows rose and quickly glanced at Henry, who was

bopping his head up and down.

"No. She's young and they hate each other."

Edith laughed again, causing Zoe to cringe.

"They don't hate each other. They detest each other and that's why Hans thought she was perfect for the job."

"Because she hated her?"

"Yes. It's common knowledge in the village. Hans thought Eva wouldn't be tempted."

"Eva is not going to be tempted; she's cured."

"Tempted to do what?" Zoe mouthed silently to Henry, who brought his finger up to his lips for her not to speak out loud.

"I know that but Hans doubted it. Did you try and get her interested?"

"I did. I got slapped."

Uta's laugh filtered through into the pantry. Zoe's eyebrows rose in an unasked question.

"Did she really?"

"Oh, yes, and it was pretty hard. I expected nothing less. I think it's genuine."

"Well, thank God for that. I fear what this would do to Hans if it didn't work."

"Sometimes it doesn't work and the only solution is to put them out of their misery."

"Well, I'm glad it did work."

"You have to get her out of the house and walking. She's refused to leave her room while I've been here."

"She walks to the church now but I've been encouraging her to go further."

"She has to. I don't want her going to the church."

Zoe shook her head and smiled. You two are so dumb, she thought.

"What about the maid? We know she's in the Resistance."

"Everyone is in the Resistance, Edith. I don't think Eva is

involved here. Not like she was in France."

Zoe quickly glanced up at Henry, who was scowling. She noticed the vein in his neck pulsate and wondered if he knew about Eva's Resistance activities.

"I don't think you were right about that. Eva was in mourning for Erik, and the last thing she would be doing was to collaborate with the French."

"Hans seemed to think she was, but here it's different, although he doesn't want her going to the church."

"The priest is in the Resistance as well?"

"Every Greek is in the Resistance."

"Young Zoe is in the Resistance and she doesn't make it a secret. The girl is not shy about telling anyone who cares to listen."

"That's why she's not a threat."

Henry looked up at the ceiling of the pantry and quietly chuckled for a moment before he glanced down at Zoe, who was wagging her finger at him.

"I hope so. I wish you could stay longer."

"As much as I would love to, I have to get back to my hellhole."

"Before you catch your train, why don't I show you Athena's Bluff and then the gorge? It's very beautiful."

"Hm, that would be nice."

Zoe's face creased into a smile as Edith and Uta walked away down the corridor. After a long moment, she glanced at Henry.

"What was that?"

"That was two escaped Harpies from hell."

"Colorful," Zoe quipped only to find that Henry's scowl had intensified. "Henry, was Nurse Edith present when you all decided to kill people?"

"I did not kill anyone."

"Was she there?"

"Yes," Henry replied quietly. "She was standing behind me."

Zoe shook her head slowly. "It was her."

Henry stood quietly and allowed Zoe to process the revelation on her own. After a long moment he put his hand on her shoulder. "It was never Eva."

"You know about that?"

"I have ears."

"You don't understand Greek."

"Yes, I do," Henry replied in Greek, catching Zoe by surprise. "A little. Eva has been teaching me."

"Just my luck," Zoe good-naturedly grumbled as she opened the door and they left the pantry. She watched Henry walk away and heard his chortle.

Zoe stood in the corridor looking down at the wooden floorboards, deep in thought. She did an about face and almost skipped down the corridor to the kitchen.

CHAPTER 21

$\mathcal{E}$va slowly made her way down the street, her guards alert as they watched the people who passed them. She was very much aware of the openly hostile looks she was getting. The last thing she wanted was for someone to get shot because of her. Major Muller had ordered her to hold her head high but it was more than a little difficult to do when hate was all that was directed at her. Muller didn't want his daughter to be intimidated by the villagers; not by them, but it was perfectly acceptable for her to be afraid of him.

"Stay here," Eva instructed Henry, who in turn gave her an outraged look. "Is there a problem? Henry, we've had this chat before," she said, and lowered the hood of her cloak.

"I have to be seen to be objecting." Henry leaned forward and whispered in Eva's ear whilst the other guard, Barkow, was busy watching the village girls. He looked surprised when Eva smiled.

"Follow me inside the house of God and I promise you that you will see the front lines faster than you can blink," Eva told him loud enough for the other guard to notice. "Do you understand me?"

The sergeant looked at Barkow, who chose to stand to attention and stay silent. "Yes, Fraulein, but I will have to report this to Captain Reinhardt."

Eva just smiled and entered the church, leaving the guards outside. She pulled out a scarf and placed it on her head before she passed the altar. She spied Father Haralambos talking to one of the elderly nuns. She patiently stood by until he had finished and then went over to speak to him. There were a few people milling around after the service, giving her the most hostile looks.

"Ah, Fraulein Muller, how nice to see you."

"Father, I hope you are well."

"Very well, my child," Father Haralambos replied with a twinkle in his eye. "How--"

Father Haralambos didn't have a chance to finish before Eva staggered forward. She was hit across her back by a short, elderly woman with a cane. The cleric grabbed Eva to prevent her fall and steadied her.

"Mrs. Elimbos! Please, we can't have violence in the house of God!" Father Haralambos said as he helped Eva to a seat nearby. "Are you okay?"

Eva merely nodded. Her back had already been on fire that morning and the blow just added to her misery. The attack brought the guards rushing into the church. They stopped when they caught Eva's eye. She motioned for them not to come in further and to stay outside. The last thing she needed was for the whole incident to be overblown and lives lost.

"Get this animal out of the house of God first!" Mrs. Elimbos replied and spat in Eva's face. Eva deliberately did not move, but let the old woman continue her tirade until she had exhausted herself. Finally, Mrs. Elimbos waved her cane at Father Haralambos and walked off quite satisfied with herself.

Father Haralambos hurriedly gave Eva a handkerchief so she could wipe away the spittle. "I'm so sorry, Fraulein."

"It's alright. I'm getting used to being hit," Eva mumbled as she took the handkerchief and wiped her face.

"Well, I'll have a word with Mrs. Elimbos next time I see her. Please, come into my office."

They entered the office, Father Haralambos helping remove Eva's cloak before ushering her into a seat. "I am sorry." He put his arm around Eva to console her. She leaned into his embrace and closed her eyes. How many times had she wished that her father would take her in his arms and hold her, tell her she was loved, and tell her everything was going to be all right? It was divine intervention she had come to Larissa; it had to be.

"You aren't at fault. Mrs. Elimbos has probably wanted to do that for a long time." Eva sighed wearily.

"I'm going to have a word with her--"

"And tell her what? That I'm your daughter?" Eva smiled. "Or that you love Germans?"

Father Haralambos scratched his beard. "You have a point." He nodded. "I do love one particular German." He smiled. "How is little Zoe doing?"

Eva grimaced. "You were right. She's very difficult when she wants to be. Henry and Zoe seem to have become friends, if you can believe that."

"Really? Now that is interesting."

"I never thought that would happen. He keeps threatening to shoot her when she annoys him but I know Henry and he does like her. It's a very strange friendship that seems to be forming."

Father Haralambos chuckled. "Henry seems to be a nice young man. At least he can be the buffer between you and Zoe if it comes to that but I don't think it will. What else has been going on?"

Eva sighed and looked down at her hands and twisted the gold ring on her finger. "My uncle sent Cerberus to visit me."

"Oh?"

"Let's not talk about her. Henry told me that she was very nice to Zoe so I don't know what game she is playing."

"How did Zoe respond?"

"Henry said she looked very confused but was nice. That's a little hard for me to picture."

Father Haralambos chuckled. "If Zoe trusts you, she will defend you even with her life. The problem is you have to earn Zoe's trust," he said.

"I don't think Zoe will ever trust me. I don't think it's even possible for that woman to trust anyone. She is so full of hate. How do I get her to trust me?"

"Be yourself." Father Haralambos smiled. "Zoe needs a friend. You need a friend and an ally in that lion's den. Zoe can be that friend, if you let her."

"That's a little difficult to do, Father, when Zoe sees me as the enemy."

Father Haralambos nodded. "You hide who you really are, and it's difficult for people to see the real you. If you let Zoe see who you are, you will find a kindred spirit."

Eva thought about Father Haralambos' words but she doubted the young woman he knew and the young woman who goaded her in her office were one and the same. "She wants to kill me."

"Zoe doesn't want to kill you. Trust me, if Zoe wanted to kill you, she would have done it."

"You mean like when she went to shoot me in the cellar?"

"Yes, well." Father Haralambos stroked his beard. "There was a reason Zoe was so angry that day."

"Isn't she like that most days?"

"No. Zoe had a very upsetting day and she was very angry. I had her cleaning the cellar to take her frustrations on the mess that was down there."

"Lucky that gun doesn't work very well."

"It works," Father Haralambos mumbled. "You have nothing

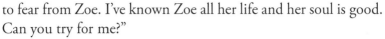

to fear from Zoe. I've known Zoe all her life and her soul is good. Can you try for me?"

Eva looked doubtful but nodded. "I will try."

"Thank you," Father Haralambos replied and kissed Eva on the cheek. "Now, why are you here? Not that I don't want you here, but I thought you were going to send Zoe? You did hire Zoe, didn't you?"

Eva pulled out the papers she had under her cloak and gave them to Father Haralambos. "Oh, yes, Zoe is perfect for the job, but Captain Reinhardt was nearby and I didn't want to arouse his suspicions." She pointed to the papers and said, "The Petrolakis family, I'm sure, will be happier."

Father Haralambos adjusted his glasses and looked at the identity papers, smiling proudly. Eva watched him. He had told her that pre-war Larissa had a large Jewish population and some had managed to flee before the Germans invaded, but others had been caught. Their neighbors sheltered the few that hadn't been captured immediately after the occupation. The penalty for hiding Jews was death and Father Haralambos tried to get them out of the country as soon as he could. Eva had managed to get her father's signature on new identity papers and the arrangement had been working quite well.

"Do you think your father suspects?"

Eva shrugged. "My stepfather suspects everything and everyone. Jurgen alerts me to my father's mood."

"He loves you."

"He does." Eva held out her hand and showed Father Haralambos the engagement ring. "He proposed two nights ago."

"I'm happy for you." The priest leaned over and kissed her on the cheek.

"My father's dream come true. Muller wants him to keep an eye on me."

"Ah." Father Haralambos stroked his beard. "You don't love

him?"

Eva glanced at him and shook her head. "I like him."

"Can I ask you a question?"

Eva smiled. "You can ask me anything you want."

"You have the chance to escape and be free of these tyrants..."

Eva sighed and smiled sadly. "I have thought about it, and you don't know how I wish to be free of him. But who will help you?"

"Are you staying just for me?" Father Haralambos asked incredulously.

"I'm staying because of you, and because it's the right thing to do," Eva replied. "Didn't you say that for everything, there is a season?"

Father Haralambos smiled. "Yes, and in our case it's a time of war."

"Our time of peace will come soon and that's what I'm holding out for," Eva replied. "I don't know what the future holds, but for now I'm going to try and help you."

Father Haralambos cupped Eva's face and kissed her on the forehead. "Your mama would have been so proud of you," he said. "Now, I think you'd better get going before your soldiers come looking for you."

Eva stood and put her cloak back on. She stood there for a moment and kissed Father Haralambos before leaving the office and the church. She mentally groaned when she saw Reinhardt with her guards. She was certain they had witnessed Mrs. Elimbos' attack on her—it would have been difficult to miss with the doors of the church wide open.

"Ah, Eva, are you all right?" Reinhardt asked as he threaded his arm around hers and led her down the steps.

"I'm fine, Jurgen."

"Why didn't you let your guards come to your rescue?"

Eva sighed. "There was nothing to rescue me from, sweetheart. An elderly woman just let her feelings be known about me being in the church."

"You were assaulted," Reinhardt persisted. "You know your guards have orders to shoot anyone--"

"I know," Eva replied. "I didn't think killing an old woman was going to achieve anything."

Reinhardt stopped and brought Eva close to him. "You are going to get killed one day."

Eva looked into his steely blue eyes and merely nodded. If the Greeks didn't get her, she was certain Muller would eventually find out the truth about her Resistance activities; it was just a matter of time.

They walked arm in arm towards the house with the guards behind them. At the entrance to the house, Reinhardt turned to Eva and kissed her chastely on the lips. "Thank you for the walk, Fraulein," he said and saluted the guards before leaving.

"I wish I could say the same," Eva whispered.

CHAPTER 22

*H*alt!"

Zoe sighed and turned to see the soldiers approaching. She had been stopped twice today already and it was beginning to get on her nerves. She put the sack she was carrying down on the ground and pulled out her identity card. Without waiting for the soldier to ask her, she handed the card over.

"You are a smart one, aren't you?" The soldier sneered as he read the papers and then glanced back at Zoe.

"No." Zoe attempted to be humble but she didn't think she could get away with it. She knew for certain she hadn't been successful when the soldier backhanded her, knocking her to the ground and spattering her clothes with mud.

The other soldiers, along with the one who had struck her, snickered. "That was for having a smart mouth. Get up!" The soldier ordered. "Where are you going with that?" He asked, pointing to the sack as Zoe struggled to her feet.

Zoe glared at him, wiping the blood from her split lip with the back of her hand.

"What seems to be the problem here, Corporal?"

Zoe glanced behind her, relieved to see Captain Reinhardt had come over to see what the commotion was about.

"Well? I'm waiting, Corporal," Reinhardt said.

"I was checking her papers, sir."

"And giving her a slap in the process." Reinhardt glanced at Zoe, and then back to the corporal. "I'll take it from here." With that he dismissed them and watched as they walked off. "You seem to attract trouble, Fraulein Lambros," he said with a smirk.

"I don't mean to," Zoe mumbled.

"Where are you going?"

"I'm going to the cemetery and then taking some vegetables back to Kiria Despina," Zoe said quietly as she felt around her lip with tentative fingers.

Reinhardt looked at Zoe and lifted her chin with his finger, inspecting her bloody lip. She met his steely eyes and then she dropped her gaze as she remembered Father Haralambos' instructions to appear meek and humble.

Reinhardt laughed. "You are a spirited little one." He chuckled. "I don't think that look is quite humble enough, though. You need to work on it."

"I will," Zoe muttered as she looked down at her muddied clothes.

Reinhardt turned away from Zoe and looked at the fields where workers were stacking the wheat harvest. "I have a favor to ask you."

Zoe stayed calm even though her heart was racing. She didn't say anything.

"I want you to make sure that nothing happens to Fraulein Muller."

"I can't promise that. What if she trips and hits her head or—"

"Or gets hit with a rock to the back of her head?"

"Something like that."

Reinhardt smiled at Zoe and she found it most disconcerting. "Come now, Fraulein, you didn't think I didn't know?" He taunted as he continued to smirk. "You are in the Resistance."

"Is there a Greek who isn't in the Resistance?" Zoe countered.

Reinhardt smiled. "Quite true, quite true." After a moment he said, "Tell whoever you talk to in the Resistance not to harm her. I like you. Don't make me shoot you."

"That would be bad for me," Zoe commented dryly, as she looked up and ran her hand through her unruly hair. "I don't think anyone wants to kill her—she's not worth two hundred innocent lives."

"So we have an understanding."

"If you say so," Zoe replied and picked up her sack and hoisted it over her shoulder.

"We understand each other, don't we?" Reinhardt chuckled.

Zoe nodded her response.

"Good. Now go on your way before your mistress starts yelling. God knows I don't want to hear that," Reinhardt said as he watched Zoe walk away down the dirt road.

The rain clouds parted to allow slivers of sun to peek through and form patterns in the clouds. In another lifetime, Zoe would have stopped and taken the time to make patterns out of the formations. She paused outside the cemetery and made a decision. She walked towards the gate and entered. As she passed an elderly woman, she nodded and walked further in. Sitting beside her parents' gravesite was the local gravedigger waiting for her. A shovel lay at his feet.

"Andreas," Zoe greeted the man and chastely gave him a kiss on the cheek. "How are you?"

"I'm better now that I've seen your beautiful face."

"You are such a flirt." Zoe gently slapped Andreas on the shoulder. She reached into her coat and pulled out an envelope. "I couldn't get these to Father Haralambos, so pass by and give them to him. I also have a favor to ask you. I've written it down."

"Alright, consider it done," Andreas replied. "I do enjoy our dates."

Zoe put her arm around Andreas and gave him a kiss. "You are my favorite boyfriend."

"I'll let the wife know she is sharing me," Andreas chuckled as he picked up his shovel and walked away.

Zoe watched Andreas walk away for a long moment before she sat on the grass.

"Morning, Mama," Zoe greeted her mother as she pulled the weeds from her grave. A simple cross adorned the grave of Helena Lambros. "I know I haven't come to see you in a few weeks, but things have moved so quickly." She paused and watched an elderly man shuffle away from a nearby grave.

"I don't know how long this war is going to last for, but we have lost so many. We kill them, they kill us. They are all dying, Mama. All my friends are dying. Be sure to kiss them for me in Heaven."

The tears started to flow freely as Zoe sat on the ground, her arms around her knees. "You won't believe what I'm doing now; even Papa would be laughing. I'm a personal maid to the beast's daughter. Can you believe it? Me, the one you kept yelling at to clean up after herself." Zoe chuckled through her tears at the memory.

"Remember Father Haralambos? Well, he gave me quite a shock. Did you know he used to have a girlfriend before he became a priest? I never thought of him as anything but a priest... funny that. Turns out that the beast's daughter isn't his daughter. She's Father Haralambos' daughter. It's worse than an ancient Greek drama. You would have loved that."

Zoe plucked some more weeds from the grave as she continued her one-sided conversation with her mother. "I was going to kill her, but now it's good I didn't. I would have killed an innocent woman. She wasn't the one that laughed while you were dying.

It was that evil nurse of hers." She stopped and plucked another weed from the grave. She sat there for a few minutes looking down at the weed in her hand. "Not to worry—tomorrow justice will be done."

Zoe stopped talking and gazed around the cemetery at some of the graves that had overgrown weeds around them.

"Her name is Eva." Zoe continued. "She has the bluest eyes I've ever seen, even bluer than Apostolos'. They remind me of the time we spent on Lymnos and the Aegean was so blue."

She sighed. "And she's tall, nearly gave me a neck pain from looking up at her. She has such a beautiful smile. I've only seen it once because she tends to scowl a lot. Aunty Despina said her family is cursed and I believe it."

Zoe stood up, picking up the sack of vegetables, and looked down at the grave. "I have to take the supplies to the housekeeper, but I'll visit you again soon. Kiss Papa and the boys for me. I hope God knows what a special person you are." She closed her eyes for a moment. "I miss you, Mama," she said before walking away from the cemetery.

Despina was bustling in the kitchen, heating pots of water for Eva's bath and trying to cook dinner, a task made all the more difficult with Zoe absent. Eva poked her head in, startling her.

"Sweet Jesus, Son of God and the Holy Ghost!" Despina exclaimed and crossed herself as Eva entered the kitchen.

Eva's eyebrows rose into her hairline at the expletive from the normally quiet housekeeper.

"I'm sorry, Despina, I was looking for Zoe. Is she back yet?"

"No, Fraulein, she hasn't returned yet. She is late and I'm—"

The door burst open and Zoe bustled in, muddied and wet. "I'm sorry I'm late," she said.

"Dear child, I thought something had happened to you," Despina said as she took the sack. She then noticed the mud and the split lip.

"What happened?" Eva queried, holding Zoe's face toward the light.

"A corporal took offense--"

"What did you do?" Eva asked as she took a piece of linen and began washing Zoe's face as soon as she sat down.

"I had been stopped by two patrols previously and so I just handed him my card. He wasn't impressed," Zoe said quietly. "It was my fault."

"You probably annoyed him with your smart mouth," Eva said as she looked down into Zoe's eyes. She was about to continue cleaning Zoe's face, but she abruptly dropped her hand as if the cloth was on fire and averted her gaze. "Despina, can you please get my bath ready? I'll see you soon," Eva said quickly and walked out of the kitchen.

Zoe glanced at Despina, who shrugged. "Come on, child, I'm late getting dinner ready and you know Major Muller hates eating late. Now empty the hot water in the buckets and take them upstairs."

Zoe nodded, but looked again at the door through which Eva had departed and frowned.

"What was that about?"

Despina turned around and glanced at Zoe. "Eva was worried about you and the curfew is due to start."

"She insulted me and you think she's worried about me? I think she just wants her bath. She is the strangest woman I've ever met. One minute she's nice and the next she races up the stairs like the devil himself was after her." Zoe helped empty the

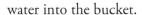

water into the bucket.

"She did not race up the stairs."

"She dropped the cloth like it was on fire. What the hell is wrong with that woman?" Zoe muttered as she picked up the bucket and slowly made her way up the stairs.

CHAPTER 23

*E*va entered her room and shut the door. She rested her forehead on the door panel and slowly banged her head against it. "Oh, that was stupid!" She muttered. When Father Haralambos said to get close to Zoe, she was sure he didn't mean to get attracted to her.

"Stupid, stupid, stupid." Eva continued to rebuke herself and hit her head with her hand. *She would gleefully kill you if you made any move,* she thought. Muller wouldn't hesitate to praise Zoe either for killing his "perverted daughter."

"Not again." Eva closed her eyes tightly, trying to keep the memory of Muller's rage being directed at her. The remembered vision of her father standing over her, his arm raised and ready to strike sent chills down her spine. That dark night her mother was murdered.

Kristallnacht.

Eva walked into the house, dropping her knapsack on the floor. She felt empty inside. Her whole world had crumbled and the only person who understood her was gone. She slumped to the floor as tears flowed freely.

She heard her father and someone else leave the house, their voices subdued. She wasn't sure how long she had been sitting on the floor. The door opened and her father walked in. He was still wearing his uniform, stained with blood...her beloved mutti's blood.

"I am going to ask you a question and I want you to answer me truthfully," Muller said as he sat on a chair across from her. Eva could see the fury in his eyes and knew that she had done something terrible, but for the life of her she could not fathom what.

"Yes, Papa," Eva replied, her voice hoarse from crying.

"Where were you tonight?"

Eva brushed away tears as she looked up at her father, who she knew was barely controlling his temper. "I went with Greta and my friends and we...we burnt a synagogue," she replied quietly.

"Didn't I tell you to be here tonight? Didn't I tell you not to go out, to stay with your mother?"

"Yes, Papa, I told her I was going to be at Greta's house and then I was going to come back--"

"You lied to her and to me. You disobeyed me!"

Eva cowered away from her enraged father, who stood over her. "Do you know what your disobedience has produced?"

Muller started to raise his voice, his face turned a bright shade of red, the veins in his neck pulsed rapidly, and the control he had held so tenuously on his temper evaporated. "You." He pointed at Eva, who was cowering in a corner. "You killed your mother!"

"Oh, Papa..." she cried.

Muller picked Eva up by the collar of her blouse and slammed her against the wall. Grabbing her by the hair, he screamed, "I will not tolerate your disobedience!" Then he slapped her so hard that it split her lip and she slumped in a heap. She dared not utter a sound and cowered against the wall.

Eva's silence only served to urge Muller on as he beat her across the back and legs for several minutes, screaming incoherently. Finally his anger was satiated for a while and he sat down heavily, his head in his hands. "You have disgraced me."

"I...I'm sorry, Papa." Eva hiccupped, tears staining her battered and bloodied face.

His voice rose as he neared the wide-eyed girl. "I will not tolerate a bastard child ruining my reputation!"

Eva looked at him, the confusion evident on her face. Muller stood and removed his belt. "I had someone tell me of your perversion. Did this person tell me the truth about you and Greta?"

When Eva said nothing to deny her father's accusations, he exploded. "You disgust me!" he spat. "Do you know what this will do to my reputation? They will send me to the front for this. And you, do you know what they do to perverts in concentration camps?"

Muller folded the belt strap, popping it for effect and leaning over her, so close she could feel his breath. He hissed, "Is it true?"

But Eva could not speak, her words frozen in fear. "Answer me, damn it!" he demanded.

Eva remained motionless, which only served to explode the rage once again boiling inside her father.

What followed was the worst, cruelest beating she had ever received. The leather belt, so mercilessly used against her back, tore her skin open. But that pain was nothing compared to the mental anguish she now suffered. She had been beaten into the bottomless pit of guilt and shame and as she lay sobbing, blood covering her back and legs, Muller's words "bastard child" tortured her until she wished she were dead.

That moment signaled the end of her freedom and the start of her longest waking nightmare. A nightmare she still endured after many months of incarceration at a research facility in Aiden, Austria. She was tortured into submission. The aversion treatments were worse than the beating she got from her father. Much worse.

"Fraulein Muller!" Despina's worried voice penetrated Eva's

consciousness from beyond the closed bedroom door. Eva shook her head to clear the memories and wiped away her tears.

"I'll be right there," Eva called out as she stood trying to compose herself. She wiped away her tears with a face cloth and undressed for her bath. She put on a robe and tied it with a sash before she left the room.

Eva followed Despina, who carried buckets of hot water from the kitchen into the bathing room. Zoe had been urged to clean up and soon began helping Despina carry the buckets of water and fill the tub. Eva walked into the room and nodded to Despina, who deposited some soap nearby.

"Thank you, Despina." Eva stood at the window watching the sun set over the quiet village. "Where is Dr. Uta?" She asked, hoping the doctor wasn't going to be there.

"Don't worry, sweetheart." Despina put her arm around Eva's waist. "She is having dinner with your father and Nurse Edith."

Eva gave Despina a relieved look and nodded. "Zoe will help you with your bath," Despina said and left before Eva had a chance to say anything.

"Are you alright?" Zoe asked quietly, watching Eva still standing by the window.

Eva remained quiet, willing herself to get better control of her emotions before facing Zoe. Turning toward Zoe, she observed her worried countenance. "I'm sorry I left so abruptly."

"You know, I've had a split lip before. I'll live," said Zoe, trying to lighten the mood. "Are you going to take a bath now, or should we get Despina to reheat it?"

Eva wondered if it had been a really bad idea to get a maid even if it was to help in the Resistance. The last thing she wanted was to disrobe in front of Zoe. With a sigh she pulled the sash open and removed her robe, hoping she wouldn't have to explain the scar that ran across her stomach or those on her back.

Those hopes were dashed when Zoe gasped at the sight of the

scars that went from Eva's shoulders to below her waist. "What happened?" Zoe whispered.

Eva didn't speak for a few moments and Zoe thought she wasn't going to get an answer. "I don't really want to discuss it," Eva told her quietly.

"They look old," Zoe continued, ignoring Eva's request. She traced one particular deep scar, causing Eva to flinch. "I'm sorry; does it hurt?"

Eva shook her head. "No."

Zoe picked up the sponge and gently began to lather Eva's back. "Who did this to you?"

Eva sighed. "Didn't Nurse Edith tell you that I was caught up in a bomb explosion in France?" She closed her eyes.

There was silence for a moment and Eva wondered if Zoe would stay quiet.

"I've seen scars like this before. I had a friend once who was beaten by her father with his belt and it left scars like this. The top one here looks different..." Zoe murmured as she gently sponged Eva's scarred flesh.

"That's from the bombing."

"Why were—"

"Zoe, please, shut up." Eva almost pleaded. Zoe's hands massaging her neck, which were both gentle and firm, almost made her leap out of the bath to try and escape from the pleasurable sensations it was causing. She knew the pleasure would turn to extreme pain if she allowed any thoughts of what Zoe was doing to her to become more than what it was.

"Lean forward," Zoe asked, catching Eva by surprise. Clutching the edges of the bathtub, Eva leaned forward, which allowed Zoe to lather her hair. Eva almost purred from the pleasurable sensation of Zoe massaging her temples and then working up to her head.

"Does that feel good?"

"Hm."

"My mama used to do this when I had terrible headaches," Zoe explained as she continued the gentle massage.

"I don't have a headache."

"You look like you do," Zoe responded and didn't say anything further as she picked up the small basin and washed off the soap from Eva's long black hair. She took the face cloth and gently wiped away the soap from Eva's eyes. "I think you may want to wash the rest of you yourself."

Eva sighed with relief as Zoe picked up the basin and turned away, leaving Eva to wash herself. She watched Zoe as she stood at the window. Zoe did not turn around until Eva signaled she was ready to get out.

Eva was surprised at the gentle way Zoe helped her out of the bath and dried her off. It was some relief when Zoe brought her robe and gave it to her.

"You have soft hands. Thank you, I did enjoy the massage," Eva said and then walked to the door to go back to her room.

Zoe smiled. "I enjoyed that myself," she mumbled before she went to the chore of emptying the bath.

Eva was combing her hair when Zoe entered her room. Without a word, Zoe picked up the hairbrush and began to comb Eva's long, dark, silky tresses.

"Why are you so nice to me?"

"You pay me to be nice," Zoe replied with a smirk. She glanced at Eva's solemn face in the mirror. "You're not who I thought you were," she observed as she brushed Eva's long hair. "No one deserves to be beaten like a dog."

"Not even someone who is a Nazi?" Eva looked back at Zoe in the mirror. "I thought that would have given you pleasure."

Zoe stopped the brushing and looked at Eva's reflection in the mirror. "It doesn't give me pleasure to see such brutality. I've never met any Nazi like you. You're not a Nazi."

"How can you be so sure?"

"You would have shot me when I threw that rock," Zoe said. They remained silent while Zoe started to braid Eva's hair.

"My father did it," Eva said quietly and looked at Zoe's reflection.

Zoe stopped braiding. "Another reason he's going to burn in Hell," she muttered. "Even if I don't believe in Hell, I think he's going to rot."

It wasn't the response Eva was expecting. "You're not going to ask me why?"

"You will tell me when you want to tell me," Zoe reasoned and continued with her task. "You're like my older brother—a clam."

"A clam?"

"Yes. Michael would speak when he wanted to speak and the rest of the time he would be quiet. You remind me of him."

"Is that a good thing or a bad thing?" Eva asked. Despite her first impressions of Zoe, it seemed it was going to be impossible not to like her. There was something about Zoe that made Eva feel comfortable, which was odd since Zoe wanted her dead.

"Bad."

"Why?"

"Because it is. You are a brooder, too. It's not a good thing to brood."

"Oh." Eva smiled and looked in the mirror to find Zoe smiling back at her.

"So why did the idiot do that?"

"I wasn't what he wanted me to be."

"I don't understand," Zoe stated, and started on another braid.

Eva was certain Zoe was going to flee screaming out of the room and she braced herself for it. "I had a disease."

"What kind of father beats his daughter if she is ill? Not even animals would do that to their young."

Eva looked down at her hands. "It's a disease of the mind."

"What kind of disease?"

Eva mentally rolled her eyes and wondered why she had started this conversation. Zoe never let up. "Do you always ask so many questions?"

"Yes."

"He found out that I had a lover," Eva whispered, her voice breaking. "He was terrified of what it would do...what it would do to his reputation."

Zoe stopped braiding Eva's hair. "He got angry because you were having sex without being married?" she asked, sounding a little surprised. "It's not good to have sex without being married, but there isn't any need to lose your mind. That's a little too Greek for a German."

"My lover was a woman."

Zoe blinked. She gazed into the mirror at Eva, who was staring back at her. "You're so beautiful. Why would you want a woman?"

Eva almost laughed at Zoe's naivety. "It doesn't matter now. I'm cured."

Zoe didn't say anything, which worried Eva, as Zoe was not short of an opinion. Zoe continued to braid her hair in silence.

"Is that what Dr. Uta was doing with you? Seeing if you were cured?" Zoe finally asked. She glanced at the mirror and saw Eva's pale face. "You are scared of her."

"Zoe--"

"The mention of her name made you look like you wanted to throw up."

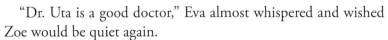

"Dr. Uta is a good doctor," Eva almost whispered and wished Zoe would be quiet again.

Zoe leaned down and whispered in Eva's ear. "She's not a good doctor because good doctors don't make people fear them."

Eva didn't respond to Zoe's comment and they both fell silent. Zoe finished what she was doing and left the room.

CHAPTER 24

oe gazed outside and leaned against the wall watching Dr. Uta Baer's luggage being loaded onto a truck. Edith was talking to one of the guards who were loading the truck.

"I hope you enjoy the ride down Athena's Bluff and to hell," Zoe said just as Uta looked up at her and waved. She waved back and smiled at the doctor. Just as she was going to push away from the wall, she noticed Henry near the truck and wondered why he was there.

"Oh, no, no, no, no," Zoe muttered. She left her room and entered Eva's study.

Eva looked up from writing the latest batch of letters for her father and noticed Zoe's smiling face. "Yes?"

"I thought you would be ready to take your walk. Why aren't you ready?"

"I'm going out later."

"Why? You know you have to go out and exercise in the morning--"

"Zoe, are you deaf? Didn't you hear what I said? I'm not going out now. I have letters to write and I don't feel like walking out in the cold."

"You need your exercise and I have my orders."

"From who?"

"Nurse Ratsger told me earlier today."

"I'm not going."

"We're not going to the church. I thought you might like to go down to the river."

"That's near the camp where the Jews are being kept. I don't want to go there," Eva replied as she continued writing.

"No, it's not near that horrid camp."

Eva sighed and put down her pen. She looked up at Zoe with an exasperated look on her face. "Why are you so eager to get me out of the house?"

"I don't want to kill you, if that's what you're thinking."

"No, you could have done this in here rather than at the river."

"Too messy and I would have to clean it up," Zoe quipped, making Eva shake her head. "It's going to be a lovely morning."

"It's cold and windy."

"A lovely fresh morning."

Eva leaned back in her chair and stared at Zoe. "I'm not sure what you are up to, but fine. I'll go out for a short time."

"I'll go and tell Henry--"

"Henry is driving Dr. Baer to Athena's Bluff."

"Alright, well, I'll go round up two guards." Zoe reached the door before Eva stopped her.

"No. I don't want other guards. Go downstairs and tell Henry to assign someone else."

"Are you sure? Henry may want a trip up the mountains."

"I don't care what Henry wants."

"Yes, ma'am." Zoe gave her a mock salute and walked out of the room. She looked back, smiled and then raced down the stairs and jumped the last two steps and landed with a thump.

She ran outside to where Henry was about to get into the truck.

"Sergeant Franz! Stop!"

Henry stopped and looked back as Zoe came rushing towards him. "Yes?"

"Fraulein Muller wants you to assign someone else to drive the car."

"Why? She said she wasn't going out this morning. We're going to be back by midday."

"She changed her mind."

Henry shook his head. "She is ruining my day."

"Trust me, she's not," Zoe muttered under her breath. Henry threw the keys to another soldier and followed Zoe back into the house. She smiled as Henry grumbled and they walked up the stairs.

Zoe walked back towards the house followed by Eva and her two guards after their brief walk to the river. They stopped in the courtyard, where several soldiers were loading a truck. Reinhardt and Muller were standing outside.

"What's going on?" Eva asked as she approached her fiancé and her father.

"There's been an accident," Reinhardt replied. He put his arm around Eva's waist. "Edith and Uta's car was hit by a landslide and they lost control."

"Oh, no."

"We're sending crews down the gorge to retrieve the car." Reinhardt kissed Eva on the cheek. "I know Uta was a dear friend; I'm sorry."

Zoe walked away and into the house. As she was walking up the stairs, she stopped, looked back, and smiled before she continued her journey up the stairs.

Walking into her bedroom, Zoe closed the door and went to the window to watch the Germans down below. "For every time there is a season, a time to live and a time to die," she said aloud.

Moments later the door opened after a gentle knock alerted Zoe. She turned to see Henry enter and close the door. He stood with his arms folded.

"It was you."

"It was me? I pushed the car down the cliff?"

"No, I meant—"

"There was a landslide. We get them and they do cause accidents. I remember a few years ago, old man Salamias got stuck in one. Took his wagon right over the edge. Terrible."

"Zoe—"

"Was Dr. Baer a friend of yours?"

"No, I hated the woman but—"

"Nurse Ratsger a friend of yours?"

"No."

"Right then." Zoe threaded her arm through the crook of Henry's elbow and looked up. "Do you know what Father Haralambos always says?"

"What does he say?"

"God works in mysterious ways. Maybe it was time for Nurse Ratsger and Dr. Baer to be called home. It just happens. I'm really glad that you were not driving that car." Zoe looked at Henry and smiled.

"Yes, so am I."

"So do we have a problem?"

Henry shook his head and walked out of the room leaving Zoe alone. "Nope, we don't have a problem," she said aloud and chuckled.

CHAPTER 25

July 1944

The electric fan whirred, making more noise than circulating any cool air. Sweat trickled down Zoe's face as she sat crossed legged on the floor in Eva's office. She was sealing envelopes, a tedious job at the best of times, but on this hot day it had become a real chore. The only way to try and keep cool, Zoe found, was to sit on the floor, which wasn't covered by any rug, and leave the door open hoping for a draft to cool things a little.

Muller had given her the job to do. The fact that Zoe was Eva's maid didn't stop him from giving her little jobs from time to time. The last six months had been a trying time with the Germans and the Resistance trading blows. The impact on the Greek population was brutal and talks of an Allied invasion were always in the forefront of any conversation.

It had also been a hard six months for Zoe, who was now working with Eva and Father Haralambos. At times it was extremely dangerous, and a couple of times Zoe thought their subterfuge would be uncovered. More luck than planning, each time something else happened that was far more important and diverted attention from their operation.

It was also six months of revelation as Zoe and Eva's often testy relationship started to slowly develop. It began on the night of that first bath when Zoe helped Eva. That night Zoe saw not the cripple or the demon's spawn, as she described Eva on numerous occasions, but a very broken soul. Zoe placed her hands on her knees and let her back rest against the sofa. She looked up at the lace curtains that were still; not a single breeze blew through the window to ruffle them.

"I hate summer," Zoe muttered as she sealed another envelope.

"You could use my desk," Eva said as she entered the office.

"It's too hot," Zoe grumbled. "I'm nearly finished anyway."

Eva went over to the desk where Despina had left a jug of lemonade. Her long dark hair was up in a ponytail which made her look much younger than her twenty-four years. Zoe watched Eva pour the lemonade into a glass for her. She looked away at the envelopes when Eva turned her way.

Eva smiled, and offered Zoe the drink. "You might like to drink this."

"Thank you." Zoe smiled and put the envelope down to accept the glass. As she did so, Eva looked down at the envelopes. She sat down on the sofa and picked up one in particular and rose to her feet. She stood in front of Zoe looking down at it. Zoe's curiosity was piqued as Eva walked over to the window and stood looking out. Something about the envelope had caused her mood to change rapidly. Zoe scanned the envelopes in front of her and the one that was missing made her sigh. "Don't you want to know what's in the envelope?" She asked.

"I know what's in it."

"What?"

"Sometimes it's best not to ask questions."

"You know me—I always ask because if I don't ask, how am

I going to know what I need to know when I need to know it?" Zoe rambled on purpose, making Eva toss the envelope on the desk and chuckle.

Zoe took a drink from the cool glass of lemonade and surreptitiously watched Eva. Eva wore a white cotton dress with long sleeves that blended with the curtains. Her long black hair ponytail contrasted with the white material. The midnight blue highlights in her hair shimmered in the sunshine as she stood at the window, oblivious to Zoe's stare. Zoe was completely mesmerized by the sight. Still clutching the drink she closed her eyes and memorized the image. She smiled.

Eva turned around and was puzzled at seeing Zoe sitting there with her eyes closed, holding the glass and smiling. "Zoe?"

Zoe opened her eyes immediately. "Um, yes?"

"What were you doing?"

Zoe drank the last of the lemonade and put the glass to one side. "Um, I...I was, um," she stammered. "Nothing," she said weakly, and smiled at the puzzled look on Eva's face.

"Alright," Eva replied, not quite sure what had transpired. "It's nearly noon. Do you want to take a break?" The daily noon siesta was a welcome relief from the heat of the day and Eva found she enjoyed the quiet that it brought. It was one Greek custom that she liked. Between noon and 3:00 p.m., the town fell quiet as everyone rested from the heat of the day.

"Yes." Zoe nodded vigorously and stood up. She braced herself against the sofa and fell into it rubbing her legs. "I think I've been sitting on the floor too long."

Eva didn't respond but watched Zoe pick up the envelopes and the fountain pen.

Zoe looked up. "You're upset."

"No--"

"You're also a very bad liar," Zoe replied matter-of-factly. She put the envelopes down on the desk. "You have your scrunchy face on."

"My 'scrunchy' face on?"

"I've seen it many times over the last six months." Zoe shrugged. "You have a little furrow between your eyes that goes all scrunchy when you're upset or you are not feeling well."

Eva brought her fingers up to massage the area between her eyes. "I didn't know you paid so much attention to me. Or is that where the imaginary target is located?"

"No, my target was a little higher up," Zoe teased. They looked at each other and then smiled. "Why are you upset?"

"It's addressed to my uncle," Eva explained and held up the envelope.

"The great Dr. Muller who cured you of your disease?"

"Yes."

"So why are you afraid of him?"

Eva shook her head. "I really don't want to talk about it, Zoe."

"Alright," Zoe replied. "I think I'll go now and have a bit of a rest."

"Are you going to your room?"

"No, I want to get out of the house and go up to Athena's Bluff."

"And then what?" Eva continued, not knowing why she was even asking since it was none of her business.

Zoe smiled. "Is this an interrogation?"

"Nein, Fraulein, an interrogation is when we use the feathers," Eva replied in German and did a mock Hitler salute. It had truly been the first time she had shown this much humor and Zoe appeared to be shocked for a moment and then started to laugh.

Eva leaned against the desk and crossed her arms across her chest. Seeing Zoe double up laughing was a nice sight and it made her feel good.

"Oh, that hurt," Zoe said in between bouts of the giggles. "I didn't think Germans had a sense of humor."

"We hide it well." Eva chuckled at Zoe's incredulous look. They both smiled at each other and Zoe was the first to break the contact by shyly looking away.

"Um, I'm going to go now."

"Where?"

Zoe looked back and smiled. "Didn't I say Athena's Bluff?"

Eva nibbled her lower lip and wondered if she could ask Zoe if she could come along. Despite her better judgment, despite everything that screamed at her to keep Zoe at arm's length, she found herself wanting to know more about this volatile youngster she had come to care for more than she should. Playing with fire, you're going to get burnt, a tiny voice echoed in her mind, but she ignored it.

"Do you want to come with me?" Zoe asked from the open doorway.

"Can I?"

"If you want to, yes, you can come with me."

"Only if you're sure…" Eva continued a little timidly. She was feeling awkward and she hated it, but she really wanted to go and get out of the house.

Zoe rolled her eyes. "I wouldn't say it if I didn't mean it."

"Oh, okay." Eva nodded and went to get her hooded cloak.

"It's boiling hot outside. You don't want that."

"Yes, I do," Eva replied and put on the cloak. She feeling very hot with the cloak on, but she pulled up the hood that shielded her face and turned back to Zoe.

"You really don't need that, Eva." Zoe grumbled. "You look

like you're about to faint away," she admonished, forgetting who Eva was.

"I have to—"

"No, you don't. Everyone knows what you look like, so you can't hide."

"Yes, I do, it keeps me feeling safe." Eva stammered. She always wore her cloak, didn't leave the house without it. She knew it was ridiculous but she felt safe, in a strange kind of way.

"Trust me, if the Resistance wanted you dead, a cloak wouldn't save you," Zoe mumbled as Eva refused to remove the garment.

Eva was about to join Zoe when she turned back and picked up her handbag.

They silently walked down the stairs and out of the building into bright sunlight and high humidity. Eva nodded to her guards, who marched behind her.

Zoe kicked a stone as if it was a ball as they walked down the cobblestone street, completely unaware of Eva's fond gaze. The plaza was eerily quiet with only the occasional cat to notice their progress along with the guards.

Zoe glanced at Eva and smiled at Eva, who was bearing up well in the heat. She was moving freely but a little slower than Zoe's stride. Zoe compensated by going slower, allowing Eva not to exert herself. Before they knew it, they were slowly making their way up the tree-lined slope to the top of Athena's Bluff.

"Are you alright?" Zoe asked. You don't look so good."

"I don't feel so good." Eva grimaced and took out a handkerchief and patted down her face. She looked back at her two guards, who weren't looking comfortable either.

"Come on." Zoe took Eva by the hand, much to her surprise, and set off in the opposite direction to the bluff.

"Where are we going?" Eva asked, and stopped, causing Zoe to skid to a stop as well.

"My cabin," Zoe replied and pointed to a log cabin only

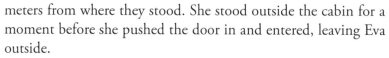

meters from where they stood. She stood outside the cabin for a moment before she pushed the door in and entered, leaving Eva outside.

"Well, are you coming in?"

"Are we allowed?" Eva asked through the open door, which caused Zoe to start laughing. "I didn't think that was funny."

"I never thought I would hear a German asking me if they were allowed to do anything." Zoe giggled. "Yes, you can come in."

Eva entered the cabin and was surprised to find it furnished and looking very inviting. The windows had lace curtains hung as limply as she felt. An old sofa dominated the largest area in the cabin with a bed at the side. A table and two chairs were off to the other side. In the middle of the floor was a large flokati rug.

"This is nice."

"This is my home." Zoe smiled and looked around the cabin. "This was my middle brother Thieri's house," she said. "He was building it himself. He was working as a builder, you know."

Eva wasn't sure what to say to the revelation and decided to stay quiet. She went over to a chair and sat down. She felt faint and tried not to show her discomfort, but Zoe came forward and knelt beside her chair.

"You should not have worn that stupid cloak." Zoe untied the clasp and removed Eva's cloak and threw it to the other end of the cabin.

"I'll be fine soon."

"Yes, you will," Zoe replied as she turned and rummaged through some clothing that was stacked against the wall in the unfinished bedroom. She came back with a towel and went outside. Eva could see Zoe walk to a large tin drum that held rain water right next to the door. Zoe dipped the towel in the water, squeezed the excess water, and came back inside.

Kneeling before Eva, Zoe tenderly wiped her face. For a brief moment their eyes met, making them smile. "On the way back you are not wearing that stupid cloak."

"How else would everyone know it's me?"

"Let's confuse them for a little while," Zoe responded and got up from the floor.

"What did Thieri look like?" Eva asked, breaking the silence.

"He had big ears." Zoe smiled. "Big ears and a big heart."

"Big ears?"

Zoe put her hands over her own ears and chuckled, which earned her a very puzzled look from Eva. "I used to tease him about his ears," Zoe continued. "I used to say that when he lost all his hair and went as bald as a rock, his ears would stick out like jug handles." She chuckled and then sighed deeply. "I won't see that happen now."

Eva was once again struck mute and didn't think she would be able to console Zoe at the loss of her brother and her family.

"Thieri had all the girls after him," Zoe continued her reminiscence. "He would sometimes get so broody he would come up here and just be by himself."

"Is that why he chose this place?"

"I guess so," Zoe replied. "He owned all the land around here, including Athena's Bluff. He cut the wood himself and built this cabin. He said once he finished it he would ask Katerina to marry him."

"Did he?"

Zoe turned to Eva and shook her head. "He never finished it," she said quietly. "When the Italians invaded, he went to fight and he never came back."

"So all of this is yours now?"

Zoe leaned against the edge of the table and nodded. "I own the farm, the fields on the west of Larissa and the east side near the farm, this cabin, and another house in town."

"How many brothers did you have?"

"Three. Michael, the oldest, then Thieri, and the youngest was Theodore. He was ten years older than me and I was closest to him."

"All redheads like you?"

Zoe grinned and shook her head. "No, Michael and Thieri resembled my father, who had dark hair and brown eyes. My mother was the redhead with green eyes. Theo and I took after her."

Both women fell silent and then Zoe spoke again. "Why don't you have a bit of a sleep? You're going to need your strength to go back down again."

"I'm alright."

"No, you're not." Zoe pushed herself away from the table and once against knelt in front of Eva. Without asking she lifted Eva's skirt and unhooked the panty hose from the garter belt from Eva's left leg. Eva shut her eyes and tried to keep calm as Zoe's soft hands brushed against her thighs. Zoe was completely unaware of what she was doing to Eva emotionally. "I don't know why you keep wearing these stockings in the middle of summer," she said as she rolled the stocking off Eva's long leg. She unhooked the panty hose from the garter belt for the right leg, which caused Eva to inhale sharply. Zoe looked up to find Eva was looking more than a little pale.

"You really should have left that stupid cloak back home," Zoe muttered as Eva rose from the chair and went to the bed and lay down. Without another word, Eva closed her eyes. She opened them moments later.

"I'm sorry, I took your bed."

Zoe smiled. "It's alright. I wanted to draw so you just have a rest while I draw and later I can show you the rest of Athena's Bluff."

"That sounds nice," Eva smiled and closed her eyes.

CHAPTER 26

*E*va woke a little groggy from her extended sleep. She opened her eyes hoping to see Zoe nearby but she was on her own. She sighed heavily as she sat up. She ran her fingers through her long hair and got up from the bed. A large note was sitting on the table. Eva picked it up and smiled on reading the neat writing.

I'm outside at the lookout; just come on over, Sleeping Beauty

Z

Eva pocketed the note and ran her fingers through her hair again. She looked around the cabin for a mirror but there wasn't one anywhere in sight. She straightened her skirt and shirt and put on her shoes. She looked around for her stockings but she couldn't see them. With a slight shrug she forgot about them and opened the door.

Henry and the other guard whose name she couldn't remember but thought was Kurt Barkow, were sitting under the shade of a tree looking very relaxed and playing cards.

Henry looked her way and smiled. He pointed to the outcrop and went back to his card game.

Eva closed the cabin door and made her way to the outcrop which was only meters away from the cabin. She stood in the clearing and admired the view. In front of her was the grand vista of Mount Ossa, tufts of white clouds ringing the summit and an expanse of blue surrounding the majestic mountain. It was the vision sitting on a blanket at the outcrop that made her catch her breath. Zoe had laid out a blanket that covered most of the rocky surface and had taken several pillows and positioned them so she could lie down. She was using one as a pillow and her legs were drawn up and were being used as a brace for her sketchpad.

Oh my god, she is so beautiful. Eva watched Zoe stop what she was doing and raise her hand. She couldn't see what she was looking at but Zoe brought her hand up close to her eyes for a moment before she smiled.

Stop it. You know where this will lead. Stop it now. Stop. Don't do anything; she is not worth the pain. My god, she has a beautiful smile, and those eyes... Eva's internal conversation with herself continued as she moved forward towards Zoe. She reached Zoe to find her talking to her hand.

"What are you doing?"

"I'm telling Lilly that I'm going to put her down somewhere other than on my hand," Zoe replied and picked up the ladybug and put her on the rock. She looked up at Eva and shielded her eyes with her hand. "Good afternoon, sleepyhead. Have a seat."

Zoe sat down cross-legged on the edge of the lookout, which was shaded by a huge overhanging tree. She beckoned Eva to sit next to her, but Eva was hesitant about getting close to the edge.

"I promise I won't throw you off," Zoe teased and patted the blanket-covered ground.

Eva sat down and took the pillow that Zoe had given her and

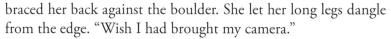

braced her back against the boulder. She let her long legs dangle from the edge. "Wish I had brought my camera."

"You have a camera?"

Eva nodded. "I have a Super Ikonata. I'm surprised I haven't shown it to you before now."

"Interesting." Zoe nodded.

Eva smiled. "You don't know what I'm talking about, right?"

Zoe shook her head. "Sounds German."

"That's because it is." Eva chuckled. "I'll show it to you when we get back."

"I don't know much about cameras. I just like to draw. I memorize things and then I draw them."

"What do you like to draw?"

"Things that touch me," Zoe replied. "I let my heart decide what to draw and my hand creates it."

Eva had never asked any artist that question even though she had spoken to quite a few when she'd visited galleries with her mother in Germany. Zoe's response wasn't what she had expected. In fact she wasn't even sure what she expected to hear. "So you draw what's in your heart?"

"Yes." Zoe nodded. "I draw my family and my friends. I love to draw landscapes. What kind of photos do you like taking?"

Eva smiled. "The sea."

"Why the sea?"

Eva looked out over to the mountain and tracked a small tuft of cloud as it lazily drifted before she answered. "I can see the power of the sea and its gentleness. Underneath its tranquil surface, there are thousands of things going on we can't see."

"That's very poetic."

"I like poetry." Eva smiled. "I write some as well."

"They say that good poets need to be really high in order to write," Zoe replied. "My brother Michael told me that, but I couldn't figure out why they needed to get high up a mountain to write."

Eva thought Zoe was pulling her leg but Zoe wasn't smiling. She just had the most puzzled expression on her face. Eva didn't laugh, even though she wanted to, at her naiveté. "I think they mean they were on drugs."

"How silly is that?" Zoe asked and shook her head. "How can you write if you can't think! If I have a headache I can't even get up to eat."

Eva chuckled. "Some people can."

"Weird," Zoe mumbled and threw a tiny pebble down the rocky outcrop.

"What were you drawing?"

Zoe reached out and brought the sketchbook to her. She flicked to the page she was working and handed the sketchbook to Eva.

Eva looked down at the pencil drawing of herself. She was standing near the window in profile back at the house. She realized that it was just a few hours ago and Zoe had memorized what she was wearing and how she wore her hair. She even added the hairclip and its intricate style.

"Wow," Eva exclaimed. "You have a very good memory. This is very good."

"Thank you. My mother used to say that I have a photographic memory and that it was a gift, especially for an artist."

"She was right. You both have a very beautiful gift..erm I mean she had," Eva quickly corrected herself. She wanted to slap herself for being so insensitive. "What was your mama like?"

Zoe smiled and closed her eyes. "My mama was the most giving, loving woman. She loved to paint and she loved beautiful things. My papa loved her so much." Zoe unclipped the chain of a small locket she wore and took it off. She opened it to reveal a small photograph inside of it. She handed it to Eva.

Eva took it and gazed at an old photograph of a much younger Zoe with her mother. The resemblance was unmistakable, and if Eva hadn't known it was Zoe's mother, she would have thought it was Zoe. "She's beautiful."

"She was." Zoe smiled. "She never left Larissa, but she loved to read and my papa used to bring her books from Thessaloniki about art and prints she liked." Zoe's voice broke with emotion.

"I'm sorry, I didn't mean—"

"No, it's alright," Zoe replied, and took a deep breath before slowly exhaling. "I miss her every day. I think about her, my papa and my brothers all the time. One day it won't hurt so much that they're gone, but I don't think that will happen until I join them."

"Do you think they're in Heaven?"

Zoe smiled and looked up at the bright blue sky. "Yes, I think so. My mama is probably asking God to paint the next rainbow." She chuckled. "I remember when a rainbow would appear and my mama would look up at it and tell me that God assigned an angel to paint it."

"That's beautiful." Eva smiled.

"Every time I looked up and there was a rainbow, I would compare it to other rainbows and try and see if the angel did a good job." Zoe laughed.

"What about your father?"

"My papa," Zoe said with a fond smile. "He was the finest man I have ever known. He died helping two Australian soldiers trying to pass the gorge during a fierce battle with the Germans." She looked out at the now somewhat peaceful vista. "In the early hours of 16 April 1941 Papa took a wagon and two Australian soldiers, one was wounded, and tried to get them across to the other side. They never made it."

"I'm sorry."

"Not your fault." Zoe glanced at Eva for a moment. "My papa died a hero trying to save our Allies. Father Haralambos tells me he will be rewarded in heaven for his bravery. When the war is over, I want to travel to Australia."

"It's on the other side of the planet."

"I know; far from this place."

The two fell silent as they both threw pebbles and pieces of wood down the gorge. After a long moment Eva turned to Zoe. "Did you really think I laughed when your mama was dying?"

"Yes. I thought it was the ugliest thing someone could do with so much death all around them."

Eva stayed silent for a moment and twisted the ring on her finger. "I didn't."

Zoe looked away into the far horizon and sighed. "I know." She turned to Eva and smiled. "I know it wasn't you."

"I thought you didn't believe me when I told you."

"I didn't," Zoe replied and played with a twig that was sticking out of the rock nearby. "I found out who did laugh."

"Who was it?"

"Nurse Gestapo," Zoe responded as she focused on Eva's face. "Is there a reason you nicknamed her Nurse Gestapo?"

"There is a reason."

"It's good that she's no longer with us, isn't it?"

Eva pursued her lips. "It was a very tragic accident."

"Very tragic." A smile creased Zoe's face. "A terrible shame they couldn't control the car and down it went into the gorge. It was also a shame that Dr. Baer was with her. She appeared to be a good friend of yours."

Eva bowed her head and stared down at the blanket-covered ground. "No, she wasn't."

"She seemed to act like it."

"She was my uncle Dieter's mistress and assistant medical director in Aiden," Eva replied as she lifted her head and met Zoe's intense gaze.

"Uncle Dieter is going to be very unhappy."

A slight smile creased Eva's face at Zoe's words. "We're in a war and she came into a war zone."

"Where is Aiden?"

"It's a small town in Austria."

"Is that where they cured you of the disease you had?" Zoe asked as she leaned forward and brought a pillow towards her. She hugged the pillow and turned her attention to Eva.

"Yes."

"Can I ask you a question?"

Don't ask me, Zoe. Please, don't ask me. Zoe was watching Eva intently. Eva often wondered if Zoe could see into her soul by the way she was looking at her.

"What happened in France?"

Phew! Eva was relieved Zoe didn't ask the most obvious question. "What about it?"

"You were working with the Resistance. Why didn't they warn you about the bomb?'

"I planted the bomb," Eva answered quietly. Zoe put her hand over her mouth in shock. "The Resistance couldn't get the bomb into the house so I volunteered."

"You were going to bomb yourself?"

"Their plan was to kill my father and my uncle, who had come to France to further his medical…work."

"What went wrong? Your father and uncle are still alive."

"Sadly, yes," Eva muttered under her breath. "The bomb went off as planned but my father had moved rooms to be with Nurse Gestapo and my uncle stayed with his mistress."

"Shit."

"And I wished for a quick death," Eva almost whispered the admission that had been a silent prayer for many years. "God did not agree with me."

"That's why you couldn't walk for a long time?"

"Yes, the ceiling collapsed on top of me." Eva nodded. "I don't know how I survived but I must have a guardian angel."

"You need to get God to sack your guardian angel—he is doing a terrible job," Zoe suggested, making Eva smile. "No, really he should."

"Everything happens for a reason."

"You really believe that? I don't know. That bombing left you in a worse condition."

"What do you mean?

"I've seen our dearly departed Nurse Gestapo and Nurse Blondie give you medication now for six months."

Eva wondered how much she was willing to tell Zoe. She knew if she said too much it might be used against her later, but then Zoe knew about her activities in the Resistance. After the past year, Zoe already had ammunition to hurt her if she wanted to. *Can I trust her more?* Eva sat silent for a long moment looking out over the horizon. "Yes and no."

"Is this one of those 'I don't want to talk about it' times?" Zoe asked and picked up another pebble and threw it over.

Eva picked up her own pebble and fingered the smooth surface for a moment. "I take it for the pain and other things," she said and threw the pebble down the slope.

"I hate taking pills." Zoe watched Eva as she threw another pebble. "You're not in pain all the time, are you?"

"I get terrible migraines and when that happens my back goes out as well," Eva admitted. "Some days I can't think straight, and I'm sorry but I take it out on you. Other days I'm fine. I'm under doctor's orders to take them all the time."

"I find that strange. If you're not in pain, why take pills for pain when you don't need them?" Zoe shook her head. "What was your mama like?" She asked, taking Eva completely by surprise at the way she had changed the subject.

"My mutti—"

"Mutti?"

Eva smiled. Mixing her German with the Greek was confusing for Zoe. Over the past year, she would throw in German words when she couldn't remember the Greek. "I'm so used to calling her that. Mutti means mommy in German," she explained.

"What was her name? You haven't spoken of her since the first day I arrived in your house and you pulled out her picture."

"Daphne." Eva smiled. "She loved art, just like your mama. She took me to the Louvre in Paris to see all the beautiful work."

"You went to the Louvre?" Zoe's eyes grew wide. "Was she an artist?"

"No, sadly my mama did not have your gift, but she tried. Yes, she took me to the Louvre. You can spend days in there." Eva loved the famous French gallery and had spent three long hot summer weeks in 1935 in Paris with her mother and grandmother. "She also loved gardening and we would spend hours out in the garden taking care of the flowers. During the summer we would go to flower shows and tour palaces with beautiful gardens."

Eva closed her eyes and the memory of summer filled days out in the garden with her mother came flooding back, memories that had been buried in the past few years. She opened her eyes and smiled at Zoe. "Sometimes we forget the good things. Being around you like this reminds me to do just that."

"So, you honestly had a maid?"

"Yes."

"I've never met anyone who was rich other than Danalos Faksomoulos. When we got news that the Italians were going to invade from Albania, he left Greece. I heard he went to America."

Eva couldn't help but smile at Zoe's easy going manner. Zoe had come a long way since that angry young woman who wanted to kill her. At the time, Eva hadn't fooled herself into thinking Zoe wouldn't kill her. But the more they got to know each other, the less likely it would be that Zoe would find her to be that "evil Nazi bitch" she used to call her. *Kill them with kindness.* Eva smiled at the memory of her best friend and his wise words from so many years ago.

"Why are you smiling? Not that I don't like you to smile, but you looked like you were very far away."

Eva turned her attention to Zoe. "I was just remembering my childhood best friend, Wilhelm. He was someone I used to talk to, just like this."

"He was a boy?"

"Oh, yes." Eva chuckled at the look on Zoe's face. "Lesbians can have friends that are boys, you know."

Zoe was momentarily stunned into silence at Eva's dry sense of humor. "That was actually funny," she said after she recovered. "But you're not a lesbian anymore. You're cured, right?"

"Y..yes," Eva stammered and hesitantly looked up to find intense green eyes gazing back at her. The two women smiled at each other for a long moment before Eva broke eye contact and looked away.

Oh, how smart is that, Eva? You almost kissed her in front of the guards! Why don't you go over to where the guards are and you can kiss her there! Eva mentally chastised herself. She spared a glance at Zoe, who had found a little lizard in the rock crag and was playing with it. Eva smiled when she saw Zoe put the lizard down on the rock and let it go.

Zoe looked up to find Eva staring at her and smiled. "Lizards need to be free as well."

"I'm sure they do."

"So, you're this rich girl. What do rich girls do with their time?"

"I went to university..."

"Really? I knew a girl who went to Athens to study at the university. She was very smart and Michael was sweet on her. So even if you were rich, you still wanted to go to university?"

"Yes. I studied languages," Eva replied proudly.

"Hmm, so Lunatic Muller let you go?"

"Is that his new nickname?"

"Yes, until I can think of something else," Zoe replied with a smile on her face that put a twinkle in her eyes.

"He had no choice. My grandmother's word was law, so I went."

"So, what did your grandfather do to become rich?"

"Has anyone ever told you that you ask too many questions?"

"Yes. You have, many times. So, if you just answer my questions, I won't have to ask so many in the future."

"That doesn't stop you—you'll find new questions." Eva smiled. "My grandfather owned the largest steel making factory. AEMullerStahl, have you heard of it?"

"No. That doesn't sound interesting." Zoe paused in thought. "You don't talk about your family a lot."

"No," Eva replied as she picked up a pebble and held it in her hand. "Sometimes I don't want to think about what my life was like before my mother died."

"If you don't think about them, how do you honor their memory?"

Eva looked at Zoe for a moment. It was true; she didn't talk about her family a great deal, even though the loss of their love was still quite raw. "My grandmother isn't dead."

"But you talk about her like she's dead."

Eva shook her head and sighed. "She isn't dead. I am."

"You look very much alive to me."

Eva smiled at Zoe's response. "I haven't heard from my grandmother for years now. I've written to her, but she has never replied. I sent letters back with my father before he was stationed in France to give to her, but I didn't hear back."

"Maybe she didn't get the letters."

"She got them. I know she did."

"We're in the middle of a war. How do you know the letters

were even delivered to her?"

Eva was silent contemplating those words. "She at least received the letters I sent with my father."

"Muller? You gave them to that crazy man? Why?"

"He's my father."

"Father H is your father, not that lunatic."

"I didn't know that at the time. I know you don't understand, but I loved that man. I think I still do. And despite everything that has happened, I do have happy memories from when he wasn't acting as crazy."

Zoe paused. "That's hard to believe. No father who loved his child would hurt his child — not like your father hurt you."

Eva was amazed at the sheer ignorance of that statement. It was so clear-cut for Zoe. So black and white — no grays or any other shade. A father loved his child and wouldn't hurt them. It was how Zoe was brought up and so different from her own history. "In a perfect world, a father would never hurt his child. We don't live in a perfect world."

"I don't understand it. Maybe Germans are different."

Eva wanted to laugh at the absurd comment, but chose not to. Zoe was a teenager living through a war and yet blissfully unaware of the realities of life other than what she saw in the village, even with the occupation. Zoe was simply a young girl and, had it been peacetime, wouldn't be any wiser. Eva envied such a blissful existence.

"Maybe they are," Eva replied and smiled. "I'm sure my father gave the letters to my grandmother, and I know why I haven't heard from her. She's ashamed of me and I don't blame her. I have shamed the entire family." She looked away, not wanting Zoe to see the tears that streamed down her face. She wiped them with the back of her hand and took a deep breath, held it, and then exhaled slowly. Losing her beloved mother was gut wrenching, but losing the love of her grandmother hurt her deeply because she knew she would be disappointed in her.

"Well, that's silly. You were a lesbian and you're cured, not a murderer."

"You don't know what that means."

"I know what it means. It means that you used to love women instead of men." Zoe shrugged. "Does it mean something else?"

"It means that you are sick and need to be cured."

Eva knew Zoe didn't understand what a "cure" entailed. "The pills — I also take pills to stop me from having feelings for women," Eva admitted. *If only that was the only way they have tried to "cure" me of these feelings.*

"Oh." Zoe nodded. "I thought you said you were cured. You don't look sick to me other than your back problem. You don't act funny, so you can't be sick in the head." Zoe paused, turning her head in thought. "I don't know why you need to be cured when you're already cured, unless you're not. So, that's why you take those pills, to cure you? Do they work?"

"Umm. They make me sick sometimes. Umm...I don't know, I guess they work," Eva responded and then looked away.

"You don't feel like thinking about women, so they must work." Zoe grinned and lightly tapped Eva on the knee, causing her to smile. "So, when you do think about women 'that way,' how does it feel?"

Eva cocked her head a little and gazed at Zoe with a smile. "Why?"

"I'm curious. I don't think I've ever spoken to a lesbian before."

Eva smiled and then started to laugh. It had been a long time since she felt so light-hearted. "I think you might have met a few, but they don't have signs on them saying 'I'm a lesbian.'"

"So did you just wake up one morning and discover you were a lesbian?"

She's awfully interested in this. Could she be...no... Zoe looked back at Eva with such innocence that Eva wondered if she was imagining something that wasn't there. "No." Eva shook her head. *Stop it, Eva. She's just curious.* "It's a long story."

"You don't want to tell me?"

"I don't want to tell you. Maybe another day."

"All right. Have you got those pills with you?"

"Yes," Eva replied and took out a small bottle she kept with her.

Zoe took it off her and read the German label. "What would happen if I took them?"

Eva found Zoe's question puzzling. "Why would you want to take them? They would make you sick because they are not for you."

"I was just curious. Do you know what would happen if you were to lose these?"

"I'd be given more."

"When?"

"I guess when Nurse Klein gets back from Thessaloniki in a few days," Eva replied, wondering why Zoe was asking.

"Good," Zoe said and promptly threw the bottle down the ravine, causing Eva to lean over a little to watch its descent.

"Oh!" Eva was surprised at Zoe's actions. "I don't think you should have done that."

"Who's going to tell on me?" Zoe grinned.

"I'm not going to tell." Eva looked over the precipice again and smiled. "I have no idea what happened to those pills. They make me very forgetful." They looked at each other and grinned. Zoe glanced at Eva for a moment and then looked away. She continued to gaze over the mountain, lost in thought or so Eva thought. It had gone very quiet; the cicadas had stopped chirping and there was a silence which unnerved Eva a little. She was startled when Zoe finally decided to speak.

"Do you really believe God has a plan?"

"Yes."

"Well, if God had a plan, why did he choose to take my mama and yours?"

"I don't know." Eva sighed. "How do you explain us being friends?"

"We're friends?"

"I think so. Aren't we?"

"You want to be friends with someone who wanted to kill you?"

"You wanted to kill me. You don't anymore...well, I hope you don't." Eva worriedly looked at Zoe, who had a mischievous look on her face. "You don't, do you?"

"I don't kill friends," Zoe replied, and reached out and tweaked Eva's chin.

Eva was completely taken by surprise by the very intimate gesture and she smiled. The only person who had ever done that before was her friend Wilhelm, who for some reason enjoyed tweaking her dimpled chin. She never understood why and now Zoe had done the same thing.

"Did I do something funny? I just find your dimple cute."

She finds my dimple cute? Oh, dear... Don't be silly, she's just being friendly. Don't get excited, you've had friends before; she's just being friendly; a little too friendly but there is nothing to it—she's young and she doesn't understand. Eva gave Zoe a very shy smile.

"You should do that more often."

"What?"

"Smile. It makes you look younger."

Is she flirting with me? Come on, Eva, stop being stupid. She's just being friendly. "You have a very nice smile as well," she said without thinking and mentally slapped herself. *Smooth, Eva. Very smooth. She's not interested in you, so stop this right now. Stop it before you get yourself killed.*

"I do?" Zoe spoke softly.

"Um...yes. When you smile, it reaches your beautiful eyes. It doesn't make you look younger because you're already young-er...I mean...uh...you're young and you have a lovely smile and umm..." Eva stammered to a stop and couldn't quite believe it was her that was acting life a goofy teenager. *Shut up! Will you just shut up!*

"Are you alright?"

"Ye...no," Eva stammered. "Let's go back; I think this heat is getting to me."

Zoe got up quickly from the rock and offered her hand to Eva, who took it. As she got up, Zoe put her arm around her waist. "I think the heat is getting to me too."

Oh, yes, it must be the heat. Eva quickly glanced at Zoe before they joined her guards for the trek back to the house — and back to being who they were supposed to be.

CHAPTER 27

October 12, 1944

The wind picked up as Zoe walked purposely towards the cemetery. It had been a few weeks since she last visited the graves of her parents and brothers. With her newfound role as Eva's maid and their resistance activities she couldn't spend as much time as she wanted at the cemetery. Today was her 16th birthday. Birthdays were not celebrated these days but she wanted to spend some time with her parents.

Zoe paused outside the cemetery and made a decision. She walked towards the gate and entered. As she passed an elderly woman, she nodded and walked further in. She made her way to her parent's gravesite and knelt beside the grave and started to pluck the weeds which had sprouted from her last visit.

"Good morning, Mama, I have some good news. It wasn't Muller's daughter but someone else who laughed when I was holding you as you lay dying." Zoe felt her throat tighten. She could barely say the words without the overwhelming feelings of anger and despair. She pushed those feelings aside to continue talking to her mother. "I took care of that heartless cow." Her voice caught. She blinked away the tears and, wiping at her eyes, she took a deep breath and continued. "She's roasting in hell as we speak."

Zoe plucked some more weeds from the grave. "Good thing I didn't kill Eva, because not only is she innocent but she's also helping us in the Resistance." She sat there for a few minutes looking down at the weed in her hand. "She is so beautiful. She has the bluest eyes I've ever seen. They remind me of the time we spent on Lymnos and the Aegean was so blue. When she looks at me, I sometimes forget what I'm doing."

Zoe smiled, and despite no one being around, she felt shy about saying these words aloud, words that had been in her mind for the last few months. "And she's tall, nearly gives me a neck pain from looking up at her so I have her sit down to talk. That way I can look at her eyes. Remember how I said I didn't like tall boys? I don't think that applies to girls," Zoe admitted and hoped that her mother wasn't disappointed with her. It had been the first time she had said aloud the reason she didn't like any of the boys that offered to marry her—it wasn't because they were not nice but because they were not the right gender. "She's not like the other girls in the village, Mama, she's different. I hope you're not upset with me. I've tried not to think about her but it's a little difficult when—um…" She stopped talking and blushed. "Maybe you don't need to know the other part," she added and gently brushed her hand over the cross on her mother's grave.

"I'm sixteen today. Didn't think I would live to see fourteen but here I am. The Allies have landed in Normandy. I didn't know where that was but Eva showed me on a map. That's her name. Eva Theresa Muller. Isn't that a beautiful name? I'm not sure why she has two names but Germans are funny. Eva says that the war is going badly for the Germans and we may soon see an end to it." Zoe watched the sky lighten and the sun begin to make its ascent.

"I have so much to tell you about what is going on in the village…"

Father Haralambos made his way down the street deep in thought. The war was still raging but the Allies had landed in Normandy in June, and that was good news. There had also been hopes of a quick end to the war, but it was now October and the hopes had evaporated. However, his job of smuggling people out of Larissa and Greece had met with some success over the past year with Zoe working with Eva. The Resistance had kept up pressure against the Germans throughout the long hot summer, frustrating the enemy.

What pleased Father Haralambos even more was the friendship that had grown between Eva and Zoe. Even though he saw a positive change when Zoe began as Eva's maid, there had been a major difference since July. The two collaborated on getting the identity papers to him even though on occasion they came close to being caught with the forged paperwork. They weren't caught though, and the work continued. He also noticed Eva was less depressed and more confident. She was smiling more. He was certain that Zoe's friendship was responsible. *They are both stubborn, but God, over time, worked a miracle!*

Eva had been a revelation, beautiful and softly spoken. She was so much like her mother. Father Haralambos wished he could turn back time and just elope with Daphne, as she had wanted, but he had been the proper ass and gone to ask her father for her hand.

Petros Mitsos was a war hero and the big man in Larissa. Father Haralambos couldn't just leave with Mitsos' daughter. *Your first mistake, you idiot,* he admonished himself. Mitsos was justifiably angry to find his daughter pregnant and outraged when he found out who her lover was. Father Haralambos wondered how he ever managed to stay alive through the tumult. He kept his sanity with the help of a German priest he had met in Athens, where he had fled to get away from gossip. Father Johan listened to him for hours and guided him through the mess he had created for himself.

"Ah, ancient history, old man," Father Haralambos muttered. Daphne had done a great job in raising Eva, and he was grateful to God for listening to his prayers. "Something has to go right," he added. He looked up into the bright early morning sun and squinted. He had a lot to do in church today and he was determined to get an early start. He rounded the corner to the small alleyway leading to the back entrance of the church, his mind on the matters of the day.

"Father."

Father Haralambos was startled at the sound of a voice coming from behind him. He turned and saw a man in his mid-twenties standing there, smiling at him. Father Haralambos embraced him and ruffled his dark hair.

Athanasios Klaras' brown eyes shone with joy.

"Thanasi, my boy, so good to see you! What are you doing here?" Father Haralambos inquired.

"I was homesick," Thanasi replied with a grin.

"Have you eaten anything?"

Thanasi shook his head.

"Well, then, we have to remedy that. Come, we will go to my home and have some breakfast and we can talk."

In deference to Father Haralambos' age, Thanasi walked slowly through the back alleys, avoiding the early morning patrols. He smiled at the man he loved as his father. Since his own parents had died when he was a young boy, Father Haralambos had lovingly filled the void. He had spent many a summer's day talking to Father Haralambos and playing backgammon. In more recent times, when he found the war too hard to bear, he would close his eyes and remember those treasured moments—summer days at the river and water fights with the other orphaned boys. Father Haralambos had run the local orphanage and made it a point that the young boys learned to play, read the Bible, and be honest, upstanding members of the school.

Thanasi was brought out of his musings when Father Haralambos stopped at a small house. He opened the door and led him into a sparsely furnished room—two rickety old chairs stood against a wooden table. A large crucifix, the only decoration in the room, hung on the wall.

"It's not much, but what is mine is yours," Father Haralambos offered.

"I have missed you so much. I can't believe I've been away for so long," Thanasi said, and gave the priest another hug.

"I've missed you too. I long for the days when I was just a priest and my only worry was how to break up water fights between you and Giorgos!" Father Haralambos laughed.

"How is that old goat? I must go and see him and Samia."

Father Haralambos frowned. "We lost Giorgos."

Thanasi sighed and glanced up at the large crucifix. "A good man."

"We also lost Kiriakos, Antonios, and Stavros. They are at peace now. The village has been hit hard. It's been a long three and a half years of occupation, but especially the last two years since you left. God only knows what our future will be." Father Haralambos he took out some cheese and bread and started to heat some water for tea. "So, how have you been?"

"I've seen better days. We've had some successes and a lot of losses...too many losses. We also have another problem—the British don't want to help us. Churchill wants the King back and I say, to Hell with the King!"

"Communism isn't the answer, my son."

"What is, Father? If we have British support, we can unite everyone and form a strong Resistance. Like the French have done. We can do it, but no one wants to sit down. Everyone is thinking about the end of the war instead of thinking about the present. We can't form a government at the end of the war if we are all dead." Thanasi picked up the cup of tea Father Haralambos had put in front of him and took a sip. "Our government can't organize a street parade, let alone this war. The King is happy and we are dying. Mark my words, Father, there will be a civil war in Greece after the krauts have been defeated. We stop one war and we begin another." His words were followed by a big sigh.

"Let's hope it doesn't come to that."

"There will be a civil war in Greece. It is a certainty."

"A civil war?" Father Haralambos repeated. "So that's the answer? More Greeks dying."

"I don't know what the answer is. We get rid of the Germans and then what? We get the King back? That loser? He sits there waiting for us to do all the dirty work."

"And the answer is Communism?"

"I don't know, but the monarchy hasn't worked. Maybe

Communism will work. But we have a more pressing problem. I was in Thessaloniki last week. A trainload of supplies and Germans are on a train that will be crossing the Gorgopotamos gorge and it will also be carrying human cargo."

"That railway line has been bombed so many times. Didn't the lads blow…" Father Haralambos stopped in mid-sentence and frowned. "Human cargo?"

"Jews. They are treated like cattle and sent to their deaths. Remember those boxcars we used to send sheep in?"

Father Haralambos nodded.

"They put those poor souls in boxcars and they go to their deaths…like sheep."

"That's what camps are for? The ones that the Germans are using out of town?"

"Yes."

Father Haralambos stared at the man in shock. "That's inhuman. But wasn't the line recently destroyed?"

"They blew it up and the Germans rebuilt it. We've played this game now quite a few times. We're going to blow up the line and the train."

"The train? You can't do that — all those people!"

"We have to destroy that line and the train. Either way, lives are going to be lost. But if we destroy the railway, we send a clear message to those monsters that we will not submit! We have to fight them in any way we can, regardless of the risk. What is life under Hitler's regime anyway?"

"What about those poor souls?"

Thanasi looked at the priest. "Those people are already dead. They're alive now, but Hitler himself has ordered their deaths. What are you suggesting? That we don't act? We don't try and stop them? If we allow this train to pass, then they will be using this method to transport troops who will murder thousands of our brothers and sisters. Didn't you tell me that it's a sin not to act when you can help a brother in need?"

"Don't quote my own sermons back at me."

"Is it a sin not to act?"

"There must be another way. Can't we bomb just the line, or liberate the train?"

"I wish we could. We don't have enough men to liberate the train. If we do that, the Germans will just start shooting and the prisoners will be killed. A few may get away but—"

"Isn't it better to let the few get away than to kill everyone?"

"Get away to where? The whole country is overrun by Germans. Where do they go? They are destined to die. The Fates have already snipped their lives short."

"You are playing God."

"If I could find a way to stop the train, I would do it in a heartbeat. We have to bomb that train. There is no other way. What do you suggest we do?"

"I don't know the solution to this particular problem. I don't have the wisdom of Solomon. I don't have the answers and I don't know what to do. If we blow up the train, how many people will be punished and killed because of it? You know they will kill fifty Greeks for every German life lost... and those poor souls—"

"If we do nothing, those on the train are destined to die," Thanasi said, looking at the distressed cleric. "As I said, I wish there was a way to liberate that train, but there isn't. We have to blow it up."

"We've been trying to get some of them out of the country," Father Haralambos said quietly.

"How? How are you getting new identity papers?"

"We have help from the inside."

"Well, that works for one or two families at a time, not for hundreds of people." Thanasi looked across at Father Haralambos. "Do I know him, this person from the inside?"

The priest smiled. "Major Muller has been doing it for us. He just doesn't know it."

More questions were left unasked, as there was a knock on the door. Thanasi quickly hid in the adjoining room as Father Haralambos went for the door.

"Father, why aren't you in church?" Zoe asked as she entered and sat down, not bothering to ask permission.

"You were going to church?"

"No. I was passing by and I saw the church closed. I came to see if you were alright." Zoe looked around and noticed the two plates and cups. "Did I interrupt anything?"

"Do you want a cup of tea?" Father Haralambos asked as he held up the teapot.

"You're not answering my question."

"One day, Zoe, your inquisitive nature is going to get you in trouble."

"That's what Eva says." Zoe giggled. "So are you—"

The other door slowly opened and Thanasi stepped across the threshold with his gun in his hand. Zoe's eyes widened and she leapt to her feet. "Ares!"

Father Haralambos looked at Zoe with a frown. "The god of war? You're reading about those pagan gods far too much."

"No, Father, not that Ares—*that* Ares." Zoe pointed to Thanasi.

"What are you talking about, my dear child? This is my friend Thanasi."

Thanasi laughed. "Ah, the Nazis know me as Ares Velouchiotis."

"You chose to name yourself after the god of war?"

"Nice touch, don't you think?" Thanasi chuckled. "I knew those stories on mythology you used to read to me would come in handy one day!"

"I think it's great," Zoe chimed in as she stared at the man she considered to be a true war hero. His exploits were legendary among the local Resistance groups and made him a man wanted by the Nazis. Father Haralambos frowned at Zoe.

"Oh, Father, stop looking at me like that. We need heroes and if he calls himself Ares, why not?"

"Ares was a blood-thirsty god—"

"I hate to break this to you, but Ares never existed, remember?" Zoe said with a chuckle.

Father Haralambos ignored Zoe's last comment. He glanced at Thanasi, who had a grin on his face and was enjoying their banter. "How did you recognize him?"

"I saw a poster of him in Captain Reinhardt's office when he interviewed me for the job, but I also remember seeing him around before he left town to fight with the Resistance," Zoe said as she continued to look at the Resistance leader. "The poster doesn't come close." She realized what she had said and began to blush.

"Did you know about that?" Father Haralambos asked Thanasi.

"They have a very old sketch of me. I wouldn't worry. The Nazis love me...problem is, I don't love them," Thanasi said with a smile and a wink at Zoe.

"What if someone saw you come into the village?"

"Don't worry, Father. No one knows I'm here."

"You are a real hero."

Thanasi sobered up and looked at Zoe. He knelt beside her chair. "What's your name?"

"Zoe."

He smiled. "You have a beautiful name, Zoe. I'm not a hero. I'm just doing what I have to do."

"Can I call you Thanasi?"

He nodded. "Or Ares," he smirked.

Zoe put her hand on his arm. "You give people hope."

"Don't romanticize what I am. God gave me the opportunity to fight for the freedom of Greece. Who am I to refuse God's request?" Thanasi asked with a wink. "Even though I don't believe in Him."

Zoe wasn't sure what to say. She couldn't fault Thanasi because she didn't believe in God either. She stood and thrust out her hand. "Thank you," she said quietly. Thanasi took her hand and held it for a long moment. His smile and the warmth of his hand flustered Zoe.

"Zoe is one our unsung heroes." Father Haralambos put his arm around Zoe's shoulders. "She and Eva have worked together to get new identity papers."

"Is that right? You are fighting for our freedom, little sister."

"The sooner we get rid of them, the better," Zoe replied. "The Allies are taking a long time."

"It won't be long; our liberation will come soon."

Gunfire and raised voices made all three look at each other before Zoe got up and stuck her head out of the door. She saw a squadron of soldiers running toward her and she quickly shut the door.

CHAPTER 28

$\mathscr{Z}$oe turned to face Father Haralambos and Thanasi and blocked the door with her body. The soldiers were running towards them, screaming incoherently and brandishing their rifles. They reminded Zoe of a pack of wolves chasing its prey. For a fleeting moment she imagined the worst— they were after her. Timidly she peeked outside to see what was happening. The soldiers, though, were not after her, but some poor soul who they had captured and were dragging through the narrow street.

"What are you doing?" Father Haralambos asked. "Close the door, Zoe."

"Oh no, the poor man. He's an escaped Jew from the camp," Zoe muttered. "I have to get back or Despina will wonder where I disappeared to." She opened the door and stuck her head out to see if there were any soldiers lurking around. She waited for a few moments, and then headed out again.

Zoe rounded the corner and stopped. She watched as two motorcycles, a car bearing the flag of a general and a truck proceeded down the street. She hurriedly made her way back to Muller's residence and watched from across the street as the general got out of his car. His aides fawned over him as they assisted him. *I wonder who that tight-assed kraut is.* Zoe went to the servant's entrance of Major Muller's quarters and entered to find that Despina was in panic mode.

"What's going on?" Zoe asked.

"Ah, there you are! Fraulein Eva was looking for you."

"What's going on?" Zoe persisted.

"Don't ask so many questions."

"I wouldn't have to ask if someone told me what was going on," Zoe muttered as she walked up the stairs and into Eva's study.

"Where have you been?" Eva asked, as she heard the door open. She continued to write.

"Good morning to you, too, Fraulein Muller. I am fine, thank you, and you?" Zoe replied. She sat on the couch and bounced in place until Eva looked up.

Eva grinned. "You know, Zoe, one of these days—"

"Don't tell me, I'll get into trouble. Trouble is my middle name, according to Father Haralambos."

"Where were you? You were up early today."

Zoe picked some nonexistent lint off the couch. "I went to the cemetery."

"Oh."

"Today is my sixteenth birthday. So I took Mama some new flowers and filled her in on what dastardly deeds we were up to." Zoe grinned at Eva.

Eva walked around the desk with a small box in her hand. She hid it from Zoe until the last moment when she sat down on the sofa. "I know," she said and gave Zoe the white box. "Um... I wanted to give you this when you woke up but you had got up early..."

Zoe couldn't stop grinning as she took the box and opened it. Inside, sitting on a bed of cotton, was an emerald colored opal. She looked up quizzically at Eva, who was smiling.

"October is your birth month and your birth stone is an opal."

"Wow." Zoe picked up the stone and held it to the light. "This is so beautiful. I didn't know there was a birth stone for the month you were born in."

"There is."

"What's your birthstone?"

"My birthstone is the garnet."

"What is a garnet?"

"It's a gemstone. My mother gave me this ring when I turned sixteen." Eva lifted her hand to show Zoe the gold ring with an emerald colored garnet at the center.

"It's beautiful."

"The color reminds me of your..er.." Eva stammered to a stop, took a breath and smiled. "The opal comes from one of your favorite parts of the world."

"Greece?"

Eva shook her head. "Your other favorite place. Australia."

"Really? Wow." Zoe held the stone in her hand and marveled at its beauty. "Where did you get this?"

"It was mine. My uncle Wilbur went to Australia when I was eight and brought me back some gifts. One of them was this opal. My aunt Marlene sent it to me recently to remind me of home." Eva replied. "Do you like it?"

"I love it!" Zoe squealed and leapt into Eva's embrace and hugged her. Eva put her arms around Zoe and laughed. "Thank you," Zoe said and gave Eva a kiss on the cheek.

"You can thread it onto your chain if--" Eva stopped speaking when Zoe took the chain around her neck and undid the clasp. She threaded the opal through where it joined the heart that held her mother's picture.

"This is beautiful, thank you," Zoe repeated and kept touching the opal, which now hung around her neck. "I don't know when your birthday is; you have never mentioned it."

"I was born January 20, but my birthday isn't important," Eva replied with a slight shrug and got up from the sofa.

"You will tell me one day why it's not important."

"You won't ever take no for an answer, will you?"

"No," Zoe replied and giggled. "If you don't ask, you never learn. Now I have another question—why is Despina in such a state this morning?"

"General Rhimes has decided to pay us a visit," Eva replied and frowned. She didn't like the overbearing German general. He always found it amusing to pinch her in the rear and give her a slap for good measure. She had hoped she would be able to get out of greeting him, but her father had insisted.

"Who is General Rhimes?"

"He is in charge of Thessaloniki and the surrounding districts."

"That bastard!" Zoe spat out. "Do you know about the stories with the Jews?"

Eva nodded. She had seen for herself when Muller and she had visited Thessaloniki before arriving in Larissa. "They aren't just stories."

"You mean they are real?"

"Yes, very real. The Jews are being hunted and exterminated. When we were in Thessaloniki I saw him shoot dead a Jewish man. Just because he felt like it."

"They can't do that! The Jews aren't animals," Zoe protested indignantly.

"They can. A Jew is a nothing in the eyes of our Führer." Eva looked up at the portrait of Adolf Hitler in disgust.

Zoe looked distressed at the revelation.

"Can I ask you a question?"

"Always, Zoe. If I can, I will answer it."

Zoe hesitated. "Do you...I mean," she stammered, "do you hate the Jews?"

Eva looked up sharply, not anticipating that question. "How can I hate the Jews when I'm helping them?"

Zoe scratched her head. "Well..."

"Not all Germans are barbarians." Eva looked down, unable to meet Zoe's gaze.

"I didn't mean to hurt you," Zoe said and went over to Eva and knelt beside her chair. "I just—"

"I know what you meant. I'm sorry. I just wasn't expecting that question. I was in the Hitler Youth, but everyone in Germany was, before the war. I don't hate the Jews." Eva looked at Zoe and their eyes met.

"I wish this war would end." Zoe sighed.

"What are you going to do when this war does end?" Eva asked with curiosity. She had been thinking about the end of the war and what she would be doing with her life. She didn't know what she wanted, but she knew she had found a friend in Zoe. Their friendship was going to come to an end as soon as the war ended and she was back in Germany.

Eva smiled as Zoe closed her eyes. Eva moved her hand to brush the red-gold hair that fell across Zoe's eyes and then stopped. Just as quickly she pulled her hand back. Zoe was completely oblivious to the small war being waged within Eva.

No matter how hard she had tried, Eva couldn't get Zoe out of her mind. The fact that she was with her every day didn't help. She found she could talk to Zoe so easily. She was tired of being lonely but she wasn't sure she could live through the torrent of abuse she knew would follow should her relationship with Zoe deepen. The more she longed to be with Zoe, the worse her migraines had become. She tried to fight it but found she wasn't able to. The best course of action was to stop thinking about her, but that was difficult as well, since they were together for most of the day. She was living in her own version of hell.

Zoe opened her eyes, almost catching Eva's fond gaze. "What will I do when the war ends?" Zoe repeated. "I want to go to Australia, create some beautiful art and I want to go back to school," she said wistfully. "I want to show the world my art."

Eva smiled. "Can I see the one you were drawing the other day?"

Zoe lowered her eyes and played with the fringe of her skirt. "Are you sure?"

"Yes."

"Really?"

Eva nodded and chuckled when Zoe ran out of the room leaving her alone. Zoe rushed back into the room a few moments later with her bag and opened it. "It's not very good," she muttered, as she handed the drawing to Eva.

Eva was very surprised to see the pencil drawing was of herself with Henry at Athena's Bluff. They were laughing. "This is great," Eva complimented. "Have you shown Henry?"

"Yes, and he says I've given him a big head. He has a big head so I just draw what I see." Zoe laughed, which caused Eva to join her. "You really like it? You were so happy that day and Henry was being so goofy that I couldn't help but draw it." Zoe sounded shy.

"It's beautiful," Eva said.

"Just like you," Zoe replied, and blushed furiously. Eva looked at her and decided she wasn't going to say anything; there wasn't much to say that wouldn't involve Eva professing her attraction to Zoe. That was a revelation best left in her dreams. "So." Zoe cleared her throat. "What do you want to do? Will you go and find your lover?"

Eva wasn't taken aback by Zoe's bluntness—she was now used to Zoe speaking her mind. "No, I don't think so."

"Why?"

Eva gazed at Zoe for a long moment. "I don't feel that way about her anymore."

"Oh, yes…the cure."

Eva wasn't sure what to make of that almost derisive declaration. "Don't you believe that's possible?"

Zoe fingered the opal around her neck and stared down at the floor for some time. "We can't change what our hearts desire."

"Our heart desires a lot of things. Some of them are not good for us. I know loving women isn't good for me."

"Well, loving women is a sickness and you have been cured," Zoe replied and with a slight shrug.

"My heart desires Captain Reinhardt and I'll be getting married soon."

Zoe shook her head. "You're going to marry someone you don't love?"

"I do love him."

"Hm, if you say so," Zoe muttered. "I don't think you love him."

"You don't?" Eva asked, knowing full well the question may lead to another one of Zoe's naïve romantic views about love and marriage.

"No, I don't. I know what you are thinking. I'm sixteen and I don't know anything about love but my mama's eyes could light up a room when she saw my papa. Your eyes don't do that."

"You're wrong," Eva replied defensively. "I love Captain Reinhardt."

"Uh huh," Zoe muttered.

Eva sighed and then looked up at the clock, grateful that she had to cut the conversation short. "I have to get ready to meet General Rhimes. Did you speak to Father Haralambos?"

"I went to find him, but he wasn't in church."

"He wasn't in church?"

"No, so I went to his house. I couldn't ask him because he had a visitor."

"Is he alright?" Eva asked, grateful for the fact they weren't discussing her upcoming marriage to Reinhardt. She was concerned for Father Haralambos. They had spent time talking, getting to know each other. She had found out he was a very gifted artist and quite a good singer. They had laughed when Father Haralambos insisted that he gave Eva his singing ability. He regaled her with his memories of a tone deaf Daphne. They had spent some time wiping the tears from their eyes as he shared memories of her mother. Memories she would treasure all her life. The times had been growing shorter and fewer with the watch of Muller and Reinhardt. Eva was happy that Zoe had been making most of the recent trips to the church to pass papers or information to the Father.

"Oh yes, he was fine; he just had a visitor," Zoe said with a grin.

CHAPTER 29

*S*o, dear friend, what brings you to my backwater?"
Muller asked as he handed Rhimes some wine.

Erik Rhimes was a big, rotund man. His uniform was stretched tight across his stomach and the buttons on his jacket appeared to want to escape. As he sat, he opened the collar of his uniform and exhaled. "Ah, that's better." He sipped his wine. "I came to warn you."

"You came all the way here to warn me? Don't tell me we have vermin?" Muller asked.

Rhimes' booming belly laugh erupted and Muller joined him. "No, no, no. You are going to get a visitor soon to your little backwater."

"Oh?"

"His name is Ares."

"The god of war is paying me a visit?" Muller chuckled. "These Greeks are so inventive. Lousy fighters, but inventive."

"Indeed. I must say that policy of fifty Greeks for one German does prove to be an excellent deterrent. I have to remember to thank General Kiefer for that idea. A stroke of genius. As I was saying, Ares Velouchiotis is coming here."

"Why?"

"To blow up the line and—"

"Again? Damn it, Erik, that line has been blown up so many times. I'm getting tired of telling my men to rebuild it!"

"They want to blow up the train as well."

"But they will be killing the Jews... I guess they will be saving us some work." They both laughed at Muller's joke. "Still, I don't understand why he wants to blow up the train."

"Well, according to our informant, to teach us a lesson."

"If it's a lesson they want, then I'll be the one to teach it. Give me the men and I'll take care of every last one of them."

"No. We're going to do something very different. I want you to put a prominent member of this little backwater on that train."

"Prominent member? How will that stop them from blowing it up?"

The door opened and Eva walked in. She had pulled her long, dark hair into a ponytail and wore an elegant suit that matched her eyes.

"Ah, Eva! How wonderful to see you." Rhimes got up and kissed Eva and then pinched her on the behind and gave her a good slap.

"Hello, General," Eva said with a forced smile.

"What is this I hear that you're getting married to Captain Reinhardt? I'm in the mood to dance. When is the happy day?"

"Very soon, sir. Of course you're invited."

"I look forward to it," Rhimes replied and motioned for her

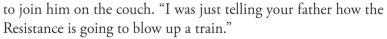

to join him on the couch. "I was just telling your father how the Resistance is going to blow up a train."

"Again?" Eva asked.

"Indeed. I think the Greeks believe in blowing something up until it doesn't exist!" Rhimes smirked. He turned to Muller and repeated his previous order. "I want you to put a prominent member of this town on that train."

"So they won't blow up the train?" Eva asked.

"You've got it. They won't blow it up if some high and mighty local is on board. Isn't that just a brilliant idea?"

Muller grinned. "I take it you have someone in mind?"

"I do. I have found that the most prominent member of the community is the local priest. I want your priest on that train."

Eva felt her chest constrict at the thought of that brave, innocent man being used as bait. In the time after finding out that Father Haralambos, the kind, gentle priest, was in fact her real father, Eva's respect had turned to love. He was everything Hans Muller could never be. When he spoke to her it was as if everything else was secondary. When she confessed her inner most thoughts to him, he listened. He didn't judge her, didn't condemn her or try to change her. Where she was expecting hate, she found love. Rejection was replaced with acceptance. The thought that Father Haralambos, her father, would be ripped away from her life again was something she couldn't accept. *I have to do something. Not again.*

"Ah, Father Haralambos. You know him well, don't you, Eva?" Rhimes asked.

"He is a very good man, General. Isn't there another way?"

"I didn't know you cared so much about these Greeks." Rhimes scowled at her. "We are at war, Eva. Even the local priest can kill you if given half a chance."

"My Eva is deeply religious. I've told her to be careful when she goes down to that church. Last year, in fact, an old woman used an opportunity while she was there to hit you," Muller said as he held his wine ready to drink and watched Eva over the rim of the glass. "I thought about making an example of her and having her shot, but I decided not to at the time. Maybe I should do it now that General Rhimes is in town. What do you think, Eva?"

"She was angry, Father, she—"

"I'm not going to waste a bullet on her." Muller chuckled and waggled his finger at Eva. "Although I am concerned that you continue to take risks each time you leave this house. You are also getting too close to that priest. Getting close to that man is not a good idea."

Eva nodded. She knew Muller was keeping a watch on her movements. Ever since Kristallnacht her father had made certain he knew who she was seeing and when. Freedom, that's what she craved, and yet Zoe's words echoed in her mind. Australia was sounding like a perfect place, if only she survived the war.

"They can easily turn and kill you where you sleep. I wouldn't trust that maid either. Spending time with them is dangerous. They fill your young mind with ideas that are contrary to what we hold in our hearts," Rhimes said as he pulled out some papers from his briefcase. "I'm sure your Father Haralambos is a God-fearing man, but he is a Greek. He is prominent in the community and he is perfect for what I have in mind."

"I will call him in tomorrow," Muller said, writing a note to himself.

"There was another matter I had to discuss with you." Rhimes handed the papers over to Muller.

"Identity papers?" Muller asked.

"Do you see anything strange about them?"

"Not really."

"Well, we found these on two of the Resistance fighters. They appear to have originated from here."

"Did you ask them?"

"Unfortunately, we killed them before asking questions. They are good forgeries. Excellent in fact. Have you seen these before?" Rhimes asked Muller again, who was studying them.

"Not that I would remember. Not unless Captain Reinhardt signed them on my behalf, but that's my signature. I don't understand it."

"Well, then you have a forger in your little backwater. A minor problem, but an annoying one. If we hadn't shot those two, you would never have known about this."

Eva tried to keep calm and disinterested in the conversation. The identity papers she and Father Haralambos created were flawless, or so they thought. She had to get word to him and quickly, and then get him to safety. She barely heard the two men talking. Her thoughts were on Father Haralambos and the dire predicament he was going to be in shortly.

Eva was brought out of her thoughts when Muller and Rhimes began to discuss the state of the war. She had heard that the Allies had landed in Normandy during the summer, but from all accounts she was led to believe that the Reich was beating back the Allied advance. She had hoped at the time that it was the propaganda machine in action again.

"So we've lost Paris?" Muller exclaimed. "When did this happen?"

"August," Rhimes said dejectedly.

"You're telling me that we lost Paris in August? Damn it! Why didn't anyone tell us sooner?"

"I think they had a lot more concerns on their minds, old friend, than telling us about Paris. We lost Bucharest, the Russian bastards have overrun Estonia, and the Americans...oh, dear God, the Americans. We are fighting on too many fronts."

Muller and Rhimes sat smoking cigars, which filled the room with smoke. Eva found the smell comforting in an odd kind of way and it reminded her of home and her grandfather.

"We are going to lose the war," Rhimes said and shook his head slowly as he watched the smoke rise from his cigar.

"Never! I don't believe that. We've had some losses but—"

"Hans, the war is going badly. Very badly. If we are lucky, we will salvage some sort of agreement. The Russians are mauling us. Barbaric people."

"What are we going to do here?"

Rhimes pulled a piece of paper from his uniform pocket and gave it to Muller.

Muller's eyebrows rose into his hairline as he read the document "That's why the train is important?" He queried.

"Yes. General Kiefer and I are organizing a slow withdrawal of troops from Athens. We are leaving only a few there. Our Jewish problem will be eliminated. The Final Solution."

"Maybe we were given wrong information—"

"The Americans have crossed into the Fatherland."

Both Muller and Eva gasped, although not for the same reasons.

"When?" Muller whispered. "Are you sure?"

"I wish I could say I was wrong, but I'm not wrong. On September 13 they marched into Germany," Rhimes said quietly.

Getting up from his chair, Muller swore and began pacing around the room.

"Excuse me, Father, General Rhimes," Eva said as she rose from her chair. "I see that you have important matters to discuss, so I will leave you."

"Yes. Yes," Muller replied absently.

Eva walked out of the office, her thoughts jumbled as the good news was replaced with the more pressing problem of getting Father Haralambos out of Greece. She walked into the kitchen, where Despina was busy preparing the noon meal. "Where is Zoe?"

"That child will be the death of me!" Despina complained exasperatedly as she pushed back her hair from her eyes.

"Do you know where she is?" Eva asked again, becoming annoyed.

"No. She ran out of here like the devil was after her and, with that child, he probably was."

Eva thanked Despina and walked up to her room to put on her cloak and hurriedly left the house, leaving her guards behind. She would have to go and tell Father Haralambos herself. She couldn't delay it any longer.

Light rain had begun to fall as Zoe headed out of the house. Despina's words still echoed in her ears while she tried to avoid any patrols. The weather had changed so dramatically that she wondered if the weather and the state of the war matched. She shook her head as she made her way to Father Haralambos' house. Avoiding the puddles that were beginning to form, she walked up to the door and tapped lightly. Adjusting her collar to keep the rain out, she impatiently wondered why Father Haralambos was so slow in answering.

"Is everything alright?" Father Haralambos asked when he finally opened the door.

"Well, we have General Rhimes here," Zoe stated as she entered through the open doorway.

Thanasi entered the room again when Father Haralambos closed the door. "Big fat pig?"

Zoe giggled at the description. He did look like an overstuffed pig. "That's him. Big fat pig had a meeting with Muller. I don't know why, but Eva was with them."

"Who is Eva?" Thanasi asked as he leaned on the table.

Zoe glanced at Father Haralambos before answering. "Eva is Major Muller's daughter."

"And this Eva is important?" Thanasi continued.

"She is very important," Zoe exclaimed. She didn't miss the surprised look on Father Haralambos' face which quickly turned into a satisfied smile.

"The important question is, why is Rhimes here?" Father Haralambos asked Thanasi.

"I wish we had a way of finding out."

"We do," Father Haralambos stated. "Eva."

"I'm now confused. How is she going to help you?"

"She is our contact."

Thanasi stared incredulously at the priest. "She is your contact?" Father Haralambos nodded. "Dear God, man. Do you realize what you have done?" Thanasi threw up his hands in frustration. "And I suppose it was her idea to help you? Right?"

"She did volunteer."

"Great. This is just great! She has set you up, Father."

"You don't understand—"

"What's there to understand? You have been duped! I bet all those people you have helped are now dead. You don't honestly believe this woman came to help you?"

"You need to stop and listen. You're getting ahead of yourself. This is not like you. You don't panic. What's the matter?"

"You don't understand." Thanasi sighed. "Does she know I'm here?"

"No, I only told her that Father Haralambos had a visitor."

"Good," Thanasi said, running his hand through his hair. "We can get you away. When you play with vipers, you get bitten. I'm not going to allow Father Haralambos to die because of this Eva," Thanasi spat out.

"I know what it means to live with vipers," Zoe retorted. "I don't want him to die either, but Eva is as honest as the day is long. She is no more a spy for the Germans than you are. She can't help it if her stepfather is a kraut." Zoe stopped when she realized what she had blurted out.

"What? Stepfather? What in God's name are you prattling about?"

Father Haralambos gave Zoe an exasperated look. "Thanasi, you need to sit and calm down. Stop getting so excited. You're going to get a nosebleed."

"But, Father—"

"Don't 'but Father' me, young man. I know what I'm doing."

"You don't! You don't know the first thing about the Resistance. You are a priest."

Zoe snorted at Thanasi's statement. "I think you don't know what is going on here in Larissa."

Thanasi scowled at her but Zoe ignored it. "You two, behave."

"You don't understand. I can't let those pigs get you. You are responsible for who I am. I'm not going to sit by and watch them kill you."

"Who said they will kill me, my son?" Father Haralambos asked.

"I am saying it!" All three jerked their heads towards the door where Eva had just entered. Thanasi immediately cocked his gun, ready to protect the priest.

"I wouldn't fire that gun—they jam with her around," Zoe muttered more to herself thank to Thanasi.

"Eva, what are you saying?" Father asked.

"Eva? That's Eva? Stand aside, Father, she means to kill you," Thanasi demanded.

"Of course I don't! What gave you that idea?" Eva retorted, but that only caused Thanasi to become bolder and more determined.

"Oh, put that away," Father Haralambos said. He grabbed

the gun from a very startled Thanasi and secured it in the chapel's offering box that had been on the table. Zoe looked at Eva, who had a very confused look on her face. "You, SIT," Father Haralambos commanded and Thanasi slumped into a chair. "And you," he leveled his gaze on Zoe, "stop smirking and behave yourself." Zoe slapped her hand over her mouth, trying to comply. "And you, what are you talking about?" He directed his question at Eva.

"Is Henry outside?" Zoe asked Eva, who shook her head. "Oh Eva! You know how he gets when you leave him behind."

"Who is Henry?"

"That doesn't matter," Father Haralambos interrupted. "Eva, Zoe said something about General Rhimes being here?"

"Well, it seems they found some of the identity papers."

"I can't believe you are trusting this kraut."

"Who are you?" Eva asked the man glaring at her.

"Athanasios Velouchiotis," Zoe said, with a laugh. "Ares to the Germans."

"THE Athanasios Velouchiotis?" Eva asked.

"You know me?" Thanasi said with some trepidation.

Eva nodded. "I know of you," she replied.

"Eva, what's the problem with the identity papers?"

Eva looked at Zoe and then back at Father Haralambos. "We have two problems actually. The first is that they shot two of our couriers. They had the papers with them."

"Those poor souls. May they rest in peace," Father Haralambos said, crossing himself. "But they can't link those back to us." He sat down across the table from Eva.

"Eventually they will find out who forged them."

"True." Father Haralambos scratched his bearded chin and sighed. "And what's our other problem?"

"There will be a train passing through here on its way from Athens to Thessaloniki, carrying troops. They are pulling out of

Athens."

Two stunned faces looked back at Eva; Thanasi merely scowled at her. "You mean they are actually pulling back?"

"Yes, I heard General Rhimes telling my father that they are slowly withdrawing troops because the Allies have taken Paris and they have crossed into Germany."

"Taken Paris? If they are in France, that means we are going to be liberated soon." Zoe's face split into a huge smile. "Our liberation is soon!"

"Hopefully soon, little sister, hopefully soon," Thanasi said with a reassuring smile.

"When is the train going to get here?" Father Haralambos asked.

"In a few days. It is how I understood it and they said something about The Final Solution—"

"The Jews...they are moving out the remaining Jews from Athens and all the way back to Germany. That has to be it," Thanasi exclaimed.

"They think the Resistance is going to blow up the train and the line."

"They know?" Thanasi asked.

"It seems so," Father Haralambos answered. "This is now a problem for us."

"They want you to be on that train, Father. If you are on it, the Resistance will think twice about blowing it up."

Shock registered on Zoe's face, while Father Haralambos and Thanasi looked at each other. "You can't go on that train!" Zoe said angrily.

"If we blow up that train, many will die but—" Thanasi said quietly.

"What utter rot! Fifty Greeks will die if you do blow it up. And what about the Jews?" Zoe spat out. "Father Haralambos is not bait. He is a living, breathing, kind man who you want to kill."

"Zoe, calm down," Eva said placing her hand on Zoe's shoulder. "That's not going to happen." She looked at the priest. "She's right."

"No, she's wrong," Father Haralambos said. The three of them looked at the priest in shock.

"Have you been drinking?" Zoe asked angrily.

"Zoe!" Eva swatted Zoe on the arm.

"Will you three please calm down? If I don't go on the train, then the Germans will know I'm in the Resistance, good people will die, and the line will be used to move the Germans out."

"A good man will die that doesn't need to die," Eva said. Father Haralambos stood and put his arm around her shoulders. "For everything there is a reason," he said quietly. "I'm going because it's the right thing to do," he said, echoing Eva's own words.

"Not when I've just found you," Eva said and hugged him.

Thanasi frowned. "We will find a way."

Father Haralambos exhaled loudly. "What part don't you understand? If I don't go on the train, Greeks die, Jews die, and I die for Resistance activities. If I do go on the train, Greeks don't die, Eva is not implicated and—"

"And you still die, the Jews will die and I couldn't give a damn about the krauts! I hope they burn in Hell!" Zoe's voice rose along with her anger with the frustration she was feeling at being unable to see a solution to this situation that did not include Father Haralambos' death.

"Either way I die."

"I don't want you to die," Zoe said quietly.

"We all die sometime, my child," Father Haralambos reiterated, just as quietly.

"How can you be so final about this?" Eva asked, suppressing her tears.

Father Haralambos looked at Eva, but he didn't answer.

"Father," Eva whispered. "Oh, Father..."

"Don't worry, Eva, everything will be all right."

"I-I want to talk to you more about this, but I have to get back to the house. They will be wondering where I have gone," Eva said, burying her head in Father Haralambos' robe. He held her closer until finally she broke away and walked to the door.

"So, you've made up your mind then?" Thanasi asked.

"I have to do what is best," the priest replied, still holding the sobbing Zoe.

"I won't let you," Zoe said, wiping away her tears. "Even if I have to kill every last German myself, you are not going to die."

"Can't you see that the train will take you out of Greece? You may end up where the Jews are headed. You will die, and damn it, I'm not going to allow that!" Thanasi yelled.

"It is for the best. The Resistance will blow up the train. We can't allow any more people to be sent to their deaths on that line."

"Please, see reason. I wanted that train blown to kingdom come, but not with you on it. I wouldn't be able to live with myself knowing I caused your death. Don't you understand?" Thanasi pleaded with Father Haralambos.

"Sometimes the burden of leading is very difficult. We all make decisions that are too hard to bear. This is your torture stake, my son. I have to do what is right."

"Father, please, listen to me!" Thanasi begged. "The Resistance will blow up that train and I can't stop it."

"No!" Zoe screamed at him and ran out of the house into the steady rain.

CHAPTER 30

oe ran. She ran until her heart pounded and her lungs ached for air. She didn't know for how long and she didn't care—she just had to run until she could run no longer. Exhaustion finally slowed her down enough to bring her to a stop in front of the cemetery. Realizing where she was, she plodded through the mud to her mother's grave.

"Oh, Mama!" Zoe cried and collapsed to the ground, sobbing. "Why is everyone leaving me?" She asked as she tried to understand what was happening. Everyone she loved was gone, and now the man who was like a father to her was also going to die.

She wiped away the tears. "This isn't fair. Eva recently found her real papa, the Germans are leaving, and now this. It's not fair."

Zoe looked to the heavens. "Dear God, I know I don't speak to you much and I know you don't have to listen, but please, I beg you...please look after Father Haralambos. I know if you let him, he will organize Heaven for you." She wiped her eyes again.

"He is a good man and I love him so much." Her voice broke as she looked down at the sodden ground. "I don't have to tell you what he has done, how many people he has saved. Please make his death as painless as possible. Don't let him suffer. I can't bear to think of him in pain and alone."

Zoe rocked back and forth in the mud as the rain continued to fall on her forlorn figure. She wasn't sure exactly how long she sat there in the mud, but eventually she realized that the pelting rain had turned to drizzle and the sun had gone down.

She was slowly making her way back to the house when she heard a soldier command her to stop. Zoe sighed and turned. She grimaced when she found herself face to face with the corporal who had manhandled her a few weeks previously.

"So Fraulein, we meet again." The corporal grinned.

Zoe gave him a wry grin in return. "So it would seem."

"Where are you going?" He inquired.

"To Major Muller's residence," Zoe responded. She was wet, cold, and emotionally spent. She just didn't have any energy left.

"What are you doing out here at this time? Don't you know about the curfew?"

"Yes, sir, I do and I'm sorry," Zoe said quietly.

The soldier looked surprised. Taken aback, he just told her to get going.

Passing the church, Zoe looked up and frowned when she saw that the door was open. She quickly ran up the steps.

The church was dark, the only light coming from the candles burning by the altar. Zoe stopped in the doorway when she noticed that Eva was kneeling in prayer. Not wanting to interrupt her, she stood by a column and waited.

Eva looked up at the image of the crucified Christ. "Lord, I can't believe that it is Your will to let Father Haralambos drink from this bitter cup." Her voice broke and she faltered. She wiped away the tears. "He's my father, Lord...I know I was brought here to find him and I know there is a reason that things happen the way they do, but I can't see how this will benefit anyone. Please, don't let him die. He has been my one saving grace in this nightmare." She choked on her words.

Tears welled up in Zoe's eyes as well, her heart going out to Eva.

"Eva…" Zoe called out as she walked down the aisle and knelt beside Eva and took her hand. "Don't' cry." She tenderly wiped a tear from Eva's cheek.

"You're wet." Eva looked down at the disheveled young woman.

"I am." Zoe shrugged. "I didn't think God would mind."

Father Haralambos hurriedly made his way to the church. He was going to make certain there was nothing left behind that could link Eva to the Resistance. He was sure he didn't have anything in his office which would incriminate her, but he wanted to double-check. Thanasi had warned him about such things before he left, and about the patrols that would stop him if he were out after dark because of the curfew that was in place. He wondered where Thanasi had disappeared to, but knew there was no use in speculating. Still, it didn't keep him from worrying about the lad.

Thanasi, God bless him. He means well but he is just too over protective. Besides, he had to make sure things were in order before tomorrow. It was just a short distance from the house to the church. What could happen? Father Haralambos rounded the corner and stopped dead in his tracks. The church doors were slightly ajar and his heart beat faster hoping that the Germans were not inside the office. He looked around and didn't see any German presence. He was sure that he had told Sister Maria to close the doors when she had finished preparing for Sunday's service. He shook his head and wearily climbed the steps.

He made his way into the church and stopped. Before the altar, two figures were kneeling, their heads covered. From their silhouettes, he was quite certain he knew who they were. He smiled. "Thank you, Father," he said quietly and crossed himself. He then noticed the trail of mud from the entrance to the altar, shook his head, and made his way out through the front door of the church. He would head into his office from around back.

Zoe and Eva rose and slowly made their way out of the church. Eva stopped and saw the muddy trail. "Do you always like to play in the mud?" She teased, making an attempt to get a grin out of Zoe.

"Only when it rains," Zoe replied. They smiled at each other and closed the church doors. They didn't encounter any patrols on the way back home. They stopped and watched as the car carrying General Rhimes sped off, and then made their way around the house and into the kitchen.

"Oh, my God!" Despina cried out as Zoe tramped the mud from her boots onto the clean kitchen floor. Zoe stood there with a sheepish grin and shrugged. "Get out of here, now! You are—" Despina yelled, but stopped in mid-sentence when she saw Eva follow Zoe inside. "Fraulein Muller, I'm sorry..."

"Sorry." Zoe took off her muddy shoes and threw them out of the kitchen door onto the rear steps. Her once white socks were now a mucky brown color.

A moment later Henry entered the kitchen and stood just inside the doorway glaring at Eva.

"Don't start," Eva said before her guard had a chance to speak. "I'm fine, just went for a stroll."

Henry shook his head and with a sigh, he turned and walked out of the kitchen.

"Get some hot water prepared for a bath, Despina," Eva requested, ignoring the glare Despina was giving Zoe as they both trudged up the stairs.

Eva ushered Zoe into her bedroom, determined to get the wet and muddy clothes off her before she developed pneumonia. Placing Zoe on the bed as if she were a child, Eva removed her socks and tossed them aside. "What were you doing? Did you run to the next village in the rain?" She asked as she unbuttoned Zoe's skirt and watched it fall around her bare feet. "I don't want you to get sick," she scolded.

Zoe tried to unbutton her blouse, but Eva pushed her hand away. "We can't have you catching a cold after..." She looked up for the first time and saw the sheepish grin on Zoe's face, "...all, uh, can we?" Not sure how to interpret that expression, Eva stepped to the side and retrieved a blanket.

"This is very romantic, isn't it?" Zoe's sense of ironic absurdity was clearly showing. "Somehow I didn't think it would be quite like this—me being wet, cold, and covered in mud, with Despina yelling at me..." Zoe teased as she tossed her blouse to the floor.

Eva smiled. "You were thinking about it...about me?" She asked, placing the blanket around Zoe's shoulders.

Zoe blushed and looked away. Eva cupped Zoe's face and turned it towards her. "You were thinking about me?" She repeated.

"Yes, sometimes."

"Why?"

"You're not a boy," Zoe replied with a tiny shrug.

"No, I can't say that I am."

"That's good because—" Zoe stopped and looked up into Eva's sparking blue eyes. "—I don't like boys."

"Oh," Eva whispered. She had resisted her feelings for so long. She had resisted giving into what her heart desired, but her mind rebelled again. Even now she felt the tendrils of fear envelop her mind, but she tried to push them aside. She would pay for what she was about to do but she was going to do it. She didn't want to get involved with anyone. She had cut herself off and maintained an icy exterior. She had built walls around her heart to prevent anyone from hurting her again and to protect herself from her father. She had managed to stay remote and aloof until she had met this young woman. Zoe had walked in and blithely disassembled the walls she had worked so hard to build. The last few months had been ones of constant pain originating from her thoughts and desires.

Eva and Zoe suddenly found themselves surrounded by the loving arms of the other. Very comfortable with the newfound intimacy, they held on to each other a few moments longer.

"I've never been interested in anyone before," Zoe said softly. "Not that way."

"Well, that's...what did you say?" Eva asked as she realized what Zoe had just said. Eva had thought that she would never hear those words again, had not dared to hope she would.

"I've fallen in Heavy Like for you," Zoe said softly but distinctly, looking into Eva's eyes. "I've never felt for anyone the way I feel about you."

"Maybe we..." Eva started hesitantly. She wanted to believe what Zoe was telling her, wanted so much to feel that finally she could love someone. A dull ache was beginning to stir within but she pushed her discomfort away.

"I'm in heavy like for you. I just admitted to you I was new at this and, well, you are just going to have to be patient with me."

"You surprise me," Eva said quietly as she gazed at Zoe, her red hair matted with mud but her eyes shining brightly. Those eyes looked at Eva with emotions that she thought she would never again see directed at her.

"Oh? How so?" Zoe asked.

"When I told you about my lover and then about my uncle..." Eva said slowly. Now, she had to make certain that Zoe knew where they were headed. She owed her that much.

"You're wondering why I didn't go running out the door, is that it?"

Eva nodded.

"Why should I run out? You were hurting and you needed a friend so badly," Zoe reminded her quietly, looking into Eva's eyes.

"You are special, very special, to me," Eva quietly said. Cupping Zoe's face in her hands, she slowly leaned over and pressed her lips to Zoe's. Gently at first, to explore the sweetness of Zoe. Eva slowly became more assertive as she could feel the excited response from Zoe and sought to quench her desire.

"Oh boy!" Zoe whispered as they parted.

"Good or bad?" Eva asked with a bit of trepidation.

"Oh, good! Better than good!" Zoe exclaimed as they shared another kiss. "Much better than when Tasos kissed me."

Eva looked at Zoe and her brows furrowed together, which caused Zoe to start laughing.

"Are you jealous, Fraulein Muller?" Zoe asked with a grin. "You should stop frowning like that," she said and playfully smoothed the furrow between Eva's eyes.

"No...I mean...yes...well...when did you kiss Tasos?"

"Let's see now." Zoe smiled. "I was ten years old and it

happened at the back of the chicken coop. Very sloppy kissing." She laughed. "My brother Michael came out and stopped us. He told me that if I kissed a boy I would have a baby."

They both laughed as Zoe continued. "Which I believed, and so I never kissed another one again."

Eva looked down at her own tall frame. "Well, I'm not a boy, so I can't get you pregnant."

Zoe looked Eva up and down. "You certainly are not a boy."

"I thought you said you didn't like boys?"

"I kissed him to see what it was like. I didn't like it." Zoe grinned. "Let me tell you something, Fraulein Muller. You definitely don't kiss like Tasos."

They looked at each other. Eva frowned. "You know this can be very dangerous for you." The thought of her father laying a hand on Zoe made her heart ache. She could withstand her 'treatments' again if she had to, but could not bear for Zoe to suffer because of her.

"For me? What about you?" Zoe asked, wrapping her blanket around Eva.

"He will hurt you if he finds out. I don't want to see you going through what I've been through. You are a very gentle soul, and if it means we can't take this further—"

"And you are a hard bitten Nazi, right? How do you feel about me?"

"I love you, but because I love you, I don't want to put you in danger. I don't want to see you hurting."

Zoe sighed. She reached up and tenderly caressed Eva's cheek. "You may not have noticed this, but we are in a war. I'm in danger just walking down the street. I can get shot for nothing more than looking at a soldier the wrong way."

"My father—"

"Your father is a psychotic man, who hurt you physically and mentally for loving someone. Father Haralambos told me that when we find love, we accept it. We don't question it, and we don't deny it."

"Father Haralambos said that?" Eva asked as her hand went to her temples and massaged them when the throbbing headache began. Her knees started to tremble and she felt a heavy weight bear down on her but she was determined to withstand it.

"Yes, he did. I don't think he was talking about us, but I do know how I feel about you. My brother Michael described it once as Heavy Like when he was talking about his newest girlfriend." Zoe chuckled. "He said, 'Zoe, there are three stages when you know it's right: Like, Heavy Like and Deep Love.' I'm in the second stage. Heavy Like. When I get to stage three you can shoot me, because I'll be useless. So I'm in stage two and I think there isn't any cure to stop it from going to level three." She grinned at Eva. "I don't want to be cured."

What happened next caught Zoe completely by surprise as Eva went to kiss her but almost passed out in her arms. Zoe grabbed hold of her as they both sank to the floor. She lost the blanket and concentrated on Eva, who was sitting on the floor with her long legs brought up to her chest and her head resting on her knees.

"You're not well, I knew that rain—"

"It's not that," Eva exclaimed. "Oh, god," she moaned.

Zoe knew what was coming and she quickly looked around the room, spotted the dustbin, and emptied it out before she brought it to Eva. Just as she did so, Eva heaved into the bucket. Zoe could do nothing but hold her, unsure of why Eva had been violently ill for the last few months.

"Go, have your bath," Eva said hoarsely as she wiped her mouth with the back of her hand.

"I can't leave you like this."

"Please go, Zoe."

Zoe didn't want to leave but she thought Eva didn't want to be seen being sick—that wasn't her way. "Alright, but I'll be quick."

"Uh huh," Eva's response could barely be heard as she had her head resting on her knees.

Zoe hesitated for a long moment before she leaned in and kissed Eva's dark head.

"Oh, god," Eva moaned. She let go of her knees and lay down on the floor. She curled into a fetal position and started to sob. Zoe picked up the blanket and left the room.

CHAPTER 31

*I*t was cold, dark, and airless. Eva took a deep breath and regretted it as her chest heaved and spasmed. She lay in the hospital bed unable to turn. She had been transferred to the hospital as soon as her back started to heal. This prison had been her world for over three months. She didn't know whether it was night or day, and after a point, she didn't care.

Eva's only means of telling time was by the visits of the nurses. If she knew their names, she didn't remember them. One particular nurse seemed to delight in injecting her with drugs that made her so sick she would retch until the pains in her chest and stomach made her cry out.

Her nurse told her that a friend was going to visit, but she wasn't told much else. For the first time in a long time, Eva looked forward to something. She was excited at the possibility that it might be a school friend. Logic didn't enter her mind to inform her anyone coming here wouldn't be doing so for a friendly visit.

The door opened once again and Eva flinched from the stark glare as the light was turned on and illuminated the small room.

Men in white coats; she didn't know their names and didn't care.

Hands grabbed her, so many hands of men in white. She fought back but she couldn't stop them from strapping her down. Her arms and legs were tied. She tried to move but it was impossible. She cried out in fear and pain but no one cared.

Eva opened her eyes to see her uncle Dieter at the head. He placed his hand on her head and whispered something to her that she could not hear—the only sound she heard was the sound of her heart. It was beating so fast, she thought it would explode out of her chest. A thick black strap kept her head immobile, a thick short bar in her mouth, and then the pain as the current went through her body like fire.

"Nooooooooooooo!" Eva screamed and struggled to sit upright. The blankets were wound around her, which caused her to thrash around, believing she was being held down. Her breath came in shallow gasps as she woke from the recurring nightmare. The door was flung open and Zoe ran inside and skidded to a stop when she found Eva doubled over, hyperventilating.

"Hey, it's okay." Zoe gently placed her arm around Eva's heaving shoulders. "Breathe into this; it works for me."

Eva breathed in and out of the pillowcase, Zoe's reassuring hand across her back. Zoe held her for what seemed an eternity but was actually only a few minutes.

Eva put the pillowcase on the floor and slumped back down to realize Zoe was holding her tightly. She turned her head and found tears running down Zoe's face.

"Sorry..."

"It's not as if you wanted to do that," Zoe replied as she wiped a tear that tracked down her face. They turned to find Henry at the door. He was wearing his uniform trousers and nothing else. He entered the room without asking and sat on the bed.

"Are you two having a party?" Henry light-heartedly asked as his gaze rested on Eva's distraught face.

"Nothing to worry about, Henry," Eva replied quietly as she reached out and took his hand.

"I'm going to go down to the kitchen—"

"No, don't. You can go to sleep."

"Are you sure?"

"Yes, it's Zoe's turn for Crazy Eva."

Henry shook his head as he rose. He leaned over to his charge and kissed her on the forehead. "Get some sleep, not so crazy Eva."

"He loves you so much."

"He is my best friend," Eva responded softly, pulling the blanket across her shoulders. She turned and gazed at Zoe, who was sitting meters from her.

"Do you want to talk about it?" Zoe asked as she reached to touch Eva. She pulled back when Eva shook her head.

"I..Zoe, don't touch me."

Zoe frowned. She looked around the room and found a chair to the side. She pulled the chair and sat at the end of the bed waiting for Eva to compose herself.

"Whatever it is, Eva, if you say it out loud, it can't hurt you anymore.'

Eva gazed into Zoe's earnest face. "It does, Zo, it does hurt."

"How? How can a nightmare hurt you?"

"You are going to think I'm crazy."

"No, I don't think you are crazy."

Eva closed her eyes. She took a deep breath, the last vestiges of the nightmare so fresh in her mind. "I was a little younger than you when my mother died and my father took out his anger at me."

"Sadistic bastard. That's when he struck you with the belt?"

"Yes, but I wish that's all he did. I was sent to Aiden in Austria. My family owns a spa there and it also has a hospital wing," Eva quietly related. Zoe leaned forward, not touching Eva but close enough to her. "My uncle Dieter—"

"That's the same one that sent Doctor Slutty, right?"

"Yes. He..ah." Eva stopped talking. "He had a cure for deviancy and I was his prize patient."

"What did they do to you?"

Eva blinked in the semi-darkness and didn't say anything for a moment. "Do you know what aversion therapy is?"

"No, but I'm going to guess it's not a good thing. You can't say the word without flinching."

"Aversion therapy is when they try and change you from a homosexual to a heterosexual."

"A heterosexual is what I'm not," Zoe said, getting Eva to look at her for a moment before a slight smile played on her lips.

"No, you're not a heterosexual."

"Right. So these people tried to change you? How did they do that?"

"They used electric shocks on me to change the way my brain worked. They wanted to stop how I felt about women. They did horrible things to me," Eva replied hoarsely and watched as Zoe's face went from confusion to rage in seconds.

Eva could see Zoe's hands were shaking and wondered if she could tell her the truth. The look on Zoe's face was one of horror but Eva saw compassion in her eyes. *If this doesn't terrify you to leave me, then nothing will,* Eva thought. All the while her gaze never left Zoe.

"I was injected with so many drugs, I didn't know my own name half the time, and the other half of the time, I didn't care what my name was."

"Are you still taking those drugs?"

Eva shook her head. "Yes, I think so. They don't tell me whether it's pain medication or those drugs."

"Is that why you have been ill for the last few months? In the morning you were fine but as the day wore on, you became so angry and ill?" Zoe asked. She reached out and then remembered, so she pulled back and sat on her hands.

"It's called aversion therapy for a reason."

"It obviously doesn't work very well."

"It does." Eva nodded. "It works the way they intended it to work. Their treatments were to try to get me not to feel sexually aroused by women."

"They can do that?"

"Yes, they can. When I kissed you earlier…"

Zoe's puzzled expression instantly changed to horror. "You are physically ill when you touch me?"

"Yes. It physically hurts me to touch you."

"That's why you were throwing up earlier?"

"Yes."

"It's why you've been sick for the last few months. You were thinking about me?" Zoe asked incredulously.

Eva nodded. "I had this dream one day that we were making love and I held you in my arms. It felt so real."

Zoe's face creased into a smile. "You were dreaming about me? About us making love?"

Eva nodded. "Yes."

"What happened when you woke?"

"I was violently ill."

"You were burning in your own version of hell."

"Yes."

Zoe sighed. "Do you want us to forget what happened tonight? I will go away and ask Father H to assign someone else; I don't want to hurt you."

"No, Zoe, I don't want you to go away."

"But I'm hurting you."

"I chose to kiss you. It's going to take me some time to overcome this but I will. If you leave, it would hurt more and they will win. I won't be able to bear that pain. What I'm feeling now, it will go away."

"Are you sure it will go away?"

"Yes, in time."

"When the war is over, we will find someone to help you. We will wait until you are stronger. This Uncle Dieter is another sadistic bastard. Is that why you are so afraid of him? When I mentioned his name as being on the guest list a few months ago, your face was so pale you were almost ready to pass out. You looked terrified of him."

"I am afraid of him because if he finds out that his cure never worked, he will take me back. I'm afraid if that happens I won't come out of Aiden alive."

"It never worked? I thought you said it did work and that's why you are ill."

"I can't change who I am, Zoe. I can't change how I feel no matter how much they torture me. What they have done is make me sick if I'm aroused by a woman, thinking about you," Eva shook her head.

"Does your father believe you?"

Eva grimaced and shook her head. "He doesn't believe I'm cured. Nurse Gestapo tried to convince him and then Dr. Uta came over and..well…"

"Horrible women. I hope they're enjoying the fires of hell." Zoe sneered. "Gestapo was the one that laughed as my mama was dying."

"She did?"

"Yes," Zoe responded as Eva's eyes closed. "I hope they enjoyed the ride down Athena's Bluff."

Eva's eyes popped open and she stared at Zoe. "What?"

Zoe stared back. "I promised to kill the woman who laughed at my mama's death. I was sorry I had to kill that Doctor but now I'm not sorry because of what they did to you."

Eva smiled. She was overcome with the feelings she was

experiencing for Zoe. "It's been a long time since anyone cared about me."

"Well, I'm going to change that," Zoe resolutely announced.

"Are you sure you want to get involved with me?" Eva whispered, hoping for all she was worth she wasn't going to hear the words that she dreaded.

Zoe didn't say anything for a few moments. "I'm sure, but I'm not the one throwing up every time you see a little flesh," Zoe gently teased making Eva smile.

"If Muller—"

"I'll kick him in the crotch and enjoy the experience." Zoe giggled.

Eva couldn't help herself and she laughed. It felt good to laugh after experiencing the familiar nightmare that seemed to haunt her.

"I told you, Evy…" Zoe said and surprised Eva by using the diminutive form of her name. She looked up to see Eva's huge smile. "You may not have noticed this, but we are in a war. Every day is dangerous." Zoe shrugged. "What's one more danger?"

"This one is different."

"I know," Zoe said. "Sometimes you have to go with your heart and let it lead you."

"You're one of a kind, Zoe," Eva replied a little hoarsely.

"The world is a safer place with only one of me," Zoe replied playfully as she fussed with Eva's blanket. "Now, go to sleep. You can worry about this tomorrow when you're feeling stronger."

Eva's furrowed brow deepened as the migraine settled behind her eyes. She watched as Zoe left the room. With a sigh she realized she was going to be spending the night alone. Moments later Zoe came back into the room with her blanket, the thick rug, and a pillow.

"What are you doing?"

"Sleeping on the floor—if I can't hold you, I'm going to be as close as I can be. I'll show these bastards that they won't win."

"God help them," Eva murmured. The last thing she saw was Zoe gazing up at her from the floor before her eyes closed.

CHAPTER 32

*M*uller sat at his desk and stared up at the ceiling. He couldn't believe what he had heard from Rhimes. If it were anyone else who had told him about the Fatherland's losses...well, he wouldn't have believed them. The Americans had crossed into the Fatherland. The very thought made his stomach hurt.

"My God," Muller muttered. "My God, what a shambles." He sighed. His thoughts were interrupted by a knock on the door, which he answered with a curt, "Come." Reinhardt entered and saluted. Muller motioned for him to sit. "Has the train arrived?" He asked.

"Yes, sir. It has three cars."

"Good. You're probably wondering why there are soldiers on that train? No?"

Reinhardt nodded.

"We have a problem," Muller said. "We're pulling out of Greece."

Reinhardt's right eyebrow twitched but he showed no outward emotion. If the situation weren't so serious, Muller would have laughed at his second in command's face.

"This is surprising to you?"

"I am surprised but—"

"Doesn't matter!" Muller snapped. "The train that came in this morning is going to Thessaloniki. Men from here will join the soldiers from General Kiefer's command. The rest will be sent via truck convoy. There will be Resistance activity to blow up the train. Bring Father Haralambos here to me. He will be on that train."

"Yes, sir. May I make a suggestion?" Muller nodded. "Why not get a hundred villagers and put them on the train? One man won't matter much to the Resistance, even if he is the priest. They will think twice about blowing up that many of their countrymen."

Muller stared at his second in command for a long moment.

"Alright. Round up a hundred villagers to go on the train," Muller said as he picked up a pen and began to sign papers. "Bring the priest here now."

"Sir, it's Sunday—"

Muller glared at Reinhardt. "So what? You don't bring priests in to me on a Sunday? Is there a problem?"

"No, sir."

"Well, go and do it then," Muller yelled.

"And so when you do a kind deed, don't let everyone know of it—just let God know." Father Haralambos finished his sermon on letting good deeds go unnoticed. His congregation was sparse today and he sighed. Only the old women and a scattering of old men were present. The young didn't have time for God with the war raging.

Even Eva was missing today, and that worried Father Haralambos. She was always there unless she was ill. He was sure that she had been well when he had seen her here last night. He was mildly startled when the doors to the church were opened and Reinhardt and six soldiers entered. He had expected to be taken from his home, not from the church.

"You're a bit late for the sermon, Captain," Father Haralambos quipped, knowing full well why the captain had come to the church.

Reinhardt grimaced. "I'm not here for that. You are to come with me."

"May I ask where to?" Father Haralambos asked, hoping to postpone the inevitable.

"Major Muller wants to speak to you," Reinhardt answered and then turned to the corporal on his left. "Gather everyone here and take them down to the train."

He led the priest out of the church as the soldiers rounded up the congregation. Father Haralambos looked back and frowned. "I said I was coming with you. What have these people done to deserve this treatment?" He tried to plead with Reinhardt, but he could see he was not going to appeal to the man's kindness.

"Don't ask so many questions. You may not like the answers," Reinhardt answered as he walked quickly back to Muller's residence.

Father Haralambos shuffled along, quite unconcerned at the hurried pace of Reinhardt. In fact, he deliberately slowed down.

"Come on, Father. Move!"

"Captain, I am old enough to be your father. Would you talk to him in that manner? And please, slow down."

Reinhardt stopped. An incredulous look crossed his face and then he laughed. "Come on, Father, Major Muller is waiting."

Reinhardt ushered Father Haralambos into Muller's office, where the major sat watching them.

"Ah, Father Haralambos."

"Good day to you, Major." Father Haralambos sat down, uninvited.

Muller frowned. "You're going on a trip," he stated, and signed some forms without looking up.

"I am? How lovely. To where?" Father Haralambos smiled.

"That doesn't concern you at the moment."

"I'm going on a trip and you won't tell me where? Ah, must be a German thing," Father Haralambos said as he folded his hands and rested them on his lap.

"Your lack of concern interests me. Why is that?" Muller tapped the pen on the desk and looked at the priest quizzically.

"Why am I not scared, or why am I looking forward to a trip when I don't know where I'm going to?"

"You are not amusing, Father."

"I'm not trying to be. I've lived a long life and I've seen a lot." Father Haralambos smiled.

Muller turned to Reinhardt. "Leave us," he said. Father Haralambos met Reinhardt's gaze for a moment before the younger man left the room.

The door closed behind the captain and Muller leaned back on his chair and looked at Father Haralambos. "What secrets do you hold?"

"I am the keeper of many secrets, most of them spiritual. I'm a simple priest."

"You're not the simple priest you want me to believe you are."

"You mean I'm not a priest? The Archbishop will be most surprised." Father Haralambos' eyes were still smiling, but Muller could sense a steely resolve. "It's a lovely dance we are dancing, Major, but I'm getting older, so why don't we say what we want to say?"

"Tell me, why does my daughter come to church so much?"

"Why do people come to church? Eva is a spiritual child."

"She is a perverted child," Muller mumbled. "I know what she has been doing."

"She has been cleansing her soul. The death of her mother caused her so much grief. I'm sure, as her father, you are aware of that. She has been in pain and she needs the solace of the Lord."

Muller watched Father Haralambos for a few moments. "What has my daughter told you about her mother's death?"

"A child is scarred from such an experience."

Muller was startled. Father Haralambos' eyes had turned cold and he could see hatred in them for a moment. Gone was the man of God and in his place he could see the hatred for him. The priest's blue eyes stared at him, and that unnerved him, more than he thought it would.

"Any child who loses a parent is devastated. Eva is no different. As I said, she has found solace in the Lord."

Muller decided to let the issue drop. He was rather unsettled by what had transpired. He fussed with some papers on his desk. "You will report to Captain Reinhardt for your train trip," he ordered, not looking at Father Haralambos.

"Ah yes, my little trip. Will I have time to let the good Sisters know I will be gone for a time?"

Muller nodded. "Tomorrow you will board the train," he said, refusing to meet the priest's eyes. "Leave," he directed, turning his chair around.

"Have a good day, Major."

Muller didn't answer as the door closed quietly. He felt that Father Haralambos had challenged him and somehow he had lost. He shook his head.

Father Haralambos was deep in thought as he made his way through the forest, the autumn chill creeping into his bones. He reached the end of the trail and settled down to gaze out across the northern horizon.

The forest that surrounded the area appeared to be succumbing to the weather — leaves were falling, leaving shriveled, bare branches to face the coming winter. He found a secluded area overlooking the northern mountains, and watched the clouds skimming across the mountain peaks, the mountains themselves looking gray and depleted. The river, a vital resource for the war-ravaged community, was a center of activity for the many local farmers, its crystal clear water and powerful currents bringing a sense of intensity and vigor to the atmosphere. The rich, opulent fields of wheat flourishing as the time for harvest neared gave an almost golden hue to the skyline. There was an eerie silence that forced his thoughts to focus on his imminent future.

He sat on the boulder and contemplated his life. He was fortunate, he thought, that he could take a moment to reflect on his life before he died. Others were not so lucky, as their lives were cut short by the violence of the war. He could find some time to organize his affairs and say goodbye to those he loved. *Maybe that's a curse and not a blessing.*

He had found his only child and now to see her being taken

away from him again hurt him a great deal. Eva was a spirited and deeply religious woman. He was proud of her. He didn't think he could ask for more in a child. He smiled. When he looked at her, he could see the love of his life, Daphne, reflected in her features.

He heard a rustling sound and he turned to see Zoe coming towards him. He smiled and she promptly sat beside him.

"I thought I would find you here," Zoe said, looking out over the valley. She had seen Father Haralambos leave Muller's residence. She had hoped to stop him before he left, but Despina held her back with some chores that needed doing, which took her some time.

"It's quiet here," Father Haralambos said, fingering the well-read Bible in his hands. They sat in silence, Zoe playing with a stick as she watched the clouds slowly pass.

"I'm going to miss you," she said quietly.

"I'm going to miss you too."

"Don't give God a hard time, okay? I know you want to organize everything." Zoe grinned.

Father Haralambos laughed. "I promise not to give God a hard time. I'll tell Him you told me to behave."

"I've already told Him," Zoe said shyly and looked away.

"Are you speaking to Him again?"

Zoe nodded and prodded some dead leaves with the stick. "I asked Him to take care of you and told Him that you are a bossy boots." She smiled at Father Haralambos, who was laughing. She hadn't seen him laugh so much in years. His whole face changed and it made him look younger.

"Can I ask you to do something for me?" Father Haralambos asked.

"Anything."

"I want you to be safe," Father Haralambos requested, as he hugged Zoe. He looked down to see tears running down her face. He kissed the top of her head and rubbed her back with his hand.

They sat like that for some time, each with their own thoughts, gazing out to the mountains. A memory surfaced as Father Haralambos smiled at the image of a very young Zoe putting her hand up eagerly to answer the question he had put to the class.

"Alright, children, what is the highest mountain in Larissa? Who can tell me?" Father Haralambos asked as he looked out at the sea of faces before him. The young children scrunched up their faces trying to think. He smiled as he watched them. A little hand shot up. Zoe's honey colored pigtails bobbed up and down as she tried to get his attention.

"Yes, Zoe?"

"Father, the highest mountain in Larissa is Mount Olympus!" She said with conviction and sat back down.

Father Haralambos. The children looked at Zoe and laughed. She was crestfallen and began to pout.

"Now, now children. Zoe is nearly right. Mount Olympus is the highest mountain in Greece and you can see it from here if you look hard enough. The highest mountain in Larissa is Mount Ossa."

"What's so funny?" Zoe asked.

"Ah, I was just remembering a very young girl and Mount Ossa," Father Haralambos said cryptically.

Zoe looked at the mountains and smiled. "Mount Olympus is the highest mountain in Greece."

She looked shyly at Father Haralambos. "Father, I have something to tell you."

"You do?"

"Yes," Zoe replied and looked away. Father Haralambos patiently waited while Zoe took her time. It wasn't usually this hard to get her to open up to him. "Zoe?"

"Remember when you said you wanted me and Eva to be friends?"

"Well." Father Haralambos smiled. "I did ask you first not to kill her."

Zoe smiled. "Well, after you told me not to kill her."

"Yes, I remember."

"I am her friend now."

Father Haralambos bowed his head and a smile creased his weathered face. He quietly said a quick prayer of thanks. He looked back up at Zoe, who was playing with a piece of twig wedged in the rock face. "Eva is a gentle soul, and I thank God that you are her friend. Then that's all I ever wanted."

"She loves you very much."

"I know."

They sat in silence for a moment. Father Haralambos picked up his Bible and turned to Zoe. "I want to read something to you." He opened his Bible and found the passage that he wanted to read to her. "When the time comes I want you to remember this."

Zoe nodded.

Father Haralambos began to read and his voice broke a little. "I am going to a better place, my child. I will not be alone. Whenever you are afraid I want you to remember what the

Psalmist wrote."

"The Lord is my shepherd; I shall not want. He maketh me to lie down in green pastures: he leadeth me beside the still waters. He restoreth my soul: he leadeth me in the paths of righteousness for his name's sake.

"Yea, though I walk through the valley of the shadow of death, I will fear no evil: for thou art with me; thy rod and thy staff they comfort me. Thou preparest a table before me in the presence of mine enemies: thou anointest my head with oil; my cup runneth over."

Father Haralambos stopped as Zoe sobbed beside him. He held her for a moment and then continued.

"Surely goodness and mercy shall follow me all the days of my life: and I will dwell in the house of the Lord forever." He finished and closed the Bible.

"I want you to have my Bible. Keep it with you and read it. I'm going to be keeping an eye on you." Father Haralambos handed her the black book, the corners upturned and well used.

Zoe took the Bible and held it close to her chest. She cradled it in her hands. "I love you," Zoe said and leaned against the priest.

"I love you too," Father Haralambos replied, holding Zoe in his arms. He was certain his prayers had been answered and that Zoe had come to realize that God was not to blame for the war or the terrible fate that had befallen the country. He was satisfied that his work was done. God had answered his prayers about his daughter and He answered them again about taking care of Eva.

care.

CHAPTER 33

"He shouldn't be too much longer."

Eva nodded and hoped Father Haralambos would arrive before she was going to be forced to go back to the house. A part of her wished she wouldn't have to face him and tell him of what had happened the previous evening. Just as she was losing hope of seeing him, his unmistakable figure walked in through the front door. She smiled but tempered her greeting because of the two guards that stood just inside the doorway of the church. They had instructions not to allow Eva to leave their sight. Eva wasn't sure if the extra measures had to do less with her security and more with Muller's wish to keep her in his invisible prison.

"Ah, Eva. Are you alright?" Father Haralambos asked as he took her hand.

"Yes." Eva turned to her guards. "You don't need to come with me."

"We have our—"

"I said you don't need to come with me. Confessions are supposed to be secret." She smiled when the guards nodded and went back to looking bored.

Father Haralambos ushered Eva into his office. "Sit, sit." He took off his black cleric's coat and hung it by the door. "How are you today?"

"Uh...we...I mean, I was late...um...getting up from sleep... and...uh," Eva stammered.

Father Haralambos turned to get a pitcher of lemonade. "You didn't sleep well?" He asked and offered her the drink. "Was your back giving you problems?"

Eva took the glass and gazed at it trying to decide if she should tell Father Haralambos about her broken promise to God and her love for Zoe. *He just came back into your life and now you've gone and thrown it away. Stupid, stupid, stupid.* She looked up to find Father Haralambos gazing at her with a puzzled look. "No... uh, my back is fine, well, as fine as it will ever be."

"I know you're angry and upset about this whole train business, but you seem flustered and not quite yourself." Father Haralambos sat down opposite Eva and took the drink from her hands and put it aside. "What is the matter?"

"No...I mean, yes...um," Eva stammered, thinking that she might as well dig a hole and bury herself in it. She hadn't thought it was going to be so hard to tell Father Haralambos. She had confided in him that she had been a lesbian. Eva wanted to laugh at the absurdity of telling her real father that she used to be a lesbian but wasn't anymore. Then she had watched the shock register on his face. She had quickly added that she was no longer a lesbian and she had been cured. Eva was certain that he would not understand the latest twist in her life. She knew she didn't understand how it had happened, how Zoe had breached her defenses, but she had, and there was nothing Eva could do about it.

"Do you want to talk about it?"

"Yes, to my priest first," Eva replied quietly.

"Alright, I'm your priest." Father Haralambos got up and went to the back of the door where he had hung his coat. Eva watched him wear the coat again and return to where she was sitting. "What's on your mind?"

Eva swallowed nervously. "Father, I've sinned against God."

"We all sin."

Eva took a deep breath and looked up at Father Haralambos with some trepidation. "You remember I told you about Aiden?"

"Yes, I remember."

"Um...I made a promise to God and I've broken that promise. I lied to God."

Father Haralambos took Eva's hands into his own and gently squeezed them. "You could never lie to God. He knows what's in your heart."

"Well, I was lying to Him."

"What did you say?"

Eva worried her lip as she struggled with the painful memories and the deep despair that had overpowered her. After several minutes of total silence in the room, she took a deep breath to steady her nerves. "I promised Him that I would never fall in love with anyone again. I promised Him that no matter what, I was no longer going to give in to my heart. All I asked was that He would save me."

Eva looked into Father Haralambos' eyes and saw the tears that formed in those deep blue eyes that mirrored her own. Her own tears made silent tracks down her cheeks, which she didn't bother to brush away. "I...uh," Eva stopped when she couldn't continue.

"Take your time," Father Haralambos told her, his voice breaking with emotion.

"I promised Him that I wouldn't let anyone control my heart, but I lost control of my heart."

"No one can control their heart. You are not perfect, nor am I. Our Lord knows this and forgives us. I know you are going to marry Captain Reinhardt—that's not a sin even if he is an unpleasant man. You can't control what your heart does."

"No." Eva shook her head. "Father, this was a promise..."

"How can you promise something to God that is out of your hands?"

"I thought it was in my power."

"You can't control your heart."

"My heart betrayed me."

"Yes, it can do that. Do you think God does not love you now that you have proven to be human?"

"I gave Him my word."

"He didn't want your word. He wants you to have faith. We all stumble, we fall, we realize we have made mistakes and we get up again."

"I have faith."

"I know you do." Father Haralambos took Eva's hand and kissed it. "You have a faith that is strong despite all the hardships you endured. Your faith is what kept you alive."

"I have to confess that my faith is warring with my heart."

"How so?"

"I've fallen in love," Eva replied and gazed at Father Haralambos for any sign of his disapproval.

"This isn't news, sweetheart. You and Captain Reinhardt are going to get married. Why are you so upset?"

"It's not Jurgen." Eva exhaled slowly.

"Oh," Father Haralambos softly exclaimed. "I see," he said and stroked his beard. "Well, that is a complication and I understand how you will be conflicted. Is there a way to break it off with this other fellow? It's not Henry, is it? I've seen the way he looks at you."

"Uh?"

Father Haralambos smiled. "That young man loves you, Eva."

"No, Father, it's not Henry." Eva shook her head and looked

down at the floor.

"Alright then. You gave your heart to this other fellow and you are also engaged to Reinhardt. It is quite a dilemma, but God will understand."

"Father, it's...I don't know how to tell you this."

"What's there to say? You have fallen in love with two men. It happens."

"It's not what you think." Eva took a deep breath and slowly released it. "It's Zoe," she said, and for a fleeting moment there was an eyebrow twitch and nothing else from the priest. Father Haralambos' expression remained neutral.

"I see," Father Haralambos finally said. "When I said you should become friends, I didn't mean that."

A slight smile played on Eva's lips despite her apprehension and anxiety over the confession. "I didn't want to."

"You didn't want to fall in love with Zoe?"

"No."

"But you did."

"Yes."

Father Haralambos stroked his graying long beard and gazed at Eva. "The medical treatment you received in Aiden didn't work."

"It did."

"Obviously not. Your heart desired what it needed the most."

"A death wish?"

Father Haralambos smiled. "No, not a death wish. I don't know a lot about your disease, Eva, but what I do know is that you can't control who you fall in love with. I fell in love with your mother and you were the beautiful gift from that. Yes, it was wrong and we sinned by not getting married first, but we can't control our hearts. You might as well petition God to stop the world from turning. Does Zoe know how you feel about her?"

Eva nodded. "She does."

"She told me you had become friends, and that's what I prayed would happen, but I didn't think you would..um..have those kinds of feelings for her."

"I didn't want to, Father, you have to believe me, I didn't want to." Eva reached out and took Father Haralambos' hand. "I tried not to think about her, but I couldn't help myself."

"Have you tried prayer?"

"Yes."

"Did you try to think of something else that will banish those desires from your mind? We can't always control our thoughts and God understands that."

Eva gazed at her father and sighed. "I tried thinking of other things. I tried to immerse myself in our work, I tried not to let my feelings for Zoe get in the way but…"

"It's very difficult with Zoe working so closely with you."

"Yes."

"Does Reinhardt know how you feel about Zoe?"

"God, no. I hope not. If he does, I'm quite sure I wouldn't be sitting here talking to you. I would be dead."

"I see. With our mission here at an end, I think it would be wise for Zoe to cease being your maid and for that temptation to be out of your reach," Father Haralambos exclaimed. "What you need to do is to remove the temptation."

Eva sat in silence with her head bowed. She didn't look up to meet her father's gaze. "It's too late for that."

"Oh."

Eva raised her head. "I kissed her."

"Oh. So Zoe now knows how you feel about her. That must have been a shock to young Zoe."

Despite the seriousness of the conversation, Eva couldn't help but smile. "No, it wasn't a shock to her. She kissed me back."

"Oh…I see. Hm. How did it happen?"

"I don't know. I was trying to resist my feelings towards her and I've been suffering for months. Trust me, this hasn't been easy for me."

"Is that why you have been ill?"

"Yes."

"You knew that by having these feelings for Zoe, you would be physically ill?"

Eva nodded. "I couldn't control my thoughts and last night I couldn't control my actions. I made a promise to God that I wouldn't love another woman and I would be what everyone wanted me to be. I can't do that even if it makes me ill."

"You were lying about falling in love with Reinhardt?"

Eva looked down at her engagement ring. "I was using him to survive. I know that was wrong but I thought that Jurgen would keep me alive."

"You didn't have feelings for Zoe when you agreed to marry him?"

"If you remember, Zoe wanted to kill me and the last thing I wanted to do was be anywhere near her."

"Yes, I remember." Father Haralambos put his arm around Eva's shoulders. "I'm sorry I put the two of you together and it has caused this to happen."

"Father, I am who I am and there was nothing you did that caused this. It was me."

"By confessing your feelings to me about Zoe, did you think I would love you less because you are different?"

"Yes," Eva answered truthfully.

"No, you're wrong. I will always love you. You are my daughter and nothing in this world will make me stop loving you. I am your father and a father never stops loving their child."

"Why?"

"Because that is what a father does. He loves his child more than life itself. God loves us as a father, and just because you think you broke a promise to Him and thought He would stop loving you, you're wrong. He knew it was a promise you couldn't keep."

"Am I going to Hell?"

"For what? Breaking a promise that you couldn't possibly be able to keep? You can't control your heart, Eva. I don't understand it but you are my daughter. That's all that matters. I also don't believe in Hell."

Eva's eyebrows rose at the declaration that came from the cleric. "The Church—"

"The Bible talks to me about a loving God. As a father I wouldn't want to hurt my child, now why would God want to hurt His children? He wouldn't. We won't tell the Archbishop that I don't believe in Hell. Nor are we going to tell him about your feelings for Zoe. Why don't I make us some tea and we can have a long chat about it?"

"Alright."

Father Haralambos nodded. He got up from his seat and left the office, leaving Eva to think about what had transpired. It wasn't what she had expected at all.

Father Haralambos closed the door and leaned against it for a moment. He crossed himself and brought the gold cross that hung around his neck to his lips and kissed it. Eva's revelation was something he wasn't expecting, nor was Eva's guilt. He sighed and quickly went into the tiny kitchen to make some tea. He leaned against the doorjamb and watched the water boil. *I did tell her to be friends but this isn't what I had in mind. Zoe and Eva? They couldn't be any more different if they tried. Zoe is a handful and*

Eva is so quiet. Dear Lord, what is to become of them when I'm gone? He took the pot and poured the tea into cups.

"Alright, let's have some tea," Father Haralambos said as he came back into his office to find Eva staring outside the window. "Eva?"

Eva turned around and rubbed her eyes before sitting down and taking the teacup. They drank in silence until Father Haralambos cleared his throat. "So, you love Zoe."

"Yes."

"Does she love you?"

"I don't know. She says she's in 'heavy like.'"

"Hmm, there is no hope for her."

"What do you think?"

"What do I think? I think you're going to be playing with fire."

"Pardon?"

"Zoe is a spirited young woman. She won't take no for an answer," Father Haralambos replied. "But she's also very loyal, loving, and will fight to the end for things she believes in."

"Are you shocked?" Eva tentatively asked.

"Am I shocked? Yes. That's the last thing I expected. I had hoped you two wouldn't kill each other. That's what I prayed wouldn't happen. You having that kind of feelings for Zoe wasn't what I was expecting," Father Haralambos replied, carefully watching for Eva's reaction.

Eva stared impassively at him, her slender fingers clasped and resting on her lap. "Yes, it was my hope that she wouldn't kill me either. I don't know how it happened but Zoe just..I don't know," she finally replied.

"As your father, I want to see you happy." Father Haralambos took Eva's hands and held them. "You and Zoe together is going to be a recipe for disaster. If you were ever found out..."

"I know. My stepfather will kill me."

"You have to end this. You have to stop. I don't want you

to suffer. We both know you will be tortured again. You have suffered enough. No more. You will get yourself and Zoe killed."

"I know, Father but—"

"Eva, my darling daughter, you can't have what your heart desires. You can't put Zoe through this either. Hasn't she suffered enough?"

Eve wiped the tears that ran down her cheeks with the back of her hand and sniffed. "I don't want to have these feelings for her, but I do. I want to be happy, I want to feel that someone loves me for who I am and not for who they want me to be."

"Even if that means that this love you have for Zoe will mean both your deaths?"

Eva turned away and looked out the window. "Yes."

"Is that what Zoe wants?"

"Zoe doesn't know what all of this means, she doesn't understand the consequences, but she has feelings for me."

"Hm." Father Haralambos put his arm around Eva's shoulders and brought her close. "I don't understand these feelings you have, Eva, but you are my daughter. I won't condemn you. I want you to be happy and at peace, even for a little while. If that means you are with Zoe, then you have my blessing. The Church says otherwise, but this time I will go with what my heart says."

"My head says to run away but my heart—"

"Listen to your heart." Father Haralambos finished her thought, placing his hand over his own heart. "I didn't listen to my heart and it meant twenty-four years of not knowing my child. I don't want you to regret not following your heart but if you do, it will have consequences; you will be found out. The truth always comes out. Are you prepared for when that happens?"

"I know what it means. Zoe doesn't, but I do."

"You should tell Zoe. Let her make the choice with all the

consequences that it will bring."

"Yes, Father," Eva whispered. "About that promise..."

"God understands. I told you He knew you couldn't keep that promise even if you thought you could."

"I don't know what to do."

"Yes, you do. You will follow your heart."

"Please, don't go."

"I have to, my child. I'm leaving tomorrow," Father Haralambos said quietly and brushed Eva's tears away with the end of his black robes.

"Maybe Thanasi can take you away."

"This is my cup, my child. I can't give it to someone else," Father Haralambos replied, knowing that no matter what he said, Eva would try and change his mind, just as Zoe had tried.

"Thanasi said they are going to blow up the train. I don't want to lose you."

"I don't want to lose you either, but my time has come. You have to be strong. You have to help Zoe as she will help you. You're not alone anymore," Father Haralambos said, trying to ease Eva's fears.

"Because I have Zoe, does that mean I have to let you go?" Eva asked, her voice breaking. "Can't I have you and Zoe in my life?"

"I can't let Major Muller know that I know what will happen to the train. He is not a stupid man. He is an evil man, but not stupid. He will make the connection. I don't want you to suffer again at his hands. Do you understand?"

"Maybe I can escape with you and then he won't be able to get his hands on either of us."

Father Haralambos sighed. "What of Zoe? Will you leave her behind?"

"No. But she—"

Father Haralambos stopped her with a finger against her lips. "My child, if I could do that, I would, but we can't all escape.

That would risk many lives. I have lived a long life, a very good life. I don't have a death wish, but Eva, my darling daughter, there is no other way. I won't sacrifice your life. You have lost too much already."

Eva sighed and sagged against him. Father Haralambos kissed her cheek tenderly. "I think you need to go to Zoe. She needs you now. You both need each other. She came to see me at Athena's Bluff. I'm sure she's still there."

Eva nodded, brushing away the tears.

"Tell her the consequences of both your actions, let her make that decision based on what is to come and trust in God," Father Haralambos said as he tenderly wiped away her tears with the handkerchief he had finally found when the sleeves of his robe had grown damp.

Eva swallowed the lump in her throat and she drank some of the now cold tea. "She is everything to me."

"I can see that. Be happy in the time you both have left. Will you do that for me?"

"Yes, Father," Eva said quietly as she held his hands.

"I want you to do something else for me," Father Haralambos continued. "If you are not found out and you survive this war, I want you to get out of Greece when the war ends. I want you and Zoe to leave. Thanasi tells me there is more bloodshed coming. He said Greece will be plunged into civil war and I don't want you two to be here. Just remember that I'll be with you in spirit. Zoe's asked me not to try and reorganize Heaven, so I will need something to occupy my time," he joked. "Take care of yourself and of Zoe," he added.

Eva nodded.

"Remember, my child, I will always love you. I thank God every day that He brought you to me." Father Haralambos brushed back the dark bangs from Eva's eyes. "Don't forget now. Remember to pray," he admonished and kissed her tenderly on the cheek.

CHAPTER 34

*E*va had an idea as she left the church. She wasn't going to give up trying to find a way to rescue Father Haralambos. She owed him that much. If she had learned anything from living in Larissa over the course of two years, it was the unyielding spirit of the Greeks against the occupation. They never gave up hope—they found ways to survive and to thwart the Germans.

She slowed as she came to the train station. It was tightly guarded on all sides. The soldiers were milling around and she wondered if they were from General Kiefer in Athens. The piteous cries coming from the boxcars broke her heart. She watched as the soldiers poured water onto the boxcars to quiet the yells and screams that were coming from inside. The weather had turned cold and it sickened her to think of the poor souls in the boxcars being drenched with the cold water. She shook her head and said a silent prayer. Turning away in disgust, she stumbled into Reinhardt, who caught her to keep her from falling.

"Ah, darling. Don't fall now. We wouldn't want that cold mud on you," Reinhardt said and grinned.

"Do they have to pour the water? It's freezing," Eva said as she tried to regain her balance.

"Yes." Reinhardt put his arm around Eva. "What are you doing here?"

"I was curious," Eva replied. She hadn't anticipated being stopped. There were some advantages to being the major's daughter. The soldiers knew her and didn't attempt to ask her questions. Except for Reinhardt.

"Curious?" Reinhardt repeated. "Would you like to see some of the scum that we took off the train?" he asked as he scrutinized Eva's face.

"No, that's fine. Nurse Klein has admonished me for not getting enough exercise." Eva made a face. "I think the woman wants me to walk around all day."

"Nurse Klein has a clean air and a clean mind approach." Reinhardt chuckled. "She was very annoyed with me for tiring you out."

Eva mentally rolled her eyes at Reinhardt's egotistical need to be told he was a good lover. As far as Eva was concerned it was far from the truth. She sighed internally and laughed at her fiancé's remarks.

"Don't be too long. I'll see you later," Reinhardt said as he watched Eva walk away.

Eva walked down the street towards Athena's Bluff. She was distracted by her thoughts of the poor Jews, Father Haralambos, and Zoe. She was unaware of her surroundings, unaware of the children playing in the street or the dog that barked at her passing. Henry and Barkow were right behind her but they might as well have been invisible.

Finally reaching the bluff, she saw Zoe sitting on the lookout, sketching. Eva smiled and took a moment to drink in the sight of this lovely young woman who filled her heart with hope and joy. She shook her head as a throbbing behind her eyes signaled the arrival of yet another migraine. With a deep sigh, she tried not to think about Zoe, but it was becoming increasingly difficult not to.

Zoe turned around and smiled when she saw Eva. She got up and walked the short distance to where Eva was standing. "Hi. You look exhausted," Zoe said. "Let's go inside the cabin."

"What's wrong with out here? I love the view."

"Well," Zoe leaned in and whispered. "You have a headache. I can see it, so I would rather you not fall down that cliff. You're taller and heavier than me."

"I'm not heavy."

"Evy, you're much taller and heavier and I can't catch you if you get dizzy. So my plan," Zoe lowered her voice, "is to get inside the cabin and do a bit of kissing. I have the bucket ready as well."

Eva couldn't help laughing as she was led inside the cabin and the door was shut. She looked around in amazement. The flokati rug had taken center stage in the middle of the room and pillows were strewn around on an old sofa. It was rather inviting.

"It looks lovely," Eva said quietly and gazed down at the rug. "I think things are going too fast for me."

"You're not regretting—"

"Oh, no, Zoe." Eva realized she had inadvertently given Zoe the wrong impression and it had frightened the younger woman. A part of her was more than a little pleased that Zoe didn't want to let her go.

Zoe leaned against the wall and regarded Eva for a long moment. "This is difficult, not being able to touch you."

Eva met Zoe's gaze and held it for a long moment. Without a word she closed the gap between them. She cupped Zoe's face and brought her lips down for a passionate kiss. She moved her kisses across Zoe's jaw and down her neck as Zoe slipped one hand into Eva's dark locks to hold her closer. They parted and smiled at each other. Eva grimaced as her head started to ache. She tried to ignore it but her knees started to tremble.

"Oh boy!" Zoe said breathlessly as they parted. "That was even better than the first time." Zoe looked at Eva. "You're getting another migraine."

"I'm ignoring it," Eva replied as she looked around and found the chair nearby. She sat down heavily and cradled her head in her hands.

"Do you have your medication with you?"

"Uh huh."

"Take it."

"No." Eva shook her head. "I want to just learn to live with it. I'm not giving you up because of a little headache."

"It's not a little anything, Evy—"

"No, I'm not taking those pills. They make me feel fuzzy and right now I can't afford to feel fuzzy."

"I can't let you do this to yourself." Zoe knelt beside the chair. "I won't be the cause of your pain. When this stupid war ends, we will find someone who can undo the damage those bastards did to you."

"I don't think it can be undone," Eva mumbled. She let her head rest against the chair's hard wooden headrest.

"I don't believe that. If they can do it, they can undo it. There has to be a doctor who can undo this."

Eva gazed at Zoe and a smile slowly surfaced. "There isn't anyone to help me."

"Why does the idea of someone helping you to overcome this scare you so much?"

Eva stared at Zoe for a long moment. "I'm scared of what they will do to get rid of this." Eva tapped herself on the side of the head.

"Why don't we wait to find out what it is before you

dismiss it?"

"I don't know—"

"You are stubborn."

Eva laughed at the absurdity of the conversation. "I'm not in your league when it comes to stubbornness, Miss Zoe Lambros."

"Is that right?" Zoe grinned, leaned over, and blew Eva a kiss. "A kiss that doesn't touch you doesn't hurt, does it?"

Eva was going to say no but stopped. "It's not just the kissing, Zo."

"What is it?'

"I'm physically attracted to you. I'm fighting myself over this. My heart is betraying me and this damaged head of mine follows."

"Oh," Zoe exclaimed softly and sat down on the floor. "How long have you been attracted to me?"

"I don't know when it happened. It just did and I couldn't stop it."

"That's amazing. All those fancy doctors with their fancy ideas of how to change who you are, and they thought they did, but they couldn't change you," Zoe replied as her gaze never left Eva. "Despite everything they did to you, you are true to who you really are."

Zoe got up off the floor and knelt beside Eva's chair again. "Who you are can never be corrupted."

"Who I am is the reason I can't kiss you without falling over in a heap."

"We will find a way to fix it. I know we will."

"This can't be fixed," Eva said quietly. "I don't want to lose you but—"

"This can be fixed; it will be fixed."

"I will believe because you believe it," Eva replied with a smile. "I saw Father today. I told him the truth about us."

"You spoke with Father H?"

"It's alright, Zoe. He understands even though he doesn't."

"Did you tell him we are more than friends?"

"Yes, I told him that I love you."

"Oh, boy. I bet that was a surprise to him."

"Yes, he was surprised. He was hoping we weren't going to kill each other."

Zoe smiled. "I was hoping I would."

"I know." Eva leaned forward and cradled her aching head in her hands. "I hoped you would end this too."

"I'm glad I didn't," Zoe said quietly and touched Eva's leg. "We will find a way to make you better."

"Zoe—"

"Don't give up hope. You survived hell and you are giving up now?"

Eva looked down at Zoe and marveled at her unbelievable strength. "If you have hope, then I have hope. I said to Father I broke a promise to God."

"What promise?"

Eva looked up at the ceiling for a long moment. If she was going to trust Zoe with her heart, she had the right to know. "I promised God that I wouldn't fall in love with another woman."

"That's just plain silly," Zoe exclaimed.

"Why?"

"Well, because it is. I can promise God that I wouldn't draw again but He gave me that gift, so how can I promise not to use it? I can't. It's a part of who I am."

Eva wasn't quite sure if Zoe truly understood. "Zoe, loving to draw is different from being a lesbian."

"I know that, but can you control your heart?"

Eva shook her head. It was plainly obvious that she couldn't. "No."

"What makes you think you can promise God something you

have no control over?"

"So you think that God made me a lesbian?" Eva asked a little incredulously.

"Did you make yourself love women instead of men?"

"I don't know. I never thought about it."

"Exactly. Now why did you promise Him that?"

"I was in a very dark place, and I just wanted…" Eva didn't want to tell Zoe about that particular memory. It was too raw and too personal. "Can we not talk about this now?"

"Maybe one day you will tell me, but until you're ready, I'll wait. Now did Father H give his approval?"

"Well, he wasn't doing handstands in his office, but he wanted us to be happy for the little time we have left."

"What little time? I plan on surviving this war and taking you with me to see what's beyond Mount Ossa." Zoe placed her hand on Eva's leg. "We will survive this. I know we will. We will find a cure for what they have done to you."

"If we are found out…"

"They won't find out, and if they do, we can escape into the mountains."

Eva gazed down and smiled. "Run away with you into the mountains."

"Yes. We will survive this war, Evy. If only Father H could be with us. There must be something we can do. What if we sabotage the train before it leaves?" Zoe asked.

"It will only postpone the inevitable," Eva responded dejectedly.

"What if Ares can get Father H out of the train?" Zoe tried again.

"I've seen the train, Zoe. It's guarded by so many soldiers no one can get close without being stopped. There are four boxcars," Eva replied, unable to dispel the image of the soldiers pouring the water into the boxcar and the screams that she had heard.

"What's in the boxcars?" Zoe asked, gazing up at Eva. She frowned when a tear rolled down Eva's face. "What's the matter?" She asked and brushed away the tear with her fingers.

"They...they hold Jews. I could hear their screams. The soldiers were pouring water into the cars to quiet them down," Eva whispered. She rubbed at her eyes.

Zoe closed her eyes and sighed.

"When this war ends, I want us to leave together, get out of here," Zoe pleaded. "We can go to Germany so you can see your grandmother."

"There's nothing there for me."

"Why don't you want to go back?"

"My grandmother disowned me. I don't want to go back. Do you still want to go to Australia?"

"Yes, but only if you are with me. It would be a very lonely journey without you."

"It's a long journey by ship. Have you ever been on a ship?"

"No, but it's going to be fun."

"I told you, Zo, I will go anywhere you want to go. I will follow anywhere you go," Eva whispered as Zoe rose and kissed her lightly despite the searing pain in her head.

CHAPTER 35

*F*ather Haralambos sat on his bed, the early morning sun shining through the threadbare curtains. His suitcase stood in the corner and he frowned. Yesterday, Sister Maria brought him a woolen scarf she had made, saying that he would need it since she had heard that the weather in Thessaloniki had turned cold. He had tried to decline, but the good Sister was quite stubborn — more so than his own stubborn tendencies — so he relented. He was again surprised when Sister Gregoria gave him a woolen jacket stating the same concern. He had spent the rest of the day writing letters to the Archbishop and getting the church ready for the Sunday sermon, which was to be delivered by the organist, since he wasn't supposed to be back in time. In fact, he knew well that he would never be back.

He was brought back from the goings on of the previous day by a knock on the door. Father Haralambos frowned and took out his pocket watch. It was only 7:00 a.m. — too early for his call to go to the train. He opened the door. Thanasi stood there thumping his feet on the ground because of the cold. Father

Haralambos ushered him inside. "What are you doing here?" He asked as Thanasi removed his scarf and coat.

"I know I said goodbye last night, but I had to see you one more time," Thanasi said.

"I thought we already had this discussion yesterday?" Father Haralambos went to the teapot to brew some tea.

"Father, please, I beg you, please, reconsider," Thanasi pleaded.

Father Haralambos sighed and turned to Thanasi. "Don't you know how much I would dearly love to stay? Do you think I haven't thought about escaping? Don't make it more difficult for me. Today I know maybe one tenth of what Jesus must have felt like in the Garden of Gethsemane. Don't you know that I would dearly love to hand this bitter cup to someone else?" He turned away from Thanasi and hurriedly brushed away the tears.

Thanasi watched as Father Haralambos poured him a cup of tea and then sat down. "I'm sorry," he apologized quietly.

"I know, my son, I know. I want you to promise me something."

"Anything," Thanasi knelt near Father Haralambos.

"I want you to promise me you will keep an eye on Zoe and Eva. Watch over them. They are going to need your help. When the war ends, I want you to take them out of the country. I don't want them to be here when the civil war starts. Can you do that for me?"

"I promise."

"Good boy. I know you don't believe in God anymore, but for a tiny moment I want you to believe. Believe in Him." Thanasi put his head on Father Haralambos' lap and began to cry. Father Haralambos held Thanasi and patted his head. "Now, now...come on, have courage." He lifted Thanasi's face and brushed away the tears with his hand.

"I love you, Father."

"I love you too, my boy. Now go and make me proud." Father Haralambos kissed Thanasi on the top of his head. He watched as he put his jacket back on and then his scarf.

Thanasi brushed away the tears and went to the door. "You are my hero," he admitted proudly, and then walked out the door and down the alleyway.

Father Haralambos watched the door close and smiled. "His hero," he repeated and shook his head. He finished his tea and cleaned the kitchen. He looked at his timepiece again. "Well, it's time I made my way to the train station."

He stopped in front of the crucifix and crossed himself. "Dear Lord, You know what is to come. Use me as You see fit in the time I have left." He kissed the icon and picked up his suitcase. "I hope Saint Peter doesn't keep me waiting at the Pearly Gates. I hate waiting," he said as he left the house.

Father Haralambos glanced up at the sky, which was cloud free, and shook his head. He shuffled along and rounded the corner of the church, stopping for a moment to watch the routine activity around him. Dimitri, the baker, was starting his day; he saw the priest and bade him a good morning. Father Haralambos raised his hand and waved back. He had watched this town's residents grow up and get married, had baptized their young and watched their young repeat the cycle. He wondered if life ever truly stopped. Probably not, he thought, and started walking again.

"Ah, Father Haralambos. Beautiful day, isn't it?"

Father Haralambos turned around and saw Captain Reinhardt. "Good day to you, Captain. Yes, it's a beautiful day," he replied and began walking.

"Are you looking forward to your trip?" Reinhardt inquired, easily keeping pace with Father Haralambos.

"Quite. I hear Thessaloniki is cold at the moment. Beautiful city. I'm looking forward to seeing Father Makarios when I get there."

Father Haralambos continued to walk towards the station while Reinhardt veered the other way. He shook his head. He glanced up at Muller's residence and spotted Eva at the window. Beside her was Zoe, who looked as though she had slept in her clothes. He smiled up at them and waved.

Eva blew him a kiss and mouthed, "I love you."

Father Haralambos nodded and walked away. He didn't want to turn back and have another look. He would lose his composure if he did. He finally arrived at the train station, where soldiers were milling about.

"Halt. This area is restricted," a young German soldier said in broken Greek.

"I am to board the train." Father Haralambos handed his papers to the soldier.

The soldier looked at the papers and after a moment he waved the priest through.

Father Haralambos stood on the platform as the chaos swirled around him. He sniffed the air and grimaced. The smell of decay was all around the train. Before he could discover the source, the door opened on one of the boxcars and a body was thrown out. The soldiers held their noses while their comrades dragged the man from the platform and threw him into the ditch near the tracks. The body rolled down the embankment and landed with a thud at the bottom.

Father Haralambos bowed his head and said a silent prayer. He looked up and met the eyes of the soldier who had pushed the man into the ditch. "Forgive them, Father," he prayed quietly.

"You!" the soldier said. "There is a space here." He pointed to the boxcar. Father Haralambos picked up his suitcase and walked to the car.

"Maybe you can convert these animals before they meet Jesus." The soldier sneered. His comrades laughed.

"I'm sure Jesus will be most happy to meet them. I'm not so sure what He will say about you," Father Haralambos said as he walked into the car, leaving the soldier slack-jawed.

The stench hit him as he stepped into the crowded car. He inhaled sharply. The occupants looked at him wearily and bowed their heads again. Their pain was too overpowering to be worrying why a Greek Orthodox priest was in the car with them. Father Haralambos found a small spot near the rear of the car, put his suitcase down and sat on it. He mentally kicked himself for not bringing food with him.

Father Haralambos bowed his head and prayed. When he looked up, he saw a young child looking at him. The little girl smiled at him. Her big brown eyes were red from crying and tears stained her grubby cheeks, her dark hair was matted, and her clothes were dirty. He tried to see if her parents were with her, but no one was paying any attention to the young girl. He smiled at her and waved her over. "What is your name?"

"Rebecca Stavrithis. What's yours?" Rebecca asked, looking at Father Haralambos' long white beard and black robe. His gold crucifix stood starkly against the black of his robe.

"Panayiotis Haralambos. Are you here alone?"

"My daddy was here, but they..." Rebecca started crying.

Father Haralambos held Rebecca while she sobbed. "Do you want me to tell you a story?" He offered as he wiped away the tears.

Rebecca hiccupped, nodded, and rubbed her eyes.

"Okay, do you know the story of the donkey that talked?" Rebecca shook her head and Father Haralambos began his tale as the train started to move.

CHAPTER 36

*P*rivate Kurt Barkow stood outside Major Muller's office, where he had been waiting for his commanding officer for the last hour. Muller had entered and then left without giving the soldier as much as a glance. Barkow wasn't sure whether to leave or stay.

"Private, why are you loitering out here?"

Barkow snapped to attention on seeing Captain Reinhardt.

"I'm here to see Major Muller."

"He's busy."

"It's important, sir."

Reinhardt waved Barkow inside the office and shut the door. He took a seat behind Muller's desk.

"Yes?"

Barkow shuffled his feet and looked pained as he stood in front of Reinhardt. "Sir, Major Muller assigned me to guard Fraulein Muller."

"Yes, I am aware of that." Reinhardt leaned back on his chair and regarded Barkow. "You have been doing a great job."

"Yes, sir, thank you."

"So other than getting praise for doing your job, what did you want?"

"Major Muller asked me to also report to him if I saw anything out of the ordinary."

Reinhardt leaned forward, his arms resting on the desk, and waited for Barkow to continue. "Yes?"

"Y—yes sir, um—"

"What is it, Private?"

"It's about Fraulein Muller, sir. I don't know how to tell you this."

"Start with the first word," Reinhardt suggested, quickly losing his temper. "Out with it before the war ends."

"I saw Fraulein Muller and Fraulein Lambros holding hands…"

Reinhardt leaned back in his chair and chuckled. "Have you been around women, Private?"

"Yes, sir, but--"

"They often hold hands and talk about nonsense things. Zoe is Eva's maid."

"They were also kissing, sir."

Reinhardt's smile disappeared. He got up from his seat and walked around the desk to stand in front of Barkow and glared down at him. "Choose your words carefully. Did you see Fraulein Muller kissing Fraulein Lambros?"

"Yes, sir."

"How?"

Barkow was puzzled by the question and stared at Reinhardt. "I don't understand the question, sir. They were kissing."

"Chaste kiss on the cheek?"

"No, sir."

"Who else saw this? Did Franz see it?"

"No, sir, Sgt. Franz went to relieve himself and didn't see anything. I didn't mention it to him because it was getting dark."

"When did this occur?"

"Yesterday, up on Athena's Bluff, sir."

Reinhardt sat on the edge of the desk and sighed. "Alright, leave it with me."

"Yes, sir." Barkow saluted and left the office closing the door behind him.

Reinhardt grimaced and shook his head. "Eva, Eva, Eva, you are still a pervert," he whispered. Muller had been right to order him to watch Eva.

His orders were clear—keep an eye on Eva and report back to her father. It wasn't a difficult job, since he enlisted the aid of her guards at various times.

"I wonder how you seduced that child," Reinhardt muttered and tried to work out what was the right time to tell Muller. There wasn't any right time, especially now that they were falling back, but it had to be done.

"What?" Muller lowered the telephone handset and just stared at it, unbelieving. Propaganda, it had to be. Propaganda made up by the Resistance. Athens couldn't fall that quickly. While it was true that the majority of the troops had left with the train bound for Thessaloniki, the troops that remained were hardened soldiers.

Muller moved his attention back to the phone and he raised the handset to his ear. "What about General Kiefer?" He asked, running his other hand through his hair and holding the back of his head. "Are you sure? Yes. ... Yes, fine. ... I'll see what I can do here." He hung up the phone and fell into his chair, pinching the bridge of his nose between a thumb and forefinger as he loudly blew out a breath.

There was a knock on the door and, after a pause, Reinhardt walked in, moving to the front of Muller's desk and patiently standing at attention for several moments.

"Athens has fallen," Muller stated, not looking up.

Reinhardt sighed. "What about General Kiefer?" He asked.

"He's dead."

The phone's shrill tone startled them both. Muller picked it up. "Yes?"

Reinhardt watched Muller's face turn a pasty white as he slumped further into his chair.

"When?" Muller asked as he glanced at Reinhardt. "Yes, General. Heil Hitler." He replaced the phone on the hook. "What else could go wrong today?"

"What happened, sir?"

"The troop train going to Thessaloniki was bombed an hour ago by the Resistance. The train fell down the gorge. The track is useless."

"What are you going to do?"

"We are pulling out. General Rhimes has ordered us to withdraw to Thessaloniki. Well, we can't catch a train on those tracks. The bridge and line have been totally destroyed. The only way out is by truck. See to it," Muller said dismissively and turned to start collecting paperwork.

Reinhardt remained still, a look of total indecision on his face. Muller frowned as he noted Reinhardt hadn't left to start carrying out his orders.

"Is there anything else, Captain?"

"Uh..."

Muller looked up sharply at the sound. "Out with it, man, I don't have all day!"

"It's about Eva, sir."

"What about Eva? Is it so important that you have to tell

me now?"

"Yes, sir. We have a problem."

"One of many, Captain," Muller growled, now annoyed with him. "Out with it, man! What problem do you have with Eva?"

"Her guard, Private Barkow, came to me earlier and told me that he had witnessed Eva kissing Fraulein Lambros."

Muller's blue eyes turned to ice. His face had turned a bright shade of red as he sat at his desk, his fists balling up in fierce anger. A problem with Eva, especially this problem, was the last thing Muller had wanted to hear about in the middle of this crisis. "I thought you told me differently in your last report?" He asked dangerously.

"Yes, sir, but I believed her. She wasn't faking anything with me."

"She obviously is a very good actress if she could fool you. What did Barkow say?"

"He saw them kissing, sir. It's not Zoe's fault, sir. I don't believe it is—I believe Eva has corrupted her."

"Mein Gott," Muller whispered, sitting back in his chair. With all that was happening, he wasn't ready to deal with Eva's betrayal again. But he knew he had to deal with it now, decisively and with no remorse. He sat back up and trained dangerous eyes on Reinhardt. "How long has this been going on? Under my very nose? In my house?" His voice rose and he thumped his desk.

Reinhardt jumped. "I-I don't believe, it's been—"

"I don't care what you believe!" Muller screamed. "I gave you an assignment to watch her, and you are engaged to her. How did you not know?" He looked daggers at Reinhardt. "I have no daughter from this moment on." His calm voice belied his rage. "I will get someone else to start the redeployment. Your assignment now is Eva. Take care of it." Muller stared at Reinhardt. He had warned Eva, had told her in no uncertain terms that if she relapsed, he would kill her.

Her betrayal of him now, when he was in such a vulnerable position, was inexcusable and Reinhardt's ineptitude compounded the problem.

Reinhardt, still standing at attention in front of his desk, was looking nervous and uncomfortable. As well he should, Muller thought. His anger flared again and he narrowed his eyes at Reinhardt. "I will deal with you after you have fixed this problem. Your incompetence astounds me, Reinhardt. Now get out of my sight!"

"How... I mean the problem, how should I handle it, sir?"

Muller cursed. "Do I have to tell you everything? How did you become a captain? Did your father buy you this commission? Kill her. She is no longer my daughter. Get the hell out of my office and go and deal with it! Now get out!"

CHAPTER 37

"Athens is free!" Apostolos declared and raised his arm in salute at the other Resistance members. They cheered loudly and began to sing "Ymnos eis tin Eleftherian," The Hymn to Freedom. Their voices harmonized even as they laughed. Finally, their dreams of a free Greece were going to be realized and the war would soon end.

Apostolos saw Zoe standing out near the edge of the group. He frowned for a moment and left the circle of celebrating men. Walking over to Zoe, he gently took her arm and silently guided her over to one side. "We got word that the line was destroyed about an hour ago."

Zoe lowered her head and Apostolos held her for a few moments. "Did anyone...?" She asked softly against Apostolos' shoulder.

"No. No survivors. The train went down the gorge," Apostolos replied, not bothering to tell Zoe that the soldiers that survived the wreck were shot dead by the Resistance. Some things were best left unsaid.

They stood there, amidst the celebrations, each feeling their own grief at losing a beloved friend. "Alright, we've been told the British are on the move. I'm not sure when they will get here, but I think it's our duty to help our German friends out the door."

Dimitri, the Thessalian Resistance leader, trying to get Thanasi's attention, yelled to be heard above the din of the celebrations.

He came over to where Thanasi, Apostolos, and Zoe were now standing, a little apart from the others. He clasped Thanasi on the shoulder and grinned. His smile turned to a scowl when he saw their faces. "What's the matter?"

"The train was blown," Zoe said quietly.

"Oh." Dimitri looked down and sighed. He had forgotten about the train amidst the good news from Athens. They had lost another hundred and one people from the village. We will mourn when the war ends, he thought. They still needed to focus on killing as many Germans as they could. He turned to Thanasi. "Leftheri has gone to Muller's place. As soon as the bomb is detonated we can begin—"

"What bomb?" Zoe interrupted Dimitri, her eyes wide with alarm.

"The one that will blow Muller straight to Hell," Dimitri replied.

"No, wait!" Zoe cried out. "Eva is in that house!"

"So?" Dimitri asked and shrugged.

"But you can't kill her!"

"She's a German. Or are you going soft on them?"

"Shut up, you idiot!" She yelled right in Dimitri's face. "You don't understand. Eva and Father Haralambos were working together!" Grabbing his arm, she pleaded with him, "When is Leftheri going to detonate the bomb?"

Dimitri checked his watch. "In ten minutes. You'd better run. You don't have much time to get her out."

"I have to stop him!" Zoe cried, running away from the

gathering and down the nearest alleyway.

Zoe's heart was beating so hard it felt as though it would explode from her chest. As she ran, her thoughts were only on Eva and reaching the house in time. Her awareness returned just in time to see the slow moving horse and cart ahead of her. It stopped, blocking the exit from the alley. Running up to the cart, she saw that its load had shifted and fallen to one side, the contents of the wheat-filled bags spilling on the ground all around the cart. There wasn't enough space to squeeze around the sides and the spilled bags blocked the route underneath. She was trapped in the godforsaken alley while precious seconds ticked away against Eva's life. Meanwhile, the old man driving the cart still hadn't moved from his seat. He was sitting halfway turned, forlornly gazing at his spilled cargo.

"Come on!" Zoe yelled. "Move!"

"What's your hurry, little Zoe? Is the devil after you? You young people have no patience," the old man grumbled, as he slowly climbed down to the cobble-stoned surface, limping around to take hold of the horse's lead and trying to coax it to move.

"Damn it, Pappou!" Zoe cursed and scrambled up the piles of wheat, slipping several times before she made it to the cart and climbed over it. Jumping off the seat to the ground, she tripped as she landed awkwardly on her ankle. She got to her feet and began to run, despite the pain shooting up her leg with every step. She had to get to Eva in time, before Leftheri blew up the house.

Reinhardt was shaken and angry. He closed the door to Muller's office and stood there for a moment trying to get his control back. The guards looked at him but didn't say a word. They had heard the yelling coming from Muller's office and were quite content to be outside rather than in there with their commanding officer.

Reinhardt straightened his uniform and checked his gun. With a scowl, he turned and stomped up the steps to Eva's rooms.

Eva stood at the window watching the trucks being loaded. The door opened and Reinhardt entered. He had composed himself and was smiling.

"Jurgen, what are the men doing?"

Reinhardt came to stand behind Eva and looked out at the soldiers loading the trucks. "Packing up; we are moving out," he said and put his arms around Eva's waist. "Athens has fallen.."

Eva turned in his embrace with a smile on her face. "You mean we are to leave this hell-hole?"

"Yes." Reinhardt nodded. "Does that please you?"

"Yes. Where are we going?"

"Thessaloniki We will try and stop the British there with General Rhimes."

Eva nodded and turned back to the men below. Reinhardt watched the back of Eva's head for a moment. "Where is Zoe?"

"She went to get my two dresses from the dressmaker. When are we leaving?"

"You will be leaving sooner than everyone else," Reinhardt replied cryptically, which made Eva turn around to face him.

Reinhardt sat at the end of the sofa with all the control he could muster and regarded his fiancée. "I know what you have done."

"What do you mean?"

"You had me fooled, Fraulein, you are a very good actress." Reinhardt slow clapped his fiancée. "You fooled Nurse Edith, you fooled Dr. Baer, and you fooled me. You never fooled your father."

Eva shook her head and smiled. "You really think I would be with a child like Zoe?"

"Who said anything about Zoe?" Reinhardt rose and came towards Eva, who took several steps back. "I didn't mention Zoe."

"You've been lied to."

"Really?" Reinhardt stopped and regarded Eva. "What lie is that? The lie that you loved me? The lie that you wanted to marry me? Have I been lied to? Yes." Reinhardt spat out and grabbed the front of Eva's shirt, "Which lie?"

"I—"

"Shut the fuck up," he yelled and backhanded Eva, who lost her footing and fell to the floor. "You are a deviant and a lying bitch."

Eva looked up in shock with a hand to her cheek where she'd been struck.

Reinhardt snarled, "Get up! You're going to write a note to your whore. You will tell her you need to meet her at Athena's Bluff, at the cabin." He was yelling the orders at Eva as he grabbed her arm painfully and yanked her to her feet.

Eva stood unsteadily, still reeling with shock, before being jerked toward her desk by the hand still tightly gripping her arm. She was shoved into her chair and a gun was waved in her face. "I said, do it!" Reinhardt screamed at her.

Her hands shaking, Eva picked up her pen and began to write the note. When she finished, Reinhardt grabbed it and folded it in half, setting it before her again. "Write 'Zoe' on it in big letters!" He demanded and then he set it on the front of her desk, prominently displaying the name to get Zoe's attention.

"Get up. You give me any trouble now and I swear, I will have that whore of yours begging me to kill her. Now move!" Reinhardt took Eva by the arm again and half dragged her downstairs. He poked his head into the kitchen where Despina was cooking.

"Despina! Fraulein Muller and I will be at Athena's Bluff. Make sure Zoe knows where we are and tell her to meet us there," he instructed and then left without waiting for a response.

Despina frowned. "That man has the manners of a pig," she spat out. A few minutes later, the kitchen door opened and a curly-topped young man entered. "Leftheri, what are you doing here?"

"Kiria Despina, I have to get you out of here!" Leftheri said and took the older woman by the arm, turning to drag her out of the house. Despina stood her ground and he fell backwards to land with a thump on the kitchen floor.

"What is going on here?"

Leftheri sighed and got up from the floor. "Look, the house is going to get bombed! Now please, can we get the hell out of here?"

"Well, why didn't you just say so?" Despina groused. She took off her apron and followed Leftheri out of the door.

They walked outside, calmly crossing the street and heading down the sidewalk toward the alleyway. It appeared they were just out for a stroll, the young man politely assisting the old woman.

The guards watched them and one of them recognized Despina. He shrugged and shifted his attention elsewhere, unconcerned. After a moment longer, the other guard did the same. Despina and Leftheri had just managed to turn the corner into the alley when the building exploded, sending debris flying everywhere causing the building to catch on fire.

Leftheri peeked around the side of the wall and grinned. "Boom, boom!" He said. He and Despina watched, staying hidden in the shadows, as the remaining soldiers ran to the burning building to try and put the fire out and look for survivors.

They never got the chance.

As the soldiers reached the front of the burning building and waited for orders, the remaining Resistance fighters began their assault from hidden positions. A gun battle quickly ensued, but the German soldiers rapidly found themselves on the losing end, many of them having foolishly left their weapons behind in the panic that immediately followed the explosion.

Leftheri, watching the battle, felt his shirt being tugged and Despina urgently calling his name. He looked at her to see her pointing in the other direction and crying, "Look! Isn't that Zoe?"

Looking down the street in the direction she was indicating, he saw a figure running awkwardly toward them. After a second, he recognized the figure as Zoe, a pained and panicked expression on her face.

"Zoe!" Leftheri yelled to get her attention, without any effect. Before Zoe reached the alley, Leftheri jumped out in front of her. He couldn't let her run right into a raging gun battle.

When Zoe still appeared to ignore him and tried to hobble past, Leftheri quickly grabbed her around the waist and carried the struggling woman into the alley.

"Eva!" Zoe screamed, seeing the remains of the building, and realizing she had been too late to save her lover.

Zoe fought against Leftheri's hold and he gripped her even tighter, enduring her blows and kicks. As she tried to twist and squirm away, he finally lost his balance, collapsing against the alley wall, still desperately hanging on to the screaming and sobbing Zoe. They slid down into a heap, Leftheri finally able to wrap his legs around hers and grab her wrists to hold her still.

Zoe was reduced to an inconsolable sobbing mass. The long run and then the struggles to get free had sapped her remaining strength. "Eva...oh, Eva..." She was half sobbing, half wailing the name.

Despina waited as Leftheri finally got the distraught woman under control and was instantly at Zoe's side, holding her and stroking her hair, trying to help Leftheri calm her feeble hysterics. "Shhh...there, there, little one." She gently tilted Zoe's face, wet with tears, so she could look at her. "You could have been hurt if Leftheri hadn't stopped you! Didn't you see the soldiers and hear the guns?" She asked, concerned.

"B-but the building...Eva...oh God...I tried to get to her!" Zoe stumbled over the words in between sobs.

"Eva wasn't there, sweet child," Despina said with a soft smile as she started drying Zoe's face with a small kerchief. "She wasn't in the building. She left a short time earlier with Captain Reinhardt." She gave Zoe a small kiss on her forehead, seeing her calming at her words.

Leftheri finally released Zoe and helped her to her feet, noticing that she was favoring one leg a bit. He helped brush her off, and then brushed off his own clothes as Zoe and Despina hugged each other.

"But," Zoe was saying, "she really wasn't there? You saw her leave?"

Despina nodded. "Eva has gone to Athena's Bluff. She and Captain Reinhardt said you were to meet them there."

Zoe looked at Despina and frowned. "Why would Eva go

with Reinhardt? Unless..." The blood drained from her face as she realized that Muller must have found out about her and Eva. "Oh, dear God!" She turned to Leftheri and grabbed his arms. "Can you run and get Thanasi? Tell him Eva is in danger and Reinhardt has her. We have to save her. Tell him to meet me at Thieri's cabin. You show him the way!"

Leftheri looked at her, confused. Zoe shook him gently, her eyes pleading with him. "Leftheri, please? Please, don't let her die! Eva has been working with the Resistance! You must find Thanasi, quickly!" She released him when he nodded at her, then started painfully running towards the bluff as Leftheri went to find the Resistance leader.

No soon had Zoe dispatched Leftheri, Henry came around the corner and collided with her. He barely had time to grab hold of her before she fell over.

"Henry! Eva is in trouble."

"Where? The house is on fire," Henry yelled as she started to remove his shirt to go to the fire. Zoe stopped him.

"She's not there, Henry. Reinhardt found out about us."

"Oh, no."

"He's gone to Athena's Bluff with Eva. I've sent Leftheri to round up some of the men. We need to rescue Eva. Did you tell them?"

"NO! Why would I betray her?" Henry yelled in response. "It must have been Kurt! That bastard, I'm going to kill him."

They started running towards Athena's Bluff until Zoe stopped when she got entangled in some washing which had come down from the line. She disentangled herself and looked up at Henry. "Take off your uniform," she said and threw him a large shirt and pants. "I would rather you didn't get shot."

Henry took the clothes and without any shred of shyness, he stripped off his uniform and threw it away. Seconds later, Zoe tapped him on the shoulder and they started running away from the burning building and the ensuing mayhem.

CHAPTER 38

*E*va's head was spinning and she felt her blood run down the side of her face from where Reinhardt had slammed her head into the wall as soon as they entered the cabin. The blows to her head and body were sickening. She tried to stay conscious. If only to see Zoe for one last time.

One of the guards who had accompanied them had tied her arms and legs tightly to the chair and placed the chair in the center of the room. Reinhardt sat across from her holding his gun across his lap.

"Does this give you pleasure?" Eva said hoarsely, trying to focus on Reinhardt. She hoped Zoe wouldn't see the note they had left on the desk.

"What a stupid thing to say!" Reinhardt sprang up from his chair and backhanded her with his pistol. Eva cried out as blood seeped into her mouth. She spat it out at Reinhardt's feet.

"This doesn't give me pleasure. I loved you and you betrayed me! You lied to me." Reinhardt grabbed Eva's hair and yanked her head back. "I gave you a chance to be an officer's wife," he said, inches from her now swollen and bloodied face. "You, worthless bitch." He spat and slapped her again.

Reinhardt sat back on his seat and wiped the blood from his hands on Eva's skirt. "You know, Eva, I did so enjoy watching Greta being pushed onto the train with those Jewish swine. I wish you could have been there to see it," he said with a grin. "She didn't look all that healthy to me."

"You bastard."

"You know, your father wanted me to kill you. Did you know that? He said that you weren't his daughter anymore." Reinhardt wanted the denunciation to hurt Eva.

"Doesn't...surprise me." Eva sighed. Her father would have killed her back in Germany if he had thought he could get away with it. But in the Fuhrer's regime, he would have appeared weak and useless if it got out. A man who couldn't even control his own daughter wouldn't be worth much to the Fatherland.

Reinhardt laughed. "Ah, yes, I suppose it doesn't surprise you. You know, I would have enjoyed watching the beating you took. It would have made up for all the times you refused my advances. You're worthless and so ugly that no man would touch you now."

Reinhardt sighed and checked his gun before looking at his watch. "You're going to die in a backwater shitty town. I'm going to hang you for the birds to feast on you, but before that happens, you'll see that Greek slut of yours die." He chuckled and the guards joined him. "Was she a virgin when you perverted her, Eva? Maybe little Zoe didn't have a good man around to show her how it's done." He sneered.

Eva was sickened by the thought of what they had in mind for Zoe when she arrived. She prayed for Zoe to be delayed, that the explosion they heard after they were outside of town would have distracted her, or that Despina would have sent her on an errand — just something, anything to keep her from seeing that note on her desk.

Eva could not focus and Reinhardt became a blur; she blinked trying to stay conscious. For a brief moment she saw her beloved mother. "Mutti," she whispered.

"You know, I have one more secret," Reinhardt told her. He took out a cigarette, lit it, and watched the smoke drift up. "One more secret. Your mother was killed on orders from your father," he said and watched Eva's face go from indifference to absolute shock. He smiled.

"He found out your mutti knew you were a deviant and she hadn't told him. She lied for you. So it's your fault she was killed."

No physical blows could come close to the absolute devastation Eva felt at that very moment. She closed her eyes and bowed her head, unwilling to give Reinhardt the satisfaction of watching her cry.

Reinhardt smiled. "My parting gift to you before I kill you. We have to wait for Zoe. It would be quite rude to start without the guest of honor. I really liked that kid, smart mouth and all. It's too bad she's been corrupted and I have to kill her." He leaned forward to rest his elbows on his knees. "Tell me, how did you seduce the poor girl? Such a sweet innocent child. Has she seen your ugliness?"

Eva's head slumped forward and she remained mute.

"You see, it is our duty to root out perversion and destroy it," Reinhardt continued. "And you; you are a freak, a perversion."

"You are a pervert," Eva managed to say, although it sounded like garbled mush to her ears.

The blow came quickly as Reinhardt punched her. It threw her head back and the pain exploded behind her eyes. She looked up at Reinhardt, who was standing over her.

Reinhart was furious. His face had turned red and the veins in his neck were visible. He backhanded her again with the hand that held his gun, the butt of the pistol striking her in the side of the head, and laying the skin open above her eyebrow. The chair fell sideways and she lay on the floor, her blood starting to pool beneath her head.

"You dare call me perverted? The Reich is my father and my mother. That is no perversion." Reinhardt bent down to yell at Eva as she lay bleeding on the floor. "You were with me in the Hitler Youth. You were touched by the Fuhrer. He stood right there in front of us and shook our hands. Didn't you feel like you were in the presence of Christ himself?"

"Didn't...wash for months," Eva retorted weakly, knowing that would infuriate Reinhardt further.

"You filthy whore! How dare you speak of our great leader like that! Oh, I am going to take great pleasure in killing you."

Reinhardt kicked Eva several times in the ribs and then sent a kick to her head. "You bitch," he spat out and prepared to kick her again when his corporal distracted him.

"Sir?" The man timidly said.

"What?"

"Sir, perhaps we should wait for the other girl," the young soldier said.

Reinhardt paused, and then nodded. The soldier was right. He straightened his jacket, which was splattered with Eva's blood, and went over to sit back down. "It's not going to work, bitch. You'll still see her die before your eyes."

Eva struggled to breathe. Her world was rapidly spinning out of control and she was close to blacking out. She was sure he had broken her ribs. She could taste the blood and the sickly smell made her want to throw up. She lay on the floor trying to get her bearings. Reinhardt signaled to the guards to haul her back up. She stifled a groan as she and the chair were roughly handled and set upright.

Reinhardt glared at her. "I've got something much better planned. Something I will enjoy a lot more," he said as he controlled his temper.

The door to the cabin opened and all eyes went to it. Eva

sighed in relief when she saw Barkow walk in. Reinhardt sighed in frustration.

Barkow entered and saluted his commanding officer. He avoided looking at Eva, who had hours ago been his charge. "Sir, that explosion we heard—"

"What now?" Reinhardt asked, glaring at Eva.

"The Resistance has bombed Major Muller's residence," Barkow blurted out, looking at the captain and then at his fellow soldiers.

"What?"

"Resistance forces have attacked the soldiers at the building after the explosion. Also, we got word that the American tanks are hours away from here."

"The British are not important. Are you sure Major Muller is dead?"

"The house was blown up and it's engulfed in flames."

Reinhardt glared at Eva for a moment.

"Corporal, have the men prepare to move out. Commandeer every available truck. We will fall back to Thessaloniki. Go!" Reinhardt ordered. He watched as the guards who were with him ran out of the cabin. He looked at Eva, his eyes filling with hate. He turned to Barkow and tossed him the rope.

"Find the tallest tree and prepare the noose," Reinhardt ordered. "I didn't want us to part this quickly, Eva, but I have other pressing matters."

Reinhardt pointed the pistol at Eva and fired. She didn't hear the gun fire, but she felt the bullet hit her in the chest. Her body reacted, causing the chair to fall over backwards. She hit the floor, still tightly bound in the chair. "Zoe," she whispered before blackness overtook her.

"Where are they?" Zoe muttered as she huddled behind a fallen tree with Henry. They had managed to come up the pass through the dense bush and away from the often-used track. Zoe's knowledge of the surrounding bush land came in useful as soldiers ran up the track to the cabin.

Zoe spun around when she heard the Resistance team coming up the same route. Thanasi was in the lead followed by three more Resistance members.

"Patience, Zoe," Thanasi counseled.

"You're here!" Zoe greeted Thanasi man with a hug before they turned their attention to the cabin. Thanasi sent one of the men to look inside through the side of the building that was the least exposed.

"They haven't killed her yet. The guards are still there," Thanasi said. He watched the scout running back, carefully dodging behind cover to hide his movement.

"They have her and there are six soldiers plus Reinhardt," the scout whispered, and then looked at Zoe. "She doesn't look good. They've beaten her quite badly. They're not doing anything now, just standing around like they're waiting for something."

"What?" Thanasi asked.

Zoe looked back at the cabin, her anger coming to the surface. "Not what. Who. He's waiting for me," she said as she looked at Thanasi, making a decision. "They want me? Well, why don't we give them what they want?"

"No way am I going to let you go in there! I promised Father Haralambos!" Thanasi said, shaking his head.

Zoe glared at him. "I don't care what you promised. Eva is in there! I'm not going to stand out here arguing with you and let that woman die. Got me?" Zoe seethed, trying to keep her volume down. "Thanasi, if she dies, I'll die. Then we can both tell Father Haralambos how we fucked it up. I'm going in there and if you want, you—" Zoe stopped talking when the cabin door opened and two soldiers ran out.

One of the soldiers went to his motorcycle, got on and roared down the track. Zoe watched the other soldier, who she recognized as Kurt Barkow, and sneered. He was looking around for something and Zoe wondered what the hell he was doing. It soon became apparent when Barkow chose a high tree and threw the rope over the lowest hanging branch.

"Oh, no, no, no," Zoe exclaimed and turned to Henry. Henry was already moving stealthily behind the cabin and around to the other side. He pulled out his gun, walked up to Barkow, and tapped him on the shoulder.

Zoe watched, with some satisfaction, as Henry said something to Barkow and seconds later the gun went off and shot him in the head. Henry stood over the dead man for a moment before more soldiers started to run out of the cabin. Henry was now shooting at his former comrades and was being joined by some of the Resistance cell.

"Now!" Zoe ordered and was stopped in her track by the sound of a single gunshot from the cabin. She was out of the bushes and heading towards the sound before Thanasi could grab hold of her.

The remaining Resistance cell followed Zoe. Thanasi shook his head as he ran and started to shoot at the soldiers. Zoe threw her gun away, since it had run out of bullets, and picked up a dead soldier's gun. There was only one place she wanted to be and she rushed through the door of the cabin.

She stood at the threshold, stunned. Reinhardt was standing, laughing over the prone body of her lover, who was tied to a chair. Blood covered Eva and pooled around her body.

"Get away from her!" Zoe yelled.

Reinhardt turned and grinned, raising his pistol in Zoe's direction. "Well. You took your time coming here. I had wanted—" Reinhardt couldn't finish his sentence because Zoe raised her gun and fired. He looked down at his chest in surprise and then crumpled to the floor. His eyes grew round as Zoe approached him. Momentarily she stood over Reinhardt, spat on him, and raised her gun again.

"An eye for an eye," Zoe screamed and fired into his head and body, emptying the clip. "Fuck off, you bastard!" She threw the gun down and it hit Reinhardt in the head, where it bounced and fell to the floor.

Zoe jumped over Reinhardt and fell to her knees in front of Eva. She untied Eva from the chair and gathered her into her arms, ignoring all the blood that had now saturated her clothes. Zoe held Eva tenderly, hoping she wasn't too late.

CHAPTER 39

*T*hree Days Later.

The rain started to fall again but Zoe didn't mind it at all. She looked out of the window and watched the muddy puddles become deeper as the British trucks rolled over them. All around her were British medical personnel treating soldiers and civilians. She had spotted some Australian soldiers as well. The temporary hospital was full of people. Greek and English voices intermingled. Zoe didn't understand a word the British were saying, but she was happy to see them. Eva was placed in a semi sitting position near the back of the makeshift hospital, and a privacy screen blocked her from the men who occupied the other beds.

It had been a tumultuous couple of days. The British had rumbled into town and some of the German troops escaped while the others surrendered to them and the Greek Resistance. Larissa was liberated. It was a dream come true, the moment Zoe had waited years to see. But she didn't see it – didn't savor the victory.

While the British were liberating her home, Zoe was trying to keep Eva alive.

It was a moment in her life Zoe would remember forever. Reinhardt standing over Eva's body enraged her. She had shot the captain so many times she didn't think anyone could recognize the kraut even if they had tried. Killing him wasn't out of vengeance for herself, but to save Eva. Zoe shook her head at how the fates must be laughing at her. She had vowed to kill Eva, made a solemn oath, and here she was killing someone to save the woman.

Waiting for help from Leftheri, who was the only medic left, Zoe held onto Eva knowing Eva could slip away from her. Zoe was grateful for Thanasi's help in the cabin. He had organized everything, and for that she would love him for all eternity. He had come through for them when she thought everything was lost. Seeing a bloodied Eva on the floor had broken her heart. She wasn't even aware of how long she sat there while Thanasi tried to stop the bleeding. It was all a blur for Zoe.

Zoe looked down at Eva and smiled. She brushed away the dark bangs. One very bloodshot blue eye opened. The other was bandaged and Eva turned her head and gave a weak smile to Zoe. "Hey," Eva whispered.

Zoe sat on the chair she had occupied for the last two days and held Eva's hand. "Do you know where you are?"

"Heaven."

Zoe laughed. "Not quite. Yesterday you were in Berlin."

"You're here," Eva rasped. She tried to smile, but winced instead. "Ow."

"You put a dent in the cabin wall. That's not how you decorate the cabin, Evy." Zoe wagged a finger at Eva, causing her to smile. Zoe heard someone coming and turned around to see Henry had hobbled over on crutches. He put his arm around her and kissed the top of her head. "How's the boss?"

"Sore," Eva replied. "What happened to you?"

"Well." Henry sat down on the seat offered to him by Zoe, who sat on Eva's bed. "I got shot."

"Did Zoe shoot you?"

Henry sat back in his chair and laughed as he ran his hand over his bald head. "No, because if she had, I don't think my mama would recognize me. My comrades shot me. Might have something to do with me shooting Barkow in the head, but that's just a guess."

Eva's eyebrow rose as she gazed at Henry for a moment before she turned to Zoe. "See, Zoe, Henry can shoot."

It took Zoe a moment before she realized Eva had made a joke and started laughing. A very familiar visitor popped his head around the privacy screen.

"Thanasi, guess who is awake and telling jokes?"

"Is she still in Berlin?" Thanasi smiled down at Eva and dropped down on his haunches to greet her.

"Morning, Thanasi," Zoe said, and glanced at the young Australian medic by Thanasi's side. His orange hair stuck up at awkward angles and the smattering of freckles on his face made Zoe grin. "Funny. Now you're a comedian."

"I try, little one, I try," Thanasi retorted and grinned. He turned to Eva. "You're looking a little less like a punching bag today. Has Zoe told you about all the excitement?"

"It's been a little busy."

"A little," Thanasi replied before he brought the man that was standing behind him forward. "This is Captain Anthony Jenkins. He's a medic. He looks like he is only fourteen, but he isn't. They breed them to look young." He turned to Anthony and repeated what he had said in English.

Anthony laughed and went to Eva's side. He stumbled over his Greek and then frowned. He turned to Thanasi. "What's the Greek word for 'examine'?"

Thanasi told Anthony and he turned back to Eva and repeated

what Thanasi had said. After he completed his examination and pulled the blanket back up around Eva, he quietly gave some instructions to Thanasi before getting up to attend to his other patients.

Anthony tried his Greek again and gazed down at Zoe. He looked puzzled when Zoe scowled at him.

Zoe was not impressed. She wasn't a married woman and he had just called her ugly. Thanasi laughed at Anthony's use of the language. He explained to Anthony what he had said and his face turned the brightest shade of red that Zoe had ever seen.

"Oh, no! Tell her I think she's beautiful," Anthony stammered.

"Come on, let's get you away before you get Hurricane Zoe going after you," Thanasi replied, and he steered Anthony away from the two women.

Zoe shook her head and Eva tried desperately not to laugh. They looked at each other and smiled.

"I agree with him."

"What? That I'm ugly?" Zoe asked.

"No, that you're beautiful." Eva smiled.

Zoe smiled back shyly as she fussed over Eva.

"It's true," Eva said.

Zoe didn't respond directly. She set about trying to make Eva more comfortable, all the while making small talk. Eva had closed her eye and Zoe's voice soothed her to sleep.

The day dragged on for Zoe, who had her own "wound" tendered to. Her ankle had swollen up after her rampage through the streets to get to Eva, but the pain was nothing compared to what she had won. Zoe sat beside Eva and tried to occupy her time. There wasn't much she could do for Eva, so she decided to go and grab a hot cup of tea and watch the world go by outside the tent.

An hour later Thanasi found Zoe sitting outside on a crate, enjoying the brief break in the rain.

"Is Eva asleep?"

"She was when I came out here," Zoe explained.

"Good," Thanasi replied and sat down on the crate beside Zoe. "I need to discuss something with you."

"Yes?"

"Well, it's about you and Eva. I made a promise to Father H and I'm determined to keep it."

"What did you promise?"

"I promised him that you and Eva would leave Greece."

"Big promise to make, Ares," Zoe teased. "I don't think there's anything left for me here anyway. Father H asked me the same thing."

"This is your home--"

"Home is where you have family, and the only family I have is Eva. I don't think she would want to stay in Larissa."

"You have me and Henry." Thanasi thumped his chest and then grinned at the effect it had on Zoe, who just laughed at him.

"You can come with us."

"I can't. I have to stay. Our work is just beginning. There is talk of conflict..."

"Aren't you sick of fighting? Come with us. I sure hope there isn't a war on."

"I have to stay..." Thanasi repeated.

"On which side?"

Thanasi looked up at the Greek flag that fluttered in the wind before he turned to Zoe. "On the right side. We have no use for the King anymore," Thanasi looked around him before he turned back to Zoe. "The British are not our friends, Zoe. They helped liberate our country but they are not our friends."

"More conflict, more death. Not what I want."

"Where are you going to go?"

"Out of Greece. As soon as the war is finally over, Evy, Henry and I are going to Egypt and then try to find a ship to Australia."

"Australia?"

"Yes. As far away from this madness as we can get."

"It's perfect," Thanasi said. "I think Father H would want you to go somewhere that's as far away from here as possible — and Australia is very far away." He got up from the crate and kissed Zoe on the forehead. "I'm going to check up on a few of the boys and see how they are fairing."

Zoe watched him leave and sat alone for a few moments. Leaving Larissa wasn't a hard decision for her. She had always wanted to go and see what was beyond Mount Ossa. Now was her chance.

Henry joined Zoe outside. He lit up a cigarette and offered it to Zoe, who shook her head. "How's the leg?"

"It's going to be fine. How are you?"

"Me? I'm fine."

"Really?" Henry asked dubiously. "Killing Reinhardt--"

"It had to be done."

"You could have let me do it," Henry replied quietly.

Zoe quietly laughed at Henry's chivalrous offer. "You're too sweet," she said and leaned against his shoulder. "Thank you, Henry. I should thank you for shooting Barkow."

"That bastard. He got what he deserved."

Zoe stared at Henry and looped her arm around his. "Are you going to get into any trouble with the British?"

"No." Henry shook his head. "Thanasi told them I was working with the Resistance."

"I've never really asked you—when did you meet Evy?"

"Paris. I was under Muller's command until he assigned me to be Eva's guard and driver."

"Did he ask you to keep an eye on Eva?"

"Yes."

"So you were his spy?"

Henry nodded. "Yes."

"You didn't do a very good job." Zoe giggled, knowing the story of Eva's activities in France and the Resistance, which included Henry.

"I know. I'm a terrible spy." Henry laughed. "I'm a better friend."

"Yes, you are. You protected Eva for a very long time."

"I did, but what she needed was more than a friend." Henry put his arm around Zoe. "You are the best thing that ever happened to her. Please, don't hurt her."

Zoe shook her head slowly. "I never will."

"Thank you, or else I will have to shoot you."

Zoe rocked back on the crate and laughed at the reference to their first meeting. "It's a good thing I didn't know how good a marksman you were."

"I'll tell you a secret. I trained as a sniper," Henry revealed, making Zoe's eyes widen in surprise.

"You were a sniper?"

"I was and then I was given the job of guarding Eva at Dr. Muller's suggestion."

"Again to spy on her?'

"That's what he thought."

"Where are you going to go? Do you want to come to Australia with us?"

Henry shook his head. "I will wait for Eva to recuperate and escort you both to Egypt, stay with you until you get on a ship to Australia. Once you are safely away, I'll head back to Berlin and see what is left."

"Are you married? You've never mentioned your girl back home."

"No, no girlfriend," Henry replied with a slight shrug.

"Time to find a girl, isn't it?"

Henry got up from the crate and kissed Zoe on the cheek. "Yes, but I want to see the two of you safely on that ship to

Australia and then I can look for the girl," he replied. "Now I'm going to eat something. I'm hungry."

Zoe watched Henry hobble away on his crutches.

"Eva, you were born under a lucky star to have a friend like that," Zoe exclaimed out loud. After a beat she started laughing at how Dr. Muller had been beaten by two kindred spirits that he arranged to spend as much time with each other as possible. She got up from the crate and, still chuckling, she went back inside. Very quietly, Zoe resumed her seat next to Eva, who stirred and opened her eye. "Hey, thought you were asleep."

"I was."

"Did I wake you?"

"No." Eva smiled. "Were you sitting here all this time?"

"Not really. I just went outside for a cup of tea. I also had a chat with Thanasi about our plans."

"Plans?"

"To go to Australia. The first truck out of here when you are well to Egypt. Or do you want to go back to Germany?" Zoe asked, hoping the answer was no. She wasn't looking forward to the prospect of living in a land that she despised.

"Not home."

"Alright, we set sail for Australia."

"Australia it is," Eva replied and shut her eye again.

After a brief silence, Zoe leaned in and whispered. "I asked Henry if he wants to come with us to Australia. He doesn't want to come to Australia."

"He wants to go back home," Eva whispered back. She opened her good eye and smiled on seeing Zoe's face.

"He wants to stay in Larissa until you are well enough and then see us to Egypt and on the ship before he goes home. You have such a good friend, Evy."

"We do," Eva mumbled and fell silent. Just as Zoe thought Eva had finally gone to sleep, Eva opened her eye again.

"What happened to Jurgen?"

"I killed him," Zoe replied. "He was taking something that didn't belong to him. You belong to me."

"I do?"

"Yes, you do." Zoe nodded. "I'm not sorry I did it. He was going to kill you." Zoe saw glistening tears in Eva's eye. "Don't cry." She brushed away the tear that had fallen. "I would do it again if I had to. I love you."

"I love you, Zo," Eva whispered back, her eye glistening with tears. After a long moment she revealed, "Reinhardt told me that Muller killed my mother."

"What?"

"He said that Muller," Eva stopped for a moment before continuing, "killed her because he found out I was--"

"That's rubbish." Zoe shook her head. "Don't believe that bastard. He only said it to hurt you."

"What if it's true?"

"It's not true." Zoe pulled the blanket to cover Eva. She straightened the covers around her and tried to make her comfortable. "Your father was a beast of a man but he loved your mama and I don't believe he hurt her."

"You think so?"

"I know so," Zoe nodded. She didn't, and it would have been a heinous crime by Muller, but he was capable of heinous crimes. The last thing Eva needed was to carry the guilt of her mother's death.

"Okay. What happened to Muller?" Eva asked.

"Leftheri bombed the house--"

"He's dead?"

"Yes, very dead."

"What about Despina?" Eva asked in alarm.

"Don't worry. Despina was taken out of the house before that. We found out that Athens had fallen and then all hell broke loose. Even little Paul...he climbed the flagpole and tore down the swastika and put the 'blue and white' up. I didn't see it, but when Dimitri told me, it brought tears to his eyes. Then the British rumbled into town and here we are. Now, I think we've talked too much. Just be quiet and rest," Zoe ordered.

Eva gave a lopsided grin at Zoe's command. She closed her eye and Zoe sat there watching her sleep until her stomach grumbled. She got up and stretched, leaving the tent for a walk outside.

They had managed to live through the war. Zoe never thought this day would come. If only Father Haralambos were here to share in her joy. "I hope you're behaving yourself, Father H," she muttered and looked to the heavens. She looked over at the flagpoles and saw the blue and white cross of Greece, her country. But now she would have a new country. She wondered how it was going to be, with new customs and language. No matter. They would manage. They had survived the war; they would survive Australia and all it had to offer.

Now, to find someone who can teach me some English before we get there. She spied Anthony and Thanasi at the mess tent and she walked purposefully over to them.

CHAPTER 40

*S*ix Months Later.

Zoe gazed at the ocean liner in awe—she had never seen a ship that large before. It was sitting serenely in the harbor at the Egyptian Port Said. The sea was tranquil compared to the sizable number of people on land. Zoe looked around at her fellow travelers—war weary and just as anxious as she was to start their new journey in Australia.

Eva stood next to her, scanning the faces of those around her. Zoe mentally sighed at Eva's obvious discomfort. Eva had a very difficult six months with her recuperation in Larissa. Zoe put her hand on Eva's back, which caused Eva to look down.

"You've been on a ship before, haven't you?"

"Yes." Eva nodded. "A few times."

"What is it like?"

"Depends if you get sea sick," Eva quipped and smiled a little at Zoe. "Also depends on where they put us. Let's hope we don't end up sleeping next to Mrs. Austerlitz," she whispered, making Zoe try and muffle her laugh by putting her hand over her mouth.

"She can't help it, Evy."

"Hm, that doesn't help when you're getting the fart in your face," Eva said in Greek making Zoe completely lose composure as she leaned against Eva and laughed.

"Alright, I have the bags, now where do we go?" Henry announced his arrival with the porter in hand. He led the way through the crowds. His bulky frame caused the crowds to part, which only made Zoe smile. Henry had been like a brother to her in the last years of the occupation and in the last six months he had proven to be an ally in Zoe's attempts to get Eva mentally and physically well.

There were so many people milling around that Zoe was feeling claustrophobic. One glance at Eva and she was certain that, given half a chance, Eva would bolt out to the deck.

"Why don't you stay here? Henry and I can go find the cabin," Zoe quietly said.

"I'm alright."

"Hm, why do you look like you're going to pass out? And it doesn't have anything to do with that god-awful ugly cloak you're wearing."

The edge of Eva's lips curled at Zoe's remarks. "I'll go and sit out on deck."

"That's a good idea." Zoe smiled on seeing Eva walk through the throng and find the nearest door.

"You are getting good at noticing her discomfort." Henry put his arm around Zoe as they walked behind the porter.

"It's one of the few times she has actually admitted she wasn't feeling well," Zoe replied while they passed other passengers down the narrow corridors. Some faces she knew well and others were total strangers. "That is progress."

"This is it," the porter announced and unlocked the door to the cabin.

Zoe stood at the threshold and glanced back at the corridor. "I think the corridor is bigger," she muttered as Henry tipped the porter to leave the luggage. The tiny cabin had room for two bunk beds, a small window, and a table with one chair. There was just enough room for their two pieces of luggage in the wardrobe behind the door.

"It is tiny."

"This is going to be a very long two months," Zoe muttered as she sat down on the lowest bunk.

"I know what you did." Henry tapped Zoe on the knee and sat in the chair that was slightly too small for his frame.

"What did I do?"

"Thanasi told me."

"Thanasi has a big mouth," Zoe replied and smiled broadly when Henry leaned forward and kissed her on the cheek.

"That was very generous of you."

Zoe waved him away and shook her head. "No, it's not. The refugee camp was hell for Eva. Sleeping in that dormitory with all those women was just…" Zoe shuddered. "You know how shy she is, and subjecting her to it again on the ship wasn't something I wanted to happen. I couldn't do anything about it at the camp but I can do something about it here."

"Have you told her?"

Zoe shook her head. "No. She still thinks we're going to be in the same cabin they assigned us when we got the letter of acceptance."

"We've come a long way since you threw that rock, haven't we?" Henry asked as he leaned back on the chair.

"We have and we survived, all three of us."

"It's been a long and difficult journey. At times I thought the three of us would get caught, and we nearly did several times, but then Muller got distracted by something."

"Did he suspect it was us?"

Henry leaned forward and took Zoe's hand. "Muller knew about the forgeries."

Zoe's eyes widened at the revelation. She leaned forward. "How?"

"General Rhimes caught two poor unfortunates with the papers. The only thing that saved us was the bombing. Muller thought it was you. I overheard him talking to Reinhardt just after Rhimes visited."

"Now that was close. They didn't suspect Eva?"

"Muller suspected, but Reinhardt said it wasn't possible. He knew Eva's handwriting."

"Muller was always quick to suspect Eva was behind everything that went wrong. If it rained, it was Eva's fault. Now as for the other idiot," she said, "how he became a Captain I'll never know."

"His father bought him the command." Henry shrugged. "His father was a general."

"So much for that. I hope they are both roasting in hell." Zoe scrunched up her face in disgust.

Henry got up from his seat and looked down at Zoe. "Kiria Despina came to me one morning and told me Eva had hired a maid. When she said it was you, I thought it was a joke."

"Is that right?" Zoe rose and looked up at Henry.

"I thought it was the worst decision she could have made, but she knew something I didn't know."

"What was that?"

"You are the second most courageous woman I've met. The two of you, working together, allowed so many to escape. I'm sorry I doubted you." Henry put his arms around Zoe and hugged her.

"I'm glad you didn't try and convince her not to."

"I did try," Henry revealed to a very bemused Zoe. "Eva told me she saw something in you and knew it would work but she didn't know what that was. As much as she disliked you, she knew it was going to work out."

"You're going to make me cry now." Zoe's voice broke as Henry kissed her tenderly on the cheek. "I'm going to miss you."

"I will write, and your German reading will improve because I can't write Greek." Henry tapped Zoe on the nose. "You will protect her, won't you? Please, don't hurt her, she will die over there and I won't be around."

Zoe nodded. "You've been in love with her since Paris, haven't you?"

"Yes, and after Erik died, I thought she might have feelings for me but I'm like her brother rather than her lover."

"She does love you a great deal."

"I know, but she loves you, Zoe. Please, tell me you feel the same way?"

Zoe gazed up at Henry and nodded. "I fell in love with her a long time ago."

"You won't allow her to brood; you know how she gets."

"I won't allow her to brood even if I have to make her angry to get her out of her mood." Zoe grinned and started to laugh on seeing Henry's eyes crinkle.

"You have figured out my ruse?"

Zoe nodded. "I figured it out when she wouldn't go out of Despina's house. You got her so angry she stormed out of the house and stayed out till late."

"She was out of the house." Henry raised his arms and shrugged.

"She was so mad at you for several days."

"Eva's anger doesn't last very long. She was just mad at herself that I outmaneuvered her." Henry chuckled.

"Why don't you change your mind? Come with us to Australia."

"I can't. I want to go home and see what's left. We have to rebuild and it's going to be very difficult."

Zoe pursed her lips for a moment. "Will you consider coming

out to Australia one day?"

"Maybe." Henry nodded. "I don't know but let's see how it goes."

"Alright." Zoe put her arms around Henry's waist and looked up at him. "I love you."

Henry smiled. "I love you too, little sister," he said in Greek, which made Zoe's smile widen.

Reluctantly they parted and Henry put his hat back on. "I'll go say goodbye to Evy and escort her back to this broom closet."

Without another word Henry turned and left the cabin, leaving Zoe alone. She sat back down and gazed at the drab and very dreary cabin.

"Hello."

Zoe turned towards the door, where a young woman stood. Her dark brown hair was tied in a ponytail. She appeared to be the same age as Zoe and her brown eyes crinkled.

"Hello." Zoe got up from the bunk.

"I'm your neighbor, two cabins to the left. My name is Elena Mannheim."

"Pleased to meet you, Elena, my name is Zoe Lambros. Come into my broom closet," Zoe introduced herself and patted the chair.

CHAPTER 41

$\mathcal{E}$va leaned against the railing and watched the water gently slap against the ship's white hull. The sun glistened off the emerald colored sea; the color reminded her of Zoe's eyes and she smiled. Her life had dramatically changed in the last two years. On a cold, damp day she noticed the young girl who defiantly stared at her during her father's killing rampage. Eva wasn't sure why she focused on Zoe but she did. Stormy green eyes stared back at her. Zoe's undisguised hatred was clearly evident. The general hubbub behind her faded into the background as Eva stared down as the last two years played out in her mind. She brought the cigarette to her lips and took a long drag. The smoke drifted as a gentle breeze blew across the deck. Eva had lost her heart to this courageous woman even before she was aware of it. The gentle Sister Abigail, whom she had met in an Aiden church, told her the heart wants what the heart wants. Eva wasn't sure what the elderly nun was talking about but she finally understood the meaning.

Eva shook her head in amazement at how the events had

transpired. Two years ago she had no hope beyond living through the day. Now, she was on a ship bound for a country she didn't know with a woman, she hoped, loved her as much as Eva loved her.

Eva heard the sound of a cane against the wooden deck and turned around to find Doctor Hannah Koch. Hannah was an older woman in her late fifties, almost as tall as Eva, with long silver hair which framed an oval face. Her amber colored eyes were hidden behind clear octagonal framed glasses. Hannah was a psychiatrist helping those who had survived Hitler's Final Solution adjust to freedom and cope with their lives after they were set free. Hannah had gained Eva's trust despite her hatred and mistrust in doctors.

"Oh, Hannah, you're here.."

"I'm getting myself settled in and I came to find you," Hannah replied as she leaned forward and gave Eva a kiss on the cheek. "Now what are you doing here all alone? Where is Zoe?"

"Henry and Zoe went to the cabin; I was feeling a little claustrophobic."

"Hm," The doctor nodded. "Probably feeling quite hot as well since you're wearing your security blanket."

Eva looked down at her cloak and then back up at her therapist with a knowing smile. "I need to wear it."

"No," Hannah shook her head. "You don't need to wear it, you want to wear it."

"I feel safe."

"I know," Hannah said as she took Eva's hand and led her to the deck chairs, where they sat down. "We haven't seen each other for a few weeks; how are you feeling?"

"Is that my friend asking or my psychiatrist?"

"A little of both. You've been through a great deal and you've made great progress."

Eva looked out the brightly colored streamers that were

festooned across the railing. "I'm still not cured."

"No, you're not, yet. That's going to take time. Undoing the damage takes time, Evy. We have been working together for only a few months; you have to give yourself time."

"Time," Eva murmured. She looked down at her hands, which rested on her lap, before she lifted her head to meet Hannah's gaze. "What if Zoe doesn't want to wait?"

Hannah burst out laughing as she clutched Eva's hand in her own and held it against her chest. "Oh my goodness, I'm sorry. We are talking about Zoe Lambros? About five feet four, with blazing red hair and green eyes. Right?"

"Yes," Eva replied, feeling a little sheepish at uttering the question.

"Goodness me, my dear Eva. Zoe isn't going anywhere. That woman will wait for as long as it takes for you to be ready. Zoe is not a patient girl, but for you, she will wait an eternity."

"But," Eva looked around the deck to see if there were any other people around them but found it empty. She glanced back at the doctor. "I can't.."

"You haven't made love to her. Yes, I know. You're not ready yet."

"I tried a few days ago but—"

"You tried but you weren't able to. Zoe understands that more than anyone else. You will get there if we continue to work together. We can't undo the damage done to you overnight. It's going to take a lot of time. Keep writing your journal, work with me and then we will see progress."

"Kissing her has become easier," Eva said shyly with a slight smile. "Like you said it would."

"Do you still feel nauseous?"

"A little, but not as bad as before. My legs go weak but I'm not sure if that's because my head is telling me to stop or if it's because I'm in love with her."

"I would say a little of both," Hannah replied with a smile as she put her arm around Eva's shoulders. "That's progress but—"

"I know, slowly slowly."

"We will work on this together, you and me. Nice and slow."

"Can't we go a little faster?"

"No. It won't be pleasant for you if we rush things. Just nice and slow."

Eva sighed and nodded. "Can you fix me before I turn forty?"

"How old are you now?"

"Twenty six."

'Oh, yes, well before then," Hannah said with a slight laugh. The two women looked at each other and smiled. "I have to go but I will see you later tonight. Alright?"

Eva nodded. "Yes."

"Good," Hannah rose and saw Henry approaching. She greeted him with a hug and left the deck leaving the two friends alone.

"So you saw the cabin?"

"I did," Henry replied and leaned back against the railing and looked up into the blue sky above him.

"And?"

"It's a cabin."

Eva smiled at her ex-guard's non-description of her new home for the next two months. "Does Zoe like it?"

Henry turned to his friend, a knowing smile creasing his lips. "Yes, Zoe likes it"

"Oh, good, then that means we won't have more than ten to a cabin."

"No, I don't think you will."

Eva gazed at her friend as she reached out and cupped his bearded face. "I'm going to miss you. You've been with me since Paris and I've trusted you."

"We've been on a long road together and now the road ends,"

Henry replied as he took Eva's hand and they both sat down on a long wooden bench. "It's time for your new life to begin."

"I never thought this day would come, Henry. I don't know what to do," Eva said, threading her arm through the crook of Henry's elbow.

"You live it. What else is there to do?"

"I don't know."

"Are you having second thoughts about Zoe?"

"NO!" Eva exclaimed, causing a couple of the passengers nearby to glance her way. "Sorry," she mumbled to Henry. "I mean, no, absolutely not."

"So what's the problem?"

"Zoe."

Henry stared at Eva with a quizzical look on his face. "Zoe is the problem?"

Eva took a drag of her cigarette and inhaled. For a long moment she didn't say a word as Henry patiently waited. "I don't know if Zoe loves me or heavy likes me or where she is on that scale of hers."

Henry chuckled at his friend and put his arm around her shoulders. "Really?"

"Don't laugh at me, Henry."

"I'm not laughing at you…no, wait, yes, I am laughing at you," Henry continued to chortle to himself. "You don't know if Zoe loves you?"

"Why are you laughing at me?"

"I'm laughing because you are so blind. Zoe loves you. She said she loves you to you, to me, to Thanasi. She roused up half the Resistance in the middle of a firestorm. Have you thought about what she did?"

"Yes, of course I've thought about it, I was there."

"No, you don't know what she did, Evy. She persuaded Thanasi and Apostolos to split up their teams and instead of both of them fighting the Germans, he sent men to rescue you. I don't know how that young woman did it. It's a good thing Zoe was on our side," Henry replied as he took Eva's cigarette and took a drag. "She killed that son-of-a-bitch for you; if that's not love then I don't know what else to call it."

"Are you in love with my girlfriend?" Eva teased her friend and pinched his cheek. They looked at each other and started laughing.

"I don't think I could handle Zoe; the woman is unstoppable. Zoe loves you so much she even put up your moods. You are not an easy woman to nurse, Eva."

"I'm not that bad," Eva mumbled but knowing Henry was right.

"Yes, you are. Zoe has seen every side of you and here she is, on a ship bound for the other side of the world. If it's not love, what is it?"

"I don't know. I just don't want to think she doesn't have options."

"Options? What kind of options? We're not going over this again, are we? Zoe was being friendly; you know she loves the Australians. She told me the story about the Australian soldiers in '41. She loves the stories they told her," Henry shook his head at his friend. "Stop thinking that you're going to lose her."

"I love her."

"I know. I've known that for a long time."

"You did not; don't be funny," Eva gently slapped her friend on the arm.

"I knew you liked her before you knew you liked her."

"What?"

"I saw your face whenever she started talking; you stood straighter, you lit up even when you were attempting to hide it; you stole a look here and there when you thought she wasn't looking."

"She wasn't looking."

Henry leaned back against the wooden beam and laughed and slapped his thigh as he tried to control himself. "Zoe is the most observant person I have ever met. She noticed."

"Isn't it a bit late to tell me now?"

"I had too much fun watching the both of you dancing around each other. The night Zoe slept on the floor after your nightmare, she showed you how much she meant to you. It was a good thing Reinhardt didn't find her on the floor because that would have been difficult to explain."

"Is that when you developed your mysterious cold?" Eva asked tapping the ex-guard on the knee. "I think you would have woken the dead by shouting so much."

"Reinhardt thought I had lost my mind. Stupid bastard. And it was a good thing Nurse Gestapo wasn't around—"

"A very good thing," Eva replied with a knowing smile which wasn't lost on her friend. He tilted his head a little and regarded her. "Zoe was responsible for the 'accident'."

"I thought it might have been Zoe who orchestrated it," Henry chortled. "Other than her hating all the Nazis, why did she choose Nurse Gestapo?"

"Zoe found out that Edith was the one that laughed as her mama was dying."

"Ah!" Henry slapped himself on the side of the head. "I was wondering why Zoe's mood changed when we were in the pantry together."

"You were in the pantry together?"

"Zoe was stacking flour and she asked me to come in and store it on the top shelf. Whilst we were in there, Edith and Uta were discussing you. Edith laughed and Zoe looked like she had had a revelation."

"She did and Edith saw the bottom of the gorge," Eva replied and snickered. "Oh, I'm horrible."

"No, you're not. I wanted to dance around like a fool when the news came through," Henry glanced down as Eva rested her head against his shoulder. "Zoe does love you."

"She doesn't love me yet; she just 'heavy likes' me."

Henry put his arm around Eva and kissed her on the cheek. "You are so blind. The woman loves you; just accept that finally something good has happened."

"Something good happened when I met you, Henry."

"You have a guardian angel looking after you, Evy. I looked after you and now it's Zoe's turn." Henry said as he put his arm around his ex-charge. The two friends sat in silence for a few minutes enjoying each other's company. Henry turned to Eva and took her hand.

"I have to get going or the ship is going to sail with me on board."

"That wouldn't be a bad thing."

Henry reached into the pocket in his jacket. "I have something for you," he said and opened the hand to reveal a ring.

"My mother's ring!" Eva exclaimed on seeing the silver band with the intricate lacing. She snatched it from Henry's hand and kissed it "How did you find it?"

"I went back into the rubble; the house was pretty much burnt down and I was looking around trying to see if my photographs were still in that tin box but I didn't find them."

"You lost all your beautiful photographs? Oh, Henry, I'm so sorry."

"That's war," Henry replied with a tiny shrug of his broad shoulders. "I did find the ring so something good came out of it."

"Thank you, my friend," Eva leaned over and kissed him on the cheek. She put the ring on her finger and admired it for a moment.

"It's a beautiful ring."

"This ring was given to her by her sister Theresa before she died in a fire in Athens two years before I was born. My mother wanted to honor her sister by giving me part of her name," Eva related as she continued to gaze at the ring.

The two friends were startled by the call for all guests to disembark. Henry got up and held out his hand to Eva, who took it. "It's time to say—"

"No," Eva shook her head. "I'm not going to say goodbye. I will see you again. It's farewell until we meet again."

Henry put his arms around her and gave her a gentle hug. "Farewell, Fräulein Muller. It's been an honor to protect you," he whispered as he held her and looked into her eyes. "I love you," Henry quietly said and gently kissed her on the cheek.

They hugged a final time before Henry smiled and walked away. He stopped and looked back at his friend for a moment before waving goodbye and disappearing down the gangway.

With a heavy sigh Eva quietly saluted her friend and decided it was time to go and find out how uncomfortable she was going to be for the next two months. Eva put up the hood of her cloak even though it was quite humid, but she didn't care.

Walking through the corridor she could see the various cabins which held six to ten bunks and winced on the thought she was going to be stuck in a cabin with no privacy. Eva rounded the corner and noted the number of the cabin. This was the number Henry had given her. No one was in the cabin, but their luggage was there.

Eva stood at the threshold with a perplexed look on her face. "This cabin is smaller than the corridor," Eva muttered to herself. "This can't be right."

"Yes, it is."

Eva turned around to see Zoe leaning against the wall and smiling at her. "How long have you been there?"

"Long enough to witness your disbelief," Zoe chuckled as she pushed herself off the wall and ducked under Eva's arm, which was braced against the doorjamb. She entered the room and crooked a finger at Eva to come in.

"Are you sure this is ours?"

"Yes, very sure," Zoe replied and closed the door. Before she turned she locked it and turned to her very confused partner. "Hello there," Zoe put her arms around Eva's waist and looked up.

"What's this, Zo?"

"This is our cabin for the next two months."

"But our letters—"

"That was before I bought us a cabin."

Eva's eyebrows rose at the revelation as she gazed down at the very satisfied look Zoe was giving her. "How?"

"I sold the fields that belonged to Michael—"

"No, Zoe, you shouldn't have done that!"

"Calm down," Zoe took Eva's hand and led her to the bottom bunk, where they both sat. Eva sat forward making sure her head wouldn't hit the top bunk. "I didn't want to share a cabin with ten other women; I've had enough of that at the camp."

"But it was your inheritance, Zo."

"Yes, and I'm quite sure my brother would think I put some dirt to good use," Zoe giggled. "It's just dirt, Evy. I couldn't bear the thought of not being able to hold you in private for two months."

"You couldn't?"

"No, I couldn't and I didn't want an audience."

Eva's face hurt from grinning so much and she tried to stop but she just couldn't force herself to do it. They both gazed at each other for a long moment before Eva threaded her hand through Zoe's red hair bringing her lover closer. She captured Zoe's mouth in a gentle kiss.

EPILOGUE

*S*omewhere out to sea between Egypt and Australia…

"Can you please stay in the bunk?" Zoe pleaded for the umpteenth time and gently pushed Eva back into the bunk. She didn't need to push hard—a gentle nudge was all it took for Eva to lie back down.

"I'm okay…argh, no, I'm not okay," Eva groaned and heaved again into the bucket Zoe held for her. Zoe patted her on the back and gave her a glass of water, then opened the cabin door to slip the bucket outside. It was bad enough that the cabin was small; they didn't need that smell in there as well.

"I need to sit up, Zo."

"You're staying in the bunk, right?"

"Uh huh."

"Any better?" Zoe asked as she helped Eva sit up. The tiny bunk, with its thin mattress, was almost too small for Eva. She had to sleep with her legs pulled up, lest they hang over the end.

"Oh, yeah, fine. Wish I could stop this cabin from spinning."

"Oh, is that all?" Zoe responded and kissed Eva on the

forehead.

"Can I ask you something?"

"No, you can't ask the Captain to stop the ship and get off. I tried," Zoe replied and got a chuckle from Eva. She perched on the edge of the bed and caressed Eva's cheek for a moment, before moving her hand up to softly stroke her dark hair. "What do you want to ask me?"

"I know it's not a good time and it's not very romantic here, but..." Eva swallowed. She got out of the bunk and fell to her knees in front of a very confused Zoe.

"What are you doing?"

"Has your Heavy Like progressed yet?" Eva asked quickly, ignoring Zoe's question.

"Huh?" Zoe replied and looked down at Eva for a moment before she realized what Eva was talking about. She went down on her knees and gazed at Eva. "I told you that I loved you in Larissa."

"You did?"

"You were asleep at the time."

"I was?" Eva asked and then sneezed, which started a coughing fit. After a few moments she looked at Zoe.

"I was waiting for the right moment and wanting to be sure that you truly felt the same. I think I passed 'Heavy Like' at Athena's Bluff."

"Before or after I redecorated it in red?"

Zoe was caught off guard by Eva's sense of humor and started to laugh. "Oh, way before that."

"Oh. You did?" Eva said in a small voice that sounded so young to Zoe, even though Eva was the older of the two.

"Eva Muller, I have bad news for you," Zoe said, suppressing a grin.

"Oh?" Eva sounded alarmed and looked up with a frown.

"I'm afraid you're stuck with me. It's too late to throw me

back, as you know. I can't swim," Zoe joked. Her eyes gentled as she gazed at the woman she had almost lost to the cruelty and hatred of war. "I love you so much that it hurts. That's how much I love you."

"Oh!" was all Eva could say.

Zoe leaned down and gently wiped Eva's face with the moist towel and kissed her. "So tell me, is that what you wanted to ask me,

love?"

"No, I mean...um...Zoe," Eva stammered.

"You know, that fever is going down. You remembered my name," Zoe teased.

"Will you be with me?" Eva asked quickly.

"I thought I was with you."

"I want to spend the rest of my life with you."

"Isn't it a bit late to ask me that? We're heading to Australia."

"No, I mean, be with me...together...um."

"We are together." Zoe was genuinely puzzled by Eva's uncharacteristic fumbling that had nothing to do with her flu.

"I want you to be my...I don't know what to call it, but if I could I would marry you."

"Um, are we allowed?" Zoe asked quietly.

"Not legally and I don't think it's allowed in Australia, but you know, in Ancient Greece it was allowed. I don't see why we can't follow your ancestors and their traditions..."

"That's good. I'm sure there was a wild woman in my past."

"So is that a yes?" Eva asked tentatively.

"To what question?" Zoe teased.

"Will you spend the rest of your life with me?" Eva asked again.

"I would spend an eternity with you, Evy," Zoe announced and took Eva's hands in her own. "I love you with all my heart and soul."

Eva smiled and produced a ring. "I promise to love you for

the rest of my life," she said as she settled the ring on Zoe's ring finger. "This was given to me by my mother and it was a gift to her from her sister."

"I love this ring," Zoe replied as she gazed at the silver band. "I don't have a ring for you."

"You already gave me everything I could ever want." Silent tears tracked down Eva's cheeks as she scooped up Zoe in her arms and kissed her. They stayed on the floor for a moment longer before Eva got back into the bunk.

"Can you please get some sleep?" Zoe fussed with the blanket and brought it up to Eva's chin. The smile that greeted her made Zoe lean down and kiss Eva. "Go. To. Sleep." She enunciated each word with a kiss.

Eva giggled and snuggled down under the blanket as Zoe left the cabin with the bucket once again.

Zoe stepped out onto the deck and took a deep breath. The sea churned as the huge passenger liner slowly and steadily made its way towards its destination. The full moon above pierced the darkness of the night sky like a beacon, overpowering most of the stars and glinting from small waves in the black sea. The Patris was a huge beast which showed the wear and tear of heavy use during the war. Used first as a troop ship and now a refugee carrier, she had carried many thousands of people. If she could talk, she would certainly have some tales to tell.

Zoe's red hair whipped around her face as she stared up at the twin funnels. She could just make out the black smoke billowing into the air. This was the first time she had sailed and she wanted desperately to be back on dry land. That wasn't going to happen for at least another month.

She braced her arms on the railing and stared off into the dark horizon. She had come a long way from Larissa. She had survived the war, lost family and many friends, but she had also gained a good friend in Thanasi and someone very precious — a lover and a best friend rolled into one very special person. Eva had come into her life and, although the circumstances were tragic, she had recognized a kindred spirit and couldn't help being drawn to her.

The refugees were packed like sardines, something Eva had mentioned to her not long after they left port in Egypt. Eva made Zoe laugh when she screwed her face up and puckered her lips like a fish. They were luckier than most, though. They had their own cabin, although it was so small Eva thought it could have been used as a broom closet.

"I wish you could be here, Father H," Zoe said quietly into the night, tears tracking down her face as she remembered the dear priest who gave up his life like so many of her compatriots. She twirled the silver ring around her finger. It wasn't much in worldly value, but it didn't need to be. It was connected to Eva, her mother and her sister, and it was from Eva, serving as a reminder of the love she had for her.

A sound made Zoe turn around and she smiled. Standing near the door was Eva with a blanket around her. Zoe wanted to scold her for coming out into the night air, but she just smiled. Eva joined her at the railing.

"I couldn't sleep and I wanted to be with you."

Zoe held out her hand. Eva took it, brought it up to her lips, and kissed it before she put her arm around Zoe. They cuddled under the blanket and watched the stars twinkle as the ship churned through the sea.

Whatever lay ahead of them was going to be quite an

adventure and they were going to face the challenges together. A new life awaited them in The Lucky Country, the land of milk and honey and new beginnings.

The End

No, this is not the end of the story of Eva and Zoe. Follow their lives to Australia in the second novel *Where Shadows Linger*

Intertwined
Souls SERIES
BOOK 2

Where
Shadows Linger

Where Shadows Linger follows the ever popular *In the Blood of the Greeks*. Having survived Nazi-occupied Greece and its liberation, Eva Muller and Zoe Lambros are still very much in love, wanting nothing more than to fulfill their dreams and hopes for the future.

Emigrating to Sydney, Australia, Eva and Zoe find themselves making new friends and forging a new life together. Eva struggles with the ramifications of her tortured past all the while trying to fit into a society marred by prejudice and the machinations of old enemies plunging them into mortal danger.

Will the unique connection between Eva and Zoe be destroyed? Will they lose their new-found friends? Or will Eva and Zoe's love prove strong enough to overcome the shadows of the past that continue to linger in their lives?

ABOUT THE AUTHOR

Mary lives in Australia and has been writing since she was eight when she rewrote her favourite tv shows when stories didn't quite end up the way she wanted. Sometimes in a world of her own, she relished the quiet to invent new stories and worlds.

Mary has written non-fiction articles for Australian and US magazines but her first love is fiction. When she's not writing, she's designing sites, creating art or being chief editor/owner of AUSXIP.com

You can find Mary's author site at http://www.nextchapter.net or the Intertwined Souls Series site at http://intertwinedsouls. nextchapter.net

45722154R00229

Made in the USA
Charleston, SC
01 September 2015